THE

TALIBAN

CRICKET

CLUB

TIMERI N. MURARI

ALLEN&UNWIN

First published in Great Britain in 2012

This paperback edition published 2013

Allen & Unwin
c/o Atlantic Books
Ormond House
26–27 Boswell Street
London   WC1N 3JZ
Phone: 020 7269 1610
Fax: 020 7430 0916
Email: UK@allenandunwin.com
Web: www.atlantic-books.co.uk

A CIP catalogue record for this book is available from the British Library.

ISBN 978 1 74331 147 9

Printed in Italy by 🦁 Grafica Veneta SpA

10 9 8 7 6

For Roger and Briony, to celebrate our long years of friendship. And for Maureen, with love.

*Cruel leaders are replaced only to
have new leaders turn cruel.*

—Ernesto "Che" Guevara

*There is no place for any act of
violence on the field of play.*

—Preamble No. 6 in the Laws of Cricket

BOOK ONE

THE SUMMONS

He hadn't forgotten me. One of his minions delivered the note to our home.

Rukhsana, daughter of Gulab, is to appear in person at 11:00 A.M. at the Ministry for the Propagation of Virtue and the Prevention of Vice, Salang Wat, Kabul, Lekshanbeh 18 Sawr 1379 at the command of Zorak Wahidi, Minister for the Propagation of Virtue and the Prevention of Vice.

No further explanation. I was just to appear in only a few hours' time on this Sunday of May 7, 2000. I had prayed, over the last four years, to slip from his mind.

"I refuse to go," I announced to my brother.

"You can't just refuse," Jahan insisted, putting on a brave face. "And I'm going with you, so you don't have to be afraid."

The slip of paper—what it said, and what it left unsaid—was a threat. Why would he summon me? What crime had I committed now? Had I revealed my face, accidentally, to a stranger? Had I, accidentally, spoken out loud in the bazaar? Had I, accidentally, revealed an ankle or a wrist? Who knew what rules were encircling us like serpents in a pit?

Or could it be that he had finally caught me doing what he had warned me never to do again. As a journalist, to keep my sanity, I had to write about what I saw and heard going on around me. But I had taken extraordinary steps to remain anonymous, undetectable. I filed my stories under a pseudonym, and never directly, with the *Hindustan Times* in Delhi. I faxed them, when the line worked, to the home of a political columnist and friend of Father's. He banked my pay and made sure the desperately needed money reached me without raising suspicion. I also contributed to the publications of RAWA, the Revolutionary Association of the Women of Afghanistan, through a complex chain of contacts.

As Jahan and I climbed the stairs to Mother's room, I replayed the day, four years ago, I had first met the minister, when he brutally dismissed me from my post at the *Kabul Daily*, and I had come home bruised and bloodied.

We tried to hide our anxiety from Mother, but despite her illness, she had an instinct for trouble. When she pressed me, I told her about the note.

"What have you done to remind him of your presence?"

"Nothing," I said innocently.

She didn't believe me. "Rukhsana, please tell me you haven't written anything recently. It has become too dangerous—you said you would stop."

"I never sign my name. I use a pseudonym," I said quietly.

"Do you think a pseudonym will protect you from someone like him?" she asked.

I heard Jahan shift uncomfortably on his feet behind me—he had reluctantly helped me, as my *mahram*, accompanying me when I needed to meet my sources.

"And your latest subject?" my mother said at last, tears coming to her eyes.

"Zarmina's execution—but, Maadar, I didn't sign it. If this is truly why I am being summoned, I will deny authorship. There were at least thirty thousand people at Ghazi Stadium. I am told there is even video footage. Any one of them could have sent the story."

"But none as reckless as my daughter." She shook her head. "Be very careful," she said, resigned. "They must have found out, somehow."

The house felt ominously quiet as we prepared to leave. While Jahan washed in the bathroom, I held the bedpan for my mother, emptied it in the toilet downstairs, and then washed her. Afterward, she lay in the large bed, a frail figure framed by white sheets. She obediently swallowed her morning medications.

"You're in the wrong profession," Mother said and smiled. "You should've been a nurse."

"I wouldn't have this patience with strangers." I drew back the curtains and opened the window to let in the morning light. She would not let me leave for the ministry with ill feelings between us.

"But you do have it for your mother. I never expected that from you." She sighed loudly. "You were always too spirited, as your grandfather said."

I leaned over and kissed her. "Dr. Hanifa will be here soon."

"By now, you should have married Shaheen, as we'd arranged, and had your own children."

He was my mother's uncle's sister-in-law's son, an only child, and we had known each other most of our lives. We were meant for each other; even from a young age we were told of the future arrangement for our lives. We had met at a wedding when I was six years old and Shaheen was ten. We were expected to bond like two small magnets. We didn't. He was a quiet, solemn child with a square face and a superior air, while I was noisy and mischievous.

Unlike me, he was always neatly dressed and made sure that his clothes remained clean throughout any games we cousins played together. His parents pampered him and he expected the same service whenever he visited our home. His father was a very successful businessman, chairman of an import-export company that traded with Iran, Iraq, Dubai, Pakistan, and India.

"Then I wouldn't be able to care for you, would I?"

I smiled as I left the room, and went to hurry Jahan along. I knocked on the bathroom door. "Save some water for me, okay?"

I looked down at the garden where our rosebushes grew wild. The fallen petals were like wounds on the lawn, which was parched, but water was as precious as life itself, and we had to survive on four buckets a day purchased weekly from a tanker.

Jahan stepped out, trying to smile, and tousled my disheveled hair. "There's enough, if you don't wash your hair."

I washed hurriedly. The bathroom had been half open to the sky for six years. Now, in summer, it was pleasant to feel the warmth of the sun through the opening, but in winter the wind would blow its cold breath through and freeze you while you washed. There was no money, or workmen to pay to repair it. A rocket exploded in our back garden in 1994 at the start of the civil war with the Taliban, the latest bloody chapter in the power struggle among greedy warlords that began when the Russians left in 1987. The rocket made the building shiver, as if with pain, and yet somehow the house stayed upright and only this part of the ceiling was destroyed. My grandparents and I were sheltered in the basement, but our servants, Asif and Sima, who had worked for our family for twenty years, refused to join us because they believed they would be safer in the outbuilding. They stubbornly remained in their home and were, mercifully, instantly killed in the explosion. We still mourned the loss of such good people.

I dressed in jeans and a blouse but did not look in a mirror. My face would be pasty, the color of watery flour, and as soft as dough. It wouldn't have the flush of health and exercise, or the light tan of an afternoon in the sun. I didn't want to look into my eyes—they would be dull, and set in deep purple circles. Like all women I existed only in the house, or else covered with my burka in the street.

We went to say good-bye to Mother, propping her door open so she would not feel trapped.

I leaned over and kissed her. "Now, don't worry, we'll be back soon," I said, stroking her forehead.

"I pray you will." And then a command: "Take Parwaaze too."

"I'm old enough," Jahan protested as he came in to kiss her. "I've been her *mahram* every time she has to go out."

"So, take another *mahram* this time, Parwaaze." Then, to me, "And keep your mouth shut, don't answer back."

"Yes, Maadar," I said meekly.

She didn't have to add that if something happened to us, she would be left all alone in the world. One of us must return.

I buried myself in my burka and Jahan and I crossed our yard, to the gate. It was the same height as our compound walls, twelve feet, to shield us from inquisitive eyes. We had a rambling old house with a stern frontage of pillars. When I was a child, two old poplar trees framed the gate, but Russian soldiers had cut them down for firewood. When Grandfather went out to protest, they merely pointed their guns at him. The Talib might have shot him for protesting. We had long been stripped of our own armed guard, so he could only mourn the loss of the trees and remain furious at the Russians for invading his kingdom.

Our ancient, white-bearded watchman, Abdul, with the resigned air of his age, came out from the guardhouse and ran his one good eye over us as we approached. In most houses, the only defense against intruders was someone like Abdul. He used to live in the old city, four streets south of the Pul-e-Khishti Mosque. His wife and children did not survive the war with the Talib. Now, he lived in the ruined quarters behind our house.

"Your ankles are showing," he announced, sounding pleased with himself. "Cover them or you'll be beaten." I tugged my burka down as far as it would go.

"I was beaten yesterday by a Talib because I did not pray. What do they expect?" He could afford to be indignant behind our compound walls. "I'm supposed to just stop doing what I'm doing and drop down to pray—five times a day too, as if I have nothing better to do and God has nothing better to do than listen to us? Before they came, I prayed once a day and went to the mosque on Fridays. God doesn't want to be reminded of our presence so often.

"You women are lucky behind your burkas," he continued. "You don't have to grow beards and pray five times a day. I was handsome without this," he said, tugging at his scruffy white beard, "and now what young girl will want to marry this old man?"

"Don't worry—they're out there waiting for you," I told him, as I did each time we received Abdul's daily litany of complaints.

"And, if you're lucky, you'll die happily in their arms," Jahan added.

"Ah, if only I could die that way." He moved toward the smaller side gate but grabbed Jahan's arm. "You too will be beaten by the Talib. Look at your *lungee!*" My brother's turban was perched— illegally—on top of his unruly hair, a show of adolescent defiance. Abdul flattened Jahan's curls and then pressed the turban down to his ears so the hair was completely hidden. He so resembled Father, with his square face, slim, straight nose, and the same gray eyes. His long eyelashes were the envy of women, including his sister. He had Father's height but not his strong build and wide shoulders. "They will cut your hair all off if they see it. And don't forget to pray when you hear the call. Where are you going, may I ask?"

"To see Parwaaze," I said quickly before Jahan could answer.

"Oh, and Dr. Hanifa will be here in a few minutes to see Mother."

He unlocked the small gate beside the larger one to let us out. He followed us to the street, watching until we were out of sight, then he would wait for Dr. Hanifa to arrive.

THE SUMMER IN KABUL IS HOT, AND WHEN THE WIND blows down from the mountains it brings with it a harsh brown dust. That morning, though, the sky was a clear indigo and little clouds floated past. Often I would go up to our roof to look out at Paghman Mountain and the Kohi Asamayi and Kohi Sher Darwaza hills. At night the mountain and hills would melt into the arms of the sky, but were forced apart, like lovers, by the harsh light of day. Between the hills, I can just glimpse the northern suburb of Wazir Akbar Khan and the rising mound of Bibi Mahro behind it. Crowning it is the huge abandoned swimming pool, complete with diving boards—but no water—built by the Russians, and nearer home the yellow brick silo they built on the border of Karte Seh, out of imperial charity, that supplied flour to their troops and subsidized our daily naan. It is such a splendid tower, our skyscraper; how the rockets missed it is both a miracle and a mystery. As a child I imagined that if I climbed to the top, I could look to a horizon, beyond the hills and mountains that encircle us.

I had no sense of the limitless world beyond until I went to Delhi. I wondered often what it must be like to stand in a desert, or by the sea, and see great distances stretching beyond my imagination. I sometimes blamed these natural fortifications for our misfortunes. They should have sealed us off from the world, made us into a Shangri-La nestled within their folds, but instead they seemed to welcome in a thousand invaders. We cannot even view the length and breadth of our city for the hills that divide us.

Jahan and I followed the winding pathway through the bomb-damaged roads toward Parwaaze's house—only two streets away. Apart from the sparrows that nested in the eaves of our house, there weren't any other birds to be seen. Over the years, we had chopped down our trees for firewood and they had fled to more hospitable habitations. It was an obstacle course of deep craters and ruts from tanks and armored carriers that had churned up the landscape around our homes. We passed our neighbors' houses, some partial ruins like ours, others reduced to rubble. Parwaaze's house had lost its entire right side; a balcony hung from it like a dislocated jaw and the front walls bled red dust from bullet holes. The green tiles along the front were all broken into shards. His windows were patched with plastic sheets or plywood. Like our house, it had once risen proudly to two floors but now crouched humbly with its many wounds.

His watchman, as old as Abdul, peered through a narrow slat and opened the small gate, but I waited by the entrance while Jahan went in. I didn't want to meet my female relatives in Parwaaze's house and listen to the familiar litany of complaints about the sapping boredom of their incarceration. Jahan came out with Parwaaze, who was rubbing the sleep from his eyes. Parwaaze was my mother's nephew and, at nineteen, five years younger than me but three years older than Jahan. At one time, he had the spirit of an adventurer and a dreamer; I think that if I had told him the story of Icarus he would have attached wings to his back and tried to fly over the mountains. But now, his shoulders drooped and he wore a permanent frown. He and his family had survived the war, but without their spirit intact. His clear gray eyes were now watchful and suspicious. Despite all this, he was still my handsomest cousin. His beard was thin, and there was a slight dent in his nose, as if it had been broken and badly set, and he was always immaculate in his dress.

"Where are we going?" he asked. I told him about Zorak

Wahidi's summons. Parwaaze grimaced. "I wish I wasn't here but was far away. I don't want to be anywhere near him—Jahan is your *mahram*."

"Maadar said you have to come with us," I insisted.

He sighed. "Okay, I will, though I doubt we'll be much protection for you. He's not going to shoot anyone, is he?"

"I hope not. No, it's only a meeting."

"Never ever look at their faces," he said to Jahan. "Don't even let them be aware of you. Otherwise, they'll grab you and . . . I've heard stories . . ." We all had heard stories about the Ministry for the Propagation of Virtue and Prevention of Vice.

"I know that," Jahan said with adolescent arrogance.

"At least they won't know I'm looking at them," I said, plucking at my burka in the heat.

"Why does Wahidi want to see you anyway?" Parwaaze said, trying to tease me gently. "Is this about your running around and writing secret newspaper stories?"

But all I could muster up in response was a shrug. "Maybe—I just don't know," I said, the fear in my voice finally registering on his face.

"Rukhsana, Rukhsana, then don't go there. You may not return."

"I have to, otherwise he'll send his police to find me."

As we left, we saw our cousin Qubad ambling up toward us. Qubad lived near Parwaaze and spent most of his waking hours with him. They were inseparable, like Don Quixote and Sancho Panza. Qubad was shorter than Parwaaze, and much fatter. He still remained well fed despite these harsh times, or they could be natural rolls that sustained him, like a camel, through the lean periods of our lives. His solemn face belied his sense of humor.

Friends since childhood, Qubad planned a career in mechanical engineering, Parwaaze in electronics. Parwaaze's father had a successful business in neighboring Shar-e-Now, selling televisions, stereos, CDs, audiotapes, and computers. I bought my tapes there when I was in school and, as family, I had a discount. Four years ago, the religious police invaded his store with their machine guns, and smashed all the television sets and stereos, broke every CD, unwound the cassettes and VHS tapes and burned them. Parwaaze's family watched this destruction of their livelihood helplessly. There was nothing they could do. It was the new law.

Qubad's father had owned the only Ford dealership in the city, and business began to evaporate in the late '90s until it finally collapsed. No one could afford cars anymore—the only wealth coming into the country was invisible in the national ledgers: profits from enormous poppy crops cultivated at the command of the warlords.

As children, we had led nervous, claustrophobic lives, playing in our gardens first amid the Russian occupation and then the civil war. I had grown up with these boys and we were still alive, but not without great loss. Qubad's father had been killed in cross fire in 1996 and so had many other relatives—fathers, mothers, and children. Our sleepless nights were punctuated by gunfire and the whine of rockets.

And with the onset of the civil war with the Taliban, Parwaaze's and Qubad's studies at Kabul University came to a halt. Young men like them who had known only war now filled the cities and the countryside, idling away their lives. The unemployment rate was above 60 percent, thus replacing their ambition with bitterness and frustration. At times, I feared they had lost the will to live. It made them all the more vulnerable to the Taliban's recruiters—I shuddered to think of my other male cousins joining their ranks.

"Where are you all g-going?" Qubad asked us.

"To be shot," Parwaaze said dourly. "Rukhsana is in trouble. The minister for the propagation of virtue and prevention of vice has summoned her but she doesn't know why."

"I'm g-going home," said Qubad, turning on his heel.

But Parwaaze grabbed him by the tail of his stained and rumpled *shalwar*, the long shirt that reached his knees. "No, no, you're coming too."

"What for? I d-don't want to be sh-shot."

"Her *maadar* said we both have to accompany her," Parwaaze lied.

We walked cautiously to the Karte Seh circle with its four wide roads leading to the compass points, pockmarked and scarred by rockets fired by both the Talibs and the Northern Alliance. The Russians entered Afghanistan in 1979 to support President Najibullah's Communist government. In the war between the Russians and the mujahedeen, our freedom fighters, we were armed by the United States. In 1987, the Russians retreated, and when General Dostum, President Najibullah's main ally, defected to form a Northern Alliance based in Mazar-e-Sharif, Najibullah resigned. Then war broke out between the Northern Alliance and various warlords, all looking to fill the power vacuum. The Taliban, an Islamist army of religious warriors recruited by Mullah Omar from the disaffected students in the madrassas, became a third player in the war in 1994. From their base in Kandahar, backed by the Pakistan army, they gradually moved north to fight the Northern Alliance. In 1996, the Talib conquered Kabul, and the Northern Alliance retreated to Mazar-e-Sharif.

Now the only color left in the city was that of the blooming roses growing wild in the gardens we passed. Afghan roses are the plumpest, sweetest-smelling roses in the world, and I breathed in their fragrance to calm my nerves. At the circle, there was a wide expanse of park to the south, along with a line of shops: bakeries,

vegetable carts, fruit shops, a restaurant (The Paradise), a car repair shop, and a pharmacy.

"It's a long walk," I said to the others. The ministry was in the
city center, just north of the river and opposite the Afghan Central
Bank. "We'll take a taxi."

Qubad took the entire front seat, so the three of us squeezed
into the back of the ancient Toyota. We slowly bounced along the
broken Asamayi Road, twisting and turning to avoid the biggest
craters and chunks of fallen masonry. The road threaded the pass
between the Asamayi and Sher Darwaza hills, washed green and
pale purple, that divided the city in two. I sweated in my burka—
from the heat and from anxiety. Would I return home or be arrested? I prayed silently that my cousins and Jahan would be safe,
whatever Wahidi wanted with me. I stared out the window—not
even the stumps of the great trees that once lined Asamayi Road
as far as the eye could see remained. I avoided looking at the Kabul
Zoo as we passed it; its grounds were neglected and overgrown,
and many of the large animals were dead, sport for the brave Talib
fighters.

There was little traffic, with very few cars and mostly bicycles,
buses, handcarts and donkey carts, and camel trains carrying bales
of cotton and sacks of grain and, probably, opium. A long line of
goats obediently followed their herdsman to their eventual slaughter. Dust blew into the car, smothering us. Qubad tried to roll up
the window but it wouldn't budge.

"You should r-repair your w-windows," he complained to the
driver.

"What are you," the driver said, laughing, "an emir? This is
good Kabuli dust. Gives us our special color and smell."

I laughed with the others, enjoying this glimpse of our lost
humor. He heard me and turned just as he avoided a deep hole.
"Sister, as much as I love the sound of your laugh, you must be

silent. I must not hear your voice. If you were alone I wouldn't even have taken you. Three days ago, I picked up a lady to take her to the old city and some religious police stopped me. They pulled her out and beat her legs with their cables and then pulled me out and beat me for traveling with a single woman who was not my wife or a relation."

We stayed silent after that.

"Where do you want me to drop you?" the driver asked.

"Just here at Pastunistan Square," Parwaaze said, not wanting to frighten the man by telling him we had been summoned to the very heart of the religious police headquarters.

Here the city was still a wasteland. In its four-year rule the Talib had done nothing to rebuild or replace what they helped destroy. The city, as fragile as any human, was gaunt with sickness; its blackened ribs jutted out at odd angles, craters of sores pitted its skin, and girders lay twisted like broken bones in the streets. Its gangrenous breath smelled of explosives, smoke, and despair. Even mosques were not spared the savagery, their skulls explosively opened to the sky. The Kabul River was a trickle of water pulsing through a muddy artery clogged with garbage. Across the river, the pale blue dome of the Timur Shah tomb was, somehow, unscathed. The tomb seemed obscene in its beauty, rising above the broken mud-brick homes and shops that had once crowded around it for protection. Rising out of those humble ruins were lines of carts selling vegetables, fruits, meat, and clothes. People clotted around them, as emaciated as the city, emerging out of the rubble to purchase a potato, a peach, a chicken leg, a sliver of meat, a bowl of rice, some dry naan.

The taxi stopped on the curve of the road leading to Pastunistan Square and we hesitantly climbed out. The two-story Ministry for the Propagation of Virtue and Prevention of Vice building stood behind crumbling walls scarred with bullet and shell holes, aloof, in an island of traffic, deceptively humble. The windows were shuttered. Farther down the road were the Ministry of Justice, the Ministry of Finance, and other government offices, their windows open for the light. We could see the walls of the president's palace from the square. Pedestrians jostled us and we headed reluctantly toward the entrance. Many whom we passed were missing hands, missing legs, and had a wild look of disorder in their eyes. There were children on crutches, jerking around like puppets, all play drained from their faces, and holding out their skinny hands for alms.

I walked a few steps behind my brother, who held our summons as protection against the whims of the police who padded along the streets like predators, armed with their canes and guns, watching us for the slightest infraction. They would strike out, as quick as snakes, to punish the transgressor of any one of their laws.

But it was the quiet that I found most disturbing, and which filled me with unease. This was once a city of music; we hummed and sang Sufi, Farsi, ghazals, qawwali, and Bollywood songs. Melodies, seducing us to enter and listen, flowed out of every shop and followed us from street to street. Now the shiny intestines of cassettes fluttered in the breeze, knotted around posts and trailing along footpaths, ripped out to teach us how fragile music was. Guns were the only culture left in the country; they were the only music, the only poetry, the only writings, the only art that nourished the children. We had been an exuberant people, loquacious, generous with our smiles and laughter, we had been gossipers and raconteurs, but now we spoke in whispers, afraid to be overheard. Suspicion soiled our daily lives. We had become a city of informers and spies. A soot of despair had settled on our souls and we could not scrub it off.

We stopped outside the ministry. "All ready?" I said bravely, but I trembled as we entered the compound. I was grateful for my three escorts. Jahan held my elbow to steady my footsteps. I could not glance at him, my burka denying me even such a simple gesture. I turned my head to peer at him through my bars.

"It'll be all right," he whispered. Two Talibs stepped in our way and quickly took the summons that Jahan held out. They were not Afghans but Arabs, either Saudis or Yemenis, surly men with dark, heavy beards. They had hooded eyes, like drowsy beasts, that awakened when they saw Jahan. I suddenly wished he had not accompanied me.

THE ANNOUNCEMENT

THEN THEIR EYES LINGERED OVER PARWAAZE AND Qubad. All three looked down. Finally, they examined me in my burka and, despite the masking mesh, I looked down too, as frightened as the boys. Satisfied that we were summoned by the minister himself, they escorted us through the building and into the rear courtyard.

Taliban edicts, tattered and frayed but still menacing in their message, were reproduced in large notices pinned to the walls:

WOMEN SHOULD ONLY BE SEEN
IN THE HOME AND IN THE GRAVE

We were only reproductive beasts to them, like goats, or chickens, or cows, fed and watered to await our slaughter should we break free. Our role was defined only by our womb and not by our thoughts and feelings. All in the name of God. How does a woman believe in God when the conduits of his messages are only men?

I straightened my back in mute defiance. I was determined not to be afraid.

In the courtyard, five men stood along the wall in the shade. I wasn't the lone one summoned here and was momentarily relieved. I recognized Yasir, my old editor from the *Kabul Daily*, among them. He was a small, burly man, Napoleonic at times with his reporters. We had our differences, but he could be kind too. Now he wore the mandatory full beard. The others must have been reporters from the Dari and Pashtu newspapers. They looked like they wanted to be there as much as we did. A sense of panic broke over me afresh—why was I being rounded up with reporters? Yasir glanced in my direction—I was the only woman there—and I could tell he knew it was me under the burka. His presence made me feel slightly better. He lifted his small finger in cautious greeting. I would have liked to have talked to him—surely he knew more than I did. He could have told me stories about the regime that I could not hear under my burka. As if he read my mind, Yasir made his way to my side. "*Salaam aleikum, Waleikum salaam.*" We quickly exchanged formal greetings, Jahan next to me.

"Why are we here?" I whispered.

"He's going to make an announcement and no doubt threaten us." He spoke quietly too, staring straight ahead like a ventriloquist's dummy. "He's called all the press on the government list, or what's left of us, and that includes you."

"But I don't work for the *KD* anymore."

"The list doesn't know that. You still get government press releases at the office."

"My summons came to the house."

"Maybe one came to the office too. Have you been writing articles?"

"No, I haven't. How can I as a woman?"

"Knowing you, a lot," he said drily. "There have been stories in the foreign press on the bad treatment of women under this regime. There are very few women journalists in the country to report on that. In fact, I know of only . . ." He lifted his index finger, and then pointed it at me.

"And they think it's me?" I said indignantly, desperate to convince Yasir. "I swear I haven't written a word since I was forced to resign."

Except that, of course, I had. With Jahan a reluctant *mahram*, I would—if not go where I wished and mingle in the bazaars to hear the gossip—follow up on the whispered stories that were passed from one to another. I could speak only to women and spoke to the men through my brother. It felt as if I was in a foreign land with a translator interpreting my questions and giving me the answers. Through these channels I interviewed Ayesha, a pretty woman a few years younger than me. She told me, "I had been walking on Chicken Street with my father when the religious police stopped me. At first, I didn't know why. I didn't know nail polish was banned; no one told me, it wasn't written anywhere. They dragged me and my father to the police station, placed my hand on a table, and with a hatchet chopped off the tip of my little finger. I screamed with pain and shock. I didn't know they would do that. And then they beat my father, as he is responsible for my behavior. See what's left of that finger?" The wound had healed and the remaining fingers were cleaned of any nail polish. I dragged Jahan to interview Frozan: "We're from Jalalabad and we fled here to escape the fighting, abandoning our home. The other day, I was passing a shop and I saw our family clock for sale in the window. I went in and told the owner that it was our clock and that he should return it. Just then, a religious policeman came in and beat me for being out without my *mahram* and then beat the shopkeeper for talking to me." I also found lighter, and defiant, stories of how we survived. A woman named Zahra told me, "We love watching smuggled tapes of Bollywood films on our television and we'd spend hours just doing that, as there was nothing else to do. One day our neighbor reported us to the religious police and they raided us. They picked up our television, threw it out of the window, and warned us not to do that again. We lived three stories up. So we moved out of that flat and into another, bought a new television, and watched our movies. We learned to keep the volume low so our neighbors wouldn't hear us."

I wrote whatever I could and I signed them all with my pseudonym. Despite what Yasir believed, I wasn't the only woman sending out scraps of news to foreign publications. There were others out there and we were a small tribe of rebellious scribes in hiding.

And under this regime, no one knew on whose side anyone was and Yasir could be tempting me to boast. Our press was putty in this regime's hands.

"I am sure there's nothing to worry about." Yasir's voice was bland in disbelief. He lowered his voice further. "But you know, print one wrong word and they beat you or imprison you."

Then he turned fractionally to me for the first time and spoke quickly. "I am sorry that I didn't defend you the day Wahidi came into the office. If I had, he would have shot me. We're not brave."

"Shot you! I thought he'd shoot me." I shivered—I was younger then, unafraid and ignorant of the nature of such men and their misshapen beliefs. "When did Wahidi become the minister?"

"Two days ago," he said, looking ahead again. "After you saw him in Kabul in ninety-six, he returned to Kandahar to serve Mullah Omar on the ruling council for two years. I heard the mullah did nothing without consulting Wahidi. Wahidi was then made governor of Kandahar province and served for another two years before the mullah sent him to Pakistan."

"Why Pakistan?"

"To be his representative in talks. He gave Wahidi the post because three or four months ago, someone attempted to assassinate him. They blew up his house, with his wife and two of his children, but he wasn't home."

"I never heard about that. So even the Talib ministers aren't safe."

I wasn't that surprised, as the Taliban's cruel regime had massacred thousands of our people, creating an army of enemies.

"You still haven't," he whispered harshly. "We can't publish such stories. He returned from Pakistan a month ago, and we don't know how the talks went because nothing was announced. The mullah doesn't like Kabul at all. He believes we are a decadent people and prefers to rule from Kandahar. So now he sends us Wahidi to keep us in line." He took a breath. "I hear he is as pious as the mullah."

"No one could be—" I stopped when I saw the Land Cruiser race into the courtyard in front of us. "Oh god."

In the back lay a man and a woman, their arms and legs bound. The woman wore her burka; the man had a sack over his head. Two Talibs, along with two police officers who had guns, stood above them. The vehicle stopped, the Talibs jumped down and pushed their prisoners out onto the ground as if they were sacks of grain. When they fell we heard their muffled cries.

The minister for the propagation of virtue and the prevention of vice, Zorak Wahidi, the man who had summoned us here, stepped out of the passenger seat and walked slowly back to the fallen couple. I felt a shudder of recognition. His beard was whiter since I'd last seen him four years ago. There was a stoop to his shoulders, as if a thousand dead souls pressed down on him. He wore a black *shalwar*, a black *lungee*, and new black sandals. He also carried a pistol. He looked down at the prisoners and then across to us. I wanted to shield Jahan from what was about to happen but he had moved to stand between Parwaaze and Qubad and watched with the fascination of any teenager. He had never witnessed an execution before—Mother had forbidden him to accompany me and Parwaaze last November when Zarmina was executed. "Look away, look away," I whispered, but he didn't hear me. Wahidi pointed the pistol down toward the man and shot him in the head. The man appeared to rise briefly before falling back. Wahidi moved to the crying woman and shot her in the head too. The shots sounded flat and harmless in the empty space surrounding us. He walked toward us holding his pistol, as casually as a man crossing a drawing room to greet his guests. The two Talibs and the policemen followed him. He turned to give them an order, and then turned back to us.

"Do you know why they were executed?" We remained silent. I felt his eyes penetrating my veil, trying to remember the face he could not see. He angrily answered his own question. "They were traitors to the Islamic Emirate of Afghanistan. They were committing adultery, which is against our laws, and they deserved to die. We will not tolerate such vices. The press too"—he paused and surveyed us, noting each one present, focusing again on me—"are responsible for projecting in the foreign media a very bad image of our legitimate government." He paced in front of us and shouted, his face snarling in fury. "From here on out, you will write exactly what I tell you." The men took out their notebooks like obedient schoolboys. I hadn't brought one.

"The ruling council of the Islamic Emirate of Afghanistan, and I, have decided to show the world that we're a fair and just people. To that end, our government has decided to promote cricket in Afghanistan. We have applied to the International Cricket Council for membership."

Like the others, I raised my head in surprise.

"We wait to hear from them on this. The Pakistan Cricket Board will support our application. Cricket will show all those against us that we too can be sportsmen. As our young men have much time to spare, we wish to occupy them to prevent any vices. We banned cricket because it was a legacy of the evil British. But we studied all sports and cricket is modest in its clothing. The uniform covers the player from his neck to his feet and covers his head as well. Therefore, we will encourage the sport, strictly according to Islamic rules of dress, and we will hold a tournament in three weeks. We will welcome an official from the International Cricket Council to observe the matches and know that we are genuine in our interest in promoting the sport, openly and fairly. The tournament is open to all Afghans and we will send the winning team to Pakistan to perfect their playing skills. They will return to teach other young men to play this sport. Women, of course, will not be permitted to play." He ended the announcement and dismissed us.

"What do you think?" I asked Yasir.

"I write what they tell me, and I do not think. But let's see how many Afghans turn up for the matches when they read about this. A free pass to leave the country—I wonder how many will return. Are you going to write this up?"

"Yasir—I don't write anymore."

When I moved to leave with the others, the two policemen grabbed me. Jahan tried to stop them, but one Talib hit him in the stomach with his gun butt. Yasir moved to help, but the second Talib pointed his gun at Yasir's chest. I struggled, trying to get a last glimpse of Jahan, but the men dragged me out of the courtyard and into a small, bare room and forced me to kneel. They pressed their gun barrels down on my shoulders so I could not move. We waited in oppressive silence. Finally, I sensed someone entering the room. I couldn't see through the mesh and tried to lift my head, but a hand pressed it back down to supplication. I smelled perfume, a cloying, sweet odor. I glimpsed dusty feet slyly circling me, and then he and his cologne walked out the door. Minutes later, Wahidi walked into the room in his black sandals. I heard the rustle of a paper, and he held a newspaper before my eyes. The English headline read "Taliban Execute Mother of Five Children." It was my story and I felt my heart miss a beat, then another. This was why I had been summoned here and he was about to kill me. But

I also knew he had no proof I had written it—it was filed under my pseudonym. *He is only trying to frighten you*, I told myself, and tried to stay calm. I did not speak; thankfully I wasn't expected to. He crushed the paper deliberately into a small ball and dropped it on the floor. Then he lowered a pistol to my line of vision, and I smelled cigarette smoke. Through the mesh, I saw his finger around the trigger, the gun like a natural extension of his hand. Its black barrel was worn gray, the butt chipped along the edges. His finger curled and uncurled as if it had a mind of its own and was thinking over the decision. The finger was surprisingly long, almost delicate, and manicured. Then the hand lifted the gun out of my small window of vision; it was somewhere above my head. I shut my eyes and waited. I tried prayers, but I couldn't form the words or sentences that would accompany me into the next life. I opened my eyes when the cigarette's smoke stung my nostrils. The cigarette lay on the floor, a serpent of smoke curling up. The ball of paper began to burn. He let it come to a small flame then crushed it with his sandal. He lowered to squat in front of me, his eyes almost level with mine. I shut mine tight and yet I felt his eyes piercing the mesh, as if searching the contours of my face. Then, with a decisive grunt, he stood up. The police lifted the gun barrels off my shoulders and followed him out.

I remained kneeling, waiting to open my eyes until I heard no further movement. The door was partially open and I was free to leave. Involuntarily, I laughed in relief. I struggled to stand, my foot caught in the edge of the burka, and I fell. I stood up, swaying, and moved to the door. I stepped out into an empty corridor. To my left, men were loading the executed couple into the back of an old Land Cruiser. For once, I was thankful for the burka. I had wet myself. My legs were rubbery and I leaned against the wall for strength. I moved cautiously out of the building, back into sunlight. Yasir was waiting by the entrance, while Jahan, Parwaaze, and Qubad were sitting on the low wall across the street, along the river. They jumped up and hurried over when they saw me. I was more concerned for the abuse Jahan had suffered, and though he walked carefully, he appeared to be all right. He lifted his arms to embrace me but dropped them quickly in embarrassment, looking around to see if such an intimate gesture was noticed by the religious police. When Yasir saw my companions, he said, "Be careful," and hurried away.

"Are you okay?" they chorused.

"Yes. Jahan, are you all right?"

"Just a stomachache. It'll pass."

"We didn't think we'd see you again," Parwaaze said, leading us away, our feet leaden on the broken pavement. "Did they hurt you?" he asked me, checking back over his shoulder.

"No, and they didn't say a word."

"Then why did they take you inside? What did they want?"

"I don't know. Wahidi came into the room, smoked a cigarette, and left." I didn't mention the gun barrels on my shoulders, the article, or the pistol. I was frightened and I didn't want to frighten them more.

"I didn't want you to see . . . that," I said to Jahan.

He was almost in tears, as he was remembering the impact of the bullets. "I didn't want to watch, but it was so sudden and I couldn't move my eyes, I couldn't even shut them."

"It's better to cry for them than just look away." I looked at the other two. They too had moist eyes, flickering with horror at what they had witnessed, and their faces were a shade paler. "Are you both okay?" I asked them, wishing I could take back everything they had seen.

"Another execution. How many more will I see before I can get out of this country?" Parwaaze asked aloud.

"Rukhsana, next time we'll be carrying out your c-corpse,"

Qubad said. "You must leave Kabul. Go to Shaheen, he's waiting for you in America. He was lucky to get out."

"I can't—there's just no way. I'm not going to leave Maadar while . . ." I didn't want Mother to die. Somehow, I had to survive and see my mother through her illness, and then escape. I prayed hard. *Please let me make it safely through Maadar's death and I will leave an instant later. Please protect me until then—just a little more time before I join my betrothed.*

"Let's get out of here," Jahan said.

We hurried toward home. My shoulders still burned from the gun barrels and I felt Wahidi's breath on my face. Why had he called me? Was he setting a trap to see if I'd report today's executions and write about the cricket announcement? If he was certain I'd written those other stories, I wouldn't be walking home. I'd be in prison.

In my preoccupation, I wasn't listening to the boys until Parwaaze's excited voice broke through my thoughts.

" . . . in three weeks and the winning team will go to Pakistan," he said. "We get out if we win that match . . . go to Australia . . . America . . . to university . . . finish our studies . . . work . . . wasting our lives here . . ."

"Then we'll have to come back here to teach the others," Jahan said.

"I'll keep going and going," Parwaaze said.

"But we have one small p-problem with that brilliant idea," Qubad said.

"We don't know how to play cricket," Parwaaze admitted, crestfallen.

"We don't," Jahan said. "But Rukhsana does."

THE CONFRONTATION

IT WAS FOUR YEARS AGO, WHEN WINTER HOVERED beyond the Hindu Kush and sent a warning chill through the streets, that I first saw Zorak Wahidi.

A rumor had been spreading along the streets, slipping through keyholes, sliding under doors, over windows, and into bedrooms. It woke me while it was still dark. It told me about a crime, one that we had long expected to happen, and which none of us could prevent.

I dressed quickly in jeans and a blouse and shrugged into a jacket. I wrapped my head in a checkered *hijab* that only partially covered my head and fell around my shoulders. I left home, as quiet as the dawn, through the back door and out the side gate while the others slept. There were no taxis waiting. I thought briefly of taking the silver gray Nissan parked in our garage but opening the main gate would wake up the whole household. So I caught the small white-and-blue tram at Karte Seh Square. A few men sat in the front, four of us women in the back. Two were nurses on their way to work; the third was a teacher with her bundle of books. I sat beside her and, after exchanging glances, we ignored each other and she sat silently as the tram swayed and tilted on its rubber wheels along Asamayi Wat toward the city center. The tram stopped frequently, either to pick up and drop off passengers or when it lost contact with the overhead cable. At Pastunistan Square, it hesitated a long time and then the driver, instead of moving north along the road like he was supposed to, continued straight on along Awali May.

"Why are you going straight?" I demanded. "What's happened? Is it true about ex-President Najibullah. Tell me . . ."

The driver looked back, and I saw the fear in his glance. The guns and rockets had fallen silent, and we sensed the eerie stillness of the city. I jumped off the tram at the next stop and walked toward Ariana Square, on my way to the office, keeping close to the high palace wall that was pockmarked with bullet holes. The mist spun a ghostly cobweb over the city, and muffled figures materialized out of the wispy net, looking back fearfully, as if pursued by demons. They vanished in an instant, leaving me alone. I wished I had ignored the rumor, pulled up the covers, and remained in bed.

Then the mist dispersed, and I saw what I thought I had only dreamed. A handful of people crossed the road to hurry past the palace gates, and turned their faces away from the mutilated corpses of ex-President Mohammad Najibullah and his brother, Shahpur Ahmadzi, hanging from the traffic-signal posts at Ariana Square. I crossed the road too, though I didn't avert my head. They wore clothes, their mouths and ears were stuffed with money, and there were unlit cigarettes stuck between their fingers. Najibullah had been a heavyset, imposing man, but death had shrunk him. I felt a sense of dread now. I had believed, like many others, that the Taliban, with their religious beliefs, would bring compassion, justice, stability, and good governance to our poor nation, but the lynching of Najibullah revealed their murderous intentions. *What would they do next?* I wondered in fear. I had a Nikon in my bag, and thought briefly of taking a photograph, but I couldn't film such terrible humiliation of human beings. Instead, I wept. Five Talibs with AK-47s and canes lounged by the wall, as proud of their craft as children would be of their paper puppets dangling from strings. They stopped those who didn't have the presence of mind to cross the road, and forced them to stare at the corpses. A whack from a cane moved them on.

When I turned the corner, I looked back. A fighter climbed out of a pickup and began to walk in my direction. Two of his men trailed him. I looked around. Apart from me no one else was in sight at this hour. I hurried now and caught a bus toward Sherpur Square, where the blackened walls on either side of the road reached up to the sky like burnt fence posts. The bus moved slowly, avoiding the potholes, and when I looked back, the three men were still following. I jumped off nimbly at my stop and ran into the office of the *Kabul Daily* on the corner of Flower Street. I was sure the men wouldn't follow me inside.

I hurried into the office, devastated by what I had seen, but aware of the responsibility I had to report breaking news. Yasir, the editor-in-chief of the *Kabul Daily*, had been a friend of my father's and granted me a small desk from which I reported on nonpolitical features: profiles of musicians, women's issues, education, civic problems, and movie reviews. But last September after I had nagged him insistently, he had permitted me to accompany him to Jalalabad to report on the fighting. We had crouched and scurried through the ruins together, talking to the wounded, tripping over the dead, being afraid and trying to stay alive. I learned that war was chaos and no one knew who was winning and who was losing.

Even at this hour, the room stank of cigarette smoke and my eyes watered. The other reporters were speaking in low whispers.

"Have you heard . . . ?" Yasir asked me.

I nodded. "I saw. It was terrible."

"Write eight hundred words to start with," Yasir said. "Then you can do a longer piece. Every detail of how they looked, readers want that." He retreated to his office, stopped at his door, and added, "Let's see what this new government will allow us to report."

"It's going to get worse, much worse, I know that. Poor Najibullah, he didn't deserve such a death," another reporter said, and they all hurried to their desks.

They pecked at their machines between puffs. The only other women employed by the paper were Fatima and Banu. They had yet to come in, and I wondered whether they would. I slipped off my jacket, dumped the *hijab* on my desk, and removed the plastic cover from my ancient Underwood typewriter. I wished I could use my laptop, on which I could cut and paste easily . . . I prayed the telephone line was working—I would need it later to fax my story to the *HT.* I reread old files, jotted down some notes, rolled paper into the Underwood, and stared at the blank space, wondering if my thoughts would flow better if I smoked.

Finally, I typed.

TALIBAN EXECUTE
EX-PRESIDENT NAJIBULLAH

The president of Afghanistan is dead. The Taliban, supported by Pakistani intelligence, captured the president, Mohammad Najibullah, and his brother, Shahpur Ahmadzi, from the UN compound and executed them. Their bodies hang from the traffic-signal posts outside the presidential palace. Fortunately, his wife and three daughters fled to New Delhi in 1992 and remain there to this day. Mr. Najibullah had been president of the Republic of Afghanistan from November 1986 to April 1992 and was supported by the Soviet Union. Prior to that, he had been chief of Afghan Intelligence (KHAD). He joined the Communist Party (PDPA) on the invasion of Afghanistan by the Soviets in 1979. On becoming president, Mr. Najibullah introduced a new constitution that embraced a multiparty assembly, freedom of expression, and Islamic law with an independent judiciary.

"I heard you actually saw them," Banu said, interrupting me.

"Hello, Banu," I said without looking away from the typewriter. She didn't go away.

"Well?"

"Yes. I did," I said.

"We heard their heads were chopped off," Fatima added.

"No, no. It was their . . . private parts," Banu corrected and looked to me for confirmation.

"They had their heads, and they were wearing clothes."

Fatima was my age, a friend from our school days. She had studied English literature at Kabul University and was a very good subeditor for the *Daily*. Banu was a year younger than us, a business graduate from Kabul University who worked in accounts. Fatima was married to an engineer, but Banu—like me—was single.

"Let me finish and I'll tell you everything," I said. They didn't return to their desks but went into a huddle at the far end of the room in the accounts section.

I reread what I had written and then continued.

In the war against the Soviet army, an estimated 1,000,000 Afghans were killed; 5,000,000 fled to Pakistan, Iran, and other countries; 1,200,000 Afghans were wounded or maimed. Land mines alone killed approximately 25,000 people, and maimed 4 percent of the population, many of them children. Over half the farmers' irrigation systems were destroyed by Soviet aerial bombings, and their livestock killed by Soviet troops. Afghanistan lay in ruins once the Soviet forces withdrew. The United States lost interest in the country and would not help in the reconstruction. This was left to Pakistan and Saudi Arabia, who formed alliances with the warlords who rose from the ashes.

I stopped writing when I sensed the silence, and looked up. Three men stood in the doorway, silhouetted against the morning light, black as shadows. They carried AK-47s and the leader scanned the room until his eyes settled on me. Buried in my writing, I had forgotten about them and never expected to see them here. The leader did not smile as he approached my desk. I remained seated, frozen, fingers poised over the typewriter's keys like a pianist waiting for the conductor's baton. The man wore black from head to toe; his turban coiled like a snake on his head. He was a fierce man, over fifty, I guessed, with unusually thick lips and dark brown eyes. A scar slashed down the right side of his face, and part of his right ear was missing.

He stopped at my desk and looked down at me with impassive eyes. I smelled the dust of war and blood on his clothes, mingled with sweat. Two fingers of his left hand, the small one and the fourth, were missing. He carried these badges of a warrior with arrogance.

"Your father must be ashamed of you, letting strangers look you in the face," he said finally in a smoke-ravaged voice.

I stood up, brushing back the hair from my eyes. "My father has no objection to my working. He's proud of me," I replied. He looked very surprised that I would answer him back. I was proud of my profession, of my degree: a B.A. in journalism from Delhi University, where my father was the deputy ambassador in the Afghan embassy.

"I am Zorak Wahidi," he announced softly.

He stared at me, waiting for me to recognize his name. Was I expected to know him from somewhere? I met his stare with my own, defiant. He looked insulted.

It wasn't a large office: a dozen desks squeezed together, papers piled on top of them and scattered on the floor. The other staff in the office were as still as statues and held their breath, waiting for whatever would come next. His men were still as well, and looked surprised that a woman should so brazenly defy their commander. He noticed Fatima and Banu across the room.

"Call them," he said.

"On whose authority?" I asked.

My defiance infuriated him. For a moment he looked puzzled and then, before I could move, he slapped me. It was so unexpected and quick, and I blinked away the tears, dazed by the sting. "Never speak back to a man. Women's faces must not be seen and their voices must not be heard."

I looked to Yasir for help. He stepped out of his office toward me but then the fighters swung their guns around, motioning him back. He hesitated until he heard the loud click of the safeties being released and he backed away, raising a hand in apologetic defeat. I reluctantly gestured for Fatima and Banu. They crossed the length of the room, holding hands for support, and then clutched mine. We three women faced Wahidi, pressed together like frightened goats awaiting slaughter, knowing there was no escape.

"Women must be seen only in the home and in the grave," he said slowly. "Return to your homes immediately. You will not leave your homes without our permission and when you do you will be accompanied by your *mahram*."

I spoke firmly. "We cannot leave our work just because—"

He slapped me again, harder. He saw the anger in my eyes and smiled, taunting me.

"Are you stupid enough to defy me and not hear what I said? You must not speak! I must not hear a woman's voice."

"I am not defying you . . . sir, I am working here and—"

He held out his hand and a fighter gave him the broken-off antenna from a car. With a well-practiced flick, the antenna slashed the air and struck my forearm. No one sprang to my defense; everyone remained rooted in fear. I didn't even cry out, though it hurt, and he watched me fight to hold back the tears.

"Go," he shouted and pointed to the door.

He tore the paper out of my typewriter and ripped it to pieces.

Fatima tugged at my hand, not saying a word. But I did not go meekly. I took my time—placing the plastic cover over the typewriter, closing my notebook, tidying my desk, collecting my handbag, covering my head with the *hijab*, each moment deliberate and slow while Wahidi and his men watched. I didn't wince when I slipped my arm into the coat sleeve. The only sounds were the whispers of feet shuffling toward the door, and every man in the room avoided meeting my eyes. I heard Wahidi talking.

"What is her name?"

"Ru . . . Rukhsana," someone answered after a long hesitation.

"Daughter of?"

After a silence, a man replied, "Gulab."

"Her home?"

"In Karte Seh."

"You should have shot her when she opened her mouth," I heard one of his fighters say harshly as we left the room. I shivered at the cruelty in his voice.

FATIMA AND BANU AND I HURRIED ALONG THE STREET, blinking at the sun's light, feeling as though we were emerging from being buried underground.

"Are you okay?" Fatima asked me when we were a safe distance away from the building.

"No, I'm not." My sleeve chafed against the welt.

"I thought he would shoot you," Banu said.

"I thought so too."

We click-clicked in our high heels toward Sherpur Square. I got angrier and angrier as the shock wore away. "You heard what he said—we may as well be dead." And then I couldn't help myself, and broke out in a rage. "They are totally mad. If they don't want to see or hear women, they should live on a 'Men Only' island and screw each other."

"Shh." Banu looked around nervously, shocked by my language. "Someone will hear you."

"I said it in English."

"And we understood. Others will too. We have to be careful."

"He seemed to know me from somewhere."

"I remember him," Fatima said in a shaky voice. "He was the man who scolded you when we came out of Cinema Park after seeing *Dushmani* in our last year at school."

I was fifteen then and remembered the film but not the man. I had come out dancing and singing, imitating the Bollywood scenes. Fatima, Banu, and three others were clapping me on.

"He shouted at your disgraceful behavior but you laughed at him and ran down the road, still singing and dancing."

"Are you sure?"

"I think it is him. Be careful, Rukhsana."

I tried to recall that moment when our lives brushed each other's but couldn't. I prayed that Fatima was wrong. It was another man, in another place.

"What are you going to do?" Banu asked before we parted ways at Sherpur Square.

"I don't know. They've only been in power a day and I'll have to wait and see. How can they stop all women from working? It's against our laws."

"They'll make up their own laws now," Fatima said.

"I can work from home if I can't go to an office."

"You'll get into even more trouble. I'm going to keep as quiet as a mouse until"—she looked around to see if anyone was near—"until I can leave."

"When's that?" Banu asked. "Tell me how too."

"I'm going to stay and do my work," I said. "I won't write under my own name, I'll invent one. I have to write and keep writing about this brutal regime."

Neither Fatima nor Banu smiled as they hurried away among the other pedestrians, praying to reach their homes safely. As I waited for the tram, I thought of my story, in shreds on the office floor. Suddenly self-conscious, I covered my face to hide the marks on my cheek.

When I got home, I averted my face from Abdul's eyes, hurried up the short flight of steps to the front door, and let myself in, hoping I would not see my grandparents. But my grandmother was just coming out of the kitchen. Even in her morning *shalwar*, she had an elegance that I admired. She had retained her youthful figure despite having borne three sons and suffered a tragedy. Her eldest, Uncle Kambiz, an army captain, had defected to the mujahedeen and died fighting the Russians. His body lay buried somewhere high in the mountains. She told me that in her dreams she went in search of his grave, but there were thousands of rectangular mounds of earth, and she could never find his. She wasn't smiling when she saw me.

"Where have you been?" she shouted. "We searched everywhere for you. Terrible things are happening."

I edged to the stairs that led up to my room. "Come back here, you're hiding something!" The slap marks hadn't faded yet and caught the morning light as I turned to her. "Who did that to you?" she asked fiercely.

"The Talib."

" . . . and we're now the Islamic Emirate of Afghanistan," my grandfather announced, walking out of his office. He had a baritone voice that intimidated witnesses, and judges, in the courtroom. "Only three countries recognize our new government—Pakistan, naturally, Saudi Arabia, and the UAE. We're shunned by the rest of the world. I warned them a hundred times this would happen. Would they listen?"

My grandfather had been in Prime Minister Mohammed Hasan Sharq's cabinet back before the war. He was the most elegant man I knew. He dressed in gray suits and pale blue shirts and matching ties, and smelled of musky cologne. He was shorter than my father but made up for his lack of height with authority. Despite his busy practice, his transport company, and his political commitments, he always had time to help me with my schoolwork in the evenings. When I had announced that I wanted to become a journalist, he encouraged me and declared to my parents that I had inherited his independent spirit. Naturally, I was insufferable for a week after that.

"I saw the president and his brother, hanging from the traffic-signal posts," I told them.

"You're a brave woman but even you should not have gone out." He pulled me closer to him, and I winced when he squeezed my arm.

"What is it?" he asked.

"Nothing."

"Take off your coat."

They grimaced when they saw the angry welt. My grandmother bathed the wound with warm salt water and Dettol soap and then applied cold cream to the welt, cooling the sting.

Grandfather moved back into his office. We trailed him like a couple of stray dogs following a scent. His office was cluttered with files piled on every flat surface, including the marble floor.

The bookshelves were crammed with legal tomes. The room was already suffocating with the fug of cigarettes. He turned off the radio. "They've taken the radio station," he reported, "and the second edict they announced was that every woman must wear a burka in public and her *mahram* must accompany her at all times. Otherwise, she will be beaten, and so will the *mahram* for not controlling her." He looked to my grandmother and attempted a grim smile. "I don't think I want that responsibility with you."

"Burka!" My grandmother was almost speechless. "I've never worn a burka and I never will."

"You had better get used to it," my grandfather said gently, an arm around her. "You can't leave the house without one. Those Talib are sadistic men and will take great pleasure in whipping women who break their laws."

"But my clothes . . ." She had a generous wardrobe of *shalwars*, skirts, and blouses, and many pairs of high-heeled shoes. "I don't even own a burka."

"Well, someone's going to get very rich selling burkas to our fashionable Kabuli ladies."

"We'll have to get them made," I said, starting to feel a depression setting in. "I was told today that the home and the grave are the only places where we can be seen from now on."

"The Talib said such a dreadful thing?"

"Yes."

My grandfather lit a cigarette. "I think it's best for you both to leave the country as soon as possible," he said quickly. "We still have friends in Delhi."

"I'm not leaving you," my grandmother said.

"Neither am I," I echoed.

"You should never have returned here," my grandmother said to me, as she had done many times. "You should've stayed in Delhi."

"I didn't want to stay in Delhi. What would I do there? Even if

I had stayed, I'd have to come home once India orders our embassy closed. Padar and Maadar and Jahan will have to return to Kabul soon anyway. Besides, Kabul is my home. This is my country. And right now they need journalists and reporters like me."

"If you are even allowed to write," Grandmother said.

My grandfather ignored the interruption. "We could all have fled when the Russians came and now where would we be? Living in tents in refugee camps in Pakistan with Rukhsana and Jahan carrying water every day for miles. I had hoped for better times, but that isn't to be." He sat behind his desk, on his throne of authority, a round-backed rosewood chair. "I'll miss you very much. But it won't be safe here for any woman. You'll be a virtual prisoner in this house."

"Padar-kalaan, you must be exaggerating."

He blew out a loud sigh of smoke to the ceiling and turned to my grandmother. "I have warned you, and God knows you make up your own mind. But I think Rukhsana must leave. I'll take her to the airport."

"I'm staying. I came here to work and not run away because of a couple of slaps—"

"And a bloody arm," he cut in.

"And what's waiting for me in Delhi?" I had not told them the real reason for fleeing the city—the heartbreak was painful enough to make the Talib seem, at that moment, tolerably less painful in comparison. "I'm not a package you can just send off somewhere," I protested. "I'm going to keep working here. There'll be a lot to write about."

"And a lot of danger when you do. Rukhsana, please be realistic— listen to what these jihadists want and look at the violence they are using."

"Danger! What about you? The Talib must know about your work in the old government."

"There's no question of my leaving. I have my transport business, my legal practice. This is my *khawk*. I will live and die in my sacred land and not in a foreign country." He rose and came around to hold me gently, making sure he didn't press on my tender arm. "But, Rukhsana, you must take a wise old lawyer's advice. Leave now, don't go to Delhi, go to Pakistan instead, it doesn't matter, just let us get you out while we can."

"When Padar returns I'll do whatever he wants me to do. Meanwhile, we'll order burkas from our tailor," I said and walked out of my grandfather's office and up to my room, trailing a hand against the blue tiles in the hall, as I had done since I was a child, tracing them from Jahan's bedroom on the top floor to my father's office, below my room. The stairs were in the exact center of the house.

On my wall were two large posters, side by side, my act of defiance against this regime. Like all who inhabit a police state, we live bland and obedient outer lives, while our inner ones seethe in rebellion. On the left was a color photograph of the Long Room of the Trinity College Library in Dublin, lined from floor to ceiling with shelves of ancient books. I longed to visit it and roam among those shelves, reading as many books as I could. The other photograph was black and white, a view of the Taj Mahal reflected in the Yamuna River, with a rowboat, lost in the shadows, approaching the great monument. Opaque light streaked the sky. It was sometimes hard to believe that a man, with a Muslim mind, had raised such an astonishing work of art for a woman he loved.

There was a narrow bed, a cupboard for my clothes, and a desk for the work I was supposed to never do again. And on a small bookshelf by my bed were novels, works of nonfiction, and a dozen or so well-worn books about cricket from my college days in Delhi—from *Beyond a Boundary* by C. L. R. James and *The Cricket Match* by Hugh de Selincourt to a collection of essays on cricket by Sir Neville Cardus. Through my readings, the game had seeped into my heart, and I dreamed often that I stood all alone, clothed in white, on an emerald oval. They reminded me of my university days and how happy I had once been on the cricket field, surrounded by my teammates, and falling in love. It seemed so long ago.

A FEW METERS OF FABRIC, SOFT, FRAGILE, AND PLIABLE, became our cell. No granite wall was more impregnable, no bars more unbreakable, no dungeon darker or more dreadful. I vanished from sight, as if a magician had passed a wand over me. I was no longer Rukhsana with a distinctive nose, a mouth, eyes, a forehead, a chin, a head of hair, but a walking shroud, identical to every other shamed and shrouded woman in the street. Under the burka it was clear that this Afghanistan had no place for women.

"Can you see at all?" I asked my grandmother. We were practicing wearing our burkas in the *zanaana*, our women's private space in the house. The floor was a rainbow of Persian carpets and divans, and bolster pillows lined all the walls. She peered out at me through the narrow mesh of her window, an opening barely large enough for her eyes.

"Just a blur. Why do they all have to be the same color?" Our burkas were pale metallic blue, stitched with a cap that fit on our heads. The corduroy-like fabric flowed down to our ankles. The tailor had made our burkas, needing to know only our heights from the top of our heads to our toes, and no other measurements.

The burka decree had come from Mullah Omar's council, through the newly created Ministry for the Propagation of Virtue and Prevention of Vice. But that was just the start—the Talib rode into our lives in their armored cars and Land Cruisers, like the Saracens on horseback, and they carried us to a land that had never existed. They had invented this new Islamic Emirate of Afghanistan through their menacing interpretation of the holy book. Everyone had to behave exactly alike. We could not think for ourselves. We had to look alike: the women in their matching burkas, indistinguishable from one another; the men with their uniform beards and dress. We could not express any individuality in our actions. We could not speak our thoughts without punishment. The Talib sheared our personalities, like fleece from sheep. The people would begin to forget themselves and live only by their fears.

"Try walking in it."

My grandmother strode forward, as she would normally in a *shalwar*. She avoided the silvery *bukhari* stove in the center of the room, but tripped over a bolster cushion and, luckily, fell on a divan. She sat there, fuming.

"I can't even see where to put my feet. Or what's in front of them."

"We'll have to practice. Come on, get up." I helped her to her feet but we bumped into each other, like circus clowns. "It's going to take a little time to learn how to navigate in these things."

"I won't live that long," my grandmother moaned. "Once upon a time," she said dramatically, "I could see all around me, up and down and from side to side! Now my neck gets a workout every time I try to take a step."

"Surely two women of such elegance and brains can handle walking," I said, teasing her. "Let's try again. If we're not careful, we'll be run over in the streets. Two women were killed by a car just yesterday because they didn't see it."

"Don't worry about me—I refuse to be seen in public in this . . ." She plucked at it disdainfully. "This . . . thing."

I held my grandmother's hand and we walked around the room without tripping or bumping into each other.

I too hated the burka. Besides being all but blind, it was difficult to breathe. But I wasn't free even without it, for the walls of my grandparents' house, with its rooms and enclosed garden, were just another prison in which we existed.

"Now . . . the stairs," I said.

Still holding her hand, I led her into the corridor to the stairs leading up to the roof. At the first stair, she took a cautious step, forgetting to lift the bottom edge of the burka, and nearly fell over. She pulled the burka off in exasperation and dropped it on the floor.

"From now on, my husband will have to drive me to the store, guide me by the hand up any steps, and sit me down on a chair when I want to sit." She crossed to her bedroom and firmly closed the door behind her.

I too removed that enveloping cape that flowed from the cap on our heads down to our ankles and retreated to my bedroom. I switched on the radio to the only station broadcasting, Radio Sharia, and listened to the commands read by the announcer.

They banned music, movies, television, computers, picnics, and wedding parties. No New Year's celebrations, or any kind of mixed-sex gathering; no children's toys, including dolls and kites, card and board games, or chess. No more cameras, or photographs, or paintings of people and animals. No more pet parakeets, cigarettes and alcohol, magazines and newspapers and most books.

People were not allowed to be with or talk to foreigners.

People could not applaud, not that there was anything to clap for.

My first article for the *HT* after I left the *KD* was on our claustrophobic, imprisoned lives.

THE GREAT GAME

On leaving the ministry, we jostled with others to get on the bus, as there were no taxis. The boys sat in the front; I took a seat in the back, behind the drab curtain that separated the sexes. My neighbors sniffed loudly and edged away from my smell. I hoped I would dry out before I reached home.

We got off the bus at our stop and I walked between Jahan and my two cousins. With each step, I felt more and more certain that I would not be able to write another word while I lived here. There was no longer a way for me to publish undetected anywhere.

"I'd love to teach you cricket," I announced, breaking the gloomy silence, "and I will teach you. You all have to play."

They stopped walking, surprised by my sudden announcement breaking into their thoughts about the game.

"I'll play on the team," Jahan said, with the same excitement as his cousins. "When we win I'll go away with them."

"We haven't started yet, Jahan, and you're already flying away," I admonished gently. He was always the dreamer.

"We know you can't play in the matches," Parwaaze said apologetically. "But if you just show us while you're still here."

"Do you know anything about it?"

They shook their heads, but Jahan said, "I saw it played when we were in Delhi, but it was so slow I fell asleep."

"It is anything but slow!" I said. They all looked so hopeful, like I hadn't seen them in years.

They were right. If the team won, Jahan could be in Pakistan in three weeks. I had been worrying about him—the papers and money Shaheen would send would only provide for my travel, for me to join him as his future wife. Jahan would be left alone here, but now was the chance to get him out too. He could leave even before I did.

We spoke hungrily about life anywhere but here.

"We can return to university." Parwaaze spoke for Qubad too.

"And I can go to a proper school and then university," Jahan said.

"Before we do all that I must get Jahan out with you."

"Let's s-start now," Qubad said as our house came into view.

Jahan knocked on our gate; Abdul peered through the slat and let us in.

"Has Dr. Hanifa come?" I asked innocently as we walked past him.

"Yes, of course. Every day, same time. You know that."

"Go into the garden," I told my cousins. "I'll be out in a sec."

As soon as I entered the house, I hoisted the burka and ran up the stairs. I looked in on Mother, who appeared to be asleep, and went to my room. I struggled out of my burka and dropped it on the floor. Then I stripped off my wet jeans and panties and hurled them in a corner. The elation I felt at teaching them cricket evaporated in an instant. I hated the man who had frightened me enough to wet myself, and I wanted to burn my clothes to erase the memory. I peered at my shoulders in the mirror, expecting to see bruises from the gun barrels, but the skin was not marked though I still sensed their weight.

I managed a cynical smile to myself. Cricket? We were not an athletic or sporting nation. As the turnstile for invading armies over the centuries—Alexander, Tamerlane, Genghis Khan, the Persians, the Mughals, the British, the Russians—we didn't have the time to cultivate a national sport apart from *buzkashi*. In *buzkashi* a headless goat is the ball and two teams of horsemen battle to carry the corpse through distant posts to score a goal. Other sports use balls of different sizes, we use dead goats. Only men played it, even before Alexander, until the Taliban banned the game.

But that the Taliban would choose this sport made it all the more insane. I could not imagine a Taliban cricket club. They would stroll onto the field wearing yellow-and-red-striped ties under their beards but, instead of cricket bats, they would carry guns as they inspected the pitch on a sunny morning. No, they could not have picked a worse sport, and that advantage was one Jahan and I could use. I dressed quickly in a *shalwar* before returning to the garden. The boys sat down in front of me.

"Why is the Taliban promoting cricket?" I said, thinking it through aloud. "You can't play cricket without understanding the essence of the game. Do the Talib know that they're encouraging the kinds of behavior they have been trying to suppress all these years? Because they are presenting us with the freedom to express who we are, to discover ourselves, to express our defiance on a playing field. It's a game that takes time, a few hours, even days, not just ninety minutes like in football, and we can roam in our thoughts and feelings without them being aware of what we're thinking and doing, even if they watch our every move. We're out of their reach on the cricket field, and when I played, I loved the freedom of a huge space with only the sky watching us. Each one is alone, yet part of something larger. It's a game that promotes individual excellence and depends on the actions and the confidence of each player. You have a captain but he isn't a dictator ordering what you must do. Cricket is a democracy of actions and reactions, and every player can question their captain's suggestions and counter them. You have a constant dialogue on the field and any player can even change the course of the game midway."

"But how do we play it?" Parwaaze asked, impatient with my introduction.

"You must understand the rules first, and the codes of behavior. For example, you can't disobey an umpire's decision—right or wrong—which is another way the sport encourages individualism over team spirit. When you play the game, the two most important individuals are the two 'warriors' battling it out on the pitch."

"It sounds like a war g-game," Qubad said warily.

"But no one's killed, of course," I said impatiently. "The two warriors are the bowler and the batsman—they are pitted against each other and only one can win. You define yourself at the batting crease or as the bowler running up to defeat the batsman." I paused, lost for a moment in thought, wanting them to fall in love with the game as I had. "Think of cricket as theater in which an action repeats itself over and over again until one character is defeated."

"So now it's like theater?" Parwaaze said. "We're getting confused."

"I mean that the other fielders do not play a role until the act of batting and bowling is over. The act then starts over again, and again. Cricket is theater, it's dance, it's an opera. It's dramatic. It's about individual conflict that takes place on a huge stage. But the two warriors also represent the ten other players; it's a relationship between the one and the many. The individual and the social, the leader and the follower, the individual and the universal."

There was a long, puzzled silence.

"Rukhsana, you do realize that we've heard about cricket but never seen it," Parwaaze said finally. "We need to learn, win that match, and get out. Do we really need to know about the warriors and the theater and the universe to learn how to play?"

I took a deep breath. Maybe he was right. This was not essential to getting on the field, but once you've played, it is impossible not to know these things deep down, like you know the feel of the ball in your glove or the bat in your hand.

How to distill a complex game into simple actions they would understand? They had only watched football matches. I picked up a twig and sketched on the ragged lawn. "Cricket is played on a large field and in the center is a flat strip sixty-six feet long and ten feet wide called the pitch. At each end of the pitch are three sticks, called the wickets. There are eleven players on each team. One team, call it Team A, is the batting team, Team B has to field. Team A has to score as many runs as it can by hitting the balls thrown, we call it bowled, by Team B."

"How do you score these runs?" Parwaaze asked.

"You get runs by hitting the ball and running up and back between the wickets. If the ball reaches the stands then you've scored four runs automatically. Team B has to get Team A's batsmen out before they score too many runs."

"What do you mean by out? How do they do that?" Qubad asked this time.

"When you hit a ball and it's caught, that's out. If the bowler's ball hits your wicket, that's also out. And when you're running to the other wicket and don't reach it before a fielder hits it, you're out. The captain of the fielding team strategically moves his players around, like chess pieces, to stop you from getting runs or tries to get you out with a catch." I smiled at them. "There, that's easier to understand, isn't it?"

They looked down at the scribbled sketch then back up.

"When did you l-learn?" Qubad asked.

"Shaheen taught me. Remember, then I tried to get you to play with me?"

"We'd never heard of the game then," Parwaaze said.

Shaheen had introduced me to cricket. He'd learned to play visiting friends in Lahore during school holidays. He wasn't an athlete—he wouldn't play hockey, football, or wrestle with us since these games could soil his clothes—but cricket had a genteel air that pleased him, and not too much physical contact. He returned from Lahore with a bat, balls, pads, and gloves, and conscripted me into his new game.

"This is our secret," he told me as he showed me the mysterious objects. "We'll play in my garden so no one will see us. If you tell anyone, I will never let you in my garden again." His family was on the same street but six houses away from us. I was just eight then and did most of the bowling. He delighted in smashing the balls to the far corners of the compound for me to fetch.

With all that bowling to Shaheen, I had become a good off-spinner and could bowl pretty fast, though my speed was never as great as his. I practiced batting a ball that I hung from a branch. I decided I would devote my young life to mastering this game.

Although Shaheen had introduced me to cricket, he did not necessarily like my excelling at it. Years later, when I told him I played cricket for my college team, I detected a strong note of disapproval in his laughter. I learned then that even good men found it hard to escape the powers that they had granted to themselves.

"She was good at it," Jahan said.

"Can we learn to play and win in three weeks is what I want to know," Parwaaze said.

"You won't be brilliant. It will take a lot of practice to learn the basics of the game—catching, throwing, hitting—but cricket really demands individual creativity, it encourages experimentation, it encourages a rebellious spirit, all within the boundaries of the game. As a batsman you hit the ball in your style, while another one will hit the ball in the way that suits him best. And as a bowler, you create your technique of bowling the ball, either fast or slow. You don't have to conform to one method."

My cousins looked dumbstruck again.

"I don't think the minister has thought about the game as you have," Parwaaze said softly. "If he thought about cricket the way you describe it, he would cancel his plan immediately."

"Well, thinking about the game this way already puts us at an advantage—this is how the best cricket is played. But more important, where will you find eleven people crazy enough to want to learn this game?" I asked.

Parwaaze waved the question away. "We have our cousins all doing nothing. Just sitting around getting depressed every day. This will be their chance." We had twenty-eight cousins scattered across the city. Ten were girls. He ticked off the boys who were around the same age. "There's Atash, Royan, Omaid, Bahram, Darab, Fardin, Namdar, and Shahdan. How many is that?"

"Eight."

"Nine," Jahan said, raising his hand.

"But not all of them will want to play," I said, deflating their enthusiasm gently. "And will they want to leave?"

"Some of them definitely will want to. We talk about nothing else but how to get out and do something with our lives."

"What do we play with?" Qubad asked.

"Bat, pads, a ball. I still have Shaheen's old kit in the basement. Just remember that the other teams have to learn the game too," I said. "So you'll be on the same level. You won't master the sport, but at least you might be better than they are. Besides, you've got me. I bet I know a lot more about cricket than any of their guys do. And I want you to win."

"What a-about you?" Qubad asked in concern. "Okay, if w-we win and l-leave, you're still here."

"I have Shaheen. He'll send the money and ticket as soon as I write him for it. He knows I must wait for Maadar before I can join him in the States. Who knows? I may not be here for the full three weeks to see the final," I said sadly. "But let's focus on the game. I'll give you a good grounding no matter what—we're not going to miss this opportunity."

"Let's start now," Parwaaze said, jumping to his feet.

"I've got to look for the kit. Tomorrow. Don't tell Maadar about what we saw today," I warned them. "I don't want her worrying."

When Jahan and I went back inside after bidding the cousins good-bye, Mother wasn't in bed but had negotiated her way down the stairs and was in the kitchen. She looked so normal sitting at the table, as if nothing was wrong. Her energy came in cycles, it seemed. She was making a *quorma*, chopping onions with the plums at her side. She would fry the onions first, and then add the meat, the plums, the vegetables, and the spices. Finally, she would add the water and allow it to simmer until it became a delicious stew. She had sent Abdul to the bakery for the naan and they were piled on the table. As always, there was enough for Abdul too and he would collect his plate and eat in his room.

She put her knife down as soon as she saw us and opened her arms for an embrace. "You're back! What happened at the ministry? What did he want?"

"Everything was fine, Maadar," I said, falling into her arms. "They summoned several of us journalists. Yasir was there. Apparently my name is still on some old list—I shouldn't have been summoned, I think."

"But what happened?" she pressed. "Are you okay? I'm so glad you're home safe."

"Yes, I'm fine! It was an announcement—apparently the government is trying to correct its image problem."

"Don't be so glib. You aren't going to write anything, are you?"

"Of course not." I saw Wahidi's gun again, felt his cigarette smoke stinging my eyes. The silence pressing down on me. He wanted me to understand that he controlled my life, that he could impose his will on my body and my mind. He was trying to imprison me in the burka, in my home, and in my thoughts. I would stick to my vow and not write another word until I left, but only to ensure our safety.

"They're going to promote cricket."

"Who?"

"The Taliban. Wahidi. He's going to hold a tournament in three weeks and the winning team will go to Pakistan to train professionally."

"Cricket! Of all things."

"For men only, of course. I'm going to teach Jahan and our cousins to play and win. Once he's out, he can join me in the States."

"You're making it sound so easy." She frowned, mulling over our plan. "And if they lose?"

"Then I'll send for him when I'm with Shaheen," I added with forced cheerfulness. "Of course, I'll only leave when you're well again and you will come too."

"That may not happen," she said quietly. "But it will make me so happy knowing you're both together," she said and smiled. "I was depressed because with you gone too, who would look after him here?"

I put my arm around her shoulders and felt her trembling. "Don't you think you should be resting? I can do the cooking."

"While I feel well, I want to cook. You do it every day. We need more vegetables for the *quorma* and a few pieces of chicken. Give Abdul the money."

I left her in the kitchen, humming to herself, without pain for this brief moment.

Outside the kitchen, Jahan stopped me and threw his arms around me. For the first time since his return to Kabul from Delhi, he looked, and even felt, exuberant.

"I'm leaving, I can't believe it!" he whispered.

"You haven't won the match yet. There's a long way to go. You'll have to apply for a U.S. visa in Pakistan before you can get there."

"We will win, with your coaching. I'm sure there's no one else in Kabul who knows cricket as well as you."

"We'll have to see," I said, hoping he was right. "I was so worried about how you would leave, and now you will. You could be out even quicker than me."

"I'll wait for you in Pakistan so we can travel together."

"No, you must go on to the States as soon as you can to join Shaheen. I won't be far behind."

"You must write to him and get things in order—who knows how soon . . ." His voice trailed off.

I nodded and swallowed, holding back the tears—it had been such a long day.

"I wrote to him two weeks ago," I said. "I don't know what's taking him so long to reply. He said he was starting a new job in a bank, so maybe that's keeping him busy. I suppose it takes time for the papers to be prepared. I will write again."

"And this time ask him to send us the name of the smuggler who helped him. He must send enough to pay those expenses."

"How much will that be?"

"I don't know. But we must find one so you'll be ready to leave."

Shaheen had left nearly one year ago. We were not officially engaged, as I had delayed the ceremony. But our families wanted this alliance and he believed in tradition. I had postponed our engagement three times, much to my family's exasperation. First for work, and then to wait for my parents to return from Delhi. But I couldn't do anything when Mother was diagnosed with cancer. Still, there was another, more desperate reason I never admitted even to myself—I was still in love with another.

Before he'd left Kabul Shaheen sent a note and I passed it around to the rest of the family in silence. The handwriting was neat, even prim.

Dear Rukhsana,

Forgive me for this hurried note. I have just learned from my father that within the hour we will be leaving Kabul for good. If I had been told earlier, I would have come to see you and tell you that no matter how far we go, I will be waiting for you to join me in America. You must leave too, as soon as you can, to meet me, as it is now too dangerous to live in this country for people like us. I wait only to see you and then we will marry.

Affectionately,
Shaheen

The note had taken me by surprise. Even if he'd had only an hour, he could have hurried over to say his good-byes. Probably, his father had stopped him in case he told me their secret plans to escape, and Shaheen was an obedient son. There were UN sanctions against international flights out of Afghanistan, apart from infrequent ones permitted to Dubai, China, and Karachi. To get on one of those the passenger needed an official clearance, and his family would not have been given permission to fly out of the country. The smuggler would have taken them by road into Pakistan, bribing border guards to let them through, and then helped them get their visas from the U.S. embassy.

Without Shaheen's help and sponsorship, I could find a way out of my country, but be denied entry into another. I would be destined to drift around the peripheries of those nations, like a lost soul seeking a final resting place. Whichever way I did it, it would cost money. Or I might not make it out of Afghanistan at all.

WRITING THE LETTER

I WOKE THE NEXT MORNING STILL SMILING FROM a dream in which I was floating high above my mountain walls, looking down on their peaks, and then Jahan joined me and we held hands, laughing at the sensation of flying.

Of course, when the time came, I would be very earthbound, with a smuggler, in the company of others fleeing our native land. I could be the lone woman and that made me afraid. I had heard that, apart from the bribe, the border guards would also demand a woman's body for their quick use, and to refuse them was to be denied passage. I imagined the journey from what I had heard through whispers—an old Land Cruiser packed with people, traveling at night, hiding in houses during the day, fearing every moment that the smuggler would abandon us in unknown terrain, among hostile strangers. Worse. He would betray us, turn us over to the Taliban who would beat and then execute us for our crime.

I dressed quickly to escape my thoughts and went down to make our breakfast. I took the tray upstairs and set it on the bed. Mother had a surprisingly good appetite and finished the pilau and all of her meat. I gave her the usual medications and she swallowed them obediently, making a face, then settled back to doze.

"I'd better go to the market and shop," Jahan said as I came downstairs.

"Send Abdul."

"No, I need a walk. And some money."

We went into Father's study where we kept our money. It was also the family library. The shutters were always closed, so the room was dark, and we always felt that we were entering a sacred place. It was a room of memories, and our shrine to him. We lit the lamp and the glow nudged the darkness to the corners of the room. The papers and files on Father's desk were still in a neat stack. I loved the dark red rosewood desk, with its wide border of inlaid mother-of-pearl. There were three drawers on either side, with a wide drawer in the center. Father teased me that the desk also had a secret drawer and, though I searched and searched, I never discovered it. Jahan also searched when he was old enough, but the drawer was hidden in Father's imagination. On a side table was Father's prayer rug, a Cowdani. The center design was a geometric *mihrab*, the arched doorway to Mecca. Inside it, the weaver had woven an abstract tree of life; the knotting was so fine that the carpet could be crumpled like a piece of cloth. Its main colors were purple, shades of peach, and a mellow light green. Father had inherited the rug from his grandfather. Now, it was Jahan's.

Out of the gloom, the telephone shrieked once and I hurried to pick it up. "*Salaam aleikum,*" I shouted into the phone. I heard a voice, a woman's I thought, lost in a snowstorm and I couldn't decipher a word. "*Salaam aleikum . . .*"

The phone died in my hand.

"Who was it?"

"Someone lost in the Hindu Kush," I said, teasing at my lower lip.

"Could it be Shaheen? Why don't you try calling him?"

I dialed his number and only heard the familiar long hum of the ether. I disconnected and hit redial, again and again. I had tried many times before. Either the phone never connected or else it rang and no one picked up. Shaheen had called two weeks back and we had shouted our "Hello, I'm fine, how are you?" He started to say, "I wanted to talk to you, Rukhsana . . ." But before we got further, the line disconnected. I waited for him to call again, and when he didn't, I wrote him a letter asking him what he had wanted to tell me. Probably my travel plans.

Once, the connection had lasted a full two minutes when my old friend Nargis called from Delhi. She was home on her vacation from Caltech, she was working on her doctorate, and she'd met a boy. I contributed little from my restricted life. And then the fatal disconnection before she could tell me what I really wanted to hear.

I dropped the receiver. It had worked for years, but now, like an arbitrary censor, it would only allow a friend or a relative to slip through a few sentences before it was silenced again. Hearing from them in fragments made missing them worse. I moved away from the phone. On a side table was our collection of family photographs in silver frames.

I picked up a photo of the four of us standing in Parki-Shahr-e-Naw, posed against rosebushes. Father had his arms around Jahan and me. I felt the grip of his strong hand on my left shoulder still, pulling me closer to him. Father and Jahan had smiles on their faces. Mother and I smiled too but you could not see our faces under the burkas. We were just two anonymous women in the company of men. How sad not to be able to see my own happiness, and my mother's, in this memory of us together.

* * *

IT WAS NOW NEARLY A YEAR SINCE MY FATHER AND MY GRAND-parents died.

Grandfather had finally determined that we should all leave the country, but he needed to say good-bye to his son, Uncle Koshan, in Mazar-e-Sharif. Father went with my grandparents but Mother had refused. There was friction between her and Koshan's wife, Zabya. The sisters-in-law had always studiously avoided each other at any large family gathering.

They left early in the morning, when the light was still gentle, and carried enough food to last them a week. Mother and I watched from the top balcony, while Jahan stood on the road, waving good-bye as the Nissan pulled away.

Four days later, someone hammering on the gate, and urgently calling out, woke us early in the morning. We heard Abdul wake and shout to the person to stop the banging.

An elderly man, disheveled from a long journey, his face fearful with bad news, waited on the steps for us.

"Forgive me, forgive me," he burst out in a long, rehearsed message. "Koshan sent me; I am Muneer, his servant." He looked at Mother. "Your *shauhar*, Gulab, and his *padar* and *maadar* have died. Three days ago, we received the news that their motorcar hit a land mine and they were killed. My master, Koshan, tried to telephone for two days but he could not reach you. I was sent by bus." He bowed low. "Forgive me."

For a long moment, we stood stiff and silent. I held tightly to Mother as she released a moan that became a scream of pain. I reached for Jahan, who stood at the door staring at the messenger, not yet believing him. I felt the emptying of my heart. We held on to each other and wept against each other's shoulders, heaving in pain.

"We will go to Mazar-e-Sharif for the funeral immediately," Jahan finally said, taking charge.

"It has been performed already," the messenger replied, and it set us weeping again, realizing we wouldn't even be allowed to see for a last time the faces of the family we loved. "It could not wait, as they had been dead already for two days. My master, Koshan, washed his father's and brother's bodies, and my mistress washed his mother's. The mullah performed the prayers." He hesitated, then added quietly, "They were not . . . whole. They are buried in the cemetery beside their ancestors. May peace be upon them."

He walked slowly back to the gate. Abdul had heard the news and he too wept as he let the man out.

We closed the door, shutting out the world, shutting ourselves in to weep and mourn for our family. Mother could barely stand, and I helped her to her bed, where she collapsed and, keening, turned her face to the pillow on which her husband had once rested his head. Jahan and I sat with her, weeping too, clutching our mother, clutching each other as if had we let go, we too would vanish. We mourned for two days, barely speaking, too numb for anything beyond tears and cries of pain. All our female relations came to weep and condole with us. The men remained outside in the garden, where Jahan received them. On the third day after hearing the news, Jahan led them to the mosque, where he performed the funeral rites for our loved ones so that peace would be on them. Mother and the other women and I waited in a hall outside the mosque. On the first Friday after this, we remained at home to receive all our relatives to remember the dead and we served an elaborate lunch. For the three following days, Jahan received more than five hundred mourners who came to pay their respects to our grandfather and father.

On the fortieth day, the whole family gathered in the house for the final prayers for the dead and served a huge feast.

My tears had long since dried, and I couldn't weep anymore when summer came, warm and dusty. Mother continued to grieve—she was weak, and the cancer, beaten back three years before with chemotherapy and radiation, returned. It had hidden in her body like a sniper waiting to ambush her. The pain had been mild at first, but Dr. Hanifa had taken Mother to the hospital anyway. But there was no oncologist there to verify Dr. Hanifa's diagnosis or prescribe further treatment. Nor were there surgeons, or anesthesiologists, or cardiologists. Only a handful of nurses remained. The hospital had lost most of its staff, an exodus of healers gone across the borders to heal other lives. Mother would die soon, of a "natural" death.

BEHIND FATHER'S DESK WAS AN IRON SAFE ABOUT TWENTY inches high and twenty across and deep enough to hold files and other precious belongings. The key was hidden behind Shirer's *The Rise and Fall of the Third Reich*. I counted out enough Afghanis for Jahan's shopping.

"What do we need?" he asked.

"Flour, onions, tomatoes, a chicken, and whatever vegetables are available for Maadar to make her *quorma*. And naan." As I told him, I realized I desperately wanted to go with him to the bazaar, to immerse myself in its sounds and smells, the jostle of people, just to get out of the house. I would touch and smell each tomato to find the best ones, check that the naan was fresh and warm from the oven, haggle, through Jahan, over the price of a few ounces of meat and win the contest, to the shopkeeper's resigned chagrin, look up and feel the sun warm my face.

"And you," Jahan said, "you must write that letter to Shaheen. Don't worry about me or Maadar, just write it so that you are ready. There is no harm in that."

"And you come straight back. Don't fool around, and be very careful." He made his usual face and rolled his eyes when I tried to give him instructions. "I'm serious. You know Maadar and I will worry until you're home. Anything can happen out there."

"I'll be fine," he said with the nonchalance of a sixteen-year-old, and closed the door. There was always such a thud of finality in that sound, which frightened me.

I stood by the door and watched him walk down the steps to the gate, exchange a few words with Abdul, and step out. He waved, without looking back, knowing I watched, pretending to be un-afraid to reassure me that nothing would happen to him.

I went to my room to compose the letter to Shaheen.

My dear Shaheen,

I paused. Could I simply say, "Please hurry up and send for me, as I want to leave the country"? I sat for half an hour trying to compose the letter—I wanted to be kind even though I was not in love. He was my future husband, alloted to me by our families, and I had to accept him. I would learn to live with him all my life, like a habit I couldn't shake off.

My dear Shaheen, I miss you very much. These are the loneliest days of my life and I wish you were near to comfort us. Mother was once such a support, but her illness has progressed and robbed her of her energy. Jahan is a wonderful brother but still a child, and the burden of being the head of a household at my age is sometimes too much for me.

I heard Jahan return. The door made a much more welcoming sound now. Jahan came in and sat beside me, glancing at the computer screen of my laptop. The bag held a few vegetables, some scrappy pieces of chicken. He had also bought the anemic four-page *Kabul Daily*. The "news" stories were government announcements and the advertisements were government tenders for bids to repair our roads and small boxes for "burkas from the finest material." Yasir's report was on the back page. He had written Wahidi's cricket announcement word for word, without a comment, and made no mention of the executions.

"The Dari and Pashtu papers have exactly the same wording," Jahan said. "I saw Parwaaze and he'd read it too. Some others who saw the story told him they were going to learn cricket to get a free trip to Pakistan. And probably, like us, apply for visas to the U.S. or Australia or England, and fly away, if they have the money. Some just want to learn the game and play for Afghanistan. Parwaaze wants to start today, and not waste any time. Where's the bat and ball?"

"In the basement."

The stairs led to a landing and then a U-turn down to the basement. Below them was a dark well. We turned right in the corridor and opened the last door, into a back room. In the dusty, gloomy room, we sneezed as we waded through the detritus of our lives. It was crammed with suitcases, cartons, broken chairs and tables. Jahan hauled out an old bat from behind some discarded lamps. It was dusty but in good enough condition. There were also two balls, almost black with use but still with a good shape.

"What else do we need?"

"Pads," I said. "And gloves—they're in my trunk." I had hoped that one day, years from now, far away from the ache I still felt at the thought of my time there, I would be able to unpack the trunk. I hoped as I aged that I could take out those old possessions and memorabilia, and tell my children stories about them. I would touch them, and friends and places would spring alive, like beautiful flowers, from dusty corners of my mind.

He looked around and saw it pushed to a far corner. I looked at the metal trunk, wishing suddenly I had never brought it from

Delhi. It was too early for that journey back, and now too late to regret that other life.

I had left Delhi three years and four months ago, but seeing the trunk, it suddenly felt as if it were just yesterday. I hadn't realized that teaching the game would rekindle so many memories and feelings. They were intertwined and inseparable. What lay buried in the trunk now were the memories of my days of freedom, the joy of being in love. Even the stale and musty air inside it would remind me of what I had lost, forever. And there was no one to blame except myself.

I followed as Jahan dragged the trunk into the dim cellar corridor, breathless from the sense of loss. "It's locked and I've lost the key," I said desperately, and turned away from the trunk, hoping at that moment that it would vanish. "We don't need it, Jahan. We can improvise. I can draw what pads look like and get them made . . ."

"I know where it is," he said, not registering my distress, and hurried upstairs.

THE BASEMENT

Jahan returned, smiling triumphantly, knelt by the trunk, inserted the key, and with a quick twist unlocked it. The lid yawned open like the jaws of a beast waiting to devour me, and I could almost smell the sultry breath of Delhi exhale in relief.

My past was in layers, like an archaeological strata of secrets. On top were books, and the articles I had written as a foreign intern with the *Hindustan Times*. A patina of fine dust covered them and Jahan impatiently brushed it away. Below were other artifacts—photo albums, letters from friends, postcards of places I'd visited, even movie theater tickets. There were also VHS tapes of films I had wanted to watch again, in French, German, Chinese, Japanese, Indian, that I could not bear to give up even though owning them was against the law. Next was my music—I didn't even want to see what I had enjoyed listening to while I worked at my desk at home in Delhi. Jahan exhumed the photo albums with their shiny red covers. He flipped one open and stopped to look at the photo of us at our house in Delhi, a happy family. We ached at seeing Father and Mother smiling, his arm around her shoulders.

* * *

AT SEVENTEEN, SEVEN YEARS AGO, IN 1993, I FLEW TO DELHI. Burhanuddin Rabbani, head of the United National Front, was our president, the Russians had retreated five years earlier, and there was a new army called the Taliban rising out of Kandahar. I was traveling alone, coiled tight with excitement. I flew over the snow-capped mountains of the Hindu Kush, their peaks as savage as incisors, and deep, dark valleys that filled the horizon as far as I could see. I could not imagine how tiny man could have discovered the narrow passages through such a wall of ice and black rock. Below was a thousand years of history. My nose was pressed to the window, and I was imagining camel caravans, loaded with silks and spices, and medieval armies shuttling back and forth between Kabul and Delhi with pendulum regularity along the fabled Grand Trunk Road. Like Kabul, commerce and blood nourished Delhi's foundations.

I peered down at Delhi as the plane circled to land. I knew there was the "New" Delhi, built by the British, but the old ones, seven empires in all, still lay visible just below the surface. It was a huge city, flat as a table, flooding to the horizon and beyond. I caught glimpses of great tombs and mosques, broken fortress walls, glittering glass palaces, the round parliament house, garden homes, large swaths of parks, and wide avenues running from north to south and east to west, filled with traffic. Nearly seven million people lived below me, a third of Afghanistan's total population. I believed I would never find my way around such a maze of streets, houses, monuments, and parks. The Yamuna, a silver rope twisting through the landscape, was wider even than the Kabul River.

I instinctively searched for recent ruins, the blackened corpses of damaged buildings that my eyes had grown so accustomed to during the Russian occupation. But the city looked complacent and whole, smug in its sense of security in the evening light. The citizens lived their daily lives without the haunting specter of sudden death. I felt envious of such a peaceful existence.

When the plane landed at Indira Gandhi Airport, my father, using his diplomatic passport, met me at the immigration desk. He was half a head taller than those around him, a handsome man, clean shaven, immaculate in a suit and tie befitting Afghanistan's deputy ambassador to the Republic of India. I laughed and waved at him from my place in the queue. We hadn't seen each other for nearly a year. When I crossed the barrier he swept me into his arms, and we both laughed with happiness. I loved him so much.

"A good flight?"

"Delayed two hours, as you know, sitting in the plane the whole time, waiting for the gunfire to die down. And my case is filled with plums, walnuts, dried fruits, pomegranates, as Padar-kalaan thinks India won't have any of them." I laughed as he hauled my case off the carousel. "I had no room for my clothes but Maadar-kalaan said I should buy them here so I will be in fashion when I go to university."

"That's what your *maadar* wants to do. Any excuse to go shopping. You have only two days before classes start."

I was the first woman in our family to study in a foreign university, breaking a long family legacy at Kabul University. Father had done his master's at Durham University in England and that had shaped his thinking.

Shaheen, in his final year at Kabul University, was unhappy that I had chosen Delhi. He had written a note, in his precise handwriting.

My dear Rukhsana,

It will feel strange not having you living close by. I have to ask you: why not Kabul U? It is as good as Delhi, and I am surprised

*that you have decided to study journalism there. It is not a woman's
profession. I would have thought a subject more appropriate would
be home science, geography, or, like your mother, English literature,
with hopes of a secure position as a lecturer in Kabul U. I'll soon
graduate and begin work in my father's business, which I look forward to very much in preparation for our life ahead. I will miss you.*
   Affectionately,
   Shaheen

Shaheen had once declared that the reason he was so drawn
to me was the sense of mischief in my eyes. I remembered that
until I was ten or eleven, we had grown in unison, and then he
had outpaced me in height. He was nearly six feet as a teenager,
a handsome young man but still a solemn one and careful with
his life. An element of shyness had entered our lives along with
adolescence, as we foresaw our future betrothal and remained re-
spectful of each other. We no longer hugged or spoke but revealed
our thoughts through our eyes and other features: a wink, a quick
smile, a raised eyebrow, a twitch of the nose. We communicated
like actors in silent movies. Though we did not see each other
except at family ceremonies, he wanted me to remain within the
confines of his city and my home, and not across mountains and
borders. I had replied:

Dear Shaheen,

   *Thank you for your sweet letter. I thought it was understood that,
as Padar is posted to Delhi, I wanted to be with my parents, since I
missed them over the last few months of my final year in school. I did
think of following Maadar into academia, even in English literature,
as she taught me so much, but I couldn't see myself as a professor of
any sort. I had also considered studying law and following my* padar-
kalaan *into practice. But to debate in a court of law intimidated me.*

I am not a good public speaker. In school, I enjoyed writing poetry,
but I also enjoyed writing essays for homework and took great delight
in research and discovering new facets of the assigned subject. And
so, after discussing it with my parents, I decided on journalism, the
fourth estate in governing, and thought I could contribute to other
Afghans something of an understanding of our country.
  Affectionately,
  Rukhsana

On the drive to our house, I watched the city streaming past
the car, marveling at the width of the roads, the bright lights il-
luminating them, the houses, the cars, the buses. It was evening,
yet the traffic hadn't abated and the city was raucous with life. I
was a villager arriving in a metropolis and everything was exciting,
strange, exotic, and intimidating and threatening, all at the same
time. By this time in Kabul, a menacing silence would be wrapping
around the city and we would lock and bar our doors and windows
to protect us from roaming gunmen searching for loot.

I was excited to see my new home, a ground-floor apartment
in New Friends Colony, and a half hour's drive from the Afghan
embassy on Shanti Path in Chanakyapuri. Mother and nine-year-
old Jahan, showing off his Montessori school uniform, waited to
embrace me. My room, next to Jahan's, was sparsely furnished—a
single bed, a cupboard, a table and chair for my studies—but I
felt instantly comfortable in it even though the walls were bare. I
would decorate it to my taste. Jahan showed me around with the
assurance of a real estate agent, opening and closing the doors.

Most of all, I loved the lawn and garden in front of the house,
with its line of mango and peepal trees against the front wall to
protect us from the brutal sun. I wished I could grow high enough
to caress these treetops and clapped my hands, delighted at the
sight of so many birds in them. There were crows, parrots, mynahs,

koels, and pigeons in this open aviary. High above, kites circled endlessly in ascending and descending spirals. From somewhere distant, I heard a strange call.

"What is that?"

"A peacock in the park," Jahan boasted. "It's very beautiful, a thousand colors, but it can't fly far. Come on, I'll show you."

He led me out of our compound and down the street to the park a hundred meters away. At this time of the day, it was deserted and I looked around nervously and that made Jahan laugh.

"It's safe here."

He searched the trees until he saw the peacock. He was happy to hear my gasp on seeing it.

"It really is the most beautiful bird I've ever seen," I said and, satisfied, Jahan led me back home.

That night, I sat on my bed and found myself listening to the quiet, turning my head from side to side like a wary animal uneasy in its new surroundings. The quiet emptied my mind of thoughts. I knew I would soon learn to love it.

In the morning, Father took me to Kalindi College, in East Patel Nagar, to help me register for classes. The college, with its pink sandstone walls, archways, and pillars, reminded me of a fortress. Girls and their parents besieged the administrative building, queuing at the different windows—B.A., B.Sc., B.Com. Father and I joined the line at the "Journalism" window where a woman behind it, like a booking clerk, checked my application, stamped it, and then took the check from Father for the first year's fees. I found myself wondering if the walls would withstand rocket fire, and I felt infinitely older than the other girls milling about and meeting their professors. They seemed carelessly, blithely unaware of any danger, like children in a fairground.

On my first day of classes, I felt as if I was at the center of a merry-go-round of bright colors and babbling voices, and for the first time I experienced a deep sense of isolation. Some girls knew each other from their school days, and hugged and laughed, chattering away. I wanted to turn and run, but I also wanted someone to acknowledge that I was there among them, an Afghan girl starting in this college. I smiled at every girl I passed, hopeful that someone would see it as an invitation to friendship. Some returned them; the elder ones passed me as if I didn't exist. At least in that sense, it didn't matter where you were from—seniors were not interested in freshmen.

I had English literature in the afternoon, and I sat in the second row, next to a girl who sprawled in her seat, drowsing in the heat. She wore faded jeans, a white T-shirt, and sneakers. On the floor between us was a kit bag with a cricket bat handle sticking out. At last, seeing something so familiar, my whole face lit up, and she saw it. The girl was beautiful, with a straight profile, light brown skin, high cheekbones, and languid eyes. She had short hair, cut almost to a young man's length. She returned a wide grin.

"I saw you at registration," she said. "You're impossible to miss, you're so tall—and you really are very fair." Then she laughed at herself. "Isn't that a typical Indian remark? We always talk about our color. Are you from Kashmir?"

"Afghanistan."

"Cool, that's really cool. From what I've read, it sounds like a scary place. I don't know how you survive there."

"Just barely," I said. It was the first time I ever heard a person use the word "cool"—I liked the sound of it. "You play cricket?"

"Have to," she said. "Father loves cricket and we had to learn it as kids. So I got quite good at it. You don't play it in Afghanistan, do you?"

"No, but I learned to play it a little."

"You did?" The girl straightened. "That's awesome. We're starting practice after this class. You have to join the team."

"I've never played with a team," I said, panicked. "I just know a little bit of bowling and batting."

"That's all you need to know." She stuck out her hand. "Nargis."

"Rukhsana," I said, taking the hand. "But I don't have any clothes, and I have to go home."

"Where do you live?"

"New Friends Colony."

"No problem. I'll drop you at home after practice. The *shalwar* is fine for the first day, and we'll find shoes for you." Her tone and voice made it impossible to disagree.

After class, I trailed Nargis to the cricket field.

And there, for the first time, I saw the pitch in the center of the grassy oval field. I wanted to run over and brush with my hand the closely mown surface, sixty-six feet in length and ten feet across, from every angle. For a batsman it was a long walk from the pavilion and seemed much longer back if he was caught out on the first ball. Off the field, in a corner, were four practice pitches, each one with netting on either side. Beside them, eight other girls were gathered around a slim, elderly man with a sad mustache and dressed in a faded blue tracksuit. He was studying his team glumly and turned when he heard us approach. His eyes settled on us appreciatively, as if we were contestants in a beauty contest and he had a couple of winners. One of the women, wearing a tracksuit that had seen better days, came to meet us; she was a little older than we were, with a square face and short-cut hair. She had a confident bounce in her step.

"I'm Gayatri, the captain," she said. "Have you come to try out for the team?"

"Yes, I'm Nargis."

"Rukhsana," I said.

"Which are you better at? Batting or bowling?" she asked Nargis.

"Bowling. Medium pace. But I can bat too, usually lower down the order." Gayatri waited for me to reply too, but Nargis spoke up for me: "Rukhsana knows about cricket but hasn't played with a team. She's from Kabul."

"Afghans don't play cricket," the coach, Sharma, snorted. He had a surprisingly deep voice for a thin man and he smoked incessantly. "They don't even know the game."

"We'll give you a tryout," Gayatri said, rolling her eyes at her coach.

"I'm a slow bowler and spin off-breaks pretty well," I said firmly. "But I haven't had much batting practice."

Gayatri then introduced us to the other girls. They stepped forward, shook hands, and told me their names—Lakshmi, Hemala, Padmini—all strange to my ears, and I repeated each name to myself, hoping I would say it correctly. At least Masooda was familiar—I knew one from home. Gayatri then tossed me a ball. I polished the red leather, faded and pitted, with a little stitching coming apart. I flexed my right arm, winding it around like a windmill to loosen my muscles, and felt all eyes on me as I walked to the bowling crease. Gayatri, wearing pads, took her stance at the batting crease.

"Just relax," Nargis whispered, jogging up alongside. "I want you on the team with me."

"You're sure you'll be chosen?"

"I'm an old pro," Nargis said, grinning. "I captained my school team."

My first two balls were wide, and bounced only halfway down the pitch, but now I was determined to join this team too and not disappoint Nargis. I couldn't believe that I finally had a chance to play for a cricket team and I couldn't let this chance slip away. My days of lonely practice were rewarded. My third and fourth balls were straighter, my fifth bounced just at the right spot and turned slightly. I knew the secret of a good bowler was in the rhythm of the run-up and delivery. As I kept bowling, I found that rhythm, a five-pace slow run, a turn of the body, the right arm arcing up and releasing the ball at the top of the arc, and then the follow-through.

"Flight it more," Sharma said. I learned later that he had played for Punjab state and once nearly made the Indian test team. He was still bitter about it, and being reduced to coaching women did not help his attitude.

It was my turn to bat then. "Bat straight, Rukhsana, your foot nearer the pitch of the ball, your head must remain still," he shouted, and I was immediately flustered. But then I concentrated on his instructions and found another rhythm here too. If Sharma was critical, he was also quick to encourage. "That's better, play the line of the ball, keep the bat straight, and follow through."

"No one will believe I have an Afghan girl on the team," Sharma said grudgingly after practice. Nargis elbowed me playfully in the ribs.

When Nargis and I got in her car, I realized that afternoon had become evening. "You'll have to explain to my mother where we've been," I said in a panic.

"No problem," Nargis said. "You have a curfew?"

"She's nervous about what might happen to me in the big city."

"She's right, you know. As a journalist you'll have to get out alone, interview real bastards," Nargis said as she drove recklessly in her battered Maruti 800, overtaking other cars with a blast of her horn as if it would magically clear a gap in the traffic. She glanced at me. "Any boyfriend back home?"

"Yes. We are supposed to marry one day. He introduced me to cricket, actually."

"You sure sound enthusiastic." Nargis laughed.

"And you?" I said, ignoring her.

"Nope. Let's see what the big bad city has to offer. Yours is arranged from the sound of it."

"Yes, parents pushing us together."

"I've already said, 'No way, Mom. I'll screw up my life on my own.' "

BACK IN OUR BASEMENT IN KABUL, JAHAN TURNED THE PAGES of the album and stopped at a picture of eleven women, all in our whites, laughing and posing after having won the intercollegiate cricket trophy. There was Sharmila, Lakshmi, Nargis, Aruna, Gayatri . . . and I was in the center, standing in the back row. The photographs had a faint purple sheen; even as memories fade, so do the bright colors of the images captured with a click. There was another photograph of me alone, padded up, gloves on, leaning nonchalantly against my bat as if I was a professional cricketer. I wondered where all those young women were now. Did they wonder what had happened to me? They would be in mid-career in Delhi, New York, Paris, and Mumbai. Lakshmi and Gayatri had corresponded with me for a while after college. I knew about Gayatri's job with Citibank and her marriage. I knew Lakshmi had gone to Harvard for her M.B.A., while Nargis, at Caltech, was working on a doctorate in geology. They would have photographs too, buried deep under the business of their lives, while mine were easily brought to light, little else of note having happened since those faraway days.

THE WAY WE WERE

"Close it," I told Jahan. But he kept turning the pages of my photo album. Me, with a gang of us, five girls and one man.

"Who's the man next to you? He's smiling at you."

I peered at the photograph. The man, half a head taller than me, casual, his hands thrust deep in his pockets, a camera hanging from his neck, was smiling.

I flushed and ached at seeing him. Where was *he* now? "I think his name's . . . Veer? . . . Yes, it's Veer . . . and he's the brother of"—I stabbed a finger at the girl standing next to him to deflect his attention—"Nargis. We all hung out together. We went to movies, sat around cafes having coffees, went to cricket matches, had a few classes together.

"Come on, Jahan, let's go. Our cousins will be here soon."

But Jahan turned more pages, studying each photograph, paying no attention to me.

At the end of the cricket season, Nargis invited the team to her house for dinner.

Nargis's father worked in communications and, though Nargis never made any mention of it, was very wealthy. She lived in a large house filled with antiques, paintings, and four playful Dalmatians that she adored. I wasn't comfortable around dogs; the ones in Kabul roamed the desolate streets as hostile survivors of the chaos. But I enjoyed the company of my teammates and we laughed and talked around the enormous polished mahogany dining table that could seat all eleven of us squeezed together.

I was sitting between Gayatri and Sushila, rehashing the recent cricket match between India and Australia, when I looked up to see a man standing at the door. He resembled Nargis, but his light brown eyes were penetrating where hers were soft. His hair was unruly and he brushed it back off his forehead impatiently. Although he scanned the table filled with chattering girls, his eyes came back to catch mine.

"What the hell are you doing back here?" Nargis interrupted the flow of conversation when she saw her brother.

"This is my home, or did Dad bequeath it to you in my absence?" His voice was low with quiet amusement.

"This is a private dinner party, and you're not invited. I'll have the cook send you up a meal to eat in your room, as you're not used to any company apart from wild animals."

"And women aren't wild?" He waved to the room, then turned, and we heard him stomp up the stairs, laughing.

"My brother, Veer," Nargis announced witheringly. "The chosen one."

"Adorable," Gayatri sighed.

"Fabulous," Mala breathed loudly.

"You hid him away from us," Sushila scolded Nargis.

"Shit, none of you has any taste at all. Believe me, he's horrible. He lives in jungles all the time, making documentaries, and has no manners." She turned to look down the table. "Rukhsana, don't you agree? Horrible."

"Very horrible." I smiled, though not in complete agreement.

The following Saturday afternoon, Veer came to watch us play a match. His presence surprised Nargis. He was shaved and looked presentable in jeans and a black shirt.

"He's never ever come to watch me play," Nargis said. She looked around at the team suspiciously. "He's come to watch one of you."

"Does he play cricket?" I asked as we took to the field.

"He played for Delhi University and was really good until he decided to make his living in the jungle."

He sat in the shade of a tree with his big black camera hanging from his neck. I noticed how alert we had all become on the field; we were all showing off for an audience of one. A New York Yankees cap was pulled down low on his forehead, shading his watchful eyes.

Every time I glanced in his direction, his camera panned the field. After the match, Veer joined the team at the college canteen for a snack and tea.

"You bowled terribly," he said to Nargis.

"Why are you here?" she demanded, hands on hips. "You totally distracted me."

"I just felt like watching a game, that's all," he said innocently. "I thought you would be delighted you had at least one person watching you play."

"Well, I didn't want you to be the one."

At first, Veer was inclusive of the other girls in his conversation at the table. He praised each one for her performance before finally congratulating me on my top score.

"How did you learn cricket in Kabul?" He spoke softly, low

enough for the conversation to be private. I remembered how he had remained at the door, looking at me.

"Something to pass the time," I replied. His attention was suddenly uncomfortable. Images of Shaheen and my parents filled my head—whatever his intentions, I had to be careful. "That's the same reason Uma and Sushila learned too. Didn't you?" I swiveled around, pleading for them to join the conversation again.

"Oh yes," they chorused and deliberately fell silent, seeing the panic in my eyes, teasing me with theirs.

"Well, it's a dangerous country, but a beautiful one. I was in the Hindu Kush three years ago photographing the gray wolf for a magazine. I had two mujahedeen protecting me. There aren't many gray wolves left, just one or two packs, and they're such magnificent creatures."

"We keep chopping away at our forests," I said sadly.

"I'll show you my shots one day."

I panicked—how to let him know this needed to stop?

"Did you see a snow leopard?" I asked, my hands beginning to shake. I wanted to leave, but that would be horribly rude.

"Not up there, but in the Himalayas. It takes a hell of a lot of patience and a lot more luck to get a shot of one. But what about you? Why do you want to be a journalist?"

Talking more calmed me down. Perhaps I had overreacted—there didn't seem to be any harm in our conversation. We were still talking when we finished our tea, left the cafeteria, and strolled slowly together across the cricket field. At this time in my life in Delhi, I had not had any long conversations with a man outside of my father, brother, and family friends, but I found myself at ease talking to Veer. The way he focused on me made me feel special. When I didn't want to talk about myself, I changed the subject to cricket. He told me about playing for his college; he'd even been given a tryout for the state cricket team. But by then he had lost interest in the game and followed his love for wildlife photography.

"When was the moment you knew you wanted to write about the world?" he said during a lull.

"One day when I was twelve, on my way to school, I saw a Russian soldier sitting on the road, all alone. He was just a few years older than I was. He had whitish blond hair and blue eyes and he was crying. Everyone could see the tears running down his face. He cried silently, not caring who saw him. He looked so tired and there were dark rings under his eyes. We are a very kind people and everyone tried to help him. Someone offered him tea, another water, another food, thinking that he needed sustenance for his body. I thought he cried because he was lost and knew it. Not in the sense that he didn't know where he was but that he was lost in the world."

"What did you think?"

"I believed he was crying for his dead friends and for his damaged soul. I wanted to speak to him but I didn't know Russian and he wouldn't have spoken Dari or even English."

"What happened to him?"

"An armored car drove by and the soldiers saw him. They had to carry him into the car as if he was a dead body. He was so lifeless, and so young too. I cried for him."

"You didn't hate him for invading your country?"

"No," I said. "I felt sorry for him. He was just a lost boy. In the old days generals—Alexander, Genghis Khan, Babur—led their armies into battle, risking their lives alongside their men. Now, the generals sit behind their desks far away and send orders to kill us." I smiled, feeling shy. "I never told anyone this story. I did write it, but I didn't submit the essay."

Our shoulders touched accidentally and I felt the heat of his body through my shirtsleeve. I stepped away but the sensation lingered. He sensed the touch too and tried to ignore it.

"And cricket? How did you learn? I didn't know Afghan women played any sports."

"We don't, we've never been encouraged to play anything. A cousin brought the game back after a visit to Pakistan and taught it to me so he'd have someone to bowl for him. I guess I wanted to be different, and cricket was certainly unheard of even in Kabul."

"So that's why you have a free-flowing style of play. The girl expressing herself outside of society's expectations."

I laughed. "I don't know what you're talking about."

"I'm a psychologist in my spare time. I can tell a person's character by the way he or she plays the game."

"And mine's free flowing?" I grinned, and when I looked at him, I felt him studying my face.

"I'd say . . ." He frowned in mock seriousness. "You're pretty focused, but you have a reckless streak."

I considered what he'd said. "I'm not reckless, but I can be impulsive at times. I should control that."

"Never do that. Just be yourself."

I felt Shaheen come and perch on my shoulder, a nagging hawk, pecking at my conscience, monitoring my reactions, grimacing at my smiles, intently listening to Veer with disapproval. "A woman," he whispered in my ear, "should never speak to strange men. Stop it at once, I order you."

Nargis was waiting for me in her car. As we approached, Veer took my floppy cap and exchanged it for his, firmly placing his New York Yankees one on my head, saying, "That's better protection from our Indian sun."

"So, what do you think of my brother?" Nargis asked when I climbed into the car.

"He seems . . . nice," I said neutrally. "You don't like him much, do you?"

"You kidding? I love him. I just like yelling at him."

"I enjoyed talking to him," I said, trying not to give anything away.

"It looked like that," she said drily.

"Doesn't he have a girlfriend, a fiancée?" I asked, hoping he had someone to distract him, yet hoping he didn't.

"Nope. He's a free spirit, wandering the earth."

That was certainly true. He called a few days later.

"Hey. It's Veer. Do you want to see a movie?"

I was alone in the house, Father at work, Mother shopping, Jahan at school.

I replied with an abrupt "I can't go out with you," and hung up. I stared at the phone, panicked, and prayed he would not call back. No one had ever asked me out on a "date."

I looked around as if expecting to see Mother step out from the shadows asking, "Who called? What did he want?"

Shaheen scolded my conscience again. "You must have encouraged him to call you." "No," I replied to his spirit, "all I did was talk to him. I didn't ask him to call me."

The phone rang again, interrupting my thoughts. I knew it was Veer calling back, and I froze for an instant before picking up the receiver.

"We were disconnected," Veer said calmly, knowing perfectly well I had panicked. "Listen, I know in your culture you can't see a man alone. Nargis is also going to the movie and so are a couple of other girls. I just thought you might like to join us. Before you say no again, I'll get Nargis to call and invite you. How's that?"

"I'll have to think about it . . ."

"And I'll sit at the far end so there'll be three girls between you and me."

I laughed.

I dressed casually, in imitation of the other girls, in jeans, a white shirt, and high heels. As if to prove her credibility as a chaperone, Nargis picked me up, coming in to talk to my father and mother.

"See what I do for my brother?" She laughed. "Playing the gooseberry."

"Gooseberry?"

"I'm the third person who spoils everything by being present on a date—it's a sour fruit. That's the only way to get you out, Veer said. He owes me a huge favor for this."

"Who else is going?"

"Just you, me, and Veer."

Veer waited at the entrance of the cinema, holding the tickets. I watched him scanning the crowd as we approached, and when he saw me, he broke into a wide smile. I couldn't help smiling too. I was so strangely happy to see this man again. I quelled any internal dialogue with the watchful Shaheen. It was only a movie, and Nargis was with us. Veer was a friend, a movie buff like me, and I would probably not see him again after this.

Nargis sat between us in the dark theater, yet I could sense Veer's presence, distracting me from the film.

On the way home, after Nargis dropped her brother off, she drove in uncharacteristic silence, staring ahead, stealing glances at me and smiling. "I think my brother's very interested in you," she said finally. "That worries me."

"Why?" I was surprised. "I'm the one who should worry. I didn't ask him to be interested."

"Sometimes it can't be helped. And you are too, though you're trying to deny it because of that guy back home, waiting faithfully for you."

"I'll stop seeing Veer," I said firmly. "It would be best for both of us."

"If that's what you want, tell him. But don't ask me to do that. You're both adults. My brother can take care of himself."

"I will then," I said, and tried to explain what I believed I felt. "I've never been out with a man, and I like him as a friend. He's interesting. That's all."

"Famous last words."

"Are you upset, Nargis?"

"Me? No. I just think it's sad, since you two seem like you're having a good time. But you do what you have to do."

I had decided, and rehearsed my words. "I'm sorry, I can't see you again, Veer. My parents will strongly disapprove. It's for the best, as there is someone waiting for me to marry him." I thought they were the right words, spoken kindly, as I withdrew from this friendship. I would spend my afternoons at home and would never answer the phone. I am relieved, I told myself. But I didn't hear from him for a whole week and then another. At first I was relieved and then angry with him. He should at least have had the grace to tell me instead of cutting me off coldly. In novels, men behaved in such a way. Didn't Heathcliff in *Wuthering Heights* just ride away without a backward glance or a good-bye? I was so angry, I refused to ask Nargis whether he was in Delhi or not. And so I spent my afternoons at home and didn't ever answer the phone. Two weeks passed, then another and another. "Are you all right?" Mother asked, not for the first time.

"I'm fine. Why?" I replied as usual.

"The frown, the distant look . . ."

"School," I said and shrugged.

"You should relax. Why don't you go shopping? That always helps me."

"I don't feel like shopping. I'll go see a movie."

I sat in the back row, and I didn't look up when a man sat down next to me as the lights went down. He handed me a Coke and I took it. "I hoped you might come."

"I followed you," he said. "Nargis called your house and your mother told her you were going to a movie, so I waited and followed your taxi."

I turned my face to Veer, and he was waiting. Our lips first touched gently, brushed each other, and then pressed more firmly, more insistently. When we drew apart, I felt as if I had been submerged in water all my life, looking up at the opaque sunlight, and the kiss had shot me to the surface to release my pent-up breath; I was no longer a girl. I had been awakened from the dreamy sleep of adolescence and innocence. That was my moment of maturity, my discovery of what it felt like to experience passion as a woman. I was unprepared for such a rush, my heart ached with the freedom. I couldn't hush it, and the remainder of the film was a blur. Afterward, we didn't speak as we walked to his car, though, for the first time, we held hands, dry palms pressed tightly against each other. When we climbed into the stifling car, cluttered with paper, his backpack, and camera case, I peered into the mirror—my lipstick was smeared.

"Why didn't you tell me?" I said, and touched up my mouth.

"You looked cute," he said. "You looked as if you'd been kissed for the first time and hadn't thought about your makeup."

I punched him gently.

He reached out and stroked back the curl of hair that fell across my eyes. I let him do that. "I wanted to do that the very first time I saw you."

He dropped me off at the corner; we blew each other good-bye kisses. Mother was home, and I told her the story of the film as proof that I had been to it, alone.

In my room, I studied my face. And then, of course, I could not escape Shaheen. He burst into the room to circle me; he was furious, he raged, his honor had been insulted. "You're a whore, a prostitute, a cheap woman. You gave your lips up to a man when that first kiss was my sole right on our wedding night."

I fought back. "It was only a kiss. It was a friendly kiss, that's all." My justifications didn't calm him.

"I know what will happen after the kiss. You'll go to bed with him, you'll give him your body next. That's what all women do. They're weak and can't control their passions."

I refused to be intimidated. "And what about men? They don't even want to kiss, they just want to take us, and that's all you want from me. You want an obedient wife who'll sit at home making babies and cooking for you. I am sick and tired of being told how I must behave as a woman." I slammed on my headphones, turned up the music, and lay back in bed, driving him out the window.

As my fury faded, I was awash with guilt, but my tongue caressed my kissed lips.

The next day, Nargis called to tease me. "What have you done to my brother? I've never seen him looking so dreamy in my whole life."

Jahan was studiously watching a cartoon, within earshot.

"Nothing . . . ," I said.

"Well, I'm inviting you out for dinner—just with me—so can you come tomorrow night?"

"As long as it's not too late and you pick me up."

We went to the university canteen and sat at our usual table. Nargis was still smiling, still teasing.

"My brother's nuts about you."

I had suspected that already, but hearing it made it even better. It felt wonderful.

"I don't believe it. He must have hundreds of girlfriends."

"No, that's just it. He's had a few but never for very long. Oh, they throw themselves at him, but you've caught him. So what happens next?"

She saw my hesitation as the smile slipped off my face. "I don't know. My family would be so angry if they knew I was seeing him and my father will forbid it . . ."

Nargis took my hand. "I know that. It's you I'm worrying about more than him. My father won't be happy, but he'll never withhold his consent. And my brother's a grown man. But I can see you're both going to be hurt when the time comes. All I can say is, be careful and enjoy yourselves."

Over the following months, Veer and I found time to be together. He traveled for work and I waited impatiently for his return. I would pace in my room, trying to suppress my longing for him, trying also to suppress the guilt of betraying my parents and Shaheen that sometimes overwhelmed me and brought me to tears. Veer was the pleasure and the pain in my life. We never talked of the future; we lived for the present. Although I never spoke the name Shaheen, he knew there was a ghost haunting me. We had our lunches and coffees, we had our movies, and we had our kisses.

As Nargis had predicted, the time, which I hoped would never come, came. I woke with dread when I should have been rejoicing. I had graduated from college and Father wanted me to return to Kabul. Shaheen awaited.

On our last afternoon together, we sat again in silence across from each other at a table, neither of us touching our food. We kissed there, in the restaurant, not with passion but with tenderness.

"I'll talk to your father? I'm sure he will understand."

"No," I said, holding his hand tightly. "He will never permit it. He is a kind and understanding man, but if he'd known about us, he would have sent me back to Kabul already. I haven't even told my mother. I cannot disobey my father like this. He will think it dishonors him. I love you so much, but I have no choice. I can't marry you."

He pulled away. "You're a coward," he said angrily. "You'll risk your life returning to Kabul and the civil war between the Talib and the Northern Alliance but won't risk staying here with me."

"Yes, I am a coward. I can't defy my family," I cried. "Please, please understand that. You know the problems I would have. My father, my family, would never forgive me. They would throw me out, maybe worse. I just wanted to love you, to experience love with you. But I have to go home."

"Things could change, we mustn't give up."

"They may. Anything can happen." But I didn't believe my words.

"We'll keep in touch," he insisted. "You will change your mind." He tried a smile, but it distorted his face. "I don't quit that easily."

We remained silent on the drive to my home, and he parked at the usual spot, on the corner, and waited for me to say something. He had said all that he could.

"You must forget me. I must forget you," I said as if it would be that easy. "Please don't write to me or call me." My voice broke. "It'll be too painful."

Tears fell from his brown eyes, and I leaned across to kiss them dry, tasting the saltiness.

He held my hand. "I won't promise that, and I won't promise that I won't call you, wherever you are, or write to you."

"If you write, I won't open the letters. And I won't speak to you if you call."

"I'll keep writing in the hope that one day you will. And calling too. You know I love you, and it's madness to know I'll never be able to say those words to you again."

I flew to Kabul the next morning and did not look down for a last glimpse of the city in which I had fallen in love. I was breathless from the pain and furious at my cowardice. I didn't have the courage to break with my family for love. I loved Veer with all my heart, and now it was tearing into pieces and the agony was unbelievable.

Grandfather met me at the Kabul airport and drove me home through a city as damaged as I felt. Grandmother noted my silence, the distraction in my eyes, and she believed me when I told her I had caught the flu. I hid away in my childhood room and waited for the sadness to drain out of me. After three weeks, I began my career in the *Kabul Daily* office, reporting on the continued fighting. I convinced myself that I'd locked Veer away in a secret corner of my mind and knew, with time, he would gradually fade to a beautiful and painful memory of my first, and only, love. I pushed him into the back of my mind, and locked him away in a very dark corner. Shaheen visited us, but as my parents were still in Delhi, we agreed to defer the engagement ceremony until they returned.

JAHAN CLOSED THE ALBUM AND LOOKED AT ME IN SURPRISE, not having known anything about Veer or my teammates.

"I should have burned these," I said, and couldn't hold back the tears.

"No." He wrapped an arm around my shoulders. "You'll want to remember Delhi. You must keep them to remind you that there were better times and that they will come again when we get out of here." He hugged me.

I leaned against him, my tears soaking into his shirt. He let me weep, uncertain as to what to do. He had never seen me crying like this—for no apparent reason. He patted my shoulders, caressed the top of my head, and held me tighter.

"I hope you're right." I sniffled.

"Aren't I always?"

At the bottom of the trunk was my cricket bag. He unzipped it and pulled out my kit. There were pads, gloves, wrinkled whites, grubby socks, and dirty boots. I had always been immaculate on the field but, after the last game, knowing I had to leave for Kabul the next day, I wanted only to forget and stuffed my kit, unwashed, into the bag.

Jahan handed me the pads and batting gloves. "Come on. Show me what these things are for."

I placed the pad on my leg and fastened the Velcro straps, then repeated the action for the other leg.

"Can you run with those on?"

"Of course. They just protect your shins and kneecaps from the ball."

I slipped on my gloves, worn, supple, and smelling of my own sweat still. I felt that I was arming myself for battle. My old accomplishments flooded back to me.

Jahan unearthed another layer of the trunk and lifted out the bat from its blue plastic sheath. He drew it out like a sword from a scabbard. He wielded it awkwardly, first like a tennis racquet and then like a hockey stick. I took it from him and held it up to the light. The foot-long round handle still had its rubber grip. The attached blade was exactly 4.25 inches in width and 26 inches in length and the flat side still retained a pale golden sheen and was liberally marked with the red stains of cricket balls. The back of the bat was curved to give it weight. Many of the hits were in the center of the blade, in the sweet spot, and I was proud that I had had a good eye for this game. My left hand reflexively gripped the top of the handle and swung it in the straight line that I had perfected. I swung it back and forth like a pendulum.

The body never forgets.

It was all rushing back to me as I held the bat. The strategy, the competition, the joy.

Now, emboldened by a good memory, I searched the trunk

for the ball, rooting through familiar objects, pulling out papers, a plastic bag, and finally finding it rolling around the bottom. It was brand new, still shiny red leather, and wrapped in tissue paper. It fit comfortably in my hand, my fingers curling around the seam.

"What is this?"

Jahan was holding in one hand the plastic bag I'd thrown aside, and in the other he held what looked like a strange furry animal.

I took the animal from him. "That's my Shylock beard from *The Merchant of Venice*. I played him in our college play." I laughed and fit the beard on my face, masking me from ears to chin. The hair was woven into a net and thin black cords slipped over my ears to hold it and the mustache in place. I took a dramatic stance.

"'Hath not a Jew eyes? Hath not a Jew hands, organs, dimensions, senses, affections, passions; fed with the same food, hurt with the same weapons, subject to the same diseases?'"

He clapped. "You made quite a man."

"I thought I was pretty good," I said modestly. "I liked doing comedy more; we could fool around then and make our audience laugh. We did a few Monty Python sketches too."

I shut the trunk firmly when we heard Abdul banging on the door and went upstairs. I slipped on the burka, with the pads still on my legs, and remained hidden behind the door, only to find Parwaaze and Qubad on the steps. They saw the bat and ball in our hands.

"So that's a cricket bat?" Parwaaze said, and I kept it out of reach. "Now can we start?"

"Azlam's forming a t-team too," Qubad said.

"Who's he?"

"He was in school and college with us. A *hila*," Parwaaze said, slightly embarrassed, meaning a cheater. "I saw him this morning and he said he was going to learn cricket. He didn't say how.

We have to beat Azlam's team if we play them." He paused and smiled. "But he doesn't know anyone who can teach him, and we have a coach who has nothing better to do." He reached eagerly for the bat again.

"First, I'll show you how to use it."

We went down the steps to the lawn. It wasn't long enough for a cricket pitch and we could break all the windows if we practiced here.

With my left hand gripping near the top and my right in the middle of the handle, I crouched over the bat, forgetting where I was, looking straight ahead, over my left shoulder, toward the bowler running up to the opposite wicket. Through the mesh, I could barely focus on a bowler, let alone the ball. But I wanted them to see the batting stance. My elbow pointed at the bowler. The ball came toward me, bounced once, and, keeping the bat straight, I lifted it back and brought it down in a perfect arc to hit an imaginary ball. I felt a sweet, joyful surge of nostalgia that nearly choked me.

"That looks easy." Jahan took the bat and tried to swing it the way I had, losing his balance.

"Don't worry," I said. "On television I've seen even the greatest cricketers lose their balance trying to hit the ball."

"Give it to me," Qubad said. He did a fair imitation of me but swung too wildly, like a golfer driving a ball.

Parwaaze grabbed the bat from him. "Let me try." He then crouched over the bat, but his feet were too close together.

Qubad took the ball first, examined it as if it were a hand grenade, and then pronounced, "This is as hard as a stone and will break my head."

"There's not much lost if that happens, and we'll stick the pieces back together," Parwaaze said, studying the leather and the parallel white stitches of the ball.

"Kn-knowing you, I'll have a nose at the back of my head," Qubad replied.

"That would improve your looks."

"Throw it at me," Parwaaze said, taking it from Qubad and tossing it to me.

"It's bowl," I reminded him. "You just need to keep your feet about a foot apart to maintain your balance." I moved about fifteen feet away from him. "It isn't that easy. And don't forget you're aiming at a ball that will bounce and could spin away."

I repeated the bowling actions of my past. I ran a few steps and turned sideways to deliver the ball. But when I tried to bowl, my right hand became entangled in the flapping garment, I lost sight of Parwaaze, and the ball flew over his head.

"You trying to kill me?"

"I can't do it properly in this," I said and removed the burka.

From their faces, I knew what they were thinking: *How is she going to teach us?*

I ignored their looks. "Ready," I said to Parwaaze. He crouched, feet slightly apart, and I bowled a gentle ball so it bounced in front of him. He pushed forward with his bat to hit it, but the ball turned and he missed.

I threw the ball to Jahan. "Now you bowl. Take a few steps, turn your body, and your right arm starts high up, then forms an arc coming down."

He concentrated hard on his bowling action, but the ball landed down near his feet and trickled over to Parwaaze, who hit it back. They took turns bowling and batting with me correcting their actions—"Raise your right hand as high as you can before letting the ball go . . . get your feet as close to the bounce of the ball as possible . . ."—and soon a sublime afternoon passed. There was still the purity and innocence of the game, which had given me such pleasure. We were back to our childhood days, playing together, laughing. I saw that they were enjoying their lesson. I imagined that Nargis and Veer would laugh and clap me on, and my old college coach, Sharma, would chuckle because his Afghan girl was teaching men to play this game.

We stopped when it was time for me to make dinner.

"Have you spoken to any of the others?" I asked Parwaaze.

"I've told Nazir and Omaid and they said they're in. I'll meet the others. We must keep the team in the family, and not let in any outsiders. We'll start learning properly tomorrow but not here."

"The university. They have a lot of space," I suggested.

I scooped up the burka and went into the house, taking the bat and ball, leaving three disappointed men who would have played all night to master this game.

THE LETTER

The next day, I deleted my first letter and began another to Shaheen.

My dear Shaheen,

I think of you often, daily, I would say. When I wake I think of you waking too, brushing your teeth, shaving, combing your hair, dressing, leaving your apartment and walking out into the street. I can see you catching the bus, sitting back and watching the scenery, thinking about your day ahead. It must be a wonderful feeling to be so free to do what you want. Do you still play cricket? I remember how well you taught me.

I am slightly concerned because I've not heard from you. I do hope all is well with your family. I am so looking forward to seeing you again soon. If you can get through, call me so I will be ready to leave. I'm sad to say Mother is not well.

No doubt, you'll understand that the cost of living has risen since you left.

I stopped. I hoped he understood what I meant. The cost of getting out was in the hundreds, I knew, but the airfare was at least a thousand dollars, and it depended on who sold you your ticket.

Do you still have a friend who will guide me to you? As I need to meet him soon, it would be great if you sent me a present, around 2K for him, so that when the time comes, I will be ready to leave in an instant.

Now, I wrote quickly.

We will marry as soon as I reach your side. I miss you so much.

There, I'd finally set the wedding date, my day of arrival. The pain was still suffocating. I fought back my tears for Veer, knowing we would never see each other again, and signed the letter.

With much affection,
  Rukhsana
  Mother and Jahan send their love.

What else could I say without telling even more lies? I reread the letter. I printed it out, folded it, and slid it into an envelope. I did not add my home address on the back, nor had I written it in the letter. If it was opened at the post office, no one could trace it back to me. I stuck a stamp on it and prayed it would reach him.

I covered the printer with a cloth and took my laptop to the basement, where Grandfather stored his old files and papers. The shelves sagged under their weight. I pressed a latch at the back of the middle shelf and a part of the bookshelf opened. It hid a dark, musty room, four feet wide and twelve long. When Grandfather built this house nearly fifty years ago, and with our long history of invasions, he had the architect design a secret room that could not be seen from the outside. Nor could it be found inside this house, unless one used a measuring tape between rooms. Not every house had one, although village homes had cellars to store grain after a harvest and hide in during an attack by a neighboring tribe. Grandfather had copied the design of his family home in Mazar. The room was our place to store the family's wealth (none left now) and conceal the women. Apart from an old divan and bolster, there was nothing in it. Only a tiny barred window, a few inches square, flush with the ceiling, leaked in light, and some air, from behind the flower bed. I returned the laptop to its concealed place under the divan and closed the secret door. In a corner of the corridor was a well-fitted slab of granite. It was no different from the rest of the flooring, except for a paper-thin gap in its four sides. Under it, three steps down, was a cellar, about five feet square, six feet high, the sides lined with brick. It was cool and dry, and we had stored dried fruits and nuts, rice and wheat down there at one time. Now, there were only empty sacks cluttering the floor. There was enough space for a few people to squeeze in there too. Should anyone search this building, they would discover the cellar and, hopefully, believe that to be our secret room. Grandfather would have created a labyrinth of escape tunnels, like the ones he saw in the old fortresses that dotted our landscape, if he could have.

Once again, I found Mother in the kitchen, this time asleep in a chair, her head down on her chest and the vegetable knife still in her hand. I touched her gently, and she came awake slowly, as if traveling a great distance through her dreams. "Come on, I'll take you to bed, you need to rest."

She stood wearily. "One moment I feel as if I can climb a mountain, the next I can't even crawl." She hooked her arm around my waist, and we shuffled slowly upstairs to her bedroom. I laid her down carefully on the bed, and drew the sheets up to her chin.

Gratefully, she closed her eyes and went back to sleep. She was breathing quietly, evenly. What would it be like when the rise and fall of her chest stopped? The dread, barely kept at bay by our hopes of escape, weighed down on my shoulders again.

I returned to the kitchen and prepared *quorma* quietly, with the plums and dal on the side. I missed Mother's company in the kitchen. We had always talked when we worked together. She had inspired my intellectual curiosity and my love of freedom, with Father's approval naturally. She had introduced me to V. S. Naipaul, Norman Mailer, Joseph Heller, Turgenev, Tolstoy, Alexander Dumas, Flaubert, James Joyce, Alison Lurie, Joan Didion, Gloria Steinem. She read me Gul Mohamad Zhowandai's short story collection *Ferroz*, and when I had enjoyed them, we read his novel *Kachkol* and spent hours discussing it. He was our most celebrated poet and writer and died in 1988. In that select company of authors and thinkers, I could imagine different worlds in which other women, and men, lived, loved, and died.

I FINISHED PREPARING DINNER AND WENT TO GET JAHAN from his room. He was at his desk in a halo of lamplight, wearing headphones, listening to his CD player. I could faintly hear Ahmad Zakir singing a Hindi song. On the wall opposite him was a large poster of Shaquille O'Neal performing a slam dunk. If the religious police raided us, they would tear it down and cane him for such a sacrilege. An orange basketball was on Jahan's bed. Some nights, I would wake to hear the ball bouncing, and the steady rhythm would lull me back to sleep.

On his bookshelf were X-Men comics and a few novels of Philip K. Dick's. I had tried to read one or two but couldn't connect with such an unemotional world. Maybe I simply lacked faith. Jahan had an unshakable faith in the future and believed, like Dick, that there was an alternate universe. Jahan's ambition was to become an astronaut, the first to slip through matter and black holes to reach this parallel universe, and never return. In that universe, I knew he hoped there would be no wars, no illness, no starvation, and no poverty. To my mind, it was the Taliban who were creating an alternate world, a violent, backward parallel universe. One of little joy, intense prayers, women kept under lock and key, the future banished, and the borders sealed from contaminating influences. They did not hate the present, they hated their inability to exist in it. Though they wanted to dismantle televisions, telephones and electricity, automobiles and planes, and all the other harbingers of corruption that they believed eroded their Islam, they knew, deep down, that time would crush them eventually.

"Have you done your homework?" I asked. Mother and I taught him at home, as the only schools open were the madrassas and we didn't want him to study there. All they taught was the Qur'an, which he would have to learn by heart. There was no math, history, geography, or science in that curriculum. So I used Mother's books to teach him and assigned his homework. Our relationship grew in such complexity—sister, surrogate mother, friend, and teacher, all rolled into one, and I had problems at times keeping them in their separate compartments.

He removed his earphones. "Almost. I just have to read the physics lesson and do the rest of these calculations. Have you written the letter?"

"Finally," I said with a sigh. "It's not my best work. I gave him a little news and warned him that it would cost more for a smuggler today."

"How much do you think?"

I shrugged. "Probably two hundred, but then he has to send air tickets also. I asked for two thousand."

He whistled. "I'm sure he'll be happy to spend that money on you." He laughed. "We must start practice early tomorrow."

"You better finish your lessons first. You have to study, whatever happens; it's very important for you."

We went to the kitchen to lay out dinner. I heated up the rice and the meat and prepared the salad. We were whittled down to such simplicity in our eating habits. I carried a tray into Mother's bedroom. Jahan helped her sit up and I placed it in front of her. Then I returned with the dishes and plates. Jahan prepared the ritual *dasaekhan*. He laid out our precious, antique Mazar-e-Sharif carpet on the floor, and then covered it with a large embroidered cloth. Jahan carried in the *aftabah wa lagan*, a copper kettle and bowl, and poured water from the kettle so that we could wash our hands over the bowl and then dry them on the small towel he handed us. He performed the ritual for Mother first, then me, and I did it for him. I served and, as usual, Mother ate a sparrow's helping. Jahan and I sat on the carpet beside her bed.

"I'm not hungry," she said.

"You don't like my cooking? You're saying I'm a bad cook?" I pretended to look hurt.

"Don't be silly, I like your cooking but . . ."

"Then show me you like it. Eat a little more. It will help you regain your strength."

"To do what? Just lie around?"

"To be with us, that's all," Jahan said. "The more you eat the more joy we have."

"You're both blackmailers." She ate a few more mouthfuls of the naan I had cut into pieces.

As we finished our meal, we heard Dr. Hanifa coming up the stairs, grumbling to herself. She was nearing seventy-three now and had retired when it became too difficult for her to visit her patients, but she lived next door and made an exception for

Mother. Kindness and compassion filled her eyes, though sadness lined her face. She always removed and left her burka on a chair by the door and donned it again when she left. Her husband, also a doctor, had died many years ago from pneumonia one severe winter. Her children had escaped to Pakistan. One was a doctor in Lahore, the other an engineer in Islamabad. They were planning to emigrate to the States. They would not sit beside her as she died, as I would by my mother.

"So how's my favorite patient?"

Dr. Hanifa took Mother's pulse and her temperature. "You young ones go and do what the young do. We'll talk awhile. Even when your mother sleeps, she's better company than my lonely house. I'll give her the medications later."

I kissed Mother good night and went to my room and lay down on my bed.

THE FIVE HUNDRED METERS

How could I teach my cousins cricket while I wore a burka? How could I show them how to bowl or bat when I could barely move? I couldn't even see a ball coming my way through the mesh.

I wasn't sure where to begin, yet currents of excitement shivered through my body. I thought about how Shaheen and my college coach had instructed me. I rolled over in bed and reached for some paper and a pencil on my desk—and I saw my letter to Shaheen. I had forgotten to ask Jahan to post it. It had to be posted tonight for the next morning's pickup, otherwise it would have to wait another twenty-four hours. I would have to disturb Jahan at his homework. It wouldn't take long. The postbox was on Karte Seh Wat. No more than five hundred meters, possibly less. It would take no more than five minutes for him to stroll there and back.

Five minutes, just five hundred meters.

It was such a short distance.

Like a sleepwalker, I went down to the basement, opened the trunk of my memories, removed the plastic bag Jahan had discovered yesterday, and hurried back to my room.

The beard was soft and seductive in my hands. I placed it on my face and firmly secured it. It was made of human hair, not animal hair. It had come from a Hindu woman's head, shorn at the temple, an act of sacrifice and humility. I'd bought it at the Broadway Theater company in Connaught Place in Delhi.

I pinned the old turban in place too, fitting it firmly on my head. I picked up the little hand mirror, and when I looked into it I saw the old moneylender looking back at me. He studied me solemnly, his gaze inching over my face as if looking for imperfections. His eyes met mine. They should have been wary, weary, cynical, and old; instead they were feminine, young, clear, and confused. I removed the turban first, then the beard, and dropped them on the floor. Shylock vanished, consigned to the stage, consigned to memories.

MRS. LAKSHMI, MY ENGLISH LITERATURE PROFESSOR IN Delhi, was a slight, small woman with a narrow face, in her midfifties. In the center of her forehead was a red, round *tilak*, the size of a coin. What she lacked in height and weight she made up for with her eyes, alight with energy and enthusiasm as she looked at her small class of a dozen students.

"You're going to do a lot of reading, and we will discuss in depth what you have read. I want your independent thoughts and not my regurgitated lectures on the writers." She spoke quickly, as if there were too many words on her tongue and she had to get them out, fast, before they choked her.

"Nargis Dhawan? Are you here?" When Nargis raised her hand, Mrs. Lakshmi dumped a sheaf of papers on her. "Hand those out. That's the required reading." And as Nargis went around distributing the papers, she continued. "Nargis, you volunteered for our theater group?"

"Yes, Mrs. Lakshmi."

"Would anyone else here like to join our theater group? We stage three or four plays a year. Some serious, some comedies, as people like comedies for no reason I can discern."

"Rukhsana," Nargis said wickedly, and pointed at me.

"Good, that's two."

"But I can't act," I said, startled to find myself volunteered.

"Nonsense," Mrs. Lakshmi said, brusquely dismissing my denial. "All women know how to act from the moment we are born. It's the gift God gave us to survive in this man's world. We have to act out our orgasms, our humility, our love when none exists, and suppress our ambitions." She looked me over from head to toe. "With a little help from me you're going to play Shylock."

"I know nothing about men!" I wailed.

"My dear girl, there is nothing to know, they are all sound and fury signifying nothing," Mrs. Lakshmi said. She waited for the burst of laughter to end. "When you leave here, observe them, watch them on the streets and in the buses and playing sports. Copy them, but don't become them, as they'll infect you with the delicate egos they suffer from. You have to believe in becoming the man, Shylock, immerse yourself in his language, his words, his arrogance at the start and humility at the end."

I WENT TO JAHAN'S ROOM CLUTCHING MY LETTER TO Shaheen. He was crouched over his books, music from the headphones pounding his ears, his unruly hair falling over his eyes. He had dozed off. I couldn't bear to wake him. Quietly, I took a *shalwar*, trousers, and his coat from a pile of clothes in a corner and left. In my room, I stripped and dressed in his clothes. The *shalwar* was loose and hung down to my knees; the jacket over it hid my feminine form. I put my hand in the pocket and found a fistful of banknotes.

I looked in my mirror: the clothes concealed my silhouette. I stood still, waiting for sanity to reclaim me. Instead, I picked up Shylock's beard and fastened the mask firmly on my face. I gathered up my hair, knotted it, and held it on the top of my head as I slipped on the turban. I pulled it down tight so that my hair wouldn't escape. I shook my head violently, from side to side and up and down. Neither beard nor turban became unfastened. Finally, I wrapped a *hijab* around my shoulders and across the bottom half of my face. I picked up the letter. I had to send it tonight, it was my lifeline.

It wasn't late, just eight o'clock. The hall was dark as I stepped through it into the kitchen. My hand shook as I reached for the keys and they eluded me, they danced out of reach, making such a loud sound that I thought my mother and Jahan would come running. I steadied one hand with the other, and took them down.

I held the key for the back door with both hands, inserted it in the lock, and twisted. The door opened. I stepped out into the cool, evening air. It seemed to take ages for me to tiptoe across the courtyard. I could hear Abdul snoring in his room. At the side gate, I held the key with both hands again, more determined now, committed to this madness, and opened that door. The street was deserted and full of shadows. The threshold seemed unnaturally high. I stepped over it, and stood in the lane. I closed the gate behind me.

When I reached the corner, I looked past the high wall of our courtyard and saw the solitary light in Jahan's room. I could still scuttle back home to safety. Instead, I kept going toward Karte Seh Wat. My breath came in short bursts and I felt as if I'd just sprinted a hundred meters.

Calm down, calm down. Remember Shylock and pace the stage.

Remember cricket: the long, solitary walk to the pitch through the mine-field of eleven hostile opponents watching and praying for you to fail.

I kept moving down the street.

Don't reveal any fear. Avoid all eye contact. Just take one step and then another. I am a young man out on an evening stroll. I will not be intimidated.

I walked as if I still wore the burka, and I was afraid that I might trip, but the streetlamps were all broken, which I had counted on to keep me hidden. I had heard of men who donned the burka to pass through dangerous war zones undetected—I had removed mine to see if I could pass undetected into danger. I had freedom even if I was also filled with dread.

Beyond the relative safety of my dark road lay the two hundred meters of better-lit streets filled with men strolling freely, laughing, gossiping, dreaming of things that men dream of. I heard distant voices and footsteps as I stood on the corner. A donkey cart passed within a few feet of me, but neither the beast nor the old man sitting on it glanced in my direction. I turned left and began walking toward Karte Seh Wat.

I smelled the dust, the kebabs, and the naan saturating the air. Men stood at stalls, drinking tea and smoking cigarettes. Their smoke drifted to me on the soft breeze. Not all the men were whole. Some were on crutches, others with an arm missing. I tried not to glance at them even though I had that freedom now. I stared straight ahead, not wanting to meet a stranger's eyes.

I recognized a few of the local shopkeepers—Kabir the baker, Akhmed the grocer, Ehsan the chemist. They were fixtures, unmoved by the wars that raged around the city. They knew how to survive and they paid no attention to the slight stranger.

Deeper in the shadows were women in their burkas, some holding out their hands for alms, others offering me their bodies. Before the Talib, our beggars were a few old men, and now they were women who did not have husbands or sons to support them. I had heard many had to turn to prostitution to survive, and the religious police would beat them and drive them away. As often as not they would first pleasure themselves for free. The women waited for them to leave the area, and then returned. "Come, young man, enjoy me. Very cheap. Thirty thousand Afghanis," they called. Some hands were gnarled, others younger and still delicate.

Another woman called softly, "Brother, please help me, give me some money. I am hungry."

I took a hurried step past her. Then stopped. I knew the voice, and it sickened me to hear her.

"Sister, what did you say?" I whispered, standing close to her.

She drew away, turning her head, ashamed. "Please help me. I'm hungry."

"Mother Nadia?"

"You know me, brother? Help me then. I am alone and can't work."

I couldn't help my tears as I took out the handful of banknotes and gave them to my old teacher.

"How did you know me, brother?"

"My . . . my . . . sister, Rukhsana, went to your school and I recognized your voice."

"Rukhsana? Rukhsana! Yes, I remember her. She was a cheerful girl, always the leader in the class, always asking questions." Her sigh penetrated my heart. "How is she? Is she safe?"

"She's well," I whispered. I remembered her voice in school, bright as a gold coin. Now, it was dull and tarnished with sadness.

"I hope she is married to a good man who cares for her. Please don't tell her about me."

She clutched the notes tightly, bowed her head, and hurried

away. I watched her with blurred eyes until she reached the corner.

The square green postbox on its stand was another fifty meters and I hurried to it, said a small prayer, and pushed the letter through the slot. I lifted my face and felt a slight breeze caress it. For the first time in three and a half years, I breathed in the cool evening air without the impediment of cloth against my nose. Just such a simple pleasure reminded me of past days.

I tried not to hurry as I returned home. I paced myself, head still averted from any lights. As I turned off to my road, a man stepped out from the darkness and fell in beside me. He walked a few steps in silence, and I did not dare turn to look at him.

"Are you mad?" Jahan whispered. "Are you stupid? They will shoot you dead and then shoot me for being your *mahram*."

"My heart nearly stopped!" I almost screamed.

"What about mine!" he continued in his furious whisper. "I've been following you this whole time. I was so scared when you spoke to that woman."

"She was my geography teacher. I recognized her voice and gave her the money in your coat pocket."

"Did she recognize your voice?"

"I whispered," I managed to stutter. I'd never seen Jahan so angry. "When you whisper . . . it's hard to tell whether you're male or female."

"You must never do this again. I forbid it, do you understand? As your brother and your *mahram*, I'm telling you this."

"What would you do if I did? Report me to the religious police and have me beaten?"

"No, I'll lock you in your room. Lock you in the house."

"I'm already locked in the house," I reminded him gently. I saw the tension in his young face as he wrestled with asserting his male authority over his sister.

"Why did you do this?"

"I had to post the letter. I forgot to give it to you and you were asleep." I took a breath. "Did I look like a man?"

"No. Like my sister in a beard," he said sourly as we walked home.

"That's because you know it's me. When we get home, tell me."

In the pale moonlight, I modeled and walked around for him.

"Well, it's night, so it's hard to say . . . but what about in the day? You walk like a woman, and look at your hands." I looked down. They were soft and pale compared to a man's hands. "And your eyes too. They are a woman's. And your feet."

"I'll wear glasses and sneakers. And I'll keep my hands in my sleeves. I'll have to study how men walk." I had to convince him. "You saw that I can't bowl or bat in a burka. I need a way to teach you how to play. This is just for cricket." I smiled at my cleverness and Jahan smiled back.

We turned the corner onto our street and stopped when we saw an unfamiliar car and a Land Cruiser parked outside our front gate. We hesitated, but two policemen saw us at the corner and motioned us over. I remained beside my brother.

As Jahan reached the car, the near passenger door opened and a thickset man with a silky black beard climbed out. He wore a black *shalwar* and a flat black *pakol* cap on his head. The driver remained at the wheel. For a few seconds the interior car light illuminated a woman sitting in the far passenger seat, clothed in her burka. She turned her head toward Jahan but vanished into the darkness as soon as the door slammed shut. A faint breeze touched the man and carried his scent to me. It was the same sickly sweet perfume of the man who had circled me in the room at the ministry, and I took a step farther back into the shadows.

The man greeted Jahan, "*Salaam aleikum*." He held out his hand and placed his left palm against his chest.

Jahan took his hand. "*Waleikum salaam.*" And he performed the same gesture.

"You are?"

"I am Jahan, son of Gulab."

"We have come to meet you," the man said to us, and gestured to the hidden woman to include her. "I am Droon, the deputy minister to my brother, Zorak Wahidi, and we wish to speak to you about an alliance between your sister, Rukhsana, and my brother."

THE PROPOSAL

THE STREET WAS DESERTED EXCEPT FOR A PASSING cyclist who swerved away when he saw the policemen.

Droon paid no attention to me as he spoke to Jahan. I was a stranger, a friend of no importance.

"That won't be possible," I heard Jahan say calmly. "She is betrothed to Shaheen, son of Nedaa Rafi."

"My brother is a minister in the government and all things are possible, my young friend." Droon had a gentle but steely voice. "This Shaheen is not here, is he?" He looked at me.

It was as if I had been punched hard in the stomach. I had to escape. What had I done to attract such a terrible fate? If Fatima was right, that laughing, dancing girl had embedded herself in his memory and out of such innocence is a man's obsession born. And then I had defied him those years ago in the office and he had remembered. I was probably the only woman who had. That's why he had called me to the press conference—to confirm his memory before he declared his true intent. Now I would become his personal slave, for him to beat whenever he wished, his property to do with as he chose. I had to escape, get out of the country. Now. I wanted to run and run, but I knew this would be a fatal move. Instead, I stood there shaking in the dark, swallowed whole by the fever of my panic.

I concentrated on Droon so that I wouldn't give myself away. Droon didn't resemble his brother. He had a fleshy nose and deep-set eyes; the beard masked the rest of his face. He must have been the son of another wife. He smiled, but it never touched his eyes.

"Still, she is betrothed to him," Jahan said, matching the steely courtesy. I had never seen my brother look more stubborn or more determined. He did not glance at me, not wanting Droon to take a further interest in his young friend. It was a strange sensation to hear myself spoken about, to be a witness to Rukhsana's life. I was still an invisible woman. Invisibility had its advantages, in over-hearing secrets and plots, but like a spirit I could not intervene in the fate of Rukhsana. I could only hover within hearing distance and remain the frightened spectator.

"My brother is a very wealthy man and he is keen for this alliance." Droon placed a friendly hand on Jahan's arm, drawing him into the conspiracy for my life. "Your sister is a fine-looking woman and he believes she will bear fine children too. He thinks of her often, which is why he makes this proposal."

"He is not family. How can he have seen her under her burka?" Jahan demanded.

"He has, before she was dismissed from the offices of the *Kabul Daily*, and so did I," Droon said sharply.

I took a step back, petrified now—how long had he been watching, waiting for this moment?

"That is why women should be hidden, so that they do not corrupt men's minds," he continued. Then he smiled. "Your family, and you, will not suffer any further from want."

"But isn't your brother married?" Jahan asked quite boldly as he took on the mantle of head of our house. "He is an elderly man."

"He was married, but his wife and eldest son were killed when their home was attacked by mujahedeen," Droon said. "It was fortunate that his two younger sons were visiting friends. He is a brave warrior who has spent the last eight years fighting for his country. Now that he plans to settle in Kabul, he needs a wife to care for his children. He will look after your sister very well, as he is, as I mentioned, very wealthy. He believes she is a very spirited woman and he could enjoy her company, though she will need to be taught a lesson or two." He looked over Jahan's shoulder to the darkened house. "Is your sister at home? My wife," he said, nodding at the woman in the Land Cruiser, "will speak to her and to your mother."

"My sister isn't here. She went to Mazar-e-Sharif to help with my female first cousin's wedding preparations. As we're a very close family, one of us had to be there for such a celebration, and she had to go. My mother is not well and, as a man, I will only be there for the wedding. Rukhsana went there with my uncle's family this afternoon. She will stay there for three weeks, maybe longer depending on the roads."

I was amazed at my brother's ability to lie with such a serious and solemn face. He could walk on the stage and convince anyone with his talent.

"When did she leave?"

"As I said, this afternoon. She went with my uncle. They left in his car."

"I see," he said, but there was a tenor of disbelief in his voice.

Droon sighed, a hiss of breath, and signaled to the two policemen. "Search the house."

"She is not at home," Jahan said. "I told you she left with my uncle . . ."

"Yes, yes, I know what you said. We just want to be certain." Droon walked past Jahan, toward our house.

"My mother is ill and I cannot permit you to disturb her."

"Your sister left your mother all alone?" He turned back and smiled in disbelief. "She isn't a dutiful daughter then."

"We have a doctor, Dr. Hanifa, who stays with my mother all day. And I am here."

Droon touched my brother's face as if to pat it gently, then closed his fingers around his jaw, squeezing hard. His middle finger was missing but that did not lessen the strength of his grip. He was hurting Jahan.

"My brother has given me the authority to do what I want. I do not need your permission. You are a young man, still not wise, and you should respect your elder's commands. Understand?" He released my brother's face, and this time patted it gently.

"Then, sir"—I detected a mocking tone in Jahan's "sir"—"may I at least warn my mother before your police search? She is old and ill and they will frighten her."

"Go with him," Droon told the policemen.

"I'll send my cousin to open the front gate," Jahan said and gestured to me.

I walked to the corner and turned down the lane. I couldn't take another step, so I leaned against the wall. My heart was beating too fast; nausea bent me double, but I couldn't retch out anything. I could not run away and disappear into the night. It would endanger Jahan and my mother. I steadied myself, sucked in deep breaths, and moved to the side gate. Abdul snored and snorted. I let him sleep; the less he knew, the better. I went through the house and across to the front side gate. I swung it open and remained behind it.

Jahan led the policemen and Droon's wife up the steps to the front door. She carried an elaborate basket filled with plums and pomegranates, on top of which was a beautiful purple and blue silk *hijab* with heavy gold-threaded borders. I waited, but Droon didn't follow them. He had settled back into the car. I closed the door and joined Jahan and the others inside. Jahan lit a lamp.

"Search where you wish, while I wake my mother," Jahan said firmly to the two policemen. And to Droon's wife, politely, "Please wait here." The woman stood as motionless as a draped statue.

I slipped past the others and upstairs to Mother's room. She was sleeping peacefully and Dr. Hanifa was reading. She looked up at me in surprise and I put a finger to my lips. I went to Mother's side and gently shook her awake. She looked up at me with no recognition. Jahan entered holding the lamp.

"The police are looking for Rukhsana," he whispered quickly in English. "I told them she went to Mazar this afternoon for a cousin's wedding. The Talib Wahidi wants to marry her. Babur, here, is our cousin, your brother's son from Kunduz. He's visiting and staying with us. Wahidi's brother, Droon, has sent his wife. She's waiting . . ."

He was silent as the policemen brought their lamp into the room, holding it high. It illuminated Mother lying in her bed, her head resting on pillows, her face gentle and serene. She looked as fragile as a flower pressed between the pages of a book, faded, and I wanted to embrace and protect her. She said nothing, allowing them to observe her as if she were a relic.

"You must not disturb her," Dr. Hanifa said sternly.

"We must ask. Where is your daughter?" one asked politely, respecting her condition.

"She went to Mazar-e-Sharif for a wedding this afternoon."

"And left you alone?"

"I'm not alone. I have Dr. Hanifa, my son, Jahan, and my nephew Babur to take care of me."

"When will she return?"

My mother considered the question with drowsy eyes. "Whenever she does. When the wedding is over, when the roads are safe, when it is time."

They accepted her reply and, with a curt nod, went out. Jahan followed, but as I moved away from the bed, Mother clutched my hand.

Dr. Hanifa stepped forward and squinted. "Is that you, Rukhsana?"

"Yes. You won't tell anyone, will you?" I pleaded. "I have to stay here to look after Maadar."

"Of course not," she replied indignantly. "You're in terrible danger." She examined me carefully and added, "But you must know that already."

"You have gone mad to be dressed up like that," Mother whispered, panic making her breath come faster. "They'll kill you." She touched the beard. "What's done is done." Her grip tightened. "And now you have to get out."

"I can't." I loosened her grip.

"You're in great danger; they will kill you in an instant if they discover this."

"I know. But—" I stepped away when Jahan led in Droon's wife.

She stood by the bed and Mother stared up at the shapeless form.

"My brother-in-law wishes to marry your daughter." She had a young girl's voice, muffled by the burka, and there was a nervous note of apology in her tone. "Your son has refused. He says she is already engaged." She held out Wahidi's gift.

"Yes, she is," my mother said politely. "I cannot accept his proposal. Please convey my regret that Rukhsana is betrothed and we must honor our word. He will understand."

The burka turned, not to leave, but to see where Jahan and I were. By the door, a safe distance away, Dr. Hanifa had returned to her chair, just out of earshot. Droon's wife stepped closer to the bed, bent over, and whispered to my mother before turning away.

"I have tried," my mother said aloud.

We made way for Droon's wife and she retreated from the room and stood quietly in the corridor. She stood with a resigned air of patience, as if trained to obey commands, the melancholy folds of her burka hanging lifeless around her.

Jahan and I followed the two policemen from room to room. The elder, with a gray beard, led his younger colleague, a man in his twenties. They wore frayed green uniforms and carried machine guns slung across their chests. I trailed well beyond the lamp's light, clothed in darkness. They opened doors, walked into rooms, and then returned to the hall empty-handed.

The policemen went to my room. They stood in the door, surveying the bed, the posters, the cupboard, the desk. In the opening pages of *The Gulag Archipelago*, Solzhenitsyn wrote that "the police come always at night when we're befuddled from sleep and vulnerable to their sudden descent on the sleeper." His police wore jackboots to trample on his books, clothes, and other objects. My police wore sandals, but they moved with the same brutish arrogance. They moved first to the cupboard, only because it was shut. They flung open the doors, revealing my kurtas, skirts, and blouses, and in the lower shelves many pairs of high-heeled shoes, dusty with disuse. They pulled out my clothes and emptied the shelves onto the floor.

They studied my bookshelf, most of the titles in English and also Dari. They lost interest, as they were looking for Rukhsana and not dissident writings—those would undoubtedly be dealt with later by my new husband. They looked at my posters, reached up, and pulled them down.

"Forbidden," they chorused, and tore both posters into halves and then quarters before scattering the pieces on the floor. Thankfully, they weren't the religious police. They left, kicking away an offending shoe. We followed them to Jahan's room and watched them rip up the Shaquille O'Neal poster too, and Jahan blankly accepted the fate of his hero's image. They shook a finger under his nose. "Be careful," a warning, and meant kindly for the young boy.

They searched the rooms in the basement and opened Grandfather's storeroom and shone their torches on the rows of books. We remained still, praying they wouldn't start pulling them out. One even went to peer at them, but like most of our police, he was illiterate.

"Law books," Jahan said to distract them.

They stepped back into the corridor, leaving the door ajar, and Jahan closed it. Then they saw the granite slab and chuckled to each other. "We found it," they chorused in triumph. One held the torch, the other knelt, and, using his knife, levered up the slab. The torch shone into the empty hole. He let the stone fall back with a thud, dusted his hands, and, in disappointment, both climbed the stairs. Droon's wife followed, still carrying her gift, with Jahan and me behind. I didn't step out of the compound with them but remained by the gate. I peered through the slat. Droon's wife got into the car, while Droon climbed out.

"She is not in the house," one of the policemen said to Droon, and added proudly, "We found the secret cellar too but it was empty."

Droon approached Jahan and stopped a foot away. "My brother is in Kandahar and will return to Kabul for the cricket match. She must be back within that time. I hope she does not try to cross any border. The guards have been told to look for her." He moved to the car and, as if he had second thoughts, stopped. "If she does not appear to marry my brother, you will be arrested and imprisoned in Pul-e-Charkhi prison for defying the police."

"But I've done nothing," Jahan said in a shaken voice.

"You are her *mahram;* you are responsible for all her actions. And we will imprison your mother too. My brother can be merciful, if you agree to the marriage."

"It must have Rukhsana's consent too." Jahan still had some defiance.

"She will consent. She will not refuse my brother." He smiled. "Or if she is too stupid, she will be arrested for reporting lies about her country in the world media. A few years in prison will help her to learn to love her country again."

He retreated to the car and a policeman hurried to open the door. He climbed in, and once more, for a brief second, I saw the upright burka beside him before it dissolved into the darkness. We remained watching the bouncing taillights until the car turned the corner. The policemen climbed into the back of the Land Cruiser and the sleeping driver woke and followed Droon's car.

"Pul-e-Charkhi," Jahan whispered in dread.

We remembered Grandfather telling us about it after he had visited a prisoner there. He looked a different man, older, wan and weary, on his return. He told us in a shaky voice, "I have seen hell and it is shaped like a huge cartwheel, with spokes leading to the prison blocks. It is crowded with men who have no reason to be there. Many are just small shopkeepers who have the misfortune to be Uzbeks. Others are in there on trumped-up political charges. I pray only that I do not end up there too one day. There are eighteen blocks and each block has a hundred and sixteen cells and each cell holds forty to fifty men packed like animals for slaughter. The prisoners are allowed to use the toilets only twice a day. One hundred and fifty Talibs guard the prison and they flog and torture the men daily for the pleasure they get from seeing such suffering. Many of the younger men are raped for days then thrown back into the cells, too ashamed to tell anyone what happened to them. Many prisoners die of starvation or torture and the Talibs take them to hospitals and declare they died of an illness, so as to pass on the blame. And even in prison, the corruption is unbelievable. The Talibs have grown immensely rich from the suffering of these men. They imprisoned my client Hassan because he wouldn't pay a bribe. I have filed papers for his release, but I don't hold out much hope of freeing him. They would not permit me to visit the women's section, and I fear there is even worse treatment there."

We still remembered Grandfather's drawn face as he told us the story.

We trudged upstairs, our steps heavy with the weight of such suffering, and returned to Mother's room.

"What did she say to you?" I asked.

"Yes, what did that little girl whisper?" Dr. Hanifa was also curious.

"She was forced to marry Droon when he threatened to kill her father if he didn't give his consent. She has not seen her family since then, and she said that you must get out of the country if you want to save yourself. They are cruel men." She stretched out her hand and I took it. "Listen to her, if not to me. You must leave me."

"I have less than three weeks, and before then I know Shaheen will send for me—I've just written to him again. I will leave that very day."

"But what if he does not get back to you in time? How will you get out then?"

"I'll find a smuggler to get me into Pakistan and wait there for Shaheen to contact me."

Then she said fiercely, "You cannot marry that Talib. I will not permit it, nor would your father. But we're helpless."

We couldn't bear to tell her about Droon's threat to imprison us if I did not marry Wahidi.

"You can't marry him," Jahan said. "I refuse to give permission."

"You can't," Dr. Hanifa added.

Suddenly nauseated, I felt his breath on my face, his bristle against my cheeks, his odor suffocating my nostrils. I was property with no rights; I had been purchased, no different from a whore. I imagined his body pressed upon me. I cannot cry out; no one can hear me, and even if they do, they won't come to my aid. I twist and turn but cannot escape the weight holding me down.

"I better go home," Dr. Hanifa said, rising. "I'll have Abdul walk me to my gate." She checked Mother's pulse. "I'll see you tomorrow. Get her to sleep, Rukhsana, and be very careful." She went out muttering about the Talibs.

Mother's instant of anger sapped her energy and she sank back into the pillows, reaching for our hands. "Rukhsana, you should not have postponed the engagement and marriage to Shaheen. I know you wanted to work before you married, but you would have been safe. You would be in America now."

She fell silent, staring up at the ceiling, her hand perspiring in mine, and she gently squeezed it. Then she turned to look me in the eyes. "You never did want to marry him, did you?"

"Of course I did," I insisted. "I just needed time. And then he didn't wait; he left."

She looked at me skeptically, with hooded eyes.

"As you say, I know we will learn to love each other once we are married." I smiled. "He wants to marry, and he expects it, as do I."

"Try to telephone him again, tell him it is even more urgent now."

"Droon said they'll be watching the borders," Jahan said.

"The smugglers will know what to do," said Mother sharply.

Mother reached for his hand and took it, enclosing it partially. "How you've grown, my beautiful son. You're such a brave boy to stand up to this Droon. You must look after Rukhsana and send her to safety."

"I will. But what can we do until we hear from Shaheen?"

"Until then she is trapped here as Babur." Mother managed a smile. "What a great name to choose for yourself. Even as a little girl you had grand ideas."

"It was Jahan who named me," I corrected her, but I was pleased with my manly name.

"Babur, the first Mughal emperor of India, now buried in this city that he loved," Mother said. "It must have been a beautiful city then, with the river flowing along its borders and all the gardens. And beautiful women, and handsome men." She looked at me and took my hand.

"You will have to remain Babur until you can leave, and I pray you will not be discovered."

"I must also teach the team cricket. It's Jahan's best chance."

"It will be dangerous. You're a good girl to care for your brother so much and risk your life. He must go, do what you can. I will pray that they win this match. I will also pray that one way or another you both do leave." She reached for me. "Let me see my brave daughter."

I removed the turban and the beard. She caressed my face with her soft hands and I felt like a small child again under her maternal touch. I kissed her good night, as did Jahan.

"I need to sleep," she whispered.

I prepared her morphine injection, lifted her arm to the light, swabbed a spot with cotton, and then gently inserted the needle into her paper-thin flesh. She was nearing sleep when we took out the lamp and left the room in darkness.

Jahan was too weary to say anything further. Defiance had drained him of energy, and we both knew the dangers ahead of us. The house was quiet, the city was quiet. I wondered how long the silence would remain.

I went into Father's office, settled myself, and dialed Shaheen's number. I didn't know what time it was in San Francisco, I didn't care. Each time the connection failed, I punched the redial button harder, but even it couldn't make that magical connection. Once, a disembodied voice came on to tell me that "The circuits are busy, please try later."

"Please, please stop being busy," I cried to the phone. "This is my life, I must get through."

I wouldn't give up, pressing redial like an automaton. I drew a pad toward me and made notes, a habit of my journalism days.

1. Hide as Babur. Only two women can be seen in the house, Mother and Dr. Hanifa.
2. Even if Shaheen's money/papers come tomorrow, stay to the day before prelim. matches.
3. Teach Jahan and team cricket up to that day so they win the final match and leave too.
4. Babur and the team? They must accept him—only way to teach them.
5. Find a smuggler so I am ready to run on that Friday.
6. Mother? I will have to leave her in Dr. Hanifa's care and pray for her forgiveness.
7. If Shaheen's money/papers too late? Borrow money from whomever. Leave and wait in Pakistan for Shaheen or Jahan.
8. Get out before Wahidi returns.

The tension exhausted me, my mind was numbed by panic, and I finally gave up on the phone.

I returned to my room, tidied it, and dumped the torn posters in the rubbish bin. There was both a Gregorian and an Afghan calendar on my desk. Nineteen days away was Sunday the twenty-eighth and I circled the date. It looked a long way off; I had lots of time and I knew my meticulous Shaheen too well. I expected that the papers and money were already on their way.

I decided to sleep as Babur should an emergency arise.

I DREAMED I WAS A CHILD AGAIN, POSSIBLY SIX OR SEVEN years old, and wearing the finery for a wedding day. Except I was alone, without parents, other relatives, or friends surrounding me. Instead of a hall or a house or a village, I was in a field of roses as far as my eyes could see. The air was sweetly scented, and I looked around with the curiosity of a child and the certainty that nothing evil would harm me. The sky was a clear blue, and I walked slowly through the field of roses, none marred by thorns, and brushed my fingers over their silken petals. I did not pluck them, as it seemed a sacrilege to despoil such perfection. The breeze that gently swayed the roses softly carried a strange and soothing music. I hummed along, and though I seemed to walk for many hours and many miles, the mood never changed. Other girls my own age appeared, who, like me, walked through the field of roses, caressing them with the tips of their fingers and humming the same tune. There was not a boy in sight, as every last one had been banished from this world of flowers.

I WAS RUNNING AWAY AND WAHIDI WAS PURSUING ME. IT was night, I was alone, and I tripped over the legs and arms of dismembered corpses. He was laughing as he fired his gun, deliberately missing me so that I was forced to duck and dodge. And after each shot he took a giant step closer, and no matter how fast I ran, I couldn't escape. He was reaching out to grab me.

* * *

I WOKE SHAKING, SWEATING, MY LEGS KICKING. I LAY STILL, waiting for my body to stop trembling. Thinking I should have married Shaheen before he left. I should have married Veer, the man I loved. I should never have left Delhi, never given up that life.

The lines of a poem by the Dari Rabi'a Balkhi ran through my mind:

> I am caught in Love's web so deceitful
> None of my endeavours turn fruitful.
> I knew not when I rode the high-blooded steed
> The harder I pulled its reins the less it would heed.
> Love is an ocean with such a vast space
> No wise man can swim it in any place.
> A true lover should be faithful till the end
> And face life's reprobated trend.
> When you see things hideous, fancy them neat,
> Eat poison, but taste sugar sweet.

Whatever happens, I will not marry Wahidi. I will eat the poison should I fail, and pray it will taste as sweet as sugar.

THE DISAPPOINTMENT

ON MY PILLOW WERE MY NOTES FROM THE NIGHT
before. It all seemed so tenuous, every hope obstructed
by impossibilities and slim chances. Suicide loomed
larger in the morning, more seductive than anything
else. I got up, went to my desk, and crossed one day
off my calendar. Eighteen days. I thought bitterly that
yesterday afternoon I had been happy teaching a game
for the sheer pleasure of recalling my past. Today, that
pleasure had knotted into panic.

It was seven in Kabul and I lay a moment calculating the time in San Francisco. Six yesterday evening.
Shaheen would be home. I ran down and called his
number. For the first five tries nothing happened. On
the sixth, a telephone rang thousands of miles away and
I prayed Shaheen would pick up. "Shaheen, help me"
would be my first words. After ten rings it stopped. I
tapped redial and I was back to an empty sound on the
line. I kept pushing the button until Jahan came into
the room. An hour was lost, another hour closing in
on me. He didn't need to ask, as he saw the despair on
my face.

"Parwaaze and Qubad are outside, waiting."

"What have you told them?"

"Nothing yet. They're ready to leave for practice. You still want to do it as Babur?"

"How else will you learn? I have to," I said in exasperation. "There's no law in the Sharia or elsewhere that states a woman can't dress up as a man."

Jahan sighed, the complications knitting his brow. "The Talib have their own interpretation of the Sharia, and if you're caught they could beat you up or even shoot you. I'll tell Parwaaze and Qubad to expect Babur."

"It's the only way I can teach you. They can only tell the team, our family, and no one else outside it."

"Of course! We'll all be dead if we tell anyone else."

I rose, still feeling fragile, and he embraced me tightly. "They'll have to wait, as I must look after Maadar first." We parted in the hall.

I held the beard and turban in my hands as I entered Mother's room. She was awake too.

"Was it a nightmare I had?"

"No, the police were here last night."

"I've been awake worrying about you. What are we going to do?"

"We wait for Shaheen. There's still time."

"Sell our jewelry," she cried. "Sell it and leave now."

"It won't be enough," I said gently, wanting to calm her. "We're worrying for nothing. Shaheen will send for me long before that."

She heaved a tearful sigh and tried to collect herself.

"You are right. I know Shaheen. He's such a good boy." She held out her frail arms and I went into her embrace.

I took the bedpan to the bathroom and emptied it. I returned with a bowl of water, and sponged her down. Then I touched her lips with lipstick, powdered her cheeks, and dabbed her with her favorite perfume, Je Reviens. "There, that will make you feel better."

"You're a good daughter, Rukhsana," she said, and added with a dry laugh, "and a good nephew, Babur."

"I'll make you some tea and your breakfast." I warmed up the food and served her, enjoying this quiet time we had together. When she finished eating I went downstairs to meet my cousins.

Parwaaze and Qubad sat on the floor in the *mardaana*, the male sanctum in the house, whispering to each other as they watched my approach. Behind them was our marble fireplace with its empty grate. Grandfather's cigarette smoke still scented the air, and had clung to the fabric of the carpets, the divans, and the pillows. The smell filled me with longing. I knelt in front of Parwaaze and Qubad, my hands resting on my thighs. I felt I was about to face a Lowya *jerga*, a meeting of elders. They resembled two wise men, puzzled frowns masking their faces. They could disown me and deliver me to the Talib for my daring to impersonate a male, to insult their manhood.

Parwaaze cleared his throat. "I was shocked when Jahan told us what you had done." He spoke solemnly. His eyes were deep and threatening. "You are not behaving like a good Afghan woman. No woman would do what you have done."

"I am a good Afghan woman," I said. "I'm sorry."

Qubad nodded. "Sh-sh-shocked, very shocked."

"Our first instinct when we heard what you had done last night was to shut our eyes and run as far as we could from you. To know about what you did, and not report you to the Talib, is to invite a beating, even death. Do you understand?"

"Yes," I said meekly.

"You must be mad to walk on the street dressed like a man," Parwaaze said. "You were always reckless, but I never expected you to do this."

"Never," Qubad echoed. "Very mad. You're too old to be a *b-baba posh*."

When I was four years old, my grandmother had me dress as a boy, a *baba posh*, as I was born a girl and she wanted people to think that I was male. Mother stopped that when I was seven. It was fun then to be a boy. There were three other girls dressed as *baba poshes* in my class.

"You have placed Jahan in great danger, since he is your *mahram* and responsible for your behavior." Parwaaze paused, and added abruptly, "But what's done is done. We can't go back in time."

"But no matter what, you can't marry the Talib," Parwaaze announced firmly. "We must get you out safely. We have three weeks before you're supposed to be back from Mazar."

"Enough time to teach you cricket before I leave so you can win the match against Azlam's team and win the final too," I said quickly. "I can't give up on that, for Jahan's sake. I can't teach wearing the burka. But, dressed like this, I can. I have the freedom to move my arms and my legs."

"You're absolutely c-crazy," Qubad said after the astonished silence. "They're looking for you and you still want to teach us cricket as Babur! You have to hide somewhere."

"But I am hiding—as Babur. I have to stay by Maadar. The best place to hide is where they have already looked."

"We could find someone else to teach us c-cricket," Qubad said to Parwaaze.

"But who?" Jahan demanded. "Even if we do find someone else, why would he teach us to play? Like Azlam, he can form his own team from his family."

I watched them waver. "They are looking for Rukhsana. If you don't want me to teach you because you're scared, that's all right with me." I stood up. "But I can't sit at home all day. If they're watching us, they'll suspect something's wrong if Babur doesn't go in and out of the house."

They put their heads together, not taking their eyes off me as they had a whispered exchange.

"Even as a child you were always giving us ultimatums," Parwaaze said, shaking his head. "You have to teach us as much as you can before you leave."

"Put on your b-beard and turban," Qubad said.

I affixed the beard to my face and piled my hair on my head before placing the turban.

"She almost l-looks like one of us." Qubad squinted at me, while Parwaaze scrutinized me from head to toe.

"Your eyes give you away."

"That's what I said," Jahan said.

"I'll wear glasses. And sneakers to hide my feet."

They couldn't say it, but I knew what they looked for, and I turned to show them my profile, with the loose coat and the shawl disguising my shape. I stood like a model for a long minute, looking away as I didn't want to embarrass them while they checked to make sure my figure was completely hidden.

"Show them how you walk," said Jahan.

I walked the length of the room.

"Take longer, stiffer steps," Parwaaze commanded.

I came to a stop in front of them. "But what about the others? You'll have to tell our cousins. I can't risk their lives without their consent."

"Would any of them betray us?" asked Jahan. They each looked from one to the other. Then Parwaaze shook his head.

"No, we are thinking about this the wrong way, like the Talib would have us think. We are Afghans and this is our family. If we wouldn't betray each other, why would they? Especially when they have a chance to get out. Why would any one of them give up that chance?"

"But what if the Talib catch on and find just one of us to bribe, to scare, or worse?" said Qubad.

"If one of them turned us in, Qubad, they know the Talib could punish us all and any other cousins loyal to our team," Parwaaze explained. "The snitch would be trapped here with the rest of our families—and they would not hesitate to take their revenge. What Afghan family wouldn't seek revenge for such treachery? So to betray us is just as dangerous as keeping quiet, and with us, they could be out of the country in mere weeks! No, they will have to protect you now if they want to win." Parwaaze rose with the authority of an elder having reached a decision.

"I think he's right," said Jahan.

"I don't think we have a choice," I said, "but we have a chance. We'll start after lunch—I have something I must do first. I also have an old tape of a match and we'll watch that later and I'll talk you through it."

"Bring it to my house tonight, after practice, so we can all see it," Parwaaze said.

"Before you leave I have a favor to ask." I had been waiting for this moment. "I know Shaheen will send the money and the sponsor letter, but if it doesn't come in time, and I have to get out, can your families give me a loan to pay a smuggler? I'll repay it as soon as I reach America."

"How much will you need?"

"About two thousand . . . dollars."

They both winced at the amount. "You know that if we had the money we would give it to you this very moment. But . . ." They looked at each other and Parwaaze continued, after Qubad's nod of consent, apologetically. "We do have some money saved, which we will need to pay for our studies when we're in Pakistan."

"We may even have enough to pay a smuggler to take us to Australia," Qubad added.

"We'll fly to Malaysia and then we take a boat from there. Many Afghans have done that. We'll ask for asylum like they did."

"If we w-win this match and fly to Karachi, it saves us some money."

"What about the rest of the team?" I asked.

"We'll only choose the cousins who have the same plans," Parwaaze said quietly. "And I know who they are. We've talked about it a lot but done nothing about it, until now. If we travel together, we could get a discount from a smuggler." He smiled for the first time. "We're buying our passports on the black market."

"And you didn't tell me?" I was hurt by their secrecy.

"We hadn't thought more about it until this tournament and your teaching us to play," he protested. "Besides, you're waiting for Shaheen to send for you, and once you're there you'll send for Jahan." Parwaaze looked at my brother. "You can come with us too."

"I must join Rukhsana," Jahan said, dismissing the invitation.

"If you lose?" I had to bring them down to earth.

"We just beg and borrow more money, spend more months here until we have enough. We will leave, one day."

I tried to swallow the hard lump of disappointment. I knew they had their own needs and had to plan for their lives. "If you win, the Talib will send a minder to make sure you return. You know that?"

"Yes, but he can't watch us day and night in Pakistan. And we'll escape when he falls asleep or goes to the toilet or . . . we pay him off."

Qubad nodded in agreement, and I saw the anguish on their faces. "We could give you what we have if you're sure you can return it in time. Of course, if we don't win the final, we'll give you the money and wait."

"By then it will be too late for me. And I'm not sure how long Shaheen's money will take."

I would wait in Pakistan for Shaheen's package. One week, two weeks . . . ? Would two thousand, which I'd suggested to Shaheen, be enough? Meanwhile, they would wait for me to return the loan, aching to leave. I could lose their money too, a lone woman wandering in an unfamiliar city.

"What about your family jewelry?" Parwaaze asked sympathetically.

"It's nearly all been sold, looking after Maadar and living our daily lives."

"We will help in any other way we can."

"I know you will." I bowed my head in gratitude. Surely there would be a smuggler somewhere who would take whatever jewelry was left—I would just have to find him.

"And how is your *maadar*?"

"Getting worse."

"Can we see her?"

I led them into Mother's room. She was reading, and put the book down when Parwaaze and Qubad approached. She put out her hand, regally, I thought, and they tenderly took it. She raised her eyebrows, and waited for her nephews to speak first.

"We will protect her, Maadar," Parwaaze said quietly.

She smiled. "I knew I could trust you. Look after her and Jahan."

"We will."

"You're l-looking well," Qubad said gallantly.

"A little makeup and perfume. I wish there was such a simple medication for the inside."

They leaned over and each kissed her forehead before backing out of the room.

When my cousins left, Jahan and I returned to our mother's room. She looked more exhausted than ever.

"Jahan, go and fetch Dr. Hanifa."

I made green tea, and returned to Mother's room. She sat up and I helped her drink it.

"I'm going to teach them cricket this afternoon."

Mother smiled. "How you loved your cricket! Playing it every Saturday in Delhi. You were happy there."

"I loved Delhi. I thought I had left it behind me but miss it even more now." I never should have opened the trunk; the spores of memories infected the whole house. "Were you happy in Delhi?"

"Yes—I just couldn't stand the summers. Remember, we had a beautiful party right in the middle of summer for your father's birthday." She cried out, "Oh god, I wish I had died with him." I held her as she wept, sobbing like a child. She stopped and sniffled. "I will be with him soon."

She sat up and wiped away the tears. "I hope you find that kind of love in your marriage, Rukhsana, like I did in mine. As you know we fell in love at Kabul University, and thankfully our parents supported us. I was never unhappy with your father, except when I became pregnant with Jahan. After two miscarriages, the doctors told me not to try again, but your father was insistent—he was desperate for a son. So I had to conjure him up out of my womb, like a magician. I was so afraid I would die in labor. Jahan was a caesarean, you know."

"I didn't know."

"You were only a child then. There are many things a child doesn't know about its parents. I love Jahan, but I was grateful whenever you looked after him—sometimes even holding him was too much of a reminder of the fear and pain I had lived through for him. You were more of a mother to him than I was in those early months."

I held her hand as she drifted back to sleep, thinking that Shaheen too would expect me to produce a son first, and not a girl child.

Jahan was born just after breakfast, but Father would not let me skip school. I wanted to be there at the very moment of the baby's birth to welcome it into the world. I was exuberant and distracted with the excitement of seeing my baby sibling. When the lunch-time bell rang, I ran out of the school, dodging people, cars, Russian trucks, donkey carts, bicycles, and buses, and was nearly run over as I made my way to the weary white facade of the hospital and down its corridors to the maternity ward. I slowly opened the door of Mother's private room and peeked in. Father stood framed by the window, against a pale blue sky, like a still-life painting, holding a tiny bundle in his arms, a broad smile on his face. I knew immediately that the baby was a boy. Mother was asleep, her face relaxed, with a hint of both a smile and triumph. Grandmother sat beside the bed and raised a finger to her lips. "Let me hold him," I whispered to Father, "please, Padar, please." Father gave me the baby and I looked down on his pink, round face, the sparse light brown hair plastered against his delicate skull. He was asleep and I kissed his forehead and then his cheeks. "I will look after you, my *braadar*," I whispered into his ear. "I will always be here for you." In his sleep, I thought he smiled. "He's going to be a happy person," I told Father and reluctantly returned the bundle to his arms. From his birth, I felt that Jahan was my baby too.

IF I WAS TO BECOME BABUR, I DECIDED TO DO IT RIGHT. I trimmed Shylock's beard to suit a more youthful man, in his late teens, so the hair was sparse but not too sparse to reveal the netting that held the hairs together. It looked worse. I needed help.

I tugged the *lungee* down on my head and wrapped a *patoo*, a heavy scarf, across half my face. I needed to be as anonymous as possible, just another man on the street. I looked in the mirror and saw not a handsome young man but a feminine one. If only I could hide my eyes, harden them into a man's eyes. I slipped on dark glasses. They would have to do. It was time to test the new Babur.

"Where are we going?" Jahan asked me as I stepped out the front door.

"I want to see Noorzia. Come on."

"Noorzia?"

"My hairdresser in the old days." I sighed for those lost, pleasurable afternoons. Her salon was on Fifth Street, in Wazir Akbar Khan. I went there every Sunday; Noorzia cut my hair, while an assistant gave me a manicure.

"You're Babur, remember," he said testily. "You don't need a beauty salon. She'll tell the Talib if she sees you dressed like this."

"No, she won't, I swear. I trust her. She could help me with this," I said, tugging at my beard. "I'll only be five minutes. Please."

"When a woman says five minutes it means an hour," Jahan said.

I felt buoyant and confident as I stepped out, until I saw Abdul in his sentry box watching the road. He turned toward us when he heard the front door open and close.

"What do we tell him?" I said, having forgotten about him.

"Let's see what he says. He may not notice."

His one inquisitive eye watched us descend the steps and cross toward him. I walked as stiffly as I could, hiding the sway of my hips. He emerged from his office to stand at the side gate and waited for us.

"I know, I know. I'll sit at the front door until Dr. Hanifa comes," he said in a testy voice. His eye squinted at me, then he frowned. "Is that you?"

"Yes," I said, frightened that he had penetrated my disguise so easily with only one eye. "I didn't think you'd notice."

"I've known you since a baby and know that only you and your brother live in the house with your mother. I'm blind but not stupid." He glanced to Jahan. "Why is she wearing a man's clothes?

If the religious police catch her dressed like a man, they will beat her. You too, probably."

"It's a long story," Jahan said.

"So tell me."

He listened carefully to the horror story from the night before. He thought it over, and Jahan and I held our breath—he could simply betray us now. But we had to trust him, as he was part of our family and would see me coming and going.

"All this happened last night?"

"Yes."

"Why wasn't I woken? It's my job to guard this gate."

"You were very tired," Jahan said diplomatically. "You won't tell anyone?"

"Your family has given me shelter and food, and may paradise shut its doors in my face if I should betray you." He faced me. "You can't marry a Talib. If my daughter were alive today and a Talib asked to marry her, I would refuse. And if I had to hide her, I would dress her in a man's clothes and send her to stay with my family, as far away as I could." He pointed at me. "You must leave too." He opened the gate. "Be very careful."

"If a letter comes for me from America, keep it carefully."

"I will."

"And if you see strangers watching the house, tell us."

"That's why I'm here. As your guardian."

As we walked a few paces down the street he poked his head out of the gate and added, "And don't talk. You sound like a girl."

I thanked God for Abdul.

THE SKY WAS A CLEAR BLUE, WITHOUT A CLOUD, AND I BE-lieved such skies were good luck. We looked back to see if anyone was following, but people were going about their lives.

From around the corner, three men, talking in low voices, came toward us. They glanced in our direction—and then passed by, continuing their conversation. Jahan and I both exhaled with relief.

"They didn't notice," I whispered.

"Just don't talk," Jahan said.

"You're more nervous than I am."

"I'm not nervous." His face shone with perspiration. "I'm scared for you and for me if you're discovered. We're both mad."

"Who isn't? And it won't happen," I said, and didn't add aloud, "I hope and pray."

We reached Karte Seh Wat to wait for a bus. A family of nomads, the Kochi, on their way south, herded their sheep and camels along the road. I was suddenly envious of their roving life. They were dusty from the long journey and looked around this ruin with wary eyes; men, women, and children moved tightly together, not wanting to be separated and lost in this strange place. I wished I could be as free as they were to move from place to place as the pastures took me, but I didn't have the courage to be a gypsy.

A crowded bus to Wazir Akbar Khan stopped and Jahan pushed his way onto it. I followed, squeezing past the men, and instinctively making my way to the curtained-off seating for the women at the back.

"Where are you going?" Jahan whispered, pulling me into a vacant seat next to an elderly man. His watery gaze lingered on my beard for what seemed a long moment before turning to stare out the window.

I pretended to doze, lowering my head, so no one could take a closer look at me. Already, I had made a stupid mistake. I had to remember to be a man, and accept his privileged front-of-the-bus position in life. Jahan stood protectively by my side.

The bus roared and wheezed along Asamayi, and bumped around the craters in the road. Stifled by the heat and the press of men around me, I actually did doze off. I started awake in fright when I felt a hand on my knee, kneading it as if it were dough.

"You're a handsome boy," the elderly man whispered in my ear. "Where do you live?"

I stood quickly, and another man, more my suitor's age, slid into the seat.

"What are you grinning about?" Jahan whispered.

"Men." And I didn't explain further.

We passed Zambak Square and the ruined buildings on either side. We got off when we reached Sherpur, jostled and pushed by men getting in and out. Reluctantly, they made way for two women, with their *mahrams*, to pass.

"How far to her salon?" Jahan whispered.

"We're going to her home. Her salon's closed."

The salon had been a palace of warmth and good company and gossip. Always elegant, simmering with laughter and encouragement, Noorzia treated every woman in her chairs like royal beauties. The gilt-framed mirrors of the salon reflected the soft pale pink walls behind our heads and the photographs of European models with sweeping hairstyles. Sometimes, Mother would come with me to have her hair trimmed and her nails painted, and it always felt special, as if Noorzia was family.

I hoped she still lived in the same house. I had been there once before to celebrate the second anniversary of her salon, nearly five years ago. It was a wonderful spring day and she had thrown a brunch for faithful clients, who were also her friends. There were thirty of us and, conscious that only other women would be in attendance, we dressed up especially for the party. I had worn a blue blouse, intricately patterned with gold thread around the neckline and along the edges of the sleeves, and a black silk crepe skirt that fell down to my ankles, and as I moved it swayed over my black high heels with semiprecious stones set in the straps.

My *hijab*, woven with gold thread along the borders, was pale gray. But, like the others, to celebrate Noorzia's handiwork, I removed it once I entered the house. The room dazzled with the vibrancy of so many colors. The air was sweetened by our perfumes, and our laughter bubbled like water from a crystal fountain as we nibbled on the food and sipped on sherbet. Where were they now? Only their ghostly laughter still echoed in my memory of that delicious afternoon so long ago.

With no reason to make myself look particularly beautiful in the last few years, I had lost touch with Noorzia too. We made it to her street without incident, and I recognized her house, but no man guarded the open gate. The garden was unkempt, the grass hip high, the rosebushes wild. It was a small house, a single floor, with a sloping roof and closed shutters crudely painted black. I knocked gently and waited. I thought of Mother Nadia—so many terrible things could have happened to Noorzia since I saw her last.

I knocked again, louder this time.

Maybe she had moved, escaped from the country.

Finally, a woman called out, "Who is it?"

"Rukhsana," I said. And then quickly, "I used to come to your salon?"

"Of course, I remember you. It's been years!"

"I know—I'm sorry."

"Wait until I've dressed," Noorzia said.

"I've come with my brother," I said. "He'll wait outside. I just want to see you for a few minutes."

She laughed, and I felt such nostalgia at that throaty sound. "You can stay as long as you want."

"I promise I won't be longer than five minutes," I said to Jahan.

The door opened slowly, yawning into an empty room. Noorzia hid behind the door. I walked in and heard her suck in her breath. Jahan waited outside.

"You said you were Rukhsana."

"I am," I said to Noorzia, who was standing stock-still in her burka.

I had completely forgotten about Babur. "See?" I said, removing the scarf, glasses, and turban.

Noorzia closed the door quickly, not even daring to peer out to the street. She took a step back and studied me.

"Rukhsana," she finally greeted me, with arms wide open in embrace and laughter in her voice.

"I'll bring your brother tea and something to read."

She took my arm and pulled me into the next room then and closed the door. She tore off her burka impatiently and tossed it onto a chair. I expected to see a bitter woman with a pallid face, slovenly hair, and melancholy eyes like mine, but she remained my idea of glamour, my movie star. Her cheeks were powdered, her lips brightly carmine, her eyebrows arched as delicately as a sparrow's wing. Her figure was trim and as supple as a dancer's and, even at home, she wore high heels that accentuated her height and shape. Her light brown hair was perfectly groomed, if slightly ruffled by her burka, and she quickly patted the stray hairs back into place. As always, she wore elegant jeans and a pale cream silk blouse. She was a beautiful woman, with smoke gray eyes accentuated by liner, a warm sensual mouth, and lovely cheekbones. Even though she was over forty, she had the exuberance of a woman half her age.

"You look exactly the same," I said, laughing with her.

She circled me, stroking the beard. "Now, you'll tell me what this is all about while I get tea and biscuits for your brother." I followed her into the kitchen. "Or would Jahan prefer a Coke?"

"I'm sure he would. He hasn't had one in years."

"It's warm," she said, and took a can out of a cupboard and piled biscuits onto a plate. "Here, you give it to him."

She also handed me a two-month-old issue of *Harper's Bazaar*, the American edition, glossy and heavy with advertising and fashions that I could never wear—or afford—in this country. I was sure Jahan would appreciate the photo shoots.

When I returned to the room, she was waiting for my story.

She listened attentively, not interrupting, until I had finished. I felt relief in this confession to my long-lost friend, a woman far more worldly than I. We were hoping for so much, tying ourselves into knots with lies and secrets—I could not help it, I began to weep. She immediately held me, and I sobbed like a child in a mother's arms. I had been brave in front of my mother, Jahan, and my cousins, but I could no longer hold in my fear.

"And now I've brought you into this—but, Noorzia, I didn't know who else to ask," I said, sniffling.

"No. You can't marry that Talib, it will be worse than hell itself—you are right to do whatever you can to get out and to get your brother out. No one is safe from someone like that. And you are right to come to me."

She took my hairy chin in her hand and turned my damp face left and right. "I think . . . I think that your skin needs darkening, as men are normally a shade or two darker than us," she said. "And your hair needs to be cut short to fit more comfortably under that turban. If the turban falls off, you'll still have a boyish head of hair. I would thicken your eyebrows with makeup. I also know I could make you a better beard than that one." She rose and went to the chair in front of the mirror. "Come on, let's take care of this."

I moved to the chair.

"Just look at you, you've neglected yourself," she scolded in her throaty voice. "You had such beautiful skin. Now it's too soft and pasty, and your lovely eyes look as if they cry all the time. Obviously you've not bothered to look after yourself."

"Who is going to notice?"

"Who is going to notice?" she said in astonishment. "You will notice! You're the one who looks in the mirror every day. Who cares about the stupid men? Do it for yourself. That's what I do. Every morning I make up my face and dress as stylishly as I can, as if I am going out to a party. I feel great when I look at myself, even if after that I sit quietly in a room waiting for a client to come, if I'm lucky. I feel even more like a beautiful woman inside. You must do the same for yourself. Fight them in secret; never give in to them. One day, we'll be free and we must be ready to open that door and step out looking as if nothing has happened. And show that they could not crush our spirit. What do you wear at home?"

I shrugged. "Sometimes jeans and a sweatshirt."

"See, that's what I mean. Dress up as if you're going to a fabulous party thrown by . . . by . . . Amitabh Bachchan, the great Bollywood movie star." She stroked her blouse. "I love the touch of silk against my skin; it's erotic, as gentle as a lover's caress."

I looked at myself in the mirror: a mess, with a beard.

I noticed then that her sitting room was almost a replica of her salon, though much smaller. There was only one washbasin with its chair and big mirror. On the shelves beside the mirror were all her usual magic potions—hair dyes, hair sprays, perfumes, powders, lipsticks, creams, combs, brushes, and scissors. On the walls were the old framed photographs of models showing off their hairstyles. I realized she was carrying on business as usual, in secret, for her most trustworthy clients.

She switched on her stereo. A Brahms concerto filled the silence. I sat back in the chair and she wordlessly gathered up my hair, studying how to cut it. I felt I was back in her salon.

"When did you have to close, Noorzia?"

She grimaced at the memory. "When eight or nine of the religious police showed up one morning four years ago. They forced me and my staff out, then opened fire on the mirrors, the washbasins, the chairs, the wall hangings. The noise was so frightening.

They smashed every bottle, stamped on every lipstick tube. Then they went outside and shot at my beautiful sign. And they laughed while they did it. There was nothing worth saving."

"Oh, Noorzia."

"That's why I defy them in here." She smiled and gestured to the room. She placed a hand on her heart. "And in here."

She draped a pink sheet over my body and tied the ends up behind my neck. She continued to ruffle my hair and fluff it out. "Rukhsana, you are a very intelligent woman and you know what you are doing. There is great danger in this impersonation, but there is great danger in simply being a woman, whether we obey their rules or not. And we know how random death is here. You must do whatever you can to leave this country, for your own safety. And your disguise will be a true shield, leave that to me." She started snipping away, the scissors sounding cheerful, as if chatting along with us too. "I may be able to help with a smuggler, but not with the money."

"Why haven't you left? What is here for you?"

"Where would I have gone? Back to Beirut, where my husband died in a bombing and all those memories? No, for a long time there was no one for me to go to. Here, I can still earn a living with my loyal clients. And I run a small business selling lipsticks, makeup, perfumes, powders, whatever women need, including tampons and condoms." She chuckled. "My smuggler, Juniad, brings in banned items from Dubai and takes out those who want to escape from the country. He has a very lucrative business."

"Is he dependable?"

"What man is dependable, Rukhsana? None. Certainly not my smuggler. He'd sell his grandmother if he could make a few more dollars." I watched her snip away at my hair, reducing it to a sad crop, close to my skull, but with enough body to give me the look of a young man. "In Beirut, I worked as a makeup artist for a television series. It was an Arabic soap opera, but I learned a lot and the pay was good. It was fun too. But there we had the Hezbollah, here we have the Talib, the mujahedeen, the warlords. Nowhere is safe." She leaned over to whisper. "But I have a plan now too. I am in touch with a friend in Australia who wants me to go there. I've said yes finally. He's sponsoring me and, like you, I'm waiting for the money and papers. It'll come any day now and I'll leave."

"How much will the smuggler cost you?"

"Up to Karachi to catch the flight, about a thousand dollars."

"One thousand!"

"Yes. If you have to go farther, then a few thousand for visas and flight tickets. And you'll need money to live on. Five or six thousand should just be enough. Will Shaheen have the money for that?"

"I've only asked him for two thousand, but at least that will get me to Karachi, and maybe somewhere just beyond the border. He works for a bank in America—I can ask him for more." But would it get here in time? I put my doubts aside. "Do you have a contact address for Juniad?"

She scribbled it on a scrap of paper and I pocketed it. She worked quickly and my hair fell to the floor. She stood back and we both studied the results. "You are a handsome young man now." She gathered up my hair carefully and placed it on a side table. "I'll make your new beard from your own hair and we'll fix it with Velcro. I'll give it enough body to make you look like a nineteen-year-old man, but not too thick. Now let's fix your skin."

She searched among her ointments and creams and found what she was looking for. The cream was a shade of pale coffee and she spread it gently over my face and along my throat. Under her magical fingers, I did become a shade darker, and my skin better matched the beard. Below the neckline, I was now startlingly white. Then she thickened my eyebrows, making them more masculine.

She capped the cream, and gave it and the pencil to me. "Here, just spread it lightly before you go out, and do your eyebrows. By the way, what do you call yourself?"

"Babur."

She nodded in appreciation. "It has a beautiful sound, Babur the emperor, the poet. Stand up."

I stood, removing the sheet covering my body. She stood to the side to view my profile. "In that loose *shalwar* and jacket I can't see your tits." She reached over to tug my *shalwar* and jacket tighter and down. Now she noticed there was the slight bulge of my breasts.

"I don't have big ones—no one is going to get that near to pull down my shirt and jacket."

"Men stumble," she said knowingly. "A man could stumble into you, knock his elbow against your tits. Men do that to me constantly but, then again, they see me as a woman. Men, you see, have highly sensitive nerves in their elbows. One bump with their elbow into your tits tells them how firm, how young, how desirable the tits are. They can even judge your cup size with an elbow. How did you protect yourself playing cricket?"

"A chest guard."

There was an impatient knock on the front door. "Ah, Babur, it's been a half hour," Jahan called out.

"I'll be with you in a minute."

"You still have your chest guard from cricket?"

I nodded.

"Better wear it so an accidental elbow doesn't find your tits." Noorzia lowered her voice. "But what about your voice?"

"I'll speak in a whisper and tell them I lost my voice in a fire, the smoke affected my throat."

I ran my fingers through my hair; it felt strange not to feel the weight and length. I was a stranger in the mirror. My darkened skin shone slightly from the cream. I hoped men wouldn't notice.

I could tell them it was just sweat. My brows curved like scimitars above my eyes, any thicker and they would cover them completely. This wasn't the wounded Shylock of the stage play but a brash young man glowering back at me. In my eyes, I noted the new surge of confidence; I would swagger, grin, and laugh like a young man who believed the world belonged to him.

I replaced the turban and my old beard and, wrapping my *patoo* around my shoulders and high enough to mask my lower face, I slipped on the spectacles. "How do you get about without a *mahram*?"

"I have an uncle who visits me once a day and takes me out for a walk, as if I were a pet dog. Without him, I'd go mad here. It was so good to see you, but you have neglected me," she scolded with a smile. "Now you'll have to come and see me regularly for the cream and for me to tend to your beard."

I stood before her in an awkward silence.

"I know what you're about to say," Noorzia said, embracing me. "Pay me when you have the money. Or better still, send me the money in U.S. dollars." She tapped my cheek. "I'll keep the accounts. One moment . . ." She took up her scissors and carefully clipped a few stray hairs off my beard. "There, that's neater."

"Let's see if he'll notice the difference in my skin color."

"Men don't notice anything different about other men, except haircuts. And here you won't be revealing yours, Babur. How old is Jahan?"

"Just sixteen."

"What a huge burden for such a boy. And your cousins?"

"Not much older."

"I'm so frightened for you," she said, tears coming to her eyes. "I'll pray one of them will not betray you. Honor is a double-edged sword for our men. They will use it to protect you and then turn it around to slash your throat. Be very careful."

We hugged. I didn't want to leave the sanctuary of her home, the pleasure of her buoyant company, the sanity of her life in her little house.

"Now, let yourself out—I don't want to have to cover myself so your brother won't turn to stone when he sees me."

"I'll do what you do from now on at home. Dress up and put on my makeup."

"You must."

When I left her room, Jahan was waiting impatiently by the front door. He stood back, scrutinizing my face. "You look darker and your eyebrows are thicker."

"And I had my hair cut."

"How can I see that under the turban? I get my hair cut in five minutes."

"Women's hair always takes longer," I said and smiled.

"You can trust her?"

"Yes. She hates the Talib. And she does have a smuggler but doesn't guarantee that he is dependable. She says I will need five thousand if I want a visa, plane tickets, a chance to get as far from Kabul as possible."

"Five . . . ," he said breathlessly. "You only asked for two."

"We'll bargain the smuggler down—and it is one thousand just to get to Karachi. I might at least be able to get over the border until I can get more from Shaheen." I gave him the paper.

"He's in the old city," he said on reading the address. "I'll meet him tomorrow and discuss the price. Then you will be ready to leave when you get the money." Jahan looked back at the house. "Can she loan us . . ."

"She doesn't have the money."

"I am worried about Noorzia talking. Women talk a lot," he added with a boy's contempt.

"She won't—you just have to trust me."

"Whatever happens I must see you married to Shaheen." He spoke with such authority. "You can't marry Wahidi, it's against mine and Maadar's wishes. I must get you out."

I was surprised by his agenda. He was now talking as if he were my father, not my little brother, carrying the burden of my future, sending the bride to the groom's home.

"That's what I've always planned to do," I said as we walked, aware that Shaheen was not in my heart but was a family obligation. Despite our closesness, I could not confess the truth to my brother. "You're risking your life too if Droon finds out you're defying him."

"I haven't forgotten that Droon threatened me, and Maadar, with Pul-e-Charkhi if I didn't agree," he continued in his commanding tone. "Father would do the same. You looked after me all these years and now I must take care of you. You're the only family I have left after Maadar."

"And you, mine. We'll make it together somehow, God willing." I wanted to take his hand and squeeze it out of my love and gratitude for his caring.

WE CAUGHT A BUS HOME, AND I FELT MORE CONFIDENT BEneath the layer of darkened skin and thickened eyebrows, believing I was now invisible among the men we passed. They didn't even glance at us.

But back at the house, in my room, I removed the turban and mourned for my hair. I had only snatched a glance in Noorzia's mirror, but now I could inspect it in private. She had left the central part, but on either side my hair lay flat and short, above my ears, exposing the sides of my head, which I had never seen before. At the back, I felt my skull and my bare nape. When I covered my face from my eyebrows down, I saw a boy's head sticking up. I carefully removed the beard and lay it on my desk tenderly, as I would a sleeping kitten. It even curled up like one. My face now had two shades, my darker makeup outlining the contours of the beard.

Still dressed as Babur, I made lunch, a pilau with *quorma*, naan, and a salad, and took it up to Mother and Dr. Hanifa.

They were playing cards.

We helped Mother sit up, and added more pillows for her back. She peered at me. "What happened to your hair?"

"Half your face looks darker—or is it the light?" Dr. Hanifa said.

"Noorzia cut it and put on darker makeup," I said.

"Noorzia!" my mother said, instantly brightening. I served my mother her usual helping. "But you had such beautiful hair." She sighed.

"It will grow back," I answered. "Eventually."

BOOK
TWO

THE TEAM

AFTER LUNCH, PARWAAZE AND QUBAD LED MY other cousins into the *mardaana*. I waited on the stairs, the wings of the house, until Jahan signaled. I counted heads; there were seven. With Jahan, Parwaaze, and Qubad that made ten. They sat on the floor with slouched shoulders and bowed heads. They were family, my childhood friends, and now my teammates, young men with incipient beards and frowns between their eyes—I had to trust them. They looked up, curious, scared, hopeful, as I entered the room. Their eyes wandered, uncertain where to settle on me—face, feet, hands, turban, chest. Finally, settling for my eyes, I held them there. I didn't let a moment pass.

"You are here to learn cricket. I can only do that dressed as a man. I am risking my life only because of Jahan. I want you to win and take him out with you. If you tell the Talib what I am doing, I will get a bullet in my head."

I began to pace slowly in front of them. "But remember, you are all implicated and you will be punished too, though not as severely as me, if we are caught. I don't have to tell you how the Talib will treat you, as you all know this regime. If any of you are afraid, tell me and leave now before any harm befalls you because of me."

The room was silent. They knew of the cruelties and I saw them hesitate. One or two wavered enough to shift uneasily, as if wanting to rise and run away before they were harmed because of me. I waited.

I asked again, "Do any of you want to leave?"

The cousins began to look at each other to see if anyone was getting up. No one moved.

Parwaaze came to my side. "We have sworn to protect you and not tell anyone. If anyone does, it will be against our family honor."

They all straightened slightly at the mention of the family.

Parwaaze continued, "They are all against you marrying the Talib and will do what they can to help you escape when the time comes."

"Thank you—I will teach you, knowing your lives are in my hands just as my life is in your hands from now on."

Each one met my eyes and held them as I asked them one last time if they were ready to join the team. I waited for each answer before moving to the next.

"Have you told your parents?" I asked them.

"I warned them not to," Parwaaze said.

"We need you," Atash said. "We have long planned to get out, and this is our chance. Why would we report you?"

"But can we win?" Namdar demanded from the back.

"Why not? You are as capable of this win as anyone else." The others murmured in agreement.

"Do they play cricket in Australia?" Bilal wanted to know.

"Yes. They are the champions today."

"Then they'll be happy to have us." Daud smiled and it passed over all their faces.

"You are a brave woman, Rukhsana," Royan said admiringly.

"We must get used to calling Rukhsana Babur," Parwaaze corrected him quickly.

"You all swear you'll look after my sister?" Jahan demanded.

"We will," they said.

"I will try my best to coach you until the day before the preliminary matches. But if it becomes too dangerous for me, I may leave earlier to join Shaheen and you'll have to teach each other. Now, I want to tell you why I love this game so much and I hope you will too as you master it." I gave them the same passionate talk I had given the day before. They listened intently and their interest flickered a bit more brightly.

After I finished, Parwaaze took me aside. "I know we're a player short, but there won't be any problem finding one more."

"Two more," I said. "A team always has twelve, even thirteen players, in case of injuries and to carry drinks and towels onto the field. Who else do you have in mind?"

KABUL UNIVERSITY WAS A FIFTEEN-MINUTE WALK AWAY AND, like children crossing a dangerous street, we looked both ways before we stepped out of the compound. The few pedestrians paid no attention to us. Parwaaze insisted on carrying the cricket bat and I distributed my pads, gloves, and ball to the others. I walked in the center of them, with Jahan beside me. I was part of this group of young men, learning to see the world with the same confidence that they possessed as their right. I copied their behavior, or tried to, the confident slouch as they moved, talking to each other, and the quick shy glances at the covered women passing us. And yet I felt detached from them, constantly aware of both my identity and the danger. I sensed their tension too as they protected me, not getting too close but always checking to see that I was still among them. And closing in when men approached, parting when they passed.

When I was gradually comfortable in their center, I studied them to work out their possible potential, drawing on the memory of our childhood days when we played together.

Parwaaze had good hand-eye coordination. He could start the batting.

Qubad, who swung a cricket bat like a golfer his club, would bat last, when we needed to make quick runs.

Namdar, handsome and stocky, looked as if he had the energy to be a fast bowler.

Bilal was slimmer and more observant, and I sensed suppleness in his movements as he walked quickly. I thought he could be the wicketkeeper.

Daud was smaller than the others and slower in his movements—I suspected he was lazy. Perhaps I could hide him far away from the batsman.

Nazir had a springy step when he moved around; he looked like a sprinter and he could have the footwork to bat with Parwaaze.

Atash was tall, slim, and had an easy grace. He had played football. I saw him as a fast bowler.

Omaid, the youngest at fourteen, walked in silence next to his brother, Royan. There was a blankness to his stare. His father and sister had been killed in front of his eyes by a rocket during the Talib attack four years ago, and his mind seemed to have gone since then. Omaid was a sweet-looking boy and I wanted to comfort him. Where could I fit him in?

Royan, like Omaid, had a very square face, one I could have drawn on graph paper with straight lines. He had the height and could be a good fast bowler.

Jahan would also bat, probably before Qubad.

They were a motley group, yes, but I could see promise in shaping them into a cricket team. But, in the way they shuffled along, I knew I would have to instill confidence in them too.

As we came to a crossroads, near the campus, we saw the religious police sitting in the back of a Land Cruiser. They were enjoying the warm sun on their faces. Our team hesitated. The leader signaled for us to approach. I felt tremors pass through the boys; even such a simple gesture had an air of menace to it. A few other pedestrians hurried past, heads averted, grateful they were not the ones summoned. These police didn't wear uniforms, their only badge of authority the guns and the electric cables they carried. They were young, not much older than Jahan, and they looked hungry and arrogant.

"Just let me do the talking," Parwaaze whispered nervously.

It wasn't us but our strange baggage that had betrayed us.

"What are you carrying?" one demanded.

Parwaaze obeyed his own advice and avoided eye contact. He lowered his head.

"Here, sir, see, this is a cricket bat." He removed it from the plastic scabbard. "We are going to play cricket." He pointed to the pads Qubad carried and the gloves, with Atash. Casually, my cousins moved to shield me from the policemen's view.

Surprisingly, the bat brought smiles to the faces of the policemen, revealing the children behind the murderous masks.

"Cricket! I saw it played in Pakistan when I was a boy."

The other, suddenly suspicious, asked Parwaaze, "But you're not Pakistani, are you?"

"No, sir," said Parwaaze, "we just want to learn the game."

"What e-else is there to do?" Qubad said.

"You will play the match?"

"Yes, that's why we're learning the game."

"Go, and good luck!" They laughed mockingly and gestured with their guns.

"Don't hurry," Parwaaze whispered. "Just walk at the usual pace. They'll be watching, I can feel their eyes on my back."

"Are you okay?" Jahan asked me.

"Just very afraid," I whispered. "I thought they were calling me out."

"We're all afraid," he said, taking my hand briefly.

"I'll pray for Babur's spirit to enter me and guide me," I said, my heart finally returning to a normal pace.

We passed Malalai Hospital, where Jahan and I were born. It looked so tired and worn out, the walls stained dark from years of rain. Just as the university gates came into view, a motorbike roared past us. The rider glanced at us, then made a U-turn to stop beside Parwaaze. He didn't turn off the engine.

"Azlam," Qubad whispered.

He was quite tall, with a patchy beard, and he wore a blue *shalwar* and a black waistcoat. The tail end of his black turban fell over his left shoulder and halfway down his chest. He had a perpetual sneer on his face. I understood right away why Parwaaze and Qubad disliked him.

"Is that a cricket bat?" he asked loudly. "Let me see it."

"No," Parwaaze said. "Find your own." Their exchange rang from the schoolyard.

"I have my team and we will win and go for training in Pakistan." He picked at his beard's patches as he spoke.

"Who's teaching you?"

Azlam laughed. "No one. It's an easy game. You hit the ball and run. We don't need teaching for that." He revved the engine. "I heard that in the preliminary matches each team will play ten overs and in the final it will be fifteen overs. I bet you don't know what an over is."

"Six balls," Parwaaze snapped. "Don't take all day to work out how many there are in ten overs."

"Are you going to the university?"

"No, to the mountain."

He revved his engine while we passed him and he seemed to be trying to remember our faces. I kept mine slightly averted, as if to talk to Jahan. Instead of continuing on his original way, Azlam rode back the way we had just come. When I looked in his direction, I saw him talking to the religious policemen. They seemed to be very friendly.

"I didn't know anyone wanted to know them," I said to Qubad, who was also looking.

"They're the only ones who would want to know A-Azlam."

The entrance gate to the campus hung on its hinges. No spirits had protected the house of learning founded in 1932. Most of the buildings were damaged, some were totally razed. They still held classes in those that remained whole. The few students were boys only, completing their final year. The Taliban had even permitted girls in their final year of study but only to complete their degrees, and then they sent them all home to waste their learning.

My cousins looked at the broken university with yearning, having had only a year of studies before the Talib won Kabul and dismissed them from classes. Now they dreamed of finishing their studies in another country.

We made our way to the eastern corner of the campus, away from the buildings. A drowsy silence greeted us. The city had fallen away. Dry leaves, brown and brittle, carpeted the dead lawns. The ground was flat enough for a cricket field and there was a footpath of hard earth that would be our pitch.

We dropped our gear—two cricket bats, one pair of pads, three cricket balls (one almost new), and a pair of batting gloves.

"We need wicket-keeping gloves. They have to be well padded to protect the fingers and the palms of the keeper. And pads."

"Daud, can your father help us with these?" Parwaaze said to him. "Can you make big gloves?"

"We can make any size gloves at the shop." He examined the pads. "These too."

As I measured out the sixty-six feet for the wicket, Parwaaze confessed he had looked up the definition of cricket in an English dictionary.

"You know how it was defined?" he said. "A jumping insect. Then, second, cricket is a game of eleven players a side. That's all. Not very helpful."

"You're just looking in the wrong book." I took out a thin volume, *The Rules of Cricket*, published by the Marylebone Cricket Club. "There are forty-two rules with a long explanation for each one."

He opened it warily and read aloud to the team, "'Cricket is a game that owes much of its unique appeal to the fact that it should be played not only within its Laws but also within the Spirit of the Game. Any action which is seen to abuse this spirit causes injury to the game itself.'"

I took it, opened the book to the appendix, and read, "'There is no place for any act of violence on the field of play.'" I returned it to Parwaaze.

"Cricket will never become popular here." Bilal broke the astonished silence and managed a laugh. "How can we live without violence?"

Standing on our "pitch," I faced my team of cousins who had never before played cricket, and I temporarily despaired. Where would I begin? The soul? The bat? The field? The positions? I picked up a ball and tossed it back and forth in my hands. "Let's start with a little fielding practice just to limber up. Parwaaze, you first."

I tossed the ball, not too high, and within his reach to see how he would catch it. "Catching itself is a skill," I said. "People open their hands like the jaws of a dog or a cat, vertically. To catch the ball in cricket, the hands should be horizontal and cupped to pouch it lovingly. With the wrong technique, the ball will come down as hard as a stone on your fingers."

Of course, Parwaaze opened his hands vertically and the ball fell to the ground after bouncing out of his hands. He winced and glared at me as if I had done something wrong.

"Throw it up to me," I said.

He tossed it up, impatient, and I caught it with cupped hands. "I know it seems an easy exercise to begin with, but catching a ball is very important in winning a game. And this is the way you catch it." I tossed it for Qubad and he fumbled, trying to imitate my actions, but did hold it. We practiced catching for half an hour. After that, even though they were impatient to learn bowling and batting, I made them run up and down our pitch, which was how they would score runs. They ran with the gait of old men, unused to such physical exertion, and were quick to bend over, panting.

"You have to be fit not only to run once up the pitch but back down and then up again. This will be three runs. And you'll have to chase balls that pass you. You are all totally unfit."

"Why should we be fit?" Royan asked. "Where can we run to without getting killed by a land mine?"

"Then jog in your garden or up and down a safe street. If you want to win, you must start training yourselves. Now I'll show you how to bowl." I took the ball, walked my five paces, and slowed down my actions. "If you bowl slowly you need only a few steps. A fast bowler will need a much longer run to generate the speed of the ball. See, I've turned sideways before I let go of the ball. My left arm is straight above my head, my right one, holding the ball, is by my side at nearly a hundred and eighty degrees. Now as I bring the right up as straight as possible—and you must not bend the elbow—my left arm goes down to keep my balance and I release the ball at the very top of the arc."

I lined them up and made them imitate my actions. They were eager but as gawky as infants learning how to walk. I moved to each one—straightening an arm, turning them more to the side. I made them run and bowl too. A team has specialist batsmen and bowlers and I would need four good bowlers. As Jahan, Parwaaze, and Qubad already knew the actions, they mastered it more quickly than the others. But I saw promise in Nazir, Royan, and, surprisingly, Omaid too.

Omaid seemed to emerge from his trance when he walked to bowl; the physical action seemed to awaken a hidden spirit in him. He surprised us all, possessing a natural talent, and he smiled with such childish pleasure that we applauded him—mutely, though, as clapping was against Talib law.

I would have to focus on bowling again later in our practice and now needed to find my batsmen. I took up the bat and they looked expectant. This is what they were here for.

I took up the position in front of them: "You see, my feet are apart to keep my balance. I'm half bent over, like a spring, so that when the ball bounces I straighten to step back, holding my bat vertically down to let the ball bounce and hit the bat. This is defensive. If you think the bounce is within your reach, you move your left foot as near the ball as possible, and bring the bat down in a straight arc to hit it."

I repeated my actions again slowly, imagining the speed and bounce of the ball. Then I handed over the bat to each one and bowled to them. As I had thought, Royan and Parwaaze were quick to copy my actions, and gradually so did Nazir. At first, he was awkward, but then as his confidence grew and he discovered how to keep his balance and hit the ball, he became more stylish and aggressive in hitting the ball. Bilal, in keeping with his nature, was slower and more stubborn—he wasn't a risk taker and he could be in the middle of the order to steady the side. Qubad, still swinging wildly, would come in near the end to hit as many balls as he could.

Royan suddenly held up his hand, turning his head one way, then another, listening. From a distance, we heard a motorbike. It seemed to be circling us, nearing and then moving away. It suddenly stopped. We knew it was Azlam, spying on us, and we looked through the trees and shrubs but couldn't spot him. We sat, waiting. Then we heard the motorbike start up and fade away.

"Even in high school and college he was always sneaking around," Parwaaze muttered.

We practiced bowling and batting all afternoon, but each time we heard the call to prayer we would stop immediately in case Azlam or even the religious police were hidden watchers. We knelt and prayed until it was time to resume the lessons once more.

I gathered the men. "As a bowler, you have only one objective—to get the batsmen out. You're alone, we cannot help you in your outthinking of the batsmen. And they are only thinking of mastering you and defeating you. You cannot lose your temper. You must think, remain calm, and bowl well."

Then I took the bat and showed them more attacking strokes— the hook shot, the square cut, the cover drive, the leg glance, the late cut—all the techniques I could remember. "As a batsman you have to think only of outwitting both the bowler and all the fielders who are just waiting to get you out. You have to focus, to concentrate, and never let anyone distract you. You too are alone on the field. You have to learn to be yourself, be bold and brave when you walk out to the middle."

Qubad, no doubt wanting to show his prowess to his cousins, grabbed the bat from me and took a batting stance. He did a good imitation—legs slightly apart, crouched over the bat, but again he held it with both fists together, as if it was a club, and not hands apart, the left elbow facing the bowler and the left hand controlling the stroke.

"Omaid," he called. "B-bowl me a slow ball and I'll hit it all the way to the Hindu Kush."

Omaid took the ball, walked slowly to the crease, and bowled. His action wasn't perfect, but near enough. Qubad, forgetting to move his feet, took a huge swing at the ball and missed. The ball bounced, turned—an off-break—and hit him squarely in the crotch. He collapsed with a strangled scream.

Oh god, I'd forgotten about that.

I could barely watch. Qubad groaned and curled up, tight as an earthworm when touched with a twig. Had I killed him? Had I ruined his life forever?

There was no such compassion from the cousins for poor Qubad; they were all laughing as he writhed on the ground, clutching his crotch. Namdar and Bilal hopped around, imitating Qubad, holding their balls, screaming with laughter. Only Omaid looked shocked and frightened, his face forming a small, tight fist. Royan, his brother, made his way out to where Omaid stood. Parwaaze and I hurried across to kneel by Qubad's side as he lay there cursing in his still strangled voice.

"You didn't tell us that we need to protect . . . ourselves," Parwaaze said accusingly.

"A cup, it's called a box in cricket," I whispered.

"What does it l-look like?" Qubad managed to say. "I need one made of i-iron."

"I'll show you tomorrow."

Omaid kept staring at Qubad, tears streaking his cheeks. I joined him and Royan.

"Qubad is okay," I told him quietly. "You're not to blame."

"See, he's getting up," Royan said and embraced his brother tightly, trying to squeeze the fear out of his frail body. "Qubad, tell Omaid it wasn't his fault."

"It wasn't your fault, Omaid," Qubad managed to wheeze. "It was m-mine. Don't worry, I'll be okay."

Omaid sniffled once and then his face relaxed. He managed a tentative smile.

Parwaaze and Daud helped Qubad to his feet. He could barely stand and remained bent over, like an old man with an arthritic back. His every pain-filled action drew even more laughter from his unsympathetic teammates. Even Jahan was laughing. Although it took the funereal looks off their faces, I couldn't understand their bizarre sense of humor. If a ball hit one of us on our breast, or anywhere else, and she collapsed with the pain, we would rush onto the field to comfort her, not roll over laughing at her agony.

"Will he be able to walk again?" I asked Parwaaze, who was himself stifling laughter.

"Of course. In five minutes he'll be back to his usual self."

"No, he w-won't," Qubad groaned. "And I'll be a eunuch and never be able to lie with a w-woman."

"Don't worry, you'll still be able to use your hands—" Namdar said before abruptly stopping, remembering that I was Rukhsana and not Babur.

"I'll bring the box tomorrow," I said.

We practiced bowling and batting, each one taking a turn. I corrected their bowling actions and their batting strokes. It wasn't as easy as they thought it would be but they worked hard. The sun was sliding down, throwing long shadows, and I decided to finish for the day. They reluctantly stopped, but the day's play had brought a healthy flush to their faces and they kept miming the actions I had taught them, smiling.

"You and the team must keep practicing—bowling and catching especially. If we practice well, we'll play well."

"Don't forget that we want to see that cricket tape," Parwaaze reminded me.

"I'll bring it after dinner. And I'm serious about practice— I want all of you to keep practicing, even in your sleep."

I WAS THIRSTY, TIRED, AND HUNGRY. I WASN'T AS FIT AS I had been when I exercised daily in Delhi.

"Any letter?" I asked Abdul eagerly as we entered our gate.

"No."

"What about a package?"

Abdul shook his head.

I had been trying not to think about the letter, but now another day was passing without news. Jahan put his arm around my drooping shoulders as we went into the house.

"What package are you expecting?" Jahan asked.

"The money, of course. How else can he send it, except through a *hawala* dealer? He won't use a bank, as the money can be traced. Besides, I don't think our banks know how to handle international transactions."

"Is there one here?"

"Of course there is, they're everywhere. It's an ancient Indian system, older than the silk route, to move money between countries without going through a bank. Shaheen will give the money to a dealer, an Afghan or a Pakistani, in San Francisco, pay him a commission, and the dealer will call his contact in Kabul, the *hawaladar*, to deliver the money to my door. It will take only three or four days once Shaheen gives the dealer the money."

"But how will they call Kabul to tell the *hawaladar* here to pay you the money? Our phones don't work for days."

"They'll have four or five phone numbers, as their business depends on that."

To keep my mind occupied, I went down to the basement and trawled through the trunk, uncovering more memories—a low-cut black dress that barely reached my knees, boldly worn at a party; Hyderabadi glass bangles bought near the Charminar bazaar; picture postcards sent by friends traveling to exotic places; papers, letters, cheap jewelry. I discovered that the memories no longer held their sting of regret now that I felt comforted, immersed again in cricket, and also knowing that soon I would be liberated. I would leave it all behind, carrying only a passport and a bundle of clothes.

I did have a box, from sheer malice, thanks to Nargis. She and Veer had picked me up at home for one of our matches. Veer was driving, and Nargis and I sat in the backseat. They were arguing— and had been arguing all morning. Nargis was so furious with her brother, she reached into his bag at our feet, took out his box, opened my kit bag, and dropped it in. "That'll teach him a lesson," she had whispered. We both laughed at her prank, although I was worried for Veer. Maybe I had kept it as a strange reminder of my memory of him, not that I needed something so tangible. I never did see him play. It just remained in my kit after that.

Finally, the box surfaced from under a layer of tracksuits and books. It resembled heavily reinforced underwear with straps to hold it in place around the lower waist and a molded pouch to protect the testicles below. I held it, as daintily as a dead mouse, by the edge of the strap and slipped it into a plastic bag. I grabbed the tape I wanted to show the boys and hid both under my *shalwar*.

I cooked our simple meal of rice and fried chicken and peas. I sent Jahan to buy fresh naan. Dr. Hanifa came downstairs and offered to wash dishes. Mother had slept most of the day, and when she was awake, they had read to each other and played cards.

After dinner, we went to Parwaaze's house and met the team in the basement. The windows were covered with blankets, and a television set and VHS player stood in the corner cupboard, now open for the show. Stuck on the walls with tape, and curling at the edges, were posters of Ronaldo, Ronaldinho, and Rivaldo, the magicians of Brazil's World Cup football team. The air stank of cigarette smoke and tea. It was a private theater for trusted friends to view banned films—the family's secret income. Parwaaze's father bought the tapes from smugglers, just as Noorzia bought her creams and perfumes.

Parwaaze switched on the television and started the tape.

"Who's playing?" Namdar asked.

"England and India."

I watched for a few minutes, forgetting the expectant company waiting for me to explain. The stage was the almost bare, dun-colored pitch in the center of the emerald oval; the wickets upright at either end; the bowling and batting marks in immaculately straight white lines, visible from the farthest seats of the stadium. The passage of the lawn mowers had left regimental stripes on the grass outfield. I loved the game's quiet rhythms, its peaks of tension, and the sudden violence that subsided back into deceptive calmness. The fans watched the two main characters, the bowler and the batsman, confront each other on center stage. Everyone waited, breaths held, for the enactment of this ritual. The sounds of the game were not raucous but muted, the bat hitting the ball a solid *thwack*, a fielder sprinting to stop it or catch it.

"Tell us what's happening!" complained Qubad.

"Sorry—start the tape again. Okay, now watch the bowler's and batsman's actions. And look at this drawing I made." I had sketched out the fielding positions before dinner. "See how the batsman guided the ball through the gap? And now he's out, caught. There are five ways to get a batsman out and I'll explain each one and why when it comes up." We watched the game progress and suddenly a batsman was given out when the ball hit him on his shin. "Here the umpire believes if his leg hadn't been in the way, the ball would have hit the wicket. It's called leg before wicket." I added softly, "LBW. The umpire's decision is final. No argument. It's not cricket."

"So who'll u-umpire our match?" Qubad asked no one in particular.

"The minister said there's supposed to be that man from the ICC," I said. "Maybe he'll umpire."

"They won't want that." Royan sighed. "They'll find some Talib goon to umpire."

"In which case it's not cricket," I insisted. "It's only cricket if we can trust the umpire to be honest. Cricket imposes the behavior of fair play, and justice for those who want to be cricketers. I've seen test matches where the batsman knows he's not out but he still has to accept the umpire's decision. He can't stand there and argue. He walks back to the pavilion."

"Cricket will never take off here then." Namdar laughed. "We don't trust anyone at all. And there is no justice."

"That's the only way to play," I snapped at him.

"We'll play the game the way Babur teaches us," Parwaaze cut in. I had been watching him listening to the discussion, not wanting to choose sides, before finally coming down on mine. "I believe Babur: if we learn to play this game properly and have that discipline, then we will win. Now, let's watch and listen."

I pressed play and Sachin walked out of the pavilion to the crease. As I described the action, my voice grew eager and loud. I imagined the thousands of people watching from the stands, and millions around the world on television. I knew from my playing days how lonely that walk to the crease was and the silence that accompanied it. "Now watch him. He's the best batsman in the world."

"He's small," Qubad said dismissively. The English players towered over the Indian.

"Height doesn't make you any better."

"Why?" Parwaaze said, leaning forward to concentrate.

"You see how he's perfectly balanced at the crease. He has perfect footwork, great hands, and a great eye. See how he leans into the ball and at the last moment guides it exactly where he wants it to go. You must watch him again and again. He's known as the Little Master."

When it was over, Parwaaze began the tape again, I made them repeat every fielding position, like children at school learning their lessons in a madrassa. I could see them imagining themselves on the field in that tape, bowling and hitting like the best in the world.

WE GOT HOME AT TEN O'CLOCK AND I WENT STRAIGHT TO bed. I dreamed I was playing cricket with my college team again and the familiar faces floated in and out of the scenes running through my head. When I woke, I wished I was still there. My calendar was waiting and I drew a line through another day, shrinking the space even more. Seventeen days.

I followed Noorzia's advice. I was not going to be indifferent about my appearance. Although I did not rouge and powder my cheeks, or trace my lips with a pale red gloss, I took care with Babur's appearance. If I was to be a man, I at least wanted to be handsome. I fussed over my skin shade, eyebrows, and beard. I adjusted my spectacles and firmly rooted the turban on my head. By this simple transformation, I felt as if I had stepped out of my body and entered another one. I wore the same clothes, and, taking Noorzia's advice, strapped on my chest protector. It would grow uncomfortable over the course of the day, but even the most sensitive elbow would not know it hid my breasts.

Before we stepped out of the house for practice, we went up to the roof and scanned the road. There were a few passing cyclists, a vegetable vendor pushing his cart, two women with their *mahrams*, and scavenging goats. It looked normal. No one even glanced at the house.

"Why would Droon watch the house?" Jahan asked. "He has searched it and didn't find you. He knows we're all frightened of the Talib and that we wouldn't defy him, not while Mother and I are here as his hostages. She's not going anywhere. Don't forget, he threatened her too."

"Just to be sure," I said and kept watching.

"The dangerous time will be a day or two before Wahidi returns, and you're still not here. That's when it will be urgent for Droon to find you for his brother."

"Then I better leave three or four days before. By then the team should be good enough. Just to be on the safe side, I'll start sleeping in the secret room."

"It won't be comfortable."

"I know that. Whatever happens, get on that field and play—it's your best chance."

As we set out for the university, we heard the motorbike. Azlam passed us without a glance but I had the feeling he had seen and remembered us from the day before. He seemed to be hovering around our neighborhood.

"I saw Azlam," Jahan told Parwaaze at the grounds.

"He wants to see how we're learning." He looked grim. "We must beat his team, we must."

I presented my gift to Qubad. He took it out and dangled it for everyone to see and examine, as if it were a work of art.

Parwaaze took it and slipped it over his pants, adjusted it, and walked around proudly. "Okay, now I will learn how to bat the ball."

"We will need another one, maybe two more," Jahan said. "There are two batsmen at the wicket, and a third one waiting to come in when one of them is out."

"Can you make two like this?" Parwaaze asked Bilal, pointing to his crotch.

"Well . . . It will take a day or two. I'll have to soak and then shape the leather to fit over the . . . parts."

"Make me a special one, I have more between my legs than any of you," Namdar boasted, and clutched his crotch. "About twice the size."

"Yes, make a special one for Namdar," Qubad added. "I don't want to catch any of his diseases."

"Okay, okay," Bilal said. "But you each pay me for this. I'm not making these for free. My father finds out I'm stealing his precious leather and he'll fire me."

Qubad looked away, and turned to Parwaaze. "Oh god, look who's c-coming."

THE PERMIT

WE ALL TURNED, EXPECTING TO SEE AZLAM. Instead, a young man with a full beard stormed across the field. Parwaaze's brother. As he got closer, we could see his face was flushed with anger. The team shuffled away from Parwaaze as his brother approached.

Parwaaze groaned aloud. "What are you doing here?"

"I want to know what you're doing," Hoshang burst out. "You should have told me."

"We're just playing a game. Now that you've seen, you can go away."

"What game?"

"Cricket," Qubad answered wearily and turned to me with a smile. "Hoshang has n-nothing better to do than follow us around."

"You shut up," Hoshang snapped at Qubad.

"Oh yes, c-caliph, I will. Now leave."

"Why cricket? Tell me, or I'll report you all."

"We're not breaking any law," Parwaaze said, exasperated. "It's a game—"

"I know that, I read the papers—"

"—and we just want to play in the matches. That's all. Now that you know, you can leave us."

"And who is that?" Hoshang jutted his beard toward me. There was a resemblance to Parwaaze, but his mood was darker and he didn't have Parwaaze's sense of humor and mischief either.

"Babur," Parwaaze said. He looked at me, then at the others. He had not told Hoshang about me and hesitated for a long moment before bursting out, "Babur is Rukhsana. She's teaching us."

Hoshang looked puzzled, believing at first that Parwaaze was playing a joke. Then he took a few steps closer to study me and a slow recognition emerged in his eyes. They blinked rapidly, in panic, I think. We weren't close as children and we'd never known each other very well—but Parwaaze seemed to know what he was doing. Protectively, the others moved closer to me. We waited tensely.

"You all know?" He looked around. Heads nodded. "Does Padar know?"

"No," Parwaaze said. "Unless you tell him." Then, resigned, he said, "And everyone else. You'll get her killed, and us too."

"Why would I do that?" Hoshang finally said. He laughed, and seemed to relax now that he had learned his brother's secret.

"We need another player," I offered, "if you want to join."

"Of course! So are we going to win or not?"

"Why else would we waste our time here? We have a full team now."

We spent the days following our routine—warm-up exercises, then batting and bowling. They still had the awkwardness of beginners and I hoped as they became more confident they would acquire the style and grace the game demanded. Jahan, Parwaaze, Qubad, Atash, and Royan showed promise as batsmen. They had the footwork and the quick eye to pick up the speed and bounce of the ball. Omaid, Daud, Namdar, and Bilal bowled well, though when Namdar and Daud tried to bowl too fast, they lost control and fell over. Control would come with more practice. I taught

Hoshang how to stand behind the wicket and stop the ball or catch it if it hit the edge of the bat. As the oldest, it gave him a sense of importance that he would be such an integral part of the game.

At the end of each day's session, I gave them fielding and catching practice, which none of them liked. They lined up thirty meters away, silhouetted against the low, dun-colored Asamayi hill, and I hit the ball along the ground until, one by one, they ran to field it and throw it back to Hoshang. By the end of the week, they moved with the easy spirit of young men.

"That was a four you let through your legs," I shouted, as Sharma had shouted to us in practice in Delhi. "The batsmen are taking three runs because you're so slow . . . you must outrun the batsmen . . . pick up and throw . . . run faster . . . expect the ball in your direction . . . faster . . . faster . . ." Then I hit high balls and, at first, they dropped every catch. "You could have gotten a man out if you'd jumped for that catch . . . Catches win matches . . ."

Each evening, when Jahan and I returned home, we exchanged the same dialogue with Abdul. "Letters? Package?" and his reply was the same. One day, I prayed, he would hold out the package and I would dance into the house and out of the country. The phone too drew me like a magnet. But it remained uncooperative. Three, four, five days passed, and each time I crossed one off my calendar; I felt as if the lines were pushing me forward and I was helpless to stop them. How long would Shaheen's letter and money take to reach me? A week, I thought, and tried to unravel the knot in my stomach.

Just as I was preparing dinner, we heard a knock on the door. Jahan looked out through the window to see who it was before he opened it. Abdul stood beside a couple, waiting on the top step. I kept behind the door when Jahan opened it and exchanged greetings with the couple.

"I'm a good friend of Rukhsana's." She had a young woman's

voice. "And as I was passing your house I thought I must see her."

"I told her that Rukhsana was in Mazar," Abdul complained.

"She's not here," Jahan said brusquely. "She's in Mazar helping with her cousin's big wedding."

"But I spoke to her just yesterday on the street."

"You couldn't have. If you give me your name I'll tell her you called when she returns."

"If she doesn't want to see me, I won't give my name," she said, now in a very hurt tone. "I was in school with her."

"You can go to Mazar then."

We watched the couple leave, followed by Abdul, grumbling at them.

"You recognize her voice?" Jahan asked as we hurried up the stairs to the top floor.

"No."

We stood at the sides of the window and looked down to the street. The couple stood outside our gate, talking, and then looked at the house before hurrying toward Karte Seh Wat.

"You were right," Jahan said, remembering our conversation from that morning. "She must be working for Wahidi and Droon."

"Next time it won't be the same couple." How long had they been watching the house? How had we missed them? I was going to be doubly cautious now. Rukhsana would never be seen in this house, even glimpsed through a window, until Babur crossed the border to safety.

It was the following afternoon when Parwaaze pointed and we saw Azlam sitting astride his motorbike, watching us. He had coasted to the side of a building and could have been there for an hour. When we noticed him, we heard his mocking laughter as he kick-started his motorbike and rode toward us. We retreated from the racket, bunching together, as he circled us, looking at our equipment. He stopped.

"Who's teaching you to play?" he shouted above the noise of his machine.

"No one," Parwaaze said and reached into his *shalwar* pocket and pulled out the Marylebone Cricket Club book of rules that I had given him. "This is teaching us how to play." He flipped through the pages. "It tells you how to bat, how to bowl, and how to move your fielders around . . ."

"Let me see." Azlam reached for it, but Parwaaze held it out of his reach.

"Find your own book."

"Where did you get it?"

"From the bookshop on Park Street." Then he added maliciously, "It was the only copy."

Azlam's eyes roved over us possessively and then settled on me. "If you're learning from the book, why is he instructing you all the time?"

"The book's in English and Babur reads it better than we do," Parwaaze said without looking at me.

"Even if you found a c-copy all you can do is look at the drawings," Qubad added, smiling at him without any humor.

Azlam gunned the bike. "My team will still win, even without the stupid book." He laughed and raced away.

We waited until the sound of his bike had faded and started again. When the light began to wane, with nine days left, we set off homeward. I prayed with each step that the letter, the package, was waiting for us.

"Which of the two is younger?" I heard Parwaaze ask Qubad.

Two women approached us.

"The one on the left," Qubad said. "She walks straighter. Maybe she is pretty."

"Which one do you think, Babur?"

How could one tell? Did men make those remarks about the

hidden me too, trying to guess my age, my looks, my shape? Of course, long ago, I noticed other women—the style of clothes, the colors, the patterns. Now I was expected to make a quick, male judgment on the women who could not be seen but only fantasized about.

"Qubad's right," I whispered. "The one on the left." Her ankles were neat and straight; the other woman had fatter ones, partially twisted by her weight.

"The younger one's looking at you." Parwaaze laughed. "See the quick glance?"

"You've sharper eyes than I do," I said. "I think she's looking at Jahan."

"No, you," Namdar insisted in a teasing voice.

"How can you tell a glance from behind the mesh?" I demanded. "She could be looking past you."

"You dream you did." Royan spoke in a longing voice. "Once, when we passed on our streets, I caught the glances of beautiful girls, some not that beautiful, and we exchanged those glances and smiled to ourselves as went on our way. Kabul women were once bold and fashionable, now they are cowed and covered by the edicts of the Taliban. I miss them, they have become invisible."

"That's your problem." Qubad laughed. "You d-dream too much."

"And you don't dream at all," Atash mocked.

"This is why I sleep well."

When we heard a woman's scream, we were a hundred yards from the hospital. At first, in the press of people, carts, and cars, I couldn't see who had cried out. Parwaaze pushed forward through a knot of men, clearing a path for us behind him. Across the street, a religious policeman was beating a woman with his cane. He was shouting, "Where is your permit to leave the house? Where is your *mahram's* letter?" The woman was screaming, weaving away from the blows. Then I saw that she clutched something in her arms, wrapped in a bright blue shawl embroidered with silvery stars. "My baby is ill, she is vomiting. I must get her to the hospital . . . emergency . . ." She clutched her baby as she twisted away from the policeman. He tried to grab her burka, but it slipped from his grasp. "Return to your home," he shouted at the woman and swung his cane, striking her back. Stubbornly, she ducked in the crowd and ran with her precious burden toward the hospital. We watched, frozen, unable to move. The policeman unslung his machine gun, and the people fell to the ground. The woman was thirty yards away from the hospital now.

I knew what was going to happen and opened my mouth to scream. Jahan saw and clamped his hand quickly over my mouth.

The policeman aimed and fired a burst of terrible consecutive cracks, like sticks breaking, and the woman staggered, tumbled, and fell. She lay half on the pavement, half on the road. She still clutched the baby in her arms and, in the silence, we could hear its mewling. The policeman slung the weapon back onto his shoulder. He looked around—a young man, heavily bearded, smirking and threatening anyone who dared to block his passage as he swaggered away. People who had fallen to avoid the bullets rose slowly to their feet and kept their distance, afraid the religious policeman would return. They stared at the body with that impassive, stoic look of shock and fear. I looked at the body as if hoping she would stir, get to her feet, and keep running. The baby still mewled, and I pushed through to reach it and picked it up, cradling it to stop its crying. The team followed me to kneel by the woman. At one time, they would have stayed in the crowd. Qubad looked around, as if searching for her family, and I saw the tears glisten in his eyes. He, Atash, Namdar, and Royan lifted up the woman between them, walking in the direction she had run from, in search of her home. Then another woman screamed. She came stumbling out of a side street and reached up for the body, weeping and crying out. She was elderly, perhaps the dead woman's mother. An elderly man, his face scarred with sadness, took the baby from my arms. He spoke to the woman, and then he stoically carried the baby toward the hospital. Stumbling and crying, the woman led the way for the team to the house the dead woman had lived in.

"Oh god" was all I could whisper as Jahan pulled me away.

ABDUL SAID, "NO LETTER, NO PACKAGE." AND WE PASSED him in silence, Jahan holding me.

When we were safe in the house, with the doors locked and barred, I screamed the scream that had been choking me on the hurried walk back to the house. Its ferocity frightened even me. I erupted with rage, hatred, and heartbreak at the injustice of my world and then I wept for the woman who had died. A shapeless tangle of clothing, like discarded laundry, on a public street.

"Someone should have stopped him," I sobbed. "Someone. Are we all such cowards that we couldn't have stopped him from killing a woman? For what? She was trying to save her baby's life. What kind of crime is that?"

"She was a woman," Jahan replied bleakly. "That was all."

He reached out to comfort me and I pulled away, as if blaming him for not saving the woman. Accusing all men for their callous indifference to a woman's murder. He dropped his arm. I wanted to be held and comforted by a woman, by my mother, who could weep alongside me for this terrible crime against us all. But such a tragic story would break her heart.

"Rukhsana, I kept thinking of you lying in that street. If you had screamed, they would have known you were a woman and god knows what could have happened to you."

I removed my turban, then carefully peeled off my beard. I scratched my head, touching the sweat that had dried from playing our harmless game of cricket, and rubbed life into my cheeks, smoothing away the prickly feel of the fine mesh.

"You can't blame the men for doing nothing," Jahan continued. "What could we do? Stand between the policeman and the woman, and get ourselves shot?"

"At least knocked his gun down, spoiled his aim. We knew what he was going to do when he swung the gun off his shoulder."

"And be killed for doing that also." Then he added stoutly, "You saw, we went to her body. I'm not afraid."

"You should be." I turned to face Jahan. "I have to help you get out of this murderous country. Even though it's madness. I cannot sit here doing nothing while waiting to hear from Shaheen," I said.

We sat on the divan, staring at the wall. Finally, Jahan tentatively reached out and I allowed him to drape his arm around my shoulder. It felt stiff from nervousness. I leaned against him.

"I hear your stomach rumbling."

"We haven't eaten since this morning," he reminded me. "Do I need to buy anything?"

I rose. "No, we have some food from yesterday, if you don't mind the chicken again. And we have some naan. I'll check on Maadar."

I went to her room; Dr. Hanifa was reading aloud from *Pride and Prejudice*. Mother smiled when I came in and the doctor put the book down.

"I heard someone shouting," she said.

"That was me. I banged my toe on the door. But the toe's not broken."

"You look tired," Mother said when I bent to kiss her.

"I'm just not fit, that's all. How are you feeling?"

"The doctor says I'm feeling fine." They both smiled. "I had some dinner with Hanifa, but you and Jahan haven't eaten."

* * *

"YOU MUST WRITE A LETTER GIVING YOUR PERMISSION FOR me to leave the house. I'll carry it around in case we get separated," I said to Jahan after dinner.

"I'll do it now," he said and went up to his room.

Although I was so tired, I went to Father's office and started dialing Shaheen's number. I would keep at it all night if necessary. After the fifth hit on redial, it connected and I heard the ringing a long distance away.

A man answered with a hello and I recognized Shaheen's father's voice. "Uncle," I shouted down the line in English. "It's Rukhsana."

"Rukhsana! How are you?"

"I'm fine." I hated this polite pleasantry, nervous that we'd be cut off before I could talk to Shaheen. "How are you and the family?"

"We're very well and happy here in America. How is your mother?"

"Not any better, Uncle." We could continue all night like this! I plunged in. "I must speak to Shaheen, it's very urgent."

"He's not home, but I'll tell him you called and he will call you back. I know he wants to speak to you. He's tried calling, but there was no answer."

I managed a smile. "You know our phones, Uncle."

"In America the phones always work and the calls are cheap," he announced proudly.

"When will he be back?"

"Soon. He'll call you."

"Tell him I'm waiting and it's very urgent." I hurried on, "Do you know if he's sent—"

The line disconnected.

I sat in the chair, staring at the phone, waiting for Shaheen to call back. I fell into a sleep of confusing images: cricket, a woman screaming, a motorbike passing. I was there in the morning, stiff and still tired, as the light slipped through the cracks in the shutters. I checked the phone and heard the stuttering dial tone.

I scratched another day off the calendar, trying not to look at the shrinking numbers. Maybe Shaheen had tried to call and couldn't get through. And if he had my letter, he would be arranging the transfer through the *hawala* dealer. I washed in cold water and that revived me, and I went down to make breakfast. Jahan appeared in the kitchen, sleepy and shuffling, but I didn't tell him I had spoken to Shaheen's father. What was there to tell? We took the tray up to Mother and ate with her, not saying much, as she looked as if she'd had a restless night too. When Dr. Hanifa joined us, I went down to the kitchen.

I heard the soft knocking on the back garden gate and reflexively looked at the battered clock on the table. It was nine thirty—I had forgotten about the girls.

Over three years ago, Mother and I had started clandestine classes for girls in and around Karte Seh. They came once or twice a week, or sometimes not at all, depending on whether or not they were free of their chores. Only a few came these days—Raishma, a cheeky girl with an impish laugh and lovely green eyes was the oldest at eight; the youngest, Sooryia, was only four, a shy, thin girl.

They broke the monotony of our restricted lives with their eagerness to learn and their gossip. It was Raishma who had told me about the woman whose fingertip, with the nail varnish, was chopped off. And a girl named Louena told me about her brother, who was given an electronic game the size of a playing card, a magical gift for his eighth birthday that he took to show off to his friends on the street. The religious police caught him. They first smashed the toy, then beat him and broke his right arm. I wrote that story too after talking to the depressed and frightened boy, his arm in a sling.

When Mother could no longer teach the classes, I continued alone. I taught them to read and write and then some geography, science, and arithmetic. We used small slates that they brought with them, hidden under their *shalwars*. Because they were that young, they could go out alone, as they didn't have far to travel. They were so proud of their skills. I thought of the priceless value of the written word. Without reading, how would they find where they were in a country, how could they read signs on a bus, read the instructions on a packet? To read a language, any language, is a wonderful gift that I had taken so much for granted. I remembered my own excitement at discovering the alphabet—first the letters formed words and then sentences, paragraphs, and pages, and ultimately they provided the pleasure of reading a whole book, even a child's story.

On two occasions women banged on our gate and told us they wanted their little girls to join the classes. As I suspected they were informers, I would blandly deny teaching any girls.

"Jahan, the girls are at the gate. I can't teach them and they mustn't see me. Tell them I'm away."

Jahan took the keys from the hook and went to the back door. I watched from the kitchen window as he opened it and stepped out—there were three here today.

Jahan closed the gate and returned to the window. "I told them you were away and they want to see Maadar," he said.

"I'll go up and hide." I retreated up the stairs as he let them in. Raishma, Sooryia, and Louena trailed after him. I ducked into Mother's room. She was propped up on pillows, and Dr. Hanifa was reading to her.

"The girls want to see you," I said and went into my room, leaving the door open just enough to listen.

They went in quietly and I heard Mother say, "Come and give me a hug."

"You look so beautiful, Maadar," they chorused.

"Never as beautiful as any one of you. I'm sorry Rukhsana's away, and I don't have the strength to teach you. Are you reviewing your lessons every day?"

"Oh yes," Sooryia said. "But we miss you teaching us."

"Isn't Rukhsana a good teacher too?"

They giggled. "But not as good as you. When will you be teaching our classes again?"

"Soon," Mother said. "Very soon. Once I get my strength back, I will teach you all everything I know so that you will be full of learning and will do wonderful things in your lives. You'll become engineers and doctors, scientists and journalists, film stars and biologists. You'll be whatever you want to be."

I knew they loved hearing her say those magical words, although they already knew that they would never fulfill those dreams. I imagined each one leaning over to kiss her and then quietly filing out of her room. They would soar on her imaginings until they reached home to crash in their prisons.

"When will Rukhsana come back?"

"Oh, in a week or two," Jahan told them as they went downstairs.

"And then she'll marry Shaheen?"

"Yes."

They always asked that question, concerned for my future. I was not just old but ancient, and still unmarried.

"He's in America," I would reply. "We'll marry when he returns here. And that could be very soon." It was a hope, of course, that instead of sending money he would send himself.

"But why would he return here? Everyone is trying to leave."

"He'll return just to marry me, and then I'll be leaving for America with him."

A dozen pairs of eyes lit up, their faces took on a dreamy look, and I felt myself reduced to their ages when we believed in fairy tales. Like them, I imagined Shaheen racing across the sky to Kabul, racing along the roads to this door, snatching me up, and racing us back to the plane and flying away. It was fairy tales that sustained us in childhood, filling in the nooks and crannies of our imaginations and soaring us into enchanted worlds, and we believed they could keep nurturing us when we became women, but we know now that those stories belonged only to that age, and that life has shorn away dreams. There are no princes riding to the rescue; there are only ferocious dragons guarding us against them, and the princes haven't the weapons or the powers to strike them down.

JAHAN AND I LEFT FOR PRACTICE A HALF HOUR EARLIER than usual to pick up my new beard at Noorzia's. While she whisked me inside, Jahan stood outside. "Don't be too long," he warned. "And don't leave without me. I'll buy the naan and vegetables and be back."

"I worry about you all the time," she said, closing the door behind us. To my surprise, she continued in English. "Safe still you are?"

"I'm still alive, yes. But why English suddenly?"

"Some English. You speak. I understand need to."

"If you want me to." I followed her into her salon. "Tell me why."

"Remember, I told you about my friend in Melbourne? I have the visa and now I wait for the air tickets. I practice must my English."

It was a broken dialogue, but I felt my envy slip through the gaps in her words. She was escaping; she would be free. I imagined Australia from seeing it in my atlas, a vast island on which a hundred Afghanistans could fit with ease. A safe, peaceful land so far from our bloody turmoil and fear. I knew its cricketers—Ponting, Warne, Gilchrist, McGrath, strong young white men—and caught glimpses of those cricket stadiums when India toured. I had also seen Melbourne when the cameras panned away from the Australian Open tennis tournament to reveal the Yarra River, tall buildings set against a clear azure sky, and a pale silvery sea.

"Who is this friend?"

"Dead husband friend," she began in English, determined to master it.

"Tell me in Dari first, and then we'll speak English."

She slipped back into her native language. "Hussein was the producer I worked for when I was a makeup artist in Beirut. Somehow, he found his way to Melbourne, and he owns a video store. He cannot work as a producer, as his English isn't good." She smiled happily. "He wants to marry me and sponsored my visa. He will send the money to pay for the smuggler to take me to Karachi. From Karachi I'll fly to Colombo, Sri Lanka, and then on to Melbourne." She switched back to English. "I need to speak good English to understand immigration questions. I speak so little, but with you I make better." She searched for her next words. "He make good . . . what is word?"

"Husband?"

"Husband. Yes. Say salon business good."

"I will miss you," I said. "I am sad."

"Sad I too," she managed. "You are safe no and every day danger, danger here." She smiled. "Protect," she pointed at my chest, struggling for the word. "Yes . . . protect your tits . . ." I lifted the shirt to show her the protector and playfully she gently dug an elbow into a breast. "No tell a tit. Muscle? Yes, only strong muscle."

She had my new beard ready, a young man's sleek fine down. The netting was almost translucent, and each hair was firmly in place, a light brown to match my own hair. She had a roll of Velcro tape, cut two strips, and stuck them on my cheeks. The beard had Velcro too and she placed it firmly against the Velcro on my face. For added safety, she had stitched flesh-colored straps to fit around my lower neck and metal hooks to hang it from my ears. When we fit it, it felt more comfortable than my old one, and much more secure. I shook my head vigorously but it remained in place.

"Will difference, see?" She was determinedly back to English.

"Will they notice the difference?"

"Will they notice the difference?"

"Dif-fer-ence. I hope not. When do you leave?"

"Oh, time not know. Days, weeks. Wait for ticket, money. Did Jahan see my smuggler, Juniad?"

"Yes." Jahan had wandered the crowded, meandering lanes in the old city, south of the river, looking for the address. When he finally found the smuggler's home, the man was very wary until Jahan used the magic password "Noorzia" and was welcomed and offered a glass of tea. "But the price has gone up. It's now one thousand five hundred dollars because of the rising cost of diesel, paying bribes, and whatever else. He said he doesn't have a schedule and makes his run only when he has a full load of people to smuggle."

"That's Juniad." She hesitated, then added, "Just be careful. I told you, you can't trust him or any other smuggler."

"Do the Talib know who they are?"

"I don't know." She returned to Dari, as her English was tiring us both. "Have you heard from Shaheen?"

"Not yet. I'm praying hard he will send the money through the *hawala* any day."

She hugged me. "I'm sure he cares for you. You'll see. Shaheen will send the money. You need a good husband. I had a good one in Tariq, he pleasured me a lot. Most men don't care for the woman enough for her pleasure; they use us for their own, brief as it is. I miss the pleasure that my husband gave me. When Shaheen sends the money, go and see Juniad. But be careful. Pay half up front, half when you cross. He's a good man at heart."

She switched back to English and I gave her a few key words—"thank you," "planes," "tickets," "please help"—until Jahan knocked and called.

DR. HANIFA LEFT WHEN WE RETURNED. MOTHER WAS happy to see us, her smile splitting her face. I sat on the bed, taking her hand, her fingers now as thin as twigs, and warmed it between my own.

"How is Noorzia?"

I told her everything in detail to entertain her and showed off the new beard, and then mentioned that Noorzia was preparing to leave to join a lover in Australia. I hadn't meant to, but it slipped out in my efforts to make her smile.

"You have someone waiting too. You must go to Shaheen." She fell silent. "I have asked Dr. Hanifa to help me leave quickly so that you can leave very soon, but she's too good a doctor to do that."

The realization of what she meant hit me.

"You cannot leave me like that," I cried. "That would be murder."

"No," she said, smiling weakly. "It would be a relief for me. You talk to her."

"I can't, don't ask me. You must not speak like that, Maadar." I didn't want to let her go, ever.

BROKEN PROMISES

Yet another day vanished, crossed out, and I wanted to tear up the calendar that now mocked me with the inexorable passing of the days. I was in my room, staring at it in the fading light, willing time to stop, when Jahan knocked on the door.

"Fatima and Arif have come to see you."

"Did you tell them I'm here? You shouldn't have . . ."

"I told her you were in Mazar. Then she asked to meet Maadar. She said it was important. I said I'd see if Maadar was sleeping. What'll I do?"

I wanted to see my oldest friend, but how could I be sure? I had trusted my life to my cousins, and Fatima, even as a child, had kept my secrets.

"Bring her here, but tell her Maadar wants to see her." I didn't light the lamp, preferring the gloom to match my mood.

She came in, carrying a bundle, and I didn't give her time to speak. "You must swear not to tell anyone you've seen me," I said. "Promise me that."

"I swear I won't," she replied, and we embraced, the bundle between us. It stirred at our movements. In her arms was a baby wrapped in a shawl, and I leaned over it in admiration, stroking its silky cheeks.

"I didn't know you had a baby," I scolded. "How did I not know this?"

I tenderly took it from her as she removed her burka. Fatima's oval face was subtly altered. Once, she had been so pretty, but now her skin had turned soft, pudgy, and a shade paler; her alert eyes were dull. She wore no makeup though once her sweet lips were a deep red, and her fluttering eyelids a pale blue.

"It's not mine, she's Masooda's child," Fatima said and began to weep. "She was . . ."

I moved to let her sit on the bed and a shaft of weak light touched the baby's shawl. It was blue, and embroidered with silvery stars.

"Oh god . . ."

" . . . killed by a . . ."

I sat beside her. "We saw it happen," I whispered and shivered at the memory. Masooda was Fatima's sister-in-law and I had met her a few times. Of course I couldn't have recognized her under her burka. I cried along with Fatima, holding each other, and the baby slept on.

"We're her guardians now. She's a girl child, and her father doesn't want her. He's become very . . . embittered. He blames Masooda for being so foolish." She lifted a fold of the baby's shawl and pointed. "That's Masooda's blood."

It was almost black, the size of the baby's fist.

"It's the only memento she will have of her mother." She paused to contain her anger. "How are you?"

I shrugged. "What can I say?"

"I so miss working. It was a dream, wasn't it?"

"Yes, it was."

I sensed she came for a purpose and was hesitating. I placed my hand on hers and we both gripped tightly. "What is it?"

"You won't tell anyone?"

"Whatever you say will remain in this room."

"We're leaving," she said, leaning over to whisper. "I can't take it anymore, not after what happened to Masooda, and I told Arif I was going mad wrapped up like a mummy. A smuggler will take us across to Iran where Arif has a cousin in Tehran. We're hoping we get to America or England from there. You have to leave too, Rukhsana."

"I will only after Maadar . . . I can't before that." Then I told her about Wahidi's proposal and she turned even paler.

"Get out, fast. He's a very dangerous man."

"You don't have to tell me that. I'm afraid every day. When are you going?"

"Later tonight. I couldn't leave without saying good-bye to you." She reached over to embrace me tightly. "If only it had been different. What have you been doing with yourself?" She leaned back. "You've cut your hair."

"It was getting too hot under the burka."

"You should go to Delhi," she said. "I thought when you returned from there you were . . . a different person."

"Of course I was. I left here after school and returned with my degree. I was proud of myself."

"No, it wasn't that. You left as a girl, and came back a woman. Something happened in Delhi. You can tell me now."

"Nothing happened. I played cricket, I studied, and that's all."

"Something happened," she insisted. "You kept postponing your engagement to Shaheen."

"I was waiting for my family to return, and then Maadar had her first bout with cancer . . ."

She ignored my excuses. "You can tell me now," she cajoled, then smiled. "I am still your best friend. I thought that under that brave face, when you fell quiet and thought no one was watching you, I sensed you were not quite so happy to be home."

"You're imagining things."

"I'm not. I can tell you fell in love with someone in Delhi." She tried to smile, but it slipped off her face. "I know because I fell in love too at university. His name was Piruz. He was in the same English language class. He wasn't handsome, but he had a good sense of humor and talked to everyone and laughed easily. He took a liking to me, and we would spend an hour after class just talking." She added quickly, "Nothing happened, we didn't even kiss. But we fell in love and all I wanted every day was just to be with him and he felt the same about me. Love is like a big balloon in your body, floating you off the ground, and you want to tell someone how wonderful it feels. I wanted to talk to you but you were away."

"You could have told me when I returned."

"I was betrothed to Arif by then; it was too late. Piruz's father was an electrician, and not rich at all. I knew my father would never give permission. We thought of running away together. But then we could have been killed for dishonoring the family." Her sigh broke both our hearts. "I married whom my father chose. I knew eleven other girls in university who also fell in love but married whom their fathers chose. We had a small club and we'd talk about the feelings of being in love. I think about Piruz whenever I feel lonely, which is most of the time." Her eyes were wretched with memories, and her voice sank as if she had no breath left. "What was his name?"

"Veer."

She touched my cheek. "He's not Muslim. That makes it more difficult. Why didn't you tell me about him? We're best friends."

"Because by telling you, I would have to remember, and I didn't want to." I looked into Fatima's pleading eyes and relented reluctantly. "He's written me a few letters."

Fatima clapped her hands. "What does he say? He loves you still?"

"Yes. And I replied. I didn't want to, but after reading his, I did reply. Over the last three years, we've kept in touch, sometimes only short notes."

"At least we both knew love once in our lives. You still have it. Don't let it go."

"I have to marry Shaheen. You know our customs, and I must obey my father's wishes."

"Then you'll be like me," she said sadly. "Always lonely, always remembering the one you love."

Jahan knocked on the door. "Arif wants to leave, it's getting late."

There was no time left, nothing else to say. We locked in a tight embrace, scarcely able to breathe. We were saying good-bye to our childhood too.

"*Khoda haafez*"—God protect us—we prayed to each other, and released our holds.

I remained sitting in my room, chewing on my lower lip, thinking about Fatima's remarks, thinking about love letters. Finally, I went to the basement and took the first letter from its hiding place. I knew I was opening his heart, and mine too, as I remembered my replies. There were six of his, six of mine, spread over three years with gaps in between as he traveled to remote jungles and mountains while I remained trapped here.

My dear Rukhsana,

I know I made a promise not to write and kept it for four months and now break it. I'd like to tell you that I think of you every minute of the day but that would be a lie. You appear in those times of the day when I am alone and have the luxury of dreaming. Maybe at the same time, even though we're thousands of miles apart, you too are having the same extrasensory experiences. I hope.

For instance, you are beside me when I wake in the morning and I see your pale emerald green eyes looking at me. I can feel your warmth, although mysteriously you have left no dent in the pillow beside mine. I do look, you know, and when I press my face against it, I can breathe in your perfume. I wonder how you managed to vanish so quickly when you had been beside me as I slept, and accompanied me on my journeys while I dreamed. We travel to strange worlds, and I feel your palm, soft as a bird's wing, enclosed in my hand. Your delicate fingers are entwined with mine and I know I will never let go.

My letters to him were in my laptop, but I remembered every word I'd written.

My dear, dear Veer,

I know I said I wouldn't open your letter if you wrote and I didn't. Not for two days. I hid it in the basement. Then I just couldn't bear not knowing how you were. I believe that sometimes words leave a taste lingering in one's mouth, sour, bitter, spicy, bland. Your letter coated my tongue and palate with honey. And I cried, for I too feel that we are both ghosts who cannot leave our separate worlds and meet somewhere else. I remember how when we walked, and were separated by a crowd, I would reach out for your hand without looking and it was there. I still reach out, but there is no hand to hold mine with that gentle warmth that yours always had. At night, I do lie beside you and tell you how I have spent my day and wish you good night with all the love in my kisses. I wake and you're not beside me and I think, "Oh, he's gone downstairs." There are many times when I stop, lost in the daydreams of being with you, and then wake with a start. Do you remember when you asked me to go with you to a wildlife reserve where you were filming elephants? Even though we'd tell my parents that Nargis would come with us (we both knew she wouldn't) I said Father would never permit me to do that. I lied.

*I knew what would happen so far from home. I would take you into
my bed. I wanted to so much, but I wanted to remain chaste until my
wedding day, even if it was to you. As of yet, I'm not married and
am still chaste . . . I can't write more.*

Love, R.

P.S. Please don't write again. I won't read it.

Dearest Rukhsana,

*The moment I read your letter, I tried to call you. No luck, but
I will keep trying and trying until I hear your voice. You made my
day, days, I should say, as I smiled with so much to be happy about
that everyone thought I was mad. I laughed too, for no reason other
than thinking of you. You read mine and replied! You are still there,
you still love me, it's there in your handwriting. And you're not
married; I dream we will be one day. I now look for you everywhere.*

*You reappear on the street, as I see you at times in other women
who pass by and they wonder why I stare at them with such intensity.
See, that girl has your color eyes—they are a light green, as soft and
elusive as a misty morning. Even if I saw a thousand veiled women
and only saw their eyes I would recognize you immediately.*

*You smile first with your eyes; the green grows a shade lighter
before the smile spreads across your face as gently as a ripple across a
clear pond. It touches your cheeks first, staining them with a delicate
rouge, and your skin glows with the amusement that you're not yet
ready to reveal but want me to know is there. You make me wait
to hear you laugh, as you know I love the sound of your laughter. It
isn't shrill and high pitched, but smoky and low, and we're sharing
a secret. Though I only caressed it once, I have often traced the tiny
moon of a scar in the center of your chin, reminding me of your
childhood, which I never witnessed, and how you fell off a bicycle and*

cut yourself. You were a bold girl. You were racing against a cousin then. Now I see you brush your hair, the very lightest brown, back from your eyes, and tuck the strands behind your ears into which I have breathed my thoughts and feelings. They are the conduits of my love, for love must always be spoken in whispers so the hearer knows the words are said especially for her and for no other to hear.

Love, V.

P.S. Will be away making a documentary on snow leopards. Write soon.

My dearest V.,

I was so happy to hear from you and I know you'll make a brilliant documentary on those mysterious and mystical animals high up in the Himalayas. I was green with envy, and I wish so much I was with you to keep you warm. We could huddle under blankets. I read that Arctic explorers often did that, slept together, for warmth.

The other day I saw a man with your nose and believed he had stolen it from you. I was with my brother in the bazaar. The man was passing by. I wanted to caress it as I did yours, from the slight frown between your brows down to the tip. His nose—it was straight, with a strong curve at the end. Both from the side and from facing him, I knew it was your nose. Except, except, his didn't have that same flare of your nostrils.

There are days when I have not thought of you and then, with a feeling of deep guilt, I am suffused with your presence and my love. A mere nose can do that.

While you scale mountains, I wing across them to be with you. That's all I can do. Days go by with little happening in my life, such a stifling stillness trapped within these four walls. You are my only company these days as I remember everything we did, every word

we spoke, every touch we touched, and every kiss we kissed. Do you
think, as I do, "I wonder what she's doing RIGHT NOW, this mo-
ment," and project your spirit toward me? I will think this is hap-
pening now, as you read my letter.

Here, I kiss the paper and send it across to you with my love, R.

I couldn't read anymore. I had told him about my father's
death, Mother's illness, and Shaheen's leaving and he had wanted
to swoop down and take me away. I couldn't answer that one, now
three months old. I folded his letters carefully and would save them
for another day when I needed to remember our love and lift my
spirits.

When I went upstairs, Jahan was waiting, a grave look on his
face.

"What is it?"

"I've been looking for you. Parwaaze and Hoshang want to see
you. They have bad news."

THE STADIUM

THEY WERE IN THE FRONT HALL AND I IMMEDI-
ately noticed the despairing hunch of their shoulders as
they paced in the narrow space.

"Hoshang knows the guard at the stadium," Parwaaze burst out. "He told Hoshang there is an official
state team in the tournament. We won't have a chance
to win against it."

"I went to the stadium just to check," Hoshang said.
"They're practicing there. The team has a Pakistani
cricketer named Imran teaching them."

"It's not Imran Khan, is it?" I asked in apprehension.
He was one of Pakistan's best cricketers. "A tall man,
well built . . ."

"No. This Imran's small and quite round."

"What difference does that make?" Jahan cut in.
"They'll win."

"Why should they just because they have a professional coach?" I wasn't in the mood for their pessimism.
"He still has to teach them how to play, just as I'm teaching you. You have to beat them, that's your only chance.
We'll watch them tomorrow before we panic."

I reached over and straightened each one's shoulders, forcing them to stand straight.

"That's not our main worry," Parwaaze said with anxiety. "They will fix it so their team wins."

"How can they, with an ICC observer? They have to stick by the rules, and you have to believe in yourselves and win the match."

He looked at me with pity. "It's the Talib, Rukhsana," he said as they went out.

Ghazi Stadium was the venue for our cricket matches and the eleven of us squeezed into an old Toyota taxi to get there. I sat on Jahan's lap, holding the passenger door closed, my *lungee* crammed down on my head and my *hijab* up to my eyes, as an added precaution, to protect me from the driver. It was cheaper than the bus.

I shivered with fear when I saw the stadium again. The Talib regularly executed people during the intervals of the football matches.

The main entrance rose like a cooling cliff of ice, and was striped with red pillars. Only Talib officials entered through the wide entrance. The huge Olympic sign of five rings was framed high on the cliff, mocking us with the pretense that we were a sporting nation.

This time the road into the stadium was deserted except for a lone guard, a young man with a cane, who stood at the gate. Hoshang and he greeted each other warmly—they played on the same football team.

"It's good to see you all," the guard said cheerfully. "It gets lonely here. But you must leave before night comes."

"Why?" Royan asked, though we had no intention of remaining that long.

The guard lowered his voice. "The spirits of the dead executed here sit in the stands and call out to each other when the sun sets."

"You've seen these s-spirits?" Qubad asked nervously.

"I have heard them. I hide out here and pray they never see me."

"What do they say?" Atash asked, also uneasy.

"They don't speak in Dari or Pashtu. They talk in the language of the dead."

"I don't believe that," Parwaaze said as we climbed the narrow steps into the stadium.

"Why not?" I said and shivered, along with the others. "Where else can they go?"

Apart from the covered stand by the main entrance, the stadium was open to the sky. It was oval shaped, a shallow saucer, and above the rim rose Paghman to the west and Maranjan to the east. A baleful sun, hazy with dust, watched over us. A neglected dirt track, with faded lane markings, surrounded the football pitch.

FIVE MONTHS AGO, PARWAAZE HAD COME AS MY *mahram* for an execution in this stadium. Mother refused to allow Jahan to accompany us. Normally, women were not permitted at public gatherings, but the government made an exception for the execution of the murderer Zarmina.

The buses were packed—even the women's section behind the drab, dusty curtain—and all along the road, crowds moved steadily toward the stadium. We had to get out of the bus and walk the last stretch to the stadium entrance. On both sides of the road were carts selling fresh fruit, smoky kebabs, naan, and children's cheap toys. I tried to judge the mood of the crowd. Some were excited, with expectation, talking and laughing; many more were silent and solemn, even fearful.

The Taliban herded us along to the gate, wanting us to hurry and not miss even a moment of their grand spectacle.

The crowd was funneled to other entrances, and Parwaaze protected me, pushing his way through the mass of people going up the narrow steps leading to the terraced seating area. There was barely a seat to spare, and we pushed our way down to the front and squeezed into a space next to a woman. I looked toward the covered stand, filled with important Talib officials, enjoying a convivial afternoon of entertainment, and then across the football field. Three Land Cruisers were parked at different positions and Talib fighters stood beside them facing the crowd, holding their guns. At either end of the football pitch were the goalposts, sagging in the center from the weight of the many men who'd been hanged there, kicking and struggling. Dark patches spotted the grass, blood being no substitute for water.

TALIBAN EXECUTE
MOTHER OF FIVE CHILDREN

Today, a crowd of around 25,000 people has gathered, many coerced by the police, to watch the Talib execute Zarmina, the mother of five children. She was accused of murdering her husband by beating him to death with a hammer. Her husband, Alauddin Khwazak, a policeman, had also owned a shop in north Kabul. Their marriage was arranged when she was sixteen and it had grown into love. She had one-year-old twins, Silsila, a female, and a male, Jawad; another son, Hawad, age eleven; and two other daughters, Shaista, fourteen, and Najeba, sixteen.

The government told everyone that the strain of the violent events in the country had affected Alauddin Khwazak, and by participating in the continued brutality, his mood had grown darker and threatening. He started to beat Zarmina frequently in front of the children. The elder girls, no longer able to bear to see their mother abused and mistreated, decided to kill their father. Najeba mixed a sleeping potion into his night meal, and when he slept, she killed him with a hammer. Zarmina claimed a robber had broken into the house and killed him.

The Taliban judge did not believe her story. To protect her

beautiful daughters, Zarmina confessed to the crime when she was tortured in prison, beaten continuously with cable wire, the normal method of torturing women who could have broken a Taliban law. Although the government claimed the murder took place a few months ago, my sources informed me that Zarmina had been in prison for the last few years, tortured and starved. Her daughters had taken her food daily, until the day they vanished.

According to custom, the two elder girls and the boy were left in the custody of Khwazak's brother, a Talib supporter. Two months ago, he told Zarmina that he had sold her beautiful daughters Shaista and Najeba for around 300,000 Pakistani rupees each to a brothel in Khost, on the Pakistan border. Zarmina had cried in despair, knowing she would never see her beloved daughters again, and beat her head against the prison walls.

On this cold November day in 1999, an open jeep entered the stadium. Zarmina, in her blue burka, stood in the back, supported by two Talibs. The crowd remained silent as the jeep circled the stadium. Then we heard the thin cries of her twin children coming from somewhere in the crowd, calling out to her, "Maadar, Maadar . . ." Her head turned, searching for her children in the crowd. "Silsila . . . Jawad," she said, trying to comfort them, but she was silenced by her captors. As if this was a sporting event, an announcer broke the silence. "Zarmina, daughter of Ghulam Hasnet, is to be executed for killing her husband with a hammer." The jeep stopped. The guards carried Zarmina down from it and escorted her to the goalposts. They forced her to sit, but she struggled to crawl away. She could see little through her burka.

The crowd now awakened. "Spare her . . . spare her . . . ," they called out, but the Talib ignored the chants. The crowd fell silent. Zarmina tried to crawl away again, a moving blue bundle. A tall Talib came to stand behind her with his rifle. His hand was unsteady. His first shot missed her, though he was only a few feet away. As she could not sit or kneel without falling over,

Zarmina cried out, "Someone, please take my arms." No one moved to help her.

The Talib took a step forward, aimed more carefully, and fired a 7.62-millimeter bullet into her head. It was a flat sound and we could barely hear it. The executioner was Zarmina's brother-in-law, the one who had sold her daughters into prostitution. (SENT BY LBW)

The crowd was silent, only the shuffle of feet was heard as we flowed out of the stadium, each cocooned in his own thoughts, and we avoided all eye contact with strangers. Even those who had come for the "entertainment" remained quiet.

We waited until we were some distance from the stadium.

"I feel sick," I whispered as a huge wave of nausea surged up into my mouth. I bent over and, hurriedly lifting my burka, puked on the street. It had been waiting from the moment I heard the children cry out for their mother. I was vomiting out my uncontrollable rage at what I had witnessed. My throat and stomach hurt as nothing heaved out. I remained bent like an old crone and waited until the wave receded. I felt Parwaaze's sympathetic hand resting on my back and finally straightened and returned to my faceless anonymity under the burka.

Parwaaze looked around before he burst out, "There were thousands of us, only a few Talibs, and we could have rushed down and saved her. Rukhsana, you must not write anything."

"I have to. I can't have her death on my hands or in my mind."

We remained silent on the bus going home and parted at my gate without speaking anymore, burdened by melancholy. I told Mother and Jahan every detail.

"Does conscience exist anymore?" I asked Mother.

"Not as far as I can see. In Dostoevsky's novel *Crime and Punishment*, Raskolnikov's punishment, at first, is not the state's punishment for his crime of killing the moneylender but is his own conscience. His conscience haunts him through his life until, no longer able to live with it, he surrenders to the police and confesses his crime . . ."

"But that's in a novel," I protested. "The brother-in-law will not even think anymore of the woman's life he's taken. He will sleep peacefully, even as other murderers sleep like innocents."

"Conscience controls our impulses to do harm," she said, taking hold of my hand to comfort me. "Our religions are meant to instruct us in what is right and what is wrong, but they can be misinterpreted, words twisted in their meanings, by those who wish to justify their killings in the name of their religion and in the name of God. Conscience does and must exist among us, as otherwise the whole world would go up in flames. You must believe in it, as I know you possess it. Never lose it."

That night, in the secrecy of my bedroom, I wrote the story, and spent half the night trying to fax it from Father's office to my contact in Delhi, the telephone sullenly unresponsive until nearly dawn, when it came to life. I disconnected, hid the modem and computer, and took to my bed. I was sick for two days after witnessing Zarmina's murder and cried for her lost daughters.

Now, I watched three men lethargically cut the grass for the wicket in the center of the football field.

It would be an uneven pitch with a variable bounce, it would take spin because of the surface and runs would be hard to get. Remembering Zarmina, I wondered whether the dead would awaken to watch the match. Would they recognize the particular black patch of grass on which a ball landed, and think that is where they had died?

From an entrance at the opposite side we saw five men drift in and take their places in the stands. I thought I recognized Azlam as one of them, and paid no further attention. There was another group of six men also watching the government's team practicing their game in the nets. Jahan, Parwaaze, Qubad, and I sat together, the others of our team scattered around as if we were just idlers, passing the time of the day, with little else to do but watch a new sport. But we weren't idle. I had coached them to study every batsman and bowler, watch for their strengths and weaknesses, and to remember everything they saw. I jotted down notes in my book.

Parwaaze pulled out a scrap of newspaper, torn out of the *Kabul Daily*. "See . . . the preliminary cricket matches will take place on Saturday and . . ."

I took the brief report. ". . . the final match will be played on Sunday the twenty-third and the winning team will be sent abroad for further training."

"It doesn't say Pakistan."

"Abroad can only be Pakistan," Parwaaze insisted. "Where else is abroad?" He looked across the stadium.

He turned his attention to the team practicing. "What do you think? Are we as good?"

There were thirteen on the state team, young men around the same ages as my cousins, dressed in green tracksuits. Only one man was immaculate in white trousers and a cream shirt, with a cap pulled low over his face to protect him from the sun. The coach. He was portly, bearded too, and he strode busily among his team. From the size of his paunch, he must have been a spin bowler. Pakistan had great spinners, and fast bowlers too, but this one in particular didn't have the build for speed.

They also had professional equipment—a few real cricket bats, many cricket balls, pads, and gloves. They had laid and rolled half a pitch, and had nets erected on either side and behind the stumps. They had chairs on which to sit and straps on their pads. The scene reminded me of our practice pitch in Delhi where we met in the late afternoons, when the sun wasn't so brutal, to hone our batting and bowling skills.

I watched the young men bowl and bat; despite their equipment, they were as new to the game as my team. The bowlers were erratic, and we could hear the coach shouting at them and pointing to the spot where they should bounce the ball. The batsmen swung clumsily or their feet got tangled up when they tried to defend. But one bowler drew my attention. He was fairly tall, a shade or two darker and older than the others. He ran up to the wicket smoothly, had a high action, and the ball whipped down the wicket to hit the stumps.

"Well? What do you think?"

"They don't look better than us," I said truthfully. "Except one of them. Now watch that bowler. See how he runs up and bowls. It's a coached action, he's played cricket before. He's the one we must watch out for. But the others are all on our level."

The tall pace bowler worried me the most. He could run through the other teams like an AK-47. The match was fixed already, with the ringer on their side. I didn't confide my fear to Parwaaze and the others when we rose to leave the stadium after a half hour. The other young men remained watching, hoping to learn the game. On the way to the university, we stayed silent in the taxi. When we reached the grounds, we sat in a circle and I waited for one of them to start the discussion. If they believed they could be beaten now, I had wasted my time. I hoped that all the training and talking I had done would influence their thinking and attitude.

They had keen eyes and had learned enough of the game to read the nuances and, without my telling them, knew the pace bowler would cause them problems. I wanted them to work out how they would play him.

"We'll have to be d-defensive when he's bowling," Qubad said.

"Play him on the back foot, as the bounce could be high on that wicket."

"Wait for the change bowler and hit him then," Namdar said, smiling.

"We should also try to hit him," Royan suggested. "He won't be accurate with every bowl, and if we hit him around, he could start bowling badly."

"He looks too cocky," Parwaaze said, also starting to smile. "We'll deal with him, so we must not worry now. We must only think of winning."

"He looks like a P-Pakistani too," Qubad said dourly. "Who's going to lead us?"

"Parwaaze should be the captain," I said.

Parwaaze grinned. "Yes, I'm the captain." He straightened and threw me a glance of gratitude for electing him as their leader.

"Why can't he be a general?" Qubad mocked. "A c-captain is very low down in an army. Generals are the ones in charge, leading from b-behind."

"Do any of you want to be captain?" I said, stopping the discussion. They hesitated and remained silent. "Then Parwaaze must be the captain." I nudged Jahan.

"I think he should," he said quickly when he caught my eye.

"What does a captain do?" Parwaaze asked, pulling me aside when we started to practice.

"He goes out with the opposing captain for the coin toss. If you call right, then you decide whether to bat or field first. That depends on the pitch. On the stadium pitch, you should bat first as it will break up after a few balls and hopefully be harder to play on in the second innings. And the captain leads the team out onto the field for a start."

"I'll never remember all this," he wailed.

I smiled in sympathy at his dilemma. A captain who knew nothing, leading his men, who knew less, into battle and off the cliff. Yet, I felt he would have an instinct for the role. "Don't worry. I'll write it all down."

We joined the others at practice and I saw how excited and motivated they had become after having seen how vulnerable the state team was. They cheered themselves when they hit a good shot and when they took a wicket. Each one had acquired different skills that rose out of their personalities. Once more, they were individuals, even in the way they walked, the swagger of their steps, turbans at an angle, the grins on their faces. As the hills melted into the arms of the sky at dusk, we practiced our fielding and catching. Where once they had been lethargic, they now ran like hares to the ball, scooping it up and throwing it back.

"We're going to win," they shouted to each other until it grew too dark to practice.

On our street corner, Jahan and I heard the motorbike behind us and kept walking, expecting Azlam to pass. Instead, he switched off his engine and, as he drew parallel, stopped.

We exchanged *salaam aleikums*, my greeting only a whisper, and waited for him to talk.

"I want you to bring the book and teach my team to play cricket," he announced, looking at me. "How much is Parwaaze paying? I'll double it."

"He's not paying us anything," Jahan said. "He's our cousin."

"You should be paid, cousin or not." Azlam hooked a leg over the petrol tank, preparing for a long bargaining session. "I'll give you ten thousand. It's a lot of money."

"I just told you, we're not doing it for money," Jahan said testily. "We love the game, and our cousins wanted to learn it, and that's enough for us."

"Twenty then, and no more."

"No."

"Can't he answer?" Azlam stared at me intently.

"He has a very sore throat and a fever," Jahan said, ending the negotiations and nudging me toward our gate.

"Twenty-five, and that's the last offer," Azlam called out.

"We're going to win the match," Jahan called back.

"We'll see," Azlam shouted and started his bike. He roared up the road, gunning it as he passed us.

"What's he going to do now?" I said, looking after him.

"What can he do? Just lose to us."

Abdul had opened the gate to see who was shouting.

"Have you seen that motorbike before?" I asked.

He shrugged. "Once or twice. It could be the same one, but I can't tell the difference."

"Any letters, packages?" I asked.

"No. Don't worry, they will come."

When we went in, Dr. Hanifa heard us and came out of Mother's room. Even in the gloom, we could read her face.

"She's sleeping, and I gave her dinner. I've increased the dosage of morphine. You'll have to give her another injection if she wakes." She touched my face, and then Jahan's, and we understood the message: death was speeding toward our mother and we would be orphaned very soon.

Jahan went out to walk Dr. Hanifa home. I cooked dinner, kebabs, rice, and a salad, a simple meal for both of us and for Abdul to eat in his quarters. When Jahan returned, we ate, and midway through we heard the telephone, crying out like a lost child. Jahan hurried to answer it and I listened to someone call "Hello" again and again until he gave up.

"Who was it?"

"Sounded like a man, but all I could hear was his hellos. Stupid phone."

"Shaheen?" I asked hopefully.

"No, I'd know his voice, even in a hello."

"Was it Uncle?"

"No, I'd recognize his hellos. It was a stranger's voice."

"Long distance?"

"There was such a buzzing on the line, it was hard to tell."

As we rose from the floor, Abdul knocked on the door and, without thinking, I ran down the stairs and waited in the well, poised to sprint into the secret room.

A SHORT NOTE

I HEARD THE FRONT DOOR OPEN AND THE MURMUR of voices.

Jahan called down softly, "Stay where you are. It's Uncle Jaweid with Auntie Badria."

Badria was Shaheen's third cousin on his father's side. It had to be a good omen. Shaheen had sent the money and papers to them and they had come to hand them over. I could leave tomorrow, if I wanted. I sat and waited in the dark.

Jaweid was a thin man, always with a frown of worry creasing his forehead; Badria, as thin, had her lips clamped in disapproval. I thought they would enter, but they remained just inside the door despite Jahan's invitation to have tea. "No, no, we just had tea," Jaweid's protesting voice. Then another rumble of words and Jahan, "Maadar's not well . . . sleeping now." A silence. "We came to see Rukhsana . . ." And Jahan replying, ". . . Mazar . . . back soon . . ." Then Badria's higher tone; she had a quarrelsome voice that always grated, "This came for Rukhsana this afternoon and we came straightaway. Shaheen asked . . . give her this . . ."

I clung tightly to her words and waited impatiently for them to leave.

"Buses are so bad . . . long waits . . ." Badria had a litany of complaints.

Finally, I heard the door close and I crept up the stairs. Jahan was holding a letter, not a package, and gave it to me. My name was on the envelope. I went to sit on the bottom stair, weighing it carefully. I held it up to the light and saw the outline of a sheet of paper.

"It could be a check inside," Jahan said.

"It could be."

I gently prised open the flap, slid out the sheet of paper, and read it. I remained holding the letter until Jahan took it from my hand.

Dear Rukhsana,

Thank you for your letter. It was good to hear from you, finally. Your mother's illness saddens me deeply and I pray that she recovers and is well soon. As I had not heard from you, and did not know whether you would ever come to America, my parents believed I could not wait much longer. You had postponed our engagement three times, and as much as I very much wanted our marriage, I have to obey my father. I married a good Afghan girl here. Her father was a great help to my father in settling in America and setting up a business together. As I now have such financial commitments to my family, I will not be able to send you the money that you requested. I pray you find another person who can be of more help than I can. Please forgive me.

My good wishes to your mother and Jahan.

With affection,

Shaheen

Jahan and I sat in silence. He reread the letter in the hope that we had misinterpreted the simple message.

"I didn't think he'd get married," I said angrily. "I didn't think he'd ever not send for me. We were committed to each other." I took the letter, crushed it into a ball, and hurled it down the hall.

"He let us down, and broke his word," Jahan said angrily. "He should have informed us before and not told us after. He has no honor."

"Don't tell Maadar, it will only worry her even more."

He put an arm around me and drew me close. We felt like two small children lost in a huge, dark, menacing world. "What do we do now?"

"I'll have to borrow as much money as I can to pay the smuggler. I'll wait for you in Pakistan." And then what would I do with my life in that limbo?

I was tired after a day of such tension and bitter disappointment and went down to the hidden room. I left the door open and slept the moment I lay down and dreamed of Zorak Wahidi again.

Surprisingly, despite the dark dreams, I woke feeling lighter, afloat in my bed, halfway to the ceiling. For a moment, I couldn't understand my sense of euphoria and lay luxuriating in it. I sat up. Of course. I was alone and I had lost my way out of the country for now, but I was free, the burden of my commitment to my family through this marriage, and to Shaheen, was gone. I could do what I wanted now—I could marry whom I wanted. Veer. I would call him now, this instant, and went down to Father's office. I tapped the Delhi number into the phone. But what should I tell him? Veer, I am free? I put the phone down. He hadn't replied to my letter sent two or three months ago; I couldn't remember the exact day I'd mailed it. Was I too late, again? Had he lost patience and married? Even now, he could be writing his letter telling me, but couching it in gentler tones than Shaheen's. This one would break my heart into tiny pieces. I bit my nails. I tried to imagine our conversation. *Veer, it's me, Rukhsana, how are you? Fine. How are you? Fine. No, I'm not. You must help me get out, I don't have much time and I need money for a smuggler. Did you get my last letter? Yes, I meant to reply but . . . but. . .*

It didn't matter—I had to tell him, now. I sat up determinedly and made the call. Even if married, at least because of our love he would send me money. I was the beggar again. I pressed redial, and each time, I only connected to a dull hum. I stopped when I heard the sound of a distant motorbike pass the house then fade away. Azlam wasn't the only one in the city to own one, but I could only think it was him, watching us. I wondered when Droon would return to make his demands, impatient with waiting, taking Jahan to prison. I redialed and held my breath as I heard a ringing phone.

A man picked up. "*Quanhai?*" He was a servant.

I replied in Hindi, "I want to speak to Veer sahib."

I heard the dreaded response. "Veer sahib out. Who is mem-sahib?"

I hesitated, not wanting to commit my name to this man. "Tell him, tell him I call from Kabul. You understand, Kabul."

It took him a long moment. "You are Kabul memsahib? I will tell him."

"When will he return?"

"I don't know, memsahib."

We both disconnected. I sat at the desk, wondering how long I should wait. All day? All week? My life was spent waiting, and each day the knot in my stomach tightened. I gave it a half hour and left when the call wasn't returned. I had to go to practice. I left the door slightly ajar to hear the phone, and stained my face, thickened my brows, affixed the beard, and put on my turban.

There was a week left to practice. We had to win; there was no other escape for Jahan. I drove them harder, criticizing each ball bowled, sneering at every batsman.

Royan rebelled. "What's happened? Why are you so angry with us?"

"I'm not angry," I said. "You're not trying hard enough. You have to beat Azlam's team and that state team." Then I announced it. "He's offered me a lot of money to coach his team."

"When was that?" Parwaaze said, startled. "What did you say?"

"What do you think I said?" I let them wait, holding their breath. "You're my family, a lazy family, and I told him I didn't want his money."

"He wasn't happy about that," Jahan said. "He even went up to twenty-five thousand."

Although it sounded astronomical, it was only a few dollars depending on that day's rate of exchange.

"So he is d-desperate," Qubad said.

"Desperate enough to hire anyone else he can find in the next week," I said. "Unless you want to lose to him, you'll have to work harder, you have to be as good as you all can be." I tossed the ball to Namdar. "Let's not waste any more time."

ON OUR WAY HOME FROM PRACTICE THE NEXT EVENING, WE shopped for food. "No letter, package," said Abdul as we came through the gate.

"They won't come," I said.

Upstairs, I visited Mother. Pain had drawn ugly graffiti on her face, but now in sleep it had been erased, and her beauty surfaced, a gift for us to remember her by. We watched her shallow breaths, counting them; breathing along with her.

"Did anyone call?" I asked Dr. Hanifa.

"I didn't hear the phone ring. My hearing's bad anyway," she said, packing up.

Jahan went to walk Dr. Hanifa home. "I'm going over to Parwaaze's to watch a Bollywood film. Do you want to come?"

"Don't watch the movie, watch the cricket tape again and again. You know the team must win the match, so don't let them waste time."

"They need to relax, even I do."

"Do it when we've escaped."

I remained awake in my room until I heard Jahan return, then went down to the basement and my stuffy cell. I left the door open and lay down.

Jahan woke me when it wasn't yet dawn.

"Shut the door," he whispered, shaking me, and his urgency brought me wide awake. "The police are banging at the gate."

THE VISITORS

I CLOSED AND LOCKED THE DOOR. THE SILENCE hummed in my ears as I strained to hear any sounds.

Wahidi was out there, he had come for me. I gave into fear and collapsed on the divan, curling tightly into a ball. In such darkness, my imagination soared out of the hiding place, seeing Jahan defying the commander, and the men dragging him away to Pul-e-Charkhi, where other men waited to violate him.

I uncurled and sat up. What if he decided to shoot Jahan?

His death would kill Mother more certainly than the cancer. I knew what I would do then: I would lock all the doors, bar all the windows and close the curtains, slide shut the bolt of my room door, perform a final *namaaz*, and die quietly.

JAHAN TOLD ME LATER WHAT HAD HAPPENED.

Abdul had awakened finally at the incessant bangs and shouts. Jahan heard him call out, "What is happening?"

"Open the gate, you stupid man."

"What do you want?" Abdul told them. "Look at the time. Come back later."

"I'll shoot you if you don't open the gate," the policeman shouted.

"So shoot. I'm an old man and my time will come sooner or later. I must ask my master whether to open it or not."

"You're a dead man."

"Open the gate, Abdul," Jahan called out to him, saving him from a bullet.

Taking his time, Abdul pulled back the three bolts—the bottom, the middle, and finally the top—that secured the small gate, while the policeman cursed him for being so slow. He pushed the gate, sending Abdul back, tripping, and stalked into the compound followed by two more policemen. They all had torches. Droon entered behind them.

"Next time, I will shoot."

"Next time, I'll probably be dead already," Abdul said.

They ran up the steps to the door, shining their torches in Jahan's face, and he had to shield his eyes. He thought they looked like the same policemen as before, but he wasn't sure.

"What do you want?" Jahan asked.

"You know what we want," Droon said, remaining by the gate. "Tell him."

"We're here to take Rukhsana, daughter of Gulab, for questioning," the policeman said.

"On what charges?" Jahan asked in his most authoritative voice.

The policeman giggled. "We'll think of them later."

"She's not here. She's visiting our uncle in Mazar-e-Sharif."

"Search the house," Droon ordered.

"We will search," the policeman said brusquely and pushed past Jahan.

"My mother is sleeping. You mustn't disturb her."

"We'll see her."

He first took them to Mother's room and permitted only one to enter.

"Not in her face," he ordered. "It will waken her." And the torch shone respectfully on the ceiling, throwing enough light on Mother to see her. He followed them into my room and the torches lit up a neat bed with plumped pillows awaiting a tired head. They went from room to room, slashing at the darkness, and then down to the basement. They opened Grandfather's storeroom and ran their light across the dusty books before shutting the door. They remembered the cellar and heaved up the slab then closed it.

When they went out, Droon was waiting. "Where is she?" he asked Jahan. He looked as if he wanted to strangle him, but he stopped himself. Jahan said that was very scary. I suppose he was thinking he couldn't kill his future brother-in-law. "My brother, the minister, has written to me asking about the progress on his marriage proposal. He is getting impatient and so am I."

"I told you, she's in Mazar-e-Sharif," Jahan said.

"Like a child repeating a lesson," Droon mocked him. "As her *maadar* is not well, why would she be so far away? She must be in the city, staying with cousins. Tell me their names."

"Which ones? We have a hundred and five here," Jahan said, exaggerating. "I'm happy to give you a list, but you won't find her with any of them."

"I'll find her. Don't forget Pul-e-Charkhi."

Droon signaled the police and they followed him out to the Land Cruiser and he got in. Abdul and Jahan waited in silence until the engines had faded into the darkness; they remained waiting, believing the police and Droon could circle back again, before it would be safe for me to come up from my hiding place.

When Jahan finished telling me what had happened, he sat beside me on the divan in the pitch blackness.

"You'll have to stay in this room," he said. "You can't move around, except when it's dark, and even then be ready to run here."

I remembered Noorzia's advice: defy them in your heart and mind. "No. I won't be locked in this room all day. I'll stay in the house and creep around like a mouse, but I must be able to look after Maadar. I'll only leave here the day before the first match, just to make sure you're ready."

"What should I tell them when you don't come with me?"

"I sprained my ankle," I said shortly, frustrated and angry at being frightened by Droon.

"And don't take off your beard or turban when you do move," Jahan said and left me to my perpetual night. Unlike the Russian police, Droon did not believe that night brought the most fear. He preferred the early dawn, while a man still slept, lost in his dreams, believing he was safe. To awaken the sleeper suddenly disoriented him or her, frightened him, and that was the time when he yielded his secrets.

THE NEXT DAY WE DIDN'T WHISPER A WORD ABOUT THE NIGHT'S invasion to Mother. She had slept, heavily sedated, and the torchlight hadn't disturbed her. I hovered like a frightened wraith in her room, ready to sprint downstairs at the slightest sound on the street. A cyclist's bell, a car's horn, or a raised voice and I was four steps down to the basement. I was angry that Droon made me tremble with such fear, but I was helpless to stop the shaking. I avoided the windows as I moved around. We told Abdul to lock the gates and we locked our doors. If Droon returned to break in, I would have time to hide, I hoped. Jahan was as free as ever and went off to the university grounds. After practice, he went to the homes of our cousins, borrowing the money I needed to escape. Parwaaze and Qubad's family gave the most, 150 dollars each; the others, needier, gave what they could to help us. By Wednesday the nineteenth, three days before the preliminary matches, we had a total of nine hundred dollars, enough for Juniad to run me over the border. Friday night would be my last in my childhood home, and my uncertain future hung over me like an executioner's sword. I knew no one in Pakistan to give me shelter and comfort; I would wander from place to place, waiting for Jahan, waiting for someone to help me. I could register as a refugee and end up in a crowded camp, a single woman, and vulnerable, among the many families. I'd eat what charity gave me and drink the contaminated water and live in my unwashed clothes for months, maybe years, until the Taliban were driven out and I could return home. But I didn't see them loosening their vicious grip on the country for many years.

The day passed in this panic-filled way. I listened for the telephone. It didn't sound all day. The servant had probably forgotten to give the message to Veer and I was too depressed to try again. Jahan and I carried the dinner I'd cooked into Mother's room. We followed the rituals of custom and Jahan and I lied about our day, telling her about cricket, shopping, books I read to pass the time. We didn't tell her I'd spent the whole day at home. The lantern cast only a small yellow halo of light around us as we ate. Above and beyond it, such a frail flame could not lift the weight of the darkness. At least it was steady in this closed room and shadows didn't leap and dance menacingly around us.

That night I lay in the secret room, in stifling heat and stale air, trying to sleep. The door was slightly ajar, near enough for me to reach out and shut it quickly, but that didn't help the air circulation. I didn't want to sleep, as I'd be tormented by nightmares, and

I tossed and turned. I must have dozed off, because I woke with a start. The early sun was a pale glow in my cell.

My calendar was up in my bedroom, and after breakfast I ran up and drew a line through another day. Thursday. Only three days were left and there was nothing I could do to stop their advance.

When Jahan left he closed the front door firmly; the sound echoed and masked another one coming from deeper inside the house. I was halfway down to the basement. At first, I couldn't place it. As I listened, I realized it was our phone, ringing urgently again. I ran up, opened the door to Father's study—the gloom pervaded here too—and groped my way to his desk.

I lifted the receiver, and remained silent, waiting for the voice of a stranger.

"Rukhsana," the voice said.

"Yes . . ." Just from the utterance of my name, that one word, I knew who it was and my breath caught. I couldn't believe it. "Veer!" It felt so wonderful to say his name. "Veer . . . ," I repeated, as stupid as a parrot with a one-word vocabulary, too astonished by the miracle of hearing his voice over this deceitful instrument.

"Jesus, I've tried this number a hundred times and could never get through." There was a new American inflection in his accent. He hurried on, "You called the house in Delhi, and it was just luck that I got home this morning. Mohan told me a Kabul memsahib had called. God, it's wonderful to hear your voice. It was like getting my first letter from you. I have a big smile on my face."

I had to smile. I'd only said, "Veer."

"To hear you say my name sounds to me like a whole poem."

"You didn't reply to my last letter."

"I have it on me, ready to post. I was stuck down in the Amazon for eight weeks." I heard his familiar laughter. "I swear I've been trying this number over the years and can never get through. And when I do I'm disconnected."

"Veer . . . Veer . . . " I gathered my strength. "I don't believe I'm talking to you. Your voice sounds exactly as I remembered."

"How are you? Are you okay? I want to see you."

I hesitated, too long, as it was a question with a very long answer, and I wasn't sure we would have the time.

"Rukhsana, you still there?"

"Yes, I'm here, Veer. I'm . . . I'm okay."

"You don't sound okay. Tell me what's wrong, please, before we get disconnected. I love you, and I've never stopped loving you."

"Oh, Veer, you don't know how just hearing that makes me feel so happy," I managed to say and began crying. I couldn't help it. Veer was there, yet out of reach, and couldn't hold me and comfort me. "I love you so much."

"I can hear you crying. I have to see you, Rukhsana. I'll come over."

"No, don't. Please don't. It's very dangerous. Promise me you won't. I couldn't bear it."

"You should know by now that I never make a promise. And don't forget that I've been there. It must be dangerous for you too. But it can't be worse than some of the jungles I've been in."

"At least there are laws in the jungle. And animals don't carry guns and rocket launchers."

"I have to see you. I know something's wrong."

"Veer, I can't see you. You can't see me. It's against the law, and they'll execute us if we're caught together. Promise me you won't come; it will place me in danger." What was I saying? I was already in danger, but I couldn't place his life in jeopardy. We would die together if he came, a small comfort, but even for love, it wasn't worth it.

"Rukhsana, my love, is there anything at all I can do to help you?"

Perversely, how does one test love? Ask for the impossible, and watch love shrivel into a dried flower, a decayed memory, a mumbled apology, and disconnection. Would he be another Shaheen?

"You can always say no, and I will understand," I said, speaking gently. "I need two thousand dollars to get out of the country."

"You got it," he said without a second's hesitation, as if he had been waiting all along for my test. "I doubt your banks work. I'll send you the money through the *hawala*. It'll reach you in two or three days."

"Thank you, Veer," I said, and I felt the tears trickle down my cheeks. "Thank you. We are desperate. Promise me, you mustn't come here. When we get out I'll find my way to you in Delhi." The phone began to hiss in impatience. "Very soon. I love you . . ."

"Rukhsana, I—"

And the connection broke.

Good-bye, good-bye, good-bye.

I tenderly replaced the receiver and stood still in the darkness. I smiled, I laughed aloud in the empty room with no one to hear my joy. And then, I wept and wept in relief. I couldn't stop and the pain bent me over. Finally, when I had no more tears left, I went to the kitchen to wash my face and prepare lunch.

Jahan returned home in the evening and saw the smile still on my face.

"You're looking happy. What's happened?"

How would I explain the money to Jahan? Should I lie? I was getting too practiced in the art of deception. I was bubbling over with the good news, the promissory note of love, the promise of the funds that would whisk me out of the country. He would have immediately become suspicious—why would a total stranger (to him) bestow the money upon us? What had I done with him that he could be so generous? Was he a lover? Had I betrayed Shaheen in Delhi and slept with this man? Why else would a man give a woman money if it wasn't in exchange for sexual favors? Men and women could never just be friends. His sense of honor could rise like a serpent and strike me down. I remembered Noorzia's warning—brothers, husbands, and fathers could be more dangerous than strangers. Sibling, marital, and filial ties were no protection against the vindictive power of despoiled honor. I thought for a long moment.

"Nargis," I said. "You remember her, don't you? I played cricket with her, and she came over to the house sometimes to pick me up. She called."

He frowned, trying to place her. He had been only eleven or twelve years old then and, at that age, boys paid very little attention to an older sister's friends. "No, I don't remember her at all. What did she want?"

I was lying, without a conscience, to my brother if only to protect myself. "She wanted to know how I was, how we were, and I told her."

"Where was she calling from? Delhi?"

"Yes. I told her my problems and she promised to help."

"How?"

"By sending me the money, as a loan of course."

"Is she rich?"

"No, she's working in America. I guess that makes her a lot richer than us." I did a little dance around the dark room to make him happy. "She's using a *hawala*."

He laughed now and held me. "As soon as it comes I'll see Juniad and make all the arrangements for you to leave. Today's Wednesday. I think it will take two or three days for the money to reach here." We didn't need to check the calendar. "So it could be here Friday or Saturday."

"That's very close. I'll leave Saturday."

"If he has a full load. He won't make a run until he does."

"Can't he just take me?" I said in impatience.

"The price will go through the roof of his old Land Rover."

"More than two thousand?"

"It carries nine or ten, depending on how many he can squeeze in. So that makes around nine thousand for just you." Jahan kept hold of me. "Even if you had that much I don't want you to travel alone with him. There'll be safety in numbers."

"I know. You come with me, there's enough for—"

"No, I can't," he said, shaking his stubborn head. "I won't let the team down, I have to play in the match. They will never forgive me for breaking my word." Then he added with a sneer, "I'm not a Shaheen who doesn't honor his word."

"You're right." I sighed. He was as obstinate as me and I knew I couldn't change his mind. I had to respect his decision. "I have to get out by Saturday night. Friday night, if we have the money. Go and talk to him and bargain. Offer him one, and if he pushes, make it two. Once I'm in Pakistan we'll meet and go to Delhi."

He looked past me, upstairs to Mother's room. "But you can't leave until . . ."

"I have to, as the alternative is . . . ," I replied. "I only pray she will forgive me."

I slept in my cell as if I was on a feather bed in an open room.

The next day too I remained at home while Jahan went to practice with the team. I was in a state of enchantment, and in a state of utter despair, remembering every word of my conversation with Veer. I wiped my eyes with my shirtsleeves. I had to occupy myself. I dusted, I cleaned, I sat dreamily staring at the walls that couldn't contain my imagination as I flew across boundaries to meet Veer.

I made a vegetable soup for Mother, and when she woke I sat beside her to spoon in the hot nourishment. When she tried to hide a grimace, I put it away and prepared the injection. Each time her flesh grew even more papery and her veins were faded blue trickles flowing through a parched landscape.

"No cricket again today?" she whispered.

"I just wanted to spend time with you. Dr. Hanifa will be in later to see you. She says you're fine . . ."

"Liar," Mother said gently. "I know it's nearer. I dream a lot now. I dream of your father mostly and I know he's waiting for me to join him."

"Don't say that," I cried and held her in my arms, as light as a small child, as fragile as crystal. "I can't live without you."

"You'll learn to live your life, even as Jahan will too, without me." She smiled and looked into my eyes. "It would happen sooner or later." She pulled me closer. "You must leave me, Hanifa will care for me."

"We'll see . . ."

"Then you must marry Shaheen, have your own children, and live a happy life. And look after Jahan."

"As my own child," I said and kept crying, rocking her gently in my arms.

She pushed away and held me at arm's length. "There's something you're not telling me. Your eyes have a glow that I haven't seen for a long time."

These were her final days and hours. I could not lie to her. I believed the last words spoken were carried into the next world, where the person had all the leisure to examine them and, if they were false, send out their displeasure to haunt the liar.

"You must tell me."

"Shaheen married another girl in America."

"Oh god." Her face crumpled. "How could he do that, he was committed . . . ?" She pushed away so the light touched my face. "Why the glow then? You should be weeping."

"I had a . . . friend in Delhi." I hurried on, "He called me yesterday."

"A friend?" Now she frowned. "The boy you were seeing in Delhi?"

"You knew?"

"I knew that radiance—a woman can tell when another woman is in love. You had it many evenings when you came home from college and after all those afternoon films. And then on your final day you were darker than night. I didn't ask his name. I knew you would behave. And you had the right to fall in love. We cannot control our emotions when the unexpected happens. And when you never spoke of him, I knew you had refused to marry him. But the more you postponed your engagement to Shaheen, the more I knew you still loved the man. What's his name? This mysterious ghost who has haunted my daughter's life."

"Veer."

She nodded understandingly. "Your father would never have given permission. He would have sent you back to Kabul if he had known."

"Would you have?"

She let me wait for her answer as she thought about it. "Yes, if only for your own safety I would have honored your father's decision. We have so many divisions among us, why add religion to break our backs? So much evil has slipped into religion and we'll never be rid of it." She reached for my hand and I held on just so I could feel its warmth. "Let me hold you, my child." I lay down beside her, my head in the crook of her arm, a child snuggled in for comfort. "I wish I had met him. He has held on to his love for you all these years."

I smiled in her embrace.

"I know you love this Veer. Go to him." She shook her head in finality. "But you cannot live in this country with him."

"I know."

I lay with her while the morphine took effect and she dozed off. I rose when I heard the front door open and sneaked out to look. It was Jahan, and he looked somber as he climbed the stairs.

"Why aren't you practicing?"

"I went there but couldn't find the team. Then I went to Par-waaze's." He took a breath. "Droon visited Parwaaze and the team early this morning."

"Oh god!" My hand flew to my mouth. "Are they alive?"

THE CRICKETERS

AN HOUR LATER, THEY CAME TO OUR HOUSE. PAR-waaze had a swollen cheek and Qubad nursed a badly cut lip and was still sucking on the blood. When I reached out in apology to caress their faces, they pulled away in pain. Their clothes were muddied and the front of their *shalwars* were spotted with blood. Jahan brought in cups of tea and Parwaaze drank his quickly, while Qubad winced at the heat.

"They woke me up from a deep sleep while it was still dark and one of them dragged me out and slammed me against the wall." Parwaaze spoke, slurring the words slightly as his tongue worried that cheek. "Another Talib hit me in the mouth and then punched his gun butt into my stomach. I swear I didn't know where I was: asleep and dreaming of pain, or wide awake and suffering it. There was a third man, grinning widely. He grabbed my hair and dragged me to my feet.

"'Where is your cousin Rukhsana?'" he asked.

"I was too surprised to answer immediately and the gun butt hit me in the lower back. Even in such pain, I knew I had to spin lies. I would not be responsible for your fate."

"I'm so sorry, so sorry that I have caused you such pain," I said, tears coming to my eyes.

"I knew that behind these men was Wahidi. I remembered your words—'Cricket is drama, it is theater, it is the conflict between one man and eleven others, and that one has to defeat the enemy surrounding him on the field. It is about the two warriors battling it out between themselves.' I was a warrior now.

"I told him, 'She went away to Mazar-e-Sharif with her uncle and . . .'

"He called me a liar and then took my face between his fingers and squeezed, nearly breaking my jaw. He said, 'You will be imprisoned in Pul-e-Charkhi, tortured and raped, if you don't tell us.'

"When I didn't show I was frightened, he went on, 'I am Droon, Wahidi's brother, and I promise I have not come to harm her. My brother only wishes to talk to her, to see if she will consider his proposal. Just tell us where she is and nothing will happen to you or to her.'

" 'Mazar,' I told him again.

"Droon gestured to a fighter and the man smiled as he pressed the muzzle hard against my head.

" 'When I lift this finger,' and Droon shook his finger under my nose, 'he will pull the trigger.'

"I was scared that would happen, but I managed a smile.

" 'He's mad,' the fighter said.

" 'Why do you smile?' Droon demanded.

" 'I'll be captain of my cricket team and teach everyone how to play the game in paradise,' I said.

" 'He is mad.'

" 'I heard about your wanting to learn this game and that you practice at the university.'

" 'Who told you?' I asked, even though I knew the answer.

" 'A friend. You entered your team in the match next week?'

" 'Yes. There will be a foreign observer and he will learn that we wanted to play, but you killed the captain so that the other team could win. Everyone will know about that when I am killed.'

" 'And how did you learn to play the game?'

" 'From books.' I pointed to the book on the floor. He picked it up and slipped it into his *shalwar* pocket.

" 'And you are a team of cousins.'

" 'Yes.'

" 'They won't be as mad as this one,' Droon said to his fighters. 'They will tell us where she is. Search the house.'

"They searched and of course didn't find you. Then he dragged me out of the room, past my father and my brother. My father stood between them and the door.

" 'What has my son done?' Father demanded.

" 'We are looking for Rukhsana. Do you know where she is?'

" 'No,' my father said.

"Droon gestured. His fighter raised the automatic and pointed it at Father's chest.

" 'Is that how you expect respect? My son says he does not know. He is not a liar.'

" 'You're all liars. I will return and your family will see ruin.'

" 'Ruin!' Father said. 'Your government has already ruined me. Your men destroyed my business. What worse can you do to me?'

"As they took me outside, Father placed his palm against his heart in farewell. They dragged me to the waiting Land Cruiser and threw me into the back like a sack of grain, and that really hurt."

"I am so sorry," I said to Parwaaze. "All because of me."

"Also cricket," he replied, trying a smile and wincing.

Qubad took up the story.

"Droon sent the police to search all our houses. He knew the whole team. He then lined us up on the road. Everyone stopped to watch before getting out of their way. Then we saw Azlam on his motorbike ride past very slowly. He didn't look, but I could see the smile on his face as he passed. I'll kill him when I see him."

I noticed in his fury that he had lost his stutter.

"Droon then slapped each of us very hard," Parwaaze continued.

"'All of you listen carefully.' Droon spoke slowly, deliberately. 'You will die very soon, when I give the order. No one can stop me from killing you, no one will care that you have died except your families. You are hiding a traitor to this great country. But you can live and be well rewarded if you tell me where we can find Rukhsana. I will guarantee that you will be paid a lot of money and you can leave the country to live wherever you wish to live. There will be no loss of honor in serving your country.'

"He stopped. When none of us said anything or even moved, he lifted his hand; the fighters lifted their guns. Royan put his arm around Omaid's shoulder.

"'I don't understand the power of this woman that keeps your mouths shut,' Droon told us. 'She is only a woman. Why die for a woman? She should die for you. Women are evil.'

"'My mother was not evil,' Omaid said. Omaid! Who could have imagined! He surprised us with his anger, and surprised Droon too. 'She was a good woman. Is your mother evil?'

"'I was not talking about her,' Droon snapped at Omaid and walked over to him.

"We thought he would shoot him.

"Then Namdar stepped forward, and he didn't speak with any fear. 'Sir, we are young men and don't know the world. If women are evil, why then is your brother so anxious to marry Rukhsana?'"

"Namdar said that?" I said. Before playing cricket, he would just shuffle his feet and look away. But once I chose him to be our fast bowler, he had gradually become more aggressive, a necessary trait.

"Yes," Parwaaze continued. "Droon did slap him but not too hard.

"Droon said, 'My brother is a pious and good man and believes he can save this woman from her bad traits.'"

Parwaaze went on: "Don't forget, his men still pointed their guns at us and I thought now he would give the order. Instead, he gestured for them to lower their guns and, like them, he looked disappointed.

"He said to us: 'You are fortunate. My brother does not want me to kill any one of Rukhsana's family, as this will cause bad blood between him and her family.'"

Parwaaze paused, holding my attention while he was blinking hard. "We relaxed when we heard that.

"Then Droon smiled and went on:

"'I promised I would not kill you, but those in Pul-e-Charkhi will. After six months none of you may be alive, such things happen there. If you win the final match—and you won't, as the state team is very good—I cannot stop you from going to Pakistan. My brother gave his word and I will not break it. But when you lose, and I know you will, and stay in the country, you will have a holiday in prison for defying my authority. Don't think you can run away and hide like that woman. I will find you; my men are watching your homes.'"

I still had my hand to my mouth when Parwaaze finished, or at least I thought he had, and didn't break the silence until he spoke again.

"There's something else Droon said, but not to us. He talked to himself and didn't think I'd overhear.

"Droon stepped back and I heard him mutter to himself, 'I should have shot her in the office if I'd known this would turn into an obsession.'"

"I was a fraction away from the bullet," I whispered. "But I had expected it from Wahidi then, not Droon, who stood behind him."

Parwaaze remained grim. "He's not forgotten you either and he will kill you when he finds you."

I couldn't even say a word. My throat was dry with fear.

"He won't do that," Jahan said fiercely. "His brother will never allow it."

"His brother won't even know," Parwaaze countered. "He finds Rukhsana, kills her, and then tells Wahidi that he couldn't find her or that she's gone to Pakistan. He believes"—he stared at me with compassion—"you've cast a spell on his brother and the only way to counter it is to kill you and free him."

None of us spoke a word. The threat was almost visible in our heads and we saw it racing toward us—for them the prison, for me the bullet. I knew that we were lost.

"Shaheen's sent the money and papers?" Parwaaze asked, breaking into our thoughts.

I told them the story, ending with the money arriving Friday, Saturday at the latest, I hoped.

They both shook their heads. "He's betrayed the family," Parwaaze announced angrily.

"He has dishonored you and Jahan," Qubad added, with the same fervor. "But Friday's a holiday. The *hawala* dealer will close."

"Then it has to be Saturday."

I turned to Jahan. "Go and see Juniad. Tell him he has to take me out this Saturday night."

"We have to win all our matches, as Droon promised that he wouldn't stop us from leaving." Qubad looked beseeching. "Before you leave, you must help us sharpen our game."

"Okay. I'll join you tomorrow." It was a reckless act, but I owed them at least this.

The next morning, after watching the road for half an hour for any suspicious-looking loiterers, Jahan and I left the house by the side gate and cut through back lanes. We kept looking back for pursuers but saw no one. It was a hazy, warm morning and I felt such pleasure at being freed from the house after days of imprisonment. *Soon, every day of my life will be free*, I thought. *I'll be with Veer and we'll live in Delhi, and I'll work as a journalist again.*

The team was waiting, eager to polish their game as much as they could while they still had their coach. We started practice immediately and I worked with them all day—correcting their batting technique, getting them to bowl straighter and bounce the ball in the right place. Namdar was bowling ferociously now, a leap in his stride as he delivered the ball; Omaid smiled and clapped when his ball bounced and turned; Royan was flamboyant, like Parwaaze, in his batting, taking steps down to hit the ball hard. Each one had grown over the three weeks and I saw how much they loved the game and believed they had a chance to win the final match. They were not just cousins but teammates and friends. Yet I was still concerned about that ringer on the state's team. He looked very good.

As the light began to fade, we had our usual fielding session with me hitting the ball high for them to run and catch. And that was when the accident happened.

RUN FOR THE BORDER

WE WERE LAUGHING AS QUBAD RAN TO CATCH A very high ball. "Faster, Qubad, faster," we shouted. "You'll get the batsman out . . ."

He wasn't going to make the catch, as he was fifteen or twenty yards away.

The ball hit the ground and the earth erupted and tossed Qubad aside like a broken toy. He remained suspended in the air almost forever, a bird in midflight clouded with dirt, the roar of a wounded earth deafening us, before he fell to the ground. We ducked instinctively and fell flat, hands shielding our heads. In the silence, we rose to stare at Qubad, lying still on the ground.

Parwaaze was the first to run to him and the others followed calling out, "Qubad, Qubad," as if their voices were the miraculous cure for such a tragedy. They crowded around him.

Jahan remained by my side. He could not leave me alone. He saw the hysteria distorting my face, my hands crushing it like putty. I couldn't breathe.

"Qubad," Parwaaze called to him, crying.

He did not move, and my pain was unbearable; it swallowed all my senses. Then I saw his foot twitch and many hands helping him to sit up. They were laughing in relief, and kept holding him as he shook like a leaf in their arms.

"He's all right," Parwaaze shouted, and we ran over to him. I pushed through the little knot of players. There was blood on his clothes, near the heart, and the dirt shrouded him. His left arm, above the elbow, was bleeding badly and he looked at it in puzzlement, as if it wasn't he who bled. And he looked around, as if it wasn't he who was alive.

"Qubad, Qubad . . ." I held him, not caring that the blood stained my clothes and crying in relief. "Oh thank god. It was my fault, hitting that ball . . . my fault if anything had happened . . ."

"So you're the one who buried the mine," said Royan, the frustrated doctor with half a degree to his name, as he ripped a strip off his *shalwar* and expertly fashioned a tourniquet above the wound to prevent more blood leaking away. "He's in shock, and we must take him to the hospital to dress the wound and put in some stitches."

"What h-happened? My head h-hurts and my ears too," Qubad said, still puzzled. "I was running and then . . ."

"I hit a high ball to you and—" I began.

"When it fell it triggered the mine—" Jahan continued.

"You were thrown back—" Daud cut in.

"You fell," Bilal ended.

I still held him. "Thank god you weren't able to catch it. You would've died."

"We'll carry you," Royan said and gestured. His cousins immediately moved to lift Qubad between them.

"I can walk." He stood, but swayed and nearly fell. He shook his head, trying to clear away the ache.

"You have a slight concussion." Royan held up three fingers. "How many?"

"Three." He held up four fingers, and Qubad said, "Four."

Royan looked relieved. "It's not a bad wound, but I don't want it to open up any further by you walking; you must rest."

Qubad sat on his cousins' linked hands and the procession hurried out of the campus. I followed, glancing back at the crater that could have killed him. It was a shallow hole, scorched around the sides and blackened at the bottom. The air was bitter with the stench of explosives. How innocent it had looked moments before Qubad nearly stepped on this spot, nothing at all to distinguish it from the surrounding area, which I scanned, looking for another mine.

It could be there, it could be here, it could be under a clump of grass. How long did they wait before they exploded? Forever? Or did they have a life span, like a torch battery, as they waited for that fatal footstep? I tried to think of the man who had buried it. He must have knelt on the earth just there, on the edge of the small crater, and dug his death hole, lowered the mine down into it tenderly, and then, lovingly and carefully, replaced all the earth he had removed. He would have smoothed that out with the flat of his palm, scattered a few pebbles across the disturbed grounds, and then stood back to admire his handiwork. He would not have thought about whom his device would kill or when, only certain that it would commit the murder for which it had been invented. I felt a surge of terrible fury at the possibility that any of us could be next—and it could be so much worse.

At the Malalai Hospital, a nurse cleansed the wound, probed it to check that there wasn't a sliver of metal still remaining, and put in eight stitches. Then she bandaged it and discharged him. The hospital didn't have any painkiller tablets left.

All the way home, surrounded by his escort, Qubad could not stop repeating himself. "I was just a few feet away and I could h-have easily stepped on it. There was only a few feet . . . I could be dead by now." He blinked back tears, more from fear than from anything else. "Just a few steps to my left and I would h-have been blown to pieces."

"It's a hard ball," Atash, the frustrated engineer, said. "It was falling at thirty-two feet per second from a height of at least thirty feet. So when it hit the ground, it had the same weight as a man stepping on the mine."

The cousins discussed the laws of physics, but we knew what each of us was thinking: I could have stepped on that mine.

"No more fielding practice," Parwaaze the captain announced. "Only bowling and batting tomorrow."

"We'll be one short," Royan said. "Qubad can't play with that arm."

"You'll just have to find another player. I told you there should be twelve or thirteen on the team."

"I know, I know," Parwaaze said, rightly distraught. "But he won't know the game."

"Hide him near the boundary then, and he'll bat last."

They all accompanied Qubad to his house except for Jahan and me. We returned home by the back lanes, deserted except for wandering dogs and a lone cyclist.

"I'll try to find Juniad again," he said. He had gone the evening before and Juniad's relative told Jahan that he was away and wouldn't say where. "Lock this gate behind you. I'll come back through the front gate."

I let myself in through the kitchen and hung up the keys. When I climbed the stairs, I heard Dr. Hanifa open the door to Mother's room.

"How is she?" I asked as she came out, closing the door behind her, blocking my way.

"She's sleeping, don't disturb her." Dr. Hanifa gently stroked the fake beard. "She worries all the time about you. Why are you still here?"

"I want to leave tomorrow night, or Saturday at the latest," I said as we walked slowly down the stairs, Dr. Hanifa leaning on me for support. "But how can I leave Maadar?"

"I'm here," she said gently. "And she'll be at peace when she knows you and Jahan are safe." At the front door, she added, "I increased the dosage again. I'll be back early in the morning to see how she is."

I made dinner and waited in the dark for Jahan to return. I thought that by this time tomorrow I would be squeezed into Juniad's car with many others, praying we would be carried safely across the border and find a new life in a foreign country. I would carry a small bag with a change of clothes to reclaim my identity. All along those dangerous roads, I knew I would think only of Mother and pray for her forgiveness. If I left Saturday night, Jahan would join me on Sunday, after winning the preliminary Saturday game and, I prayed, the final match. I would wait in Karachi for him and we'd leave for Delhi.

I was so lost in thought I didn't hear Jahan return until he was standing beside me, scaring me for a moment.

"Juniad's not at home," he said wearily, and my stomach knotted. "I asked when he'd be back, but no one would tell me."

"You'll have to try again tomorrow."

We sat and ate in the gloomy light, both fatigued and depressed by the day. He had a boy's appetite and finished all the rice and chicken, while I could only manage a mouthful with a cold salad.

THE GOOD-BYE

IN THE MORNING, HAVING DOZED FITFULLY IN THE cramped space, eyes burning from tiredness, I made tea and took it to Mother's room.

A pale glow, falling softly across the bed, filtered through the drawn curtains, and it was from the silence that I knew my mother had passed from this world to the next. I placed the glass and the plate of biscuits down on a table with surprisingly steady hands and stood by her bedside.

Mother was beautiful, the pain lines vanquished, and she even seemed to be smiling. Her right hand crossed her chest, the left lay by her side. I leaned down to kiss the cool forehead and brush my palm against the chilled cheeks. Mother could have died early in the morning, even while I lay hidden in the room far below. If only I could have been beside her to hold her hand, a last touch before life left. I didn't cry, the tears would come later, and was relieved Mother had finally escaped the pain that had ravaged her.

Mother had given me so much and now whom could I talk to? No one. I would still tell Mother everything, even though my words would fall into silences. I had revealed my deepest secret to my mother—Veer—and she understood and blessed me. I wished they could have met, Mother would have liked Veer.

I went to Jahan's room. He was huddled in sleep and I watched his strong, steady breathing before sitting on the bed. I shook him gently awake and he knew from my face why I woke him. He sat up and we held each other, the orphans now alone in the world.

"When?"

"In her sleep. When I went to give her tea, she wasn't with us. How are you feeling?"

"I dreamed I was Qubad and had taken those twenty or thirty steps, and the earth had opened its jaws and swallowed me."

I led him downstairs to Mother's room and Jahan leaned over and kissed her cold forehead. He looked steadily at his mother's face, wanting to remember it and carry the serene image with him for the remainder of his life. When tears blurred his vision, he wiped his eyes on his sleeve and sniffled into it.

"You must call Uncle Koshan in Mazar and tell him. And then send Abdul to go to our cousins' homes and inform them."

He went to the telephone; he would probably spend the morning there, while I sat beside Mother. I wept after kissing her again but made sure that not a tear dropped on her body, as its bitterness would be carried into the next world. Dr. Hanifa came in, looked down at Mother with just a slight smile, and then held me in her arms so I could cry against her.

"It's for the best," she said.

"Did you help her . . . ?"

"As a doctor, I did not," she protested, with little conviction, and I didn't press her. I knew they had conspired in this eventual moment.

She helped me perform the *ghusl*, gently bathing Mother with scented water. I caressed the shrunken frame, remembering

Mother as a robust woman who once had heavenly warm flesh to cuddle and cradle me.

"You must think only that she has escaped from this world finally and left her pain behind," Dr. Hanifa said as we performed the rituals.

"I know. I only wish I'd been beside her at the time."

"You are now, you are saying your good-byes." Dr. Hanifa sighed. "Who will say farewell to me when I go? My children are so far away." She saw me about to reply. "And don't tell me you will look after me, because your mother wanted you to leave. You must get away."

"I will, tonight or tomorrow."

When we finished the *ghusl*, we dressed Mother in clean clothes and then tenderly wrapped her in a pure white sheet, again, not allowing a tear to stain it. We covered her face and tied the straps around the ankles, across the stomach, and over the chest to keep the sheet in place. We stood back to study our handiwork, a white shroud vaguely shaped like a woman lay on the floor beside us. Jahan came in and we knelt on either side of our mother. We looked down at her earthly outline and then up at each other's distressed face. Jahan wiped away his tears with his sleeve, head averted, reminding me of him as a small boy. We were alone now, forever, with no parent to witness him grow into a man or to witness my marriage. We lifted her tenderly, Mother as light as a soul in flight, and then, alone, refusing my outstretched arms, he carried her down the stairs to place her in the *zanaana* for our female relatives to pay their last respects. Dr. Hanifa accompanied him downstairs to receive the female mourners in my place.

I looked numbly at the unmade bed, and the table cluttered with medications and syringes. I emptied them into a wastebasket. I lay on the edge of the bed, as I always had, and caressed the indentation in the pillow, breathing in her spirit. It had not left yet. When I heard the gates open and the murmur of approaching mourning voices, I closed the door; the click of the latch sounded so final. I retreated down to the basement.

"Where's Rukhsana? Why isn't she here?" Qubad's mother.

"In Mazar, I called her . . ." Jahan.

"She should have been here, beside her *madaar*." Parwaaze's mother scolded in between crying.

"She'll be here as soon as she can." Jahan.

"Her *madaar*'s more important than a wedding . . . very uncaring girl . . ." Daud's father.

Others spoke too, men and women, as they crowded into the house. I wanted to walk up and tell them all, "I'm here." But Mother whispered her reminder in my ears, "Keep your mouth shut." And I clamped my ears against hearing the censure heaped on my head.

Although it was Friday, Mother had to be buried as soon as possible. I listened to the muffled sounds above my head and the weeping increase as they carried Mother out to the waiting van. Her spirit, which had filled this home and sustained me for so many years, even from her sickbed, accompanied her and slipped out the door. I was, for the first time, alone in our house, a child abandoned. I leaned against the wall for support, slid down to sit, clutching my knees tightly, bending my head, protecting myself from the loneliness.

I knew the rituals from the past. The men would carry the body to our local mosque, a small, unpretentious building only slightly damaged. A few bullet holes were lodged in its side and there was a large crack in the dome. The women would wait in an adjoining hall. Jahan and his cousins would lower Mother's body to the floor, just within the entrance of the mosque. The old mullah, who knew the family, would slowly move to them, dragging his left foot, clutching the holy book. "This is a woman," he would announce to all within hearing. He would not remove the covering on her face, and would pray over the body. The brief ritual over, the funeral procession of men would move along Asamayi Wat. They would travel in silence along the dusty road, steadying the body for the bumps and ruts in the road.

I listened; something had fallen—a cup, a book—carelessly left on the edge of a table.

I returned to my thoughts, accompanying my mother to her grave. The procession would take half an hour to reach the cemetery, which began by the roadside. It sloped gently up the hill, forested with headstones, some protected by iron railings, and one day the graves would reach the summit and flow down the other side. The van would turn onto a narrow road, with graves on either side, a carpet of mounds, headstones, and iron railings protecting the graves of the more affluent. Halfway way up the slope, hidden by a grove of trees, was a small shrine. I thought Mother would lie, looking down at the city she had loved, and wished Father lay beside her too. To love and then be separated by such a distance in death saddened me. One day, we would disinter Mother and take her to lie near her husband, or at least in the same cemetery. But now, they would have dug a fresh grave and lowered her body into it so that her head pointed toward Mecca. Then Jahan would—

I stopped.

The *zanaana* door was opening upstairs, sly, hesitant, menacing. A whisper of feet. Then another door opened, the latch loud as the safety flicked off a weapon, and another sound of feet. I remained glued against the wall, unable to free myself. There were thieves in the house. They had mingled with the crowd of mourners, knowing that in the confusion they could remain hidden.

"She could have gone to the funeral too," a woman said, not even whispering. I recognized the voice. The one who had claimed to be my friend.

"We're searching there too," a man replied. "We'll start from the top, see if you can find anything that will tell us where she is."

When I heard them climb, unhurried, knowing they had hours of privacy, talking to each other as if on the street, I managed to stand with the wall's support. I edged away from the stairs—the faintest sound would carry—and moved to the storeroom. Above, I heard them opening a door. I waited, then, as gently as I could, inch by inch, I twisted the handle and stepped into the room. I closed it as quietly as possible and in the darkness finally started breathing again. Panting for air, I crossed to the secret room, the door ajar, a sepia glow of light coming from it, and locked myself in. I sat on the divan, still sucking in air. I controlled myself, silencing even the sound of my breathing. These were not illiterate policemen and I stared at the frail door protecting me, expecting it to crash open. I didn't move, as even the sound of a sleeve brushing my arm sounded so loud. I don't know how long it took them before I heard their murmurings in the basement. The storeroom door opened.

"Nothing but useless books," the woman said. "They should be burned."

I didn't hear it close and I sensed she was prowling among the books, reading titles, pulling them out.

"There's a cellar here," the man called to her.

I heard her leave and then the man grunting to pry open the granite slab.

"Empty," the woman said in disgust and the slab fell back into place, causing the floor to vibrate. "She'll have to be back soon for the other ceremonies."

I didn't hear them leave; they could be standing still, as alert as predators waiting for the prey to run. I was uncomfortable, my legs cramping from the tension, but I wouldn't move. Stay still, stay still, they're listening.

They were there, at the outer door. They had found the secret latch. Who had told them? The door opened slowly. I shrank back.

"Rukhsana!" Jahan was faintly outlined in the frame. When I couldn't move, he knelt in front of me. "Are you okay?"

"Two of them were here," I said, surprised by my own calm. "The woman who said she was a friend and the man with her. They searched for me." I stretched up my hands. "Help me up, I think I have a cramp in my legs." He held and steadied me as I stretched. "They weren't here when you came in?"

"No." He helped me walk. "The police went into the women's hall searching for you. A woman went with them. She wanted all the women to reveal their faces, and they were angry at being disturbed on such a sad occasion. But they had to when the police threatened them."

"I want to see her grave one day."

"We must place a marble headstone on it," he said and then went on. He gestured dejectedly. "Now there's a police car parked opposite our gate."

THE DEAD END

Jahan trudged upstairs to wait for mourners to pay their respects. I knew death was draining, it stole a part of the living to take into the next world as memory, and we needed to mourn Mother alone, but that would have to wait.

I was exhausted by the end of the day. I broke into tears each time I thought of my mother, trying to make believe she had just gone to visit a friend and would return home soon. Now I waited for Veer's money to save me.

I returned to the room and lay down. I started to fall asleep, praying to escape the pain that pursued me with the same lethal zeal as Wahidi. I had forgotten him until his name and image detonated through the grinding plates of grieving to surface in my consciousness. I paused in my sad flight, a bird struck by a catapult's stone, tumbling down to the earth. And then as my vision grew darker, Mother appeared, smiling and opening her arms. I slipped into those arms and Mother rose, carrying me into a blue sky. We were laughing as we flew . . .

"Rukhsana," Jahan called from a distance, and I sat up. "What time is it?"

"Nearly five. Noorzia wants to see you."

"Are you sure it's her?"

"Of course. I recognize her voice." He waited patiently for my decision.

Should I see her? Why had she come? I wanted to feel her invigorating presence that had filled me with defiance before. "She can't see me in this room. We'll meet in the corridor."

I followed him out, closing both the doors, and waited for her. She swept down the stairs with such elegance, despite the burka. I knew that only she could move with such confidence.

"My Babur," she said, removing the garment to reveal her stylish self beneath it. Designer jeans, a silk blouse, perfumed, touching her hair back into place. She brought her own light into this gloomy hallway, and when she opened her arms, I went into them.

"I did not know about your mother. I am so sorry."

"It was a release from her suffering," I managed to say.

She drew back and caressed my beard. "It's kept its shape."

"It's my lifesaver."

"I came to say good-bye. I am leaving tonight and couldn't go without seeing you."

"You have your ticket and papers?" I said, suppressing my envy.

"Yes." She laughed, and then stopped. "I couldn't find Juniad to take me. No one knows where he is, and I have to leave."

"Jahan tried to find him too. So how will you go?"

"Remember? I told you about my uncle. He has an old car and he's said he'll drive me. He knows the passes well. He will take me to Karachi and from there I'll fly to Colombo and then to Melbourne. I'll be married there. Now, what about you?"

I told her everything that had happened until the moment she came in and she listened gravely.

"You have nothing to keep you here now. Go, go quickly to

Veer." She stopped and clapped her hands. "I know. You come with me right now. Be my Babur and I'll have two *mahrams*."

Her excitement was contagious and I didn't hesitate a moment. "I can perform Maadar's third-day ceremony in a mosque in another country." I hesitated, the practical raising its objections. "But I don't have enough money yet."

"I have enough for food for us on the journey and we can share a hotel room in Karachi. But I can't loan you any."

"By then the money will be here and Jahan can bring it when they win the match." I sobered from the intoxicating feelings. "*If* they win. I told you Qubad can't play, and he was a big hitter for us. Now they have to find just another body to make up the eleven."

"So? If they lose, Jahan can use the money to join you."

"You're right. The others will be bitterly disappointed though."

She grabbed my hand. "Come on, we mustn't waste time. The police car in the road will think of you as just another male mourner leaving the house." She put on her burka. "Oh, to see the world without blinkers."

We hurried to the stairs. I needed my passport, which was in Father's study, and I wanted to say good-bye to Jahan, Dr. Hanifa, and Abdul. My life was reduced to these essentials. I would call Veer from Karachi and tell him that I was on my way.

We were halfway up, giggling like schoolgirls, when we met Jahan coming down.

"At least someone sounds happy." He managed a smile through his mourning and looked down at me. "Veer's waiting to see you."

NO GREATER LOVE . . .

"VEER!" MY HAND FLEW TO COVER MY MOUTH TO hide both the panic and the smile fighting to shape my lips. "Oh god, I didn't expect him. He's Nargis's brother and—"

Noorzia breathed his name as I did, "Veer."

"I know who he is," Jahan said.

"What do you know?"

"Mother told me." And when he saw the surprise in my face, he smiled. "Everything. You're not the only one who talked to her and held her hand. We talked. She told me he had phoned and spoken to you. Why didn't you tell me all this?"

"Because . . . because I was afraid."

"Of me?"

"Yes."

He frowned, puzzling over the remark. "I was angry when Mother told me, but only because you hadn't," he admitted. "I promised her I would look after you, and I'll keep that promise. Why didn't you trust me?"

"I do, but sometimes men are difficult to understand, and I wasn't sure. Your mind was set on my marriage to Shaheen."

"I thought that was what you wanted."

"No. That's what the family wanted."

"I will never understand you." He smiled. "You better see him . . ."

Noorzia pushed past Jahan, taking his hand as she went up. "You two are the only ones left in this family and you mustn't squabble. Obey each other's wishes." She laughed. "Now, I have to meet Veer, I can't leave without doing that."

"I can't like this . . ." I looked down at my crumpled *shalwar*, touched my bearded face, and sniffed my body. I hadn't bathed, only washed quickly, as I was afraid I'd be trapped in the bathroom. "Give me five minutes . . ."

"No five minutes," Noorzia said. "You can't beautify yourself into Rukhsana, and I don't have the time. Where is he?"

"In the *mardaana*."

"May I enter?"

She didn't wait for an answer and crossed the hall. I followed quickly, now pushing Jahan aside. My Veer was here. I was a step behind Noorzia and saw a bearded man, wearing a black turban, a white, crumpled, dusty *shalwar*, and an equally rumpled coat.

He came to his feet lightly, moving toward Noorzia's covered shape. "Rukhsana . . ."

Noorzia's laughter stopped him. It wasn't my laugh. "I'm not Rukhsana, and now I wish I was. She's the youth behind me."

I was still at the doorway, watching him, devouring him, and felt an overwhelming need to be held and protected by him. I didn't know what to say except that I loved him.

"Rukhsana?" He stepped around Noorzia, ignoring Jahan, to stop a foot before me.

He held out his arms to embrace me, and I wanted to run into them and have him hold me. Then our laughter was stifled as we remembered Mother. Instead of embracing me, Veer placed his palms together in the Hindu act of obeisance, and bowed his head.

"I am very saddened, Rukhsana. Please accept my deepest condolences. I wish I could have met her."

"So do I." I took a step closer to him and placed my palms on either side of his. Just the touch was exhilarating.

He looked up and saw my eyes and the shape of my mouth emerge from out of the shadows and the beard. "I've waited so long to see you, and you've grown a beard since I saw you last." He had the same smile I remembered. "I'll take you even with that beard."

"And so have you . . ." We both reached to touch the hair on each other's faces. "If you tug mine, it will come off."

"Then I will."

"No, you can't, not yet." But I did tug on his.

"It's my own. I hadn't shaved for a month and was going to when we talked. The beard is mandatory here, so I kept it."

I remembered my letter and slowly ran my finger from his brow to the tip of his nose, meaning to land it on his lips for a kiss.

Noorzia coughed gently and broke our aura. "I have to go."

I stepped back, having forgotten her. "I'll come to the door . . ."

"And no further now." She embraced me tightly and whispered, "Go with him."

"I will. You will keep in touch? Where will I find you?"

She opened her purse and took out a scrap of paper. "That's my friend's address and phone number in Melbourne."

"*Khoda haafez*," we said to each other and she hurried out with Jahan.

I forgot her again the next moment as Veer kissed me, gently, the second we were alone. Just the soft brush of his mouth and I pressed against him, having waited so long in my dreary solitude.

"I'll get tea," Jahan called out.

We remained in an embrace, both afraid to let go in case we would never find each other again. We both thought the same thing: *I love you, I love you.*

I pulled away to whisper the words and then had to tell him, "Veer, Veer, I don't believe you're here, holding me, but you shouldn't have come. It's dangerous if they find you here."

"I had to deliver my letter," he said and pulled out a creased envelope. "The one I was writing and meant to post if I could find a postbox in the Amazon." Out of another pocket he pulled a roll of dollar bills. "Your beard's driving me crazy, and that turban . . ." He swept it off my head and looked astonished. "I loved touching your hair, brushing it off your face . . ." He ran his hand over the cropped hair and opened it to the air.

"Noorzia," I said and took off his turban, his hair falling over his brow. "At least yours is still there." I brushed it back and kissed him. "Tell me what you wrote."

"That I love you . . . that I'll do whatever it takes to be with you . . . that there are nights I dream you're beside me . . ."

"I dream too . . . we're close and touching . . ." I touched his face. "We're not dreaming, are we? I'm not going to wake up and find myself in that dark room . . ."

"No, we're not. Even if we are, we're in the same dream and we'll wake together."

"How's Nargis?" I remembered to ask.

"She sends her love and her prayers for us."

We parted only when we heard Jahan pushing on the door. Veer led me to sit beside him on the divan, his hold tight on my hand in case I flew out the window. I drank the tea greedily, my throat parched from the fear an hour back and now with the love that swelled my tongue.

"How did you get here?" Jahan sat opposite, noticing our clutched fingers.

"I flew into Karachi. I still had a month left on my visa, and then I had my mujahedeen friend pick me up. He knows the passes through the mountains that only birds can see. And here I am." He leaned against the bolster. "Now tell me everything."

We took turns in our telling. He listened intently, turning from one to the other as we told our tale. When we fell silent, he sat up.

"We leave now, this moment." He started to stand in his hurry to get me out, pulling on me. "Jahan, I'll take her to Delhi, but before that I need to ask your permission, as her *mahram*, to marry your sister, Rukhsana."

"I give it," Jahan said and smiled. "But there is one condition."

"What's that?"

We both stopped, half risen, and I saw a calculating look in my brother's eyes that I'd not seen before.

"You're a good cricketer?" Jahan said quietly.

"I played a lot once, and I was good, but it's a long . . ." Veer stood up straight. "I know what you're going to ask. The answer is no. We have to get her out."

Jahan ignored him. "You must play for us. It's the only chance the team has of winning the matches and leaving."

"You come with us too. We'll cross the border in four . . . five hours."

"No," Jahan said firmly. "I cannot abandon my cousins, my family, for my own safety. It is against my honor."

Veer looked at me. "Honor! Is he crazy? He wants me to play in a match while you're being hunted by this Talib who wants to marry you?"

"Veer," Jahan added with such finality. "If you won't play, I will not give my permission."

"We'll marry without that."

Jahan glanced at me and then back to Veer. "Look at her face."

I knew what was in my eyes. Jahan was the only one of my family left and I would not marry Veer without my brother beside me on the wedding day. He would never forgive me and would never speak to me again if I went against his wishes. Losing my brother would throw a dark shadow over my love for Veer.

"Rukhsana . . ."

"I can't," I whispered.

"Veer, you are going to become part of my family." Jahan was the only calm one in the room. "If you marry Rukhsana. Here, family is all important, and if you want to belong you must play."

"This is blackmail," Veer said, still angry.

"No, this is Afghanistan," Jahan replied.

Veer sat down, looking from one of us to the other, puzzled, struggling to understand. He nodded his head. "I'll play."

"Then we'll win our matches." Jahan lost his solemnity and was a boy again, excited by his success.

"Listen, Jahan, there's no guarantee that just because I play you'll win the matches. Cricket is a very unpredictable game and I've played it many more times than either of you. One day you win, the next day something goes wrong and you lose. A catch is dropped, a batsman run out, a bowler is on a lucky streak."

"But with you, they have a better chance to win than without you. And you're playing for me too."

"Two blackmailers," he growled. "What kind of family am I marrying into?"

"One you'll love," I said and squeezed his hand.

"You told me there's a good fast bowler on their side," Veer said, coming to grips with his commitment. "How good? Young?"

"Both. I think he can bat well too."

Veer groaned. "Young, good, and I haven't touched a bat for years."

"But you never forget."

"Then, this being Afghanistan, can this Droon, Wahidi, fix the match? Cricket, like any other sport, is open to that."

"There'll be the International Cricket Council man watching the matches."

"Ah, to have such faith as you have in an Englishman," Veer said cynically and then focused his attention on Jahan. "Okay, here's the deal and I want to make sure you understand. I play and, win or lose, you give your permission to marry?"

"Yes, on my word."

"When you win, your team is sent to Pakistan and I will take Rukhsana with me and cross the border. And if you lose the first match, we leave Saturday night?"

"Yes. But we won't lose against the other team."

"Let's say you do." Veer was not to be distracted. "We leave, then what do you and the team do?"

"Jahan will come with us, of course," I said.

"No."

"Jahan, listen to Veer and me now."

"I can't leave just by myself. If we lose, the team must go with you. You have a car and a driver."

Veer hit his forehead with the palm of his hand. "Why not take the whole stadium? It's only an old Jeep—it won't seat twelve people. It can take another three or four, but not more without cracking an axle on those high-pass dirt tracks." Veer paused, looking at Jahan. "If you all want to leave, why play in these matches? We can go now. I brought the money and we can hire a minibus. I'll check with my driver, Youseff. He must know someone who'll make that run."

"We thought we had a smuggler, Juniad, but he's disappeared," I said and then had a scary thought. "They must have followed Jahan to Juniad and arrested him."

"I thought so too but didn't want to frighten you. You saw the police car outside, they will follow me when I leave. You and Babur can leave, as they'll think you're two mourners. But if I leave too, they'll believe I could lead them to Rukhsana. Mother's not here anymore and I'm the only way they have to find you."

"They'll follow you to the matches . . ."

"Yes," he said, waiting for Veer to continue.

". . . and if your team wins . . ." Veer looked to me too. "They won't let you on that flight on Sunday."

"I'll come home," he said quietly and simply. "And if we lose, take Rukhsana and my cousins out."

"Jahan, you can't do that," I said, my voice cracking in horror. "I won't let you."

"What's the alternative?" he asked gently. "You marry Wahidi? I won't give permission, and neither did Mother. You're my sister and I must get you out. You will marry Veer." He tried to smile. "And I'll be there for it. When you're safe in Delhi, you will send the money for me."

I saw Veer struggling to understand the implications of what we had said. He was more familiar with the noble savagery of tigers and cheetahs than the cruelty of men.

"And will they put a bullet in your head?" Veer asked quietly.

"Droon will send Jahan to Pul-e-Charkhi," I said, and even Veer winced at that name.

"They won't," Jahan said with what he thought was confidence. "Wahidi wouldn't allow that to happen to family."

"Jahan, you know who you are dealing with," I cried out. "They won't blink an eye. I can't let you do this."

"We must take you too," Veer said.

"You can't." Jahan was determined now. "I'm the one they're watching." He saw the tears in my eyes. "I'm a good liar, and they have to sleep sometime. I'll slip out and hide here or even in Mazar and let you know where I am." He rose. "I think you should leave. We'll meet tomorrow at the stadium. Babur will be there too."

"I should stay here," I said in panic. "I can't be seen in public as Babur."

"I can't leave you alone in the house," Jahan said. "They could come again, even bomb the house in revenge. At least with the team around you, you'll be safe and you'll be the twelfth man."

"I'll pick you both up," Veer said.

"No. I don't want your face to become familiar here. Meet us at the stadium."

We heard Abdul knock on the door and call out. Jahan faced Veer. They embraced, parted, placed their hands on their hearts, and Jahan went to see who had come.

"We can't let him do this, I can't let him sacrifice himself for us," I said and hugged Veer tightly, not wanting to let him go out into the night.

"You talk to Jahan, dissuade him; we must find a way to get him out too. If the team wins or loses, we both leave after the match and take Jahan with us." He thought a moment. "We can bribe the cops. It always works in India."

"It will work here too."

"I'll get Youseff to find another smuggler and we'll negotiate with the cops." Veer kissed me. "He's a brave kid, setting himself up as bait for you and your cousins."

Jahan came back into the room, closing the door softly. "Droon's outside."

THE MOURNER

EVEN THE SOUND OF HIS NAME SHOCKED MY heart, and I was sure he was outside, listening to us. He had heard every word.

"Rukhsana, go down, quickly," Jahan said, remaining composed. "I haven't opened the door, I saw him through the window. Veer . . . your turban." He waited until Veer replaced it and Jahan tugged it down to meet his eyebrows. He adjusted the tail so that half of it fell across Veer's face. "Don't look at him. We'll embrace at the door, you're a mourner, and you pass him."

I reached for Veer's hand and found his searching for mine too, as it had long ago.

"I love you, I'll come for you," he whispered as we went out together.

"I love you." I moved behind their backs and, even though the door was still closed, I felt Droon's eyes piercing the wood. I let go and darted for the stairs, not looking back, to vanish down into the darkness. But I didn't run to the room. I stayed in the well, pressed against the wall, within hearing. I heard the door open, a murmur— Jahan saying good-bye to Veer. I prayed Veer wouldn't respond.

"Come in, sir," Jahan said. "I will fetch tea to the *mardaana*."

"No, no, I won't stay long," Droon replied. "I came only to pay my condolences for your *maadar*. After all, we'll be family soon."

"You are most thoughtful," Jahan said quietly, even though I shivered at his arrogant presumption.

"Your sister has still not returned?"

"No. As you know, she is still in Mazar and not in this house or at the mosque. I managed to get through to her late today—the phones don't work well here—and she wept when she heard the news. She went immediately to pray outside the shrine of Hazrat Ali for my *maadar*'s soul and to beg forgiveness."

"You're a very clever boy." Droon's voice took on an edge of menace. "When will she return?"

"Sunday evening, if she can leave tomorrow morning, but as you know, the roads are bad and it could be later. They are also danger-ous. My father and my grandparents were killed on that road."

"Yes, I know. Tell me where she is staying in Mazar. I will send a message for her escort."

"I will write it down."

"No, tell me," said Droon, insistent.

"It would be better to write it . . ."

Mazar, like other cities and towns, including Kabul, did not have street names, apart from the main roads. A stranger asking for directions would be given landmarks to follow and decipher.

"Tell," Droon demanded, and in that insistence he also revealed that he was illiterate, unlike his half brother.

"Do you know Mazar?"

"Yes."

I doubted that—the Taliban government did not have full con-trol of the northern parts of the country. The Talib had killed a few thousand there when they took it, and Mazar was still an anti-Talib city.

"You know the Akbar business center, it's a new building half a mile west from the shrine, on the main road. There you turn right, and after three streets . . . no, four streets . . . you turn left. After the second street, you'll see a postbox. You pass that and you'll see a large red building. There is a lane opposite it and my uncle Koshan's house is the fourth one. It's a very old, large house built by my great-grandfather, and it has a large rosebush just inside the gate. You can't miss it."

To protect ourselves, we have polished the art of telling only half truths to our interrogators. Jahan had confidently given Droon just one misdirection, and he did sound convincing. The postbox was after the third street. Great-grandfather's house, built in 1901, also had a cellar with a short, narrow passage that led out into the back garden. As children we played in it and pretended that it led into another world.

"I will send a message to Mazar for my fighters to pick her up. Where is your cousin? He still lives here?"

"Yes. Babur went out to buy fresh naan." Jahan paused, having a thought. "You must stay and eat with us. It won't be much, as we are alone, but it will honor us greatly to have you—"

He had to extend our tradition of hospitality, *melmastia*, to every visitor, even to the enemy. I stopped breathing and I knew Jahan had too, as he waited for Droon's reply.

"I won't," Droon said, cutting him off harshly. "I'm informed there is a woman in the house."

"Dr. Hanifa, she looked—"

"I will see her," Droon snapped.

I heard Jahan move to the kitchen and then the scrape of a match. Droon sucked on the cigarette, exhaled, and a slight tendril of smoke drifted down to me. He moved stealthily along the corridor and stopped at the top step leading to the basement. I wanted to melt into the wall, because if he did reach the landing, he would see me. It was too late to run without him hearing.

The kitchen door opened and I smelled the dinner Dr. Hanifa was making. I was almost sick from the perfume of the meal; I hadn't eaten all day. Dr. Hanifa followed Jahan to Droon.

"Are you ill?" she asked in a belligerent tone. "I'm a woman's doctor and don't treat men."

"No, I'm not." I sensed Droon take a step back.

"Then why did you send for me and waste my time?"

She returned to the kitchen, grumbling to herself about "stupid men" and I felt even more faint from hunger. The front door opened for Droon to leave.

"You will be at the match tomorrow?" Jahan asked.

"No. Only Sunday." He was laughing as he pronounced his prediction for the match. "Your team will not win and you will not leave Kabul."

The door closed and I waited to hear the gate open and close too before I went upstairs. I had to talk to Jahan—my mind was on fire with his plan.

But Dr. Hanifa called out, "Rukhsana, Jahan, you must eat."

We went in and Jahan laid out our carpet and Dr. Hanifa set out the dishes—fried chicken in the center, along with mutton kebabs, *ashak* dumplings filled with yogurt and tomato sauce, naan, and steaming yellow rice. Jahan performed the rituals for us to wash our hands and then neither of us spoke as we ate, stuffing the food in our mouths, with Dr. Hanifa piling on more when our plates were empty. I felt a terrible loss, as the custom after a funeral was to have a dinner for all our relations and I felt I was once more betraying Mother. The day was so compressed that I couldn't believe she had died this morning, was buried, and that this was the first night for the rest of my life that she was not with us. And my happiness about Veer was tied to an anchor of guilt.

"I'm too tired to go home," Dr. Hanifa said when we finished.

"You can stay in our grandparents' room." I went to it and quickly made the bed. Even before I had finished she lay down with a tired sigh.

"I saw the man you love," she said when she saw the droop in my shoulders.

"How do you know he is the man?"

"Your mother told me," she said and, when she saw the surprise in my face, laughed. "We old women didn't just play cards and read to each other. We talked too. She was disappointed you didn't marry Shaheen, but when you told her about . . . Veer? . . . she decided to give her blessings. You do love him?"

"Very much. But what can I do with Wahidi and Droon watching and waiting?"

"Go away with him, quickly."

"I'm trying to."

I went to close the door and had to ask, "Did you love your husband?"

Hanifa smiled and shook her head. "I got used to him, and he got used to me. I did fall in love once in college. He was studying engineering, and then he had to marry a cousin. It's not only us women who have to obey our fathers. The men do too."

She fell asleep in an instant. Jahan was halfway up the stairs.

"Jahan, we have to talk. I can't let you do this."

"It's the only way. And I am very tired." He came down to me. "I was wondering what it is in you that these men see—Veer, Shaheen, Wahidi? You're my sister and I think you are beautiful, but you're not as beautiful as a Bollywood star like Aishwarya, yet these men fall in love with you. I don't know that feeling, as I've never fallen in love and don't understand its power. What do they see and feel that I can't because you're my sister? I think it's the way you speak, your passion for life, how you carry yourself, and the warmth of your easy laughter. Our cousins adore you. I'm telling you this because I know what you're thinking. You will not give yourself to Wahidi to save me now. If you do that, I will not speak to you again. Now go to bed."

We held each other, as I could not speak. I went up on tiptoe and kissed his forehead then watched him walk up slowly until he was out of sight. I went down to my cell, exhausted, but still thinking about how to get him out with us.

I couldn't sleep, knowing my dreams would be filled with Veer and the nightmares with Wahidi. I lit the candle I'd brought down with me; the light was a small shield against the blackness, and didn't flicker and dance in the stillness. I couldn't bear the thought of Jahan ending up in Pul-e-Charkhi because of me. I would live with that guilt all my life, and it would be far worse if he didn't survive. I had found Veer again and didn't want lose him. If our plans failed, I had to choose. Veer? Jahan? I knew Jahan meant what he'd said—he wouldn't speak to me ever again if I married Wahidi. Yet at least I'd know he was safe and alive somewhere in the world. I would serve Wahidi like a servant, serve him as a whore, serve him with his children, knowing that in this service Jahan and I would survive. I took my notepad and looked at it again. I wrote carefully in the candle's glow.

1. Marry Wahidi, if the plan doesn't work, to save Jahan.
2. Tell Veer.
3. Commit suicide. Hundreds of Afghan women kill themselves to escape the purgatory of their lives.

I removed my beard; I hated it now. It had become like a loathsome fungus on my face, sucking out my life, my identity, my very sex. I had put it on to amuse myself, and teach my cousins a game, and now it caged me. I had to escape it, one way or another.

THE DROPOUT

I woke, wretched with fear. It had been with me as I slept, dreaming now that Droon was killing Veer. He had to leave, at least then I'd know he too was safe and alive. I wanted to climb the stairs to Mother, lie beside her and ask her guidance. If only she could reach down from heaven and move us, like chess pieces, out of danger's way.

"Please, Maadar, look after us," I prayed. "Take us all away to safety. I thought last night of giving myself to Wahidi to save Jahan. I don't want to do that, it's against your wishes, so please guide me in these days ahead."

I didn't need to look in a mirror to note the dark circles under my eyes, but I tried to hide them with even darker makeup to match the rest of my face. The team assembled in the front hall had a funeral air. They were as immaculate as they could manage in their white *shalwars*, sneakers, and white *pakols* for their first match. I too was in white and feeling much worse, worrying that I would be picked out, even in a crowd. I would stay as close to my team as possible. Qubad had his arm in a sling.

"How is it?" I asked.

"Hurting." He removed his arm from the sling, flexed it, and slipped it back in. "And I had d-dizzy spells too—"

"Jahan told us we have a new player, Veer," Parwaaze impatiently cut in.

"Is he any good?" Namdar asked.

"Will he win the match?" Daud wanted to know.

"Can he get us out?" Atash demanded.

"He's a very good cricketer." I did exaggerate a bit about Veer's talent, never having seen him play. "He played for his university, but he can't win these games all by himself. You too are good players, and I know how you are feeling. It's in your faces. Don't think of Droon at all because then you'll try too hard and tense up. Stay calm. Just enjoy playing the game and you'll win."

It was a warm day, with a clear blue sky and a slight breeze to cool us. When we went out, the police car slowly followed us up the road. We didn't look back and, as usual, I remained in their center. They too were quiet and I didn't want to waste any words until we reached the stadium. Veer would have to guide them once they were on the field, and I believed that he would have the talent and the ability to inspire them. We caught a taxi at Karte Seh Wat, and when we craned our heads back, we saw the police car trailing us.

The first match was set to start at eleven and we reached the stadium by ten thirty to limber up and study the opposition. The stadium looked deserted when we stopped at the gate and got out. The police car pulled up behind and two bored-looking policemen climbed out to lean against it and light their cigarettes. They were poor men and I was certain they would accept a bribe to look the other way. There was also a battered olive green Jeep in the car park, and a tired-looking minibus parked beside it. It had a banner on its side that said AFGHAN STATE CRICKET TEAM. Veer, mopping his face with an old towel, hurried over to us trailed by his driver,

Youseff, thickset and gray bearded. Veer was looking only for me among the youths; seeing me in the center he gave that beautiful, joyful smile. I returned it through the wretched beard. Jahan stepped between us before we could even formally shake hands.

"Veer, I want you to meet the team."

With grave formality, Veer shook hands with each of them, touching his heart, as they also did when he let go, and I saw them eyeing him hopefully. They saw a tall man, supple still, with an easy smile and a balance in his movements that reassured them. He could play cricket; after all, he was an Indian and they all excelled at the game, like the Pakistanis.

He finally shook mine, squeezing it, and I wanted to keep holding it and not let go. But there were watchers, and when I did let go, he placed his hand against his heart and held it there longer than he had for the boys.

"I've been here since dawn, trying to get back into shape," he said, dabbing his face again. "And I was waiting for you, desperate to see you."

"I knew you'd be here, and even if we can't speak, I want to just look and look at you. You'll know what I am thinking from my eyes, if not from my lips."

I would not think of anything else. These might be the last, most precious hours of my life. I wanted so much to be with him, forever. I couldn't tell him now what I would have to do if our plan didn't work. I would just vanish, a coward who couldn't bear the pain of looking at his distraught face.

He managed to slip in beside me and our hands touched and held as the team entered the grounds. The policemen shuffled along behind Youseff and us. Jahan moved to Veer's other side.

"Did your driver find someone to take the team?"

"Yes. He has, but it's going to be expensive. More money than I have on me, but I figure I can talk Youseff into giving me credit.

The smuggler's ready anytime. If we lose today, we're all ready to move. Youseff will talk to the cops to sound them out. He's an expert in bribery."

He pointedly looked at Youseff, who was drifting toward the two policemen. We saw him greet them courteously, offer them cigarettes, and settle down beside them. Apart from them, there were no Talib fighters with AK-47s, lounging against Cruisers, or religious police playing with those electric cables and caressing their guns. The quiet was innocently peaceful.

There were three other teams already on the field. They stood, well separated, around the pitch. Standing apart from them were two official-looking men, one clutching a file, and in between them a tall *khaareji*. He wore a pale cream linen suit and an elegant straw hat a shade darker than his suit, a red-and-yellow-striped band around the brim. His tie was the same pattern as the hatband.

"He's a member of the Marylebone Cricket Club," Veer muttered. "Not that anyone here will recognize that tie."

We moved to also stand near the pitch, keeping our distance from the others. I had thought there would be a few more teams. We had a fair sprinkling of spectators and we spotted our other cousins and friends, around fifteen to twenty of them, sitting together. The team waved and they returned the wave. The fans and supporters of the other teams were scattered around. I guessed that all in all we had a hundred or more spectators. If this had been a football match, the stadium would be packed; it was still the only other sport, and entertainment, permitted in this deprived country.

One of the officials approached us first. He opened a file, plucked a pen from his top pocket, and was poised to write.

"Your team name?"

"Taliban Cricket Club," Parwaaze announced.

"Player names?" The official wrote our names, including Babur, without reacting to the team's name. Parwaaze changed Veer's name to Salar to blend in with the others.

The official moved on to the others. The state team was the Afghan State Cricket Team. Without doubt, they were the smartest among us. They wore new white trousers, shirts buttoned to their wrists, white *pakols* on their heads, and new sneakers, while the others, like us, were in our white *shalwars* and ordinary shoes. Only some of us had sneakers.

Azlam's team was the Azlam Cricket Club and he was one player short. Deliberately, he removed the *Rules of Cricket* book from his pocket and waved it at Parwaaze. The fourth team was the Karta-i-Aryana Cricket Club, named after their suburb. They looked around them with uncertainty, as if not sure why they stood in the middle of a football field beside a bare strip of pitch.

The official, a clerk in the ministry, an elderly man, addressed us, saying, "The man who has the keys to the dressing rooms hasn't come today." He pointed to the tunnel leading into the stadium's interior. "He may come tomorrow. Today, you change outside. I have noted your team names and the observer will pick which teams play against each other." He looked down at his file. "Each side has ten overs." He looked back to us, hoping we understood, even if he did not, that mysterious sentence. "In tomorrow's final match each side has fifteen overs. The match starts at two P.M."

"Let's look at this pitch," Veer said to Parwaaze, and we moved together to stand beside it and pace its length.

It was sixty-six feet long and ten feet wide, three new wickets were planted at both ends, and there were white chalk lines for the batting and bowling marks.

"What do you think?" he asked me.

"It will wear quickly since it's not been rolled well," I said and looked to Captain Parwaaze. "What will you do?"

"Try to bat first," he said, and checked with Veer, who nodded. "The ball will bounce badly."

The Englishman too came to inspect the pitch with the other official by his side, a younger man, neatly dressed in a blue *shalwar*, a black waistcoat, and a black turban. The Englishman looked at ease in these surroundings, as only one of an imperial race, whose blood had soaked this land more than a century ago, could. His confidence seemed to announce that he knew us from our past history and belonged here. He crouched and poked a knowledgeable finger into the pitch and looked back at his companion.

"It's going to break up," he also pronounced. "We must send you one of our experts to help you lay a proper pitch. You'll have to dig this up, then lay down gravel, then layers of clay, and sow good grass to bind it. I'm sure we can provide that too. And lots of water until the grass has grown, then mown to its correct length, and . . ."

His companion nodded to each word and murmured, "Yes, yes," as if he understood what the man was talking about, and looked doubtful that this would ever happen.

The Englishman stood and looked at us as we edged nearer. "My name is Phillip Markwick and I've been sent by the International Cricket Council as an observer. We at the ICC are delighted that your government has applied for an associate membership. We will do everything possible to encourage cricket here, and we welcome every new nation that wants to learn this splendid game into the growing family of cricket-playing countries. Cricket today is played in more than eighty-nine countries, even in the United States of America." He stopped to turn to his companion. "Do they understand English?"

The other official looked across and saw mostly blank faces. "No."

"Pity, I thought they would have," Markwick complained. "They do in India and Pakistan. Now please translate what I am saying." Markwick turned back to us and began again. "My name is . . ."

The translation was hesitant and the interpreter stumbled from the start over Markwick's name and many more words, finally giving us just the gist of the speech.

"As you all know," Markwick continued when the interpreter stopped. "Your country is known as the graveyard of empires." He laughed and drew smiles from the teams, though not all understood since the translator waited. "My great-grandfather is here in one of your graveyards, the British Cemetery in Kabul. A tribesman assassinated him in 1867. So, as you see, my family, among many other English ones, does have a long relationship with Afghanistan."

"I knew he'd say that," I whispered to Veer.

"Well, I won't keep you from the game any longer." Markwick went among us, shaking all our hands, murmuring his "good lucks." "I'll leave the ministry person to schedule the play." He returned to his interpreter and we overheard him say, "I must visit my great-grandfather's grave before I leave the country."

"It will be arranged for you tomorrow, sir."

The elderly official had written down the team names on strips of paper, folded them neatly, and jumbled them in his cupped palms. He approached Markwick and made his offering. Markwick picked out a slip, opened it, frowned, and passed it to his interpreter. It was written in Pashtu.

"The Afghan State Cricket Team will play the first match against . . ."

He waited for Markwick to draw another slip, and we held our breaths. We didn't want to play them in the preliminary nor did the other two teams.

I didn't believe the state team would be better, except for their ringer. Through the grapevine we knew his name was Wasim Khan, a nephew of their coach, Imran, and he played for his college in Rawalpindi. He stood, relaxed, a cricket ball in his hand, looking over the opposition with a satisfied air.

They were no competition for him, until he scanned us. He passed over Veer, and then returned to settle on him. Veer sensed someone watching and turned to see Wasim; a smile lifted both their mouths as they recognized each other's nationalities and knew it would be another historical confrontation in this game between India and Pakistan. We would be spectators in their conflict.

Markwick was pulling out another slip and passing it on.

" . . . the Karta-i-Aryana Cricket Club," the official announced. "These two teams will play first. The Taliban Cricket Club will play the Azlam Cricket Club following this match."

"Now we can see how the Afghan state team plays," Veer said to Parwaaze, who was still smiling in relief that we had to play his old nemesis Azlam.

"We must beat Azlam," he insisted. "We must thrash him."

Markwick waited for the two playing captains to stand in front of him, and then took a coin out of his pocket.

"Call," he said, ready to toss it, and waited for the interpreter to explain this little ritual to start the match.

The Afghan State Cricket Team won the toss and decided to bat first.

"Who'll be the umpire with me?" Markwick asked no one in particular but from his tone demanded an answer.

The Afghan team coach, in his tracksuit, stepped forward, and the two men walked out to the pitch to await the start of play. We expected, in the spirit of the game, the coach would be impartial in his judgments.

Wasim and his teammates strode out, impressive in their clothes and equipment. We settled in the lowest stand, Veer next to me, our knees touching, to watch the match.

"I still can't believe you're beside me," he whispered.

"I always was, even when we were apart."

His presence, and a sense of foreboding, distracted me.

Our plans might not work and we will all be caught, including Veer.

I pushed the thought to the back of my mind. Here was the simple pleasure of watching a game of cricket with Veer once more, and secretly wishing I was playing too.

The Karta team was in shambles, trying to set their fielders in the right positions, changing their minds even before they bowled the first ball. It didn't even bounce and Wasim took a step forward and hit it into the stands.

"Oh, good shot," Markwick said and clapped; though he was supposed to be the neutral umpire, he wanted to encourage the players. In cricket it was the normal, courteous way of showing a spectator's appreciation. He was the only one to do it in the stadium but didn't appear to notice the silence. He did it whenever he thought a player needed praise.

Those in the stands shouted, "*Khub, khub,*" and waved their arms to show their approval. I thought that in a packed stadium in a football match there would be an unnerving hush after someone scored a goal. Apart from shouts of "*Khub, gol*" and a lot of hand waving and sad sighs from the losing fans, the matches were watched in silence.

We had to get Jahan out, the cops must take the bribe.

Wasim hit the other five balls in the over too. But the other batsman wasn't so confident, and trying to imitate Wasim hit a catch and was out, much to the delight of the fielding side.

"Wasim's good," Namdar said, looking dejected as once more Wasim hit the ball with ease.

"That's because the bowling's bad," I said to cheer him up. "We have Veer, and Omaid is going to be our secret weapon."

The ten overs passed quickly. Sadly, the Karta team couldn't check the runs, and the Afghan team, Wasim mostly, scored seventy-five runs. It didn't take Wasim long to run through the Karta batting with his bowling, even if only two overs by the rules, he took six wickets. They were out for fifteen runs.

"He bowls a very good line," Veer said. "Straight at the wicket."

Parwaaze and Azlam looked belligerently at each other when Markwick tossed the coin. Azlam called and won and, taking his cue from the Afghan side, decided to bat first. But before he left, he slid the *Rules of Cricket* book out of his *shalwar* and held it out like a gift to Markwick. Droon had given him our confiscated book.

"Please . . . please," he said, fawning, half in obeisance.

"*The Rules of Cricket*, published by my club." Markwick was delighted and took it.

Azlam spoke to the interpreter. "I want him to sign the book for me. I will treasure it all my life with his name in it."

"He's an expert in bribery too," Veer said sardonically.

"Of course I will," Markwick said when he was told, and signed it with a flourish, saying to Azlam, "With the best wishes from the MCC to Azlam."

I remained close by Qubad, sitting on the grass, as our team went to field. Wasim stood a few feet away, waiting to see Veer play. Parwaaze consulted with Veer in placing his fielders. They had decided to have Namdar bowl first.

I cannot leave Jahan behind here, they will kill or imprison him.

Azlam and his partner went in. In the way he prepared himself, it was obvious Azlam had not read the cricket book. Just possessing it, and depriving Parwaaze of it, was his only strategy. He held the bat like a club; he was going to hit the ball as hard as he could. Namdar ran up to bowl and Azlam did connect; though the ball didn't reach the stands, they made two runs.

With his next ball Namdar hit Azlam's wicket, and both he and Parwaaze jumped high in joy. Namdar took another two wickets, and I was so proud of him. In three weeks, he was now an accurate bowler, bouncing the ball in the right place. Veer came on to bowl at a medium pace. I thought that in all the years in Delhi I had never seen him play and here he was in Ghazi Stadium. His first was wide and he windmilled his right arm to loosen up. His next was straighter and bounced high. With his third one, he hit the wicket.

Qubad and I shouted, "Good, good," waved, and followed every ball with "Stop the run," "Catch the ball," "Good, good."

When we heard the call for prayer, the game stopped and everyone on the field, and in the stadium, performed *namaaz*. Veer was taken by surprise and stayed standing until I gestured for him to kneel and he did so quickly. Markwick remained the lone upright figure, waiting patiently for prayers to finish. Everyone stood when *namaaz* was over and continued playing.

However, after every over bowled, the team would gather in a tight circle to talk. It was normal in cricket to discuss strategy, but these conferences didn't seem to be about the match, as they frequently looked at the dozing policemen or else surrounded Jahan. I wondered what they discussed. When they broke up, I signaled for Jahan to come over but he ignored me.

I will insist we marry only after Jahan is safe and after the forty days of mourning for my mother.

Hoshang, as wicketkeeper, caught two catches from nicked balls and danced with delight. Azlam's team managed to score twenty-five runs, and my Omaid got three wickets, much to his joy.

When our turn came to bat, Jahan and Parwaaze went to the pitch. At first, they played cautiously, but when they soon saw that Azlam's team didn't have any good bowlers, quickly began to hit the ball hard. Parwaaze was out first, with our score on fifteen, when Veer went to join Jahan. Veer had a stylish technique and hit the ball with ease. We scored twenty-seven runs and won.

Jahan will leave then, and will never see my face again.

Markwick congratulated the two winning teams, consoled the losers and told them not to give up playing this great game.

Azlam stared furiously at a sweetly smiling Parwaaze. For a moment, I thought he would stick out his tongue.

"Be careful," Bilal whispered. "He hates you now."

"He always has."

Then Markwick gave another speech on bringing cricket to the country and said that he would see us tomorrow for the final. He was escorted out to a waiting car and we were left to celebrate our first victory with our fans, other cousins, and their friends, who crowded around us.

"You'll be in Pakistan tomorrow night . . . don't forget us . . . well played," they were saying as they patted everyone, including Qubad and me, on the back.

We moved toward the exit, and the two policemen woke from their long afternoon siestas to trail us. They looked for Jahan among us and when they saw him, relaxed. Youseff fell in beside Veer, and spoke softly.

"Youseff says it won't be a problem tomorrow," Veer told me. "They both need money, but he hasn't made an offer. They're on duty tomorrow too. And the smuggler will pick up the team from your house tomorrow morning in his minibus."

The team, in unison, slowed down, leaving a widening gap between our fans and the other spectators trickling out of the stadium.

"We can't leave Jahan behind," Parwaaze said in a steady voice. "If he has to stay, we all stay. We discussed and agreed on that when we were fielding." He looked at the others and had affirmative nods from them all.

"Then you'll all go to Pul—" I started.

"Wait," Veer broke in. "Parwaaze and the team are going to talk to the cousins and friends who were in the stands today. They'll come tomorrow and they will dress in white *shalwars*, and sneakers, if they have them. But they'll wear black *pakols* or *lungees*, with *hijabs*."

"Like today, they'll come onto the field after the game," Royan said, taking it up.

"They'll carry white *pakols* too to wear and put them on when we're ready. Twelve of them will then take our place in the smuggler's minibus," Namdar said, eyes glistening with the risk.

"The cops will follow the minibus back to Karte Seh," Bilal continued.

"We hide in the tunnel until they've gone," Veer said. "When it's clear, we take the Jeep to the airport when we win. If we lose we take it for the border and hope it won't smash an axle with the load."

"But they'll be looking for Jahan," I said sharply.

"Yes, they will be looking for me," Jahan said. "I'll get into the bus first so they can see me inside, and then when all the cousins start crowding in, I'll slip out the back door of the bus. We'll have our friends surrounding it to cheer the team, and I will then mix with them. The bus drives off and the cops follow it. And I'll join you."

"What about the bribes?" I was determined to puncture their dreams.

"They'll be paid," Veer said. "Then they'll swear he was on the bus."

"Have you got another plan then?" Atash asked, querulous.

They looked at me expectantly.

"No," I said. It had to work to save us all.

"We're going to talk to our cousins and our friends this evening," Parwaaze said.

"Will they agree?" I asked.

"To save Jahan, why not?" Qubad said. "We're family."

"They can always say they didn't know Jahan wasn't on the bus," Omaid said quietly.

We moved to join the crowd as it drifted to the main road. I lifted Veer's hand to my mouth and kissed it quickly, caressing his hand against my bearded cheek.

"Are you comfortable where you're staying?" I asked in a normal voice, a polite inquiry, not wanting to think about tomorrow and possibly my last day with him.

"A cheap guesthouse Youseff knows. I've stayed in worse."

"I wish you were staying with us, close to me."

"It won't be long before we'll be together always. No more good-byes." He quickly kissed my hand. "Be ready to leave tomorrow, and we will take Jahan with us."

It was dusk by the time we reached home in another taxi and the police car slid into its usual position, across the road. The two men settled back in their seats to continue sleeping once they saw Jahan and me enter the compound and the gate close behind us.

Dr. Hanifa, who had decided to stay and help with our final preparations for escape, had surpassed herself and we immediately sat down to eat. We regaled her with stories of the match, Markwick, and our winning the game. She didn't understand a word about cricket but knew we now had a chance to escape the country if we won.

"Will it work?" I asked Jahan after Dr. Hanifa had gone to bed in Grandfather's room.

"It has to. What else? I know I sounded brave saying I'd stay behind, but I want to be out too, and not face Droon alone."

"I don't want you to either. I couldn't live knowing you were in prison or—"

Abdul interrupted us from the front step, calling, "Parwaaze and the other cousins are here."

The team shuffled in and we closed the door.

"We've spoken to our cousins and their friends," Parwaaze announced. "They will do what we ask to help Jahan."

Jahan clapped his hands, bringing smiles to all our faces. Now he would just have to slip off the bus and join us. But my cousins lingered in the hall, watching me, watching Babur. They turned to Parwaaze, nodding their heads like puppets.

"What is it?" I asked.

Parwaaze looked both embarrassed and pleading at the same time. "Hoshang won't be playing tomorrow. Father said if the team wins and we go to Pakistan, he cannot lose both his sons. One son must stay in Kabul to look after the business and care for the family should anything happen to him. As Hoshang is the older son, he has to stay."

"But he loved being behind the wickets!"

"He's very disappointed. But Father is right. One of us must stay home. He can't lose both of us."

"Then you'll have to play with one of the others dressed like us."

"But we have to win," Omaid said quietly.

"We can't risk losing the game by having someone who doesn't know how to play," Daud echoed.

Omaid stepped forward. "We want you to play in place of Hoshang."

"I can't," I answered immediately. "They'll see I'm a woman very quickly on the field and arrest me."

"No, they won't," Nazir said. "Hoshang was our wicketkeeper. You'll be in the center of the field, behind the wickets the whole time when we're fielding and not anywhere near the stands."

"And you don't have to run for the ball," Royan said.

"You bat last," Parwaaze added quickly. "If we win before you bat, then you won't have to be on the field."

"You're placing yourselves in great danger, and me, and Veer, by asking me to play," I warned. But the chance to help them win and get Jahan to safety was percolating through my mind, eroding my reluctance.

"You must," Qubad said in a no-argument tone. "I'll be twelfth man."

They were waiting expectantly, their eyes pleading with me to agree. They were so hungry to win and escape and I couldn't deny them. It was a risk I had to take. "I'll play."

They clapped and smiles lit up their faces.

"You have played wicketkeeper?" Royan asked as they moved to leave.

"Many times," I said cheerfully, although I'd done that only twice when Lakshmi, our college wicketkeeper, had fallen ill. It was a great position—the wicketkeeper was constantly a part of the action, and I could help the bowler decide which ball to send down.

I felt a surge of adrenaline at the thought of playing the game again, and not just teaching it. I went down to my stuffy room, thinking about the game, strategizing it, knowing I would be playing a game I loved, with a man I loved.

THE GREAT GAME

As was our habit now, when we woke, Jahan and I went up to the roof to check the street.

We expected to see the police car, but instead we saw a Land Cruiser with two Talib fighters, AK-47s cradled in their arms, smoking and waiting for us to leave. How would Jahan escape them? A battered pale blue minibus pulled up in front of it and they went to the driver to talk to him. We waited, holding our breaths. Would the driver back off and drive away? The chat was brief and the fighters returned to the Land Cruiser. The driver of the minibus slid back in his seat to nap.

"What do we do?" I panicked and pulled back from the edge.

"We'll have to talk to the others. It might not work with the Talibs."

"They take bribes too," I said, almost hopefully.

"Youseff will have to see."

Jahan turned me around and held my shoulders, looking into my eyes.

"Whatever happens now, you will go with Veer. Do you understand that?" He shook me as if I was asleep. "Promise me that."

"I will," I said.

"No, you must promise, otherwise I won't speak to you. Ever."

"Promise," I said. I was near tears. "But what about you?"

"I can look after myself," he said. "And look after you too. So don't break your promise to me."

"I won't."

"We must go and play the game," he said after a long study of my face.

We had a morning to take our minds off the dread haunting us, and we went to the basement to practice. Although the light was gloomy, we didn't want to play in the garden, as the Talibs would hear bat against ball and want to find out what we were doing.

I remembered that first time I'd thrown the ball to Jahan, so long ago it seemed, and now when I did, he played it expertly. I threw it slow, then faster, as we both thought more of facing Wasim in the match, and we varied the bounce. We took turns batting and throwing the ball, correcting each other. If I was to bat, I needed more practice, as all I had done for three weeks was coach, and not play the game. I focused on every ball, remembering my old days and also how Veer had played yesterday. Footwork, straight bat, defense, attack.

We only stopped when Dr. Hanifa called down to us for lunch.

After lunch, I dressed in my crisp white pants with the pride of a matador and slipped on the white *shalwar*. Then, with meticulous care, I thickened my brows with the pencil and then darkened my skin with the cream. I ran a comb through my short hair, thinking of Noorzia. Had she reached safety? Was she alive? Had Fatima reached Tehran? I had not heard, even from Fatima, to say they had found safety somewhere. Were they . . . ? I could drive myself mad with the unanswered questions.

I focused on the present and lightly rubbed a drop of oil over my beard, giving it the glow of healthy life, and affixed the Velcro strips to my face. I gave the beard a slight tug; it held. I scrutinized the young man looking back at me, avoiding the troubled eyes and only studying the skin, the eyebrows, the mouth. I chewed on my lower lip; it looked pouty, feminine; I could be gay, and this was always acceptable to the Talib. They screwed boys, *bacha bareashs*, beardless boys, on Thursdays and prayed for forgiveness of their sins at Friday prayers. Now, crowning myself, I settled the white *pakol* on my head and pressed it down so that it slid to rest just above my eyebrows. I thought my glasses gave me a more scholarly look, more solemn, a madrassa student possibly filled with piety. I shrugged into my coat, and wrapped the shawl around my shoulders to mask half my face. This was the last time I would be Babur.

I went to Mother's room. Pale streaks of light filtered in to stripe the neatly made bed. I had not plumped the pillows, wanting the indentation of her beautiful head to remain there forever. She had just gone away on a short journey and would be back soon; this was how I still thought of her. I had cleared away all the medications, opened the windows, and now the air smelled of her favorite perfume. I knelt by the bed and performed my *namaaz*, and told her I was leaving and prayed for her guidance on this dangerous journey. I rose, locked the door, the click a final sound in the silence, and went down to the basement. I reformatted the hard drive on my laptop, instantly erasing my past, and tucked Veer's letters deep into my *shalwar* pocket.

My final pilgrimage was to Father's study to remove what was left of my depleted inheritance—emerald and ruby earrings and a gold necklace—from the safe, and tucked them into another pocket. I found our passports in the top drawer and caressed his desk for the last time. I locked this door too and joined Jahan.

Dr. Hanifa was waiting for us. "This is the day you will both leave. Don't return until the Talib lose power. I know that day will come."

We both embraced her and I couldn't help my tears. Without her, I could not have carried the terrible burden of my mother's illness. *Khoda haafez*.

The team waited for us in the front hall, as immaculate as they could manage in their white *shalwars*, sneakers, and white *pakols*. I was proud that they had grown in such confidence. They would walk out onto the field and play cricket the very best they could, and I prayed we would win. I had to help them win, whatever happened to me after the game, and I had to see their triumphant faces.

It might be my final appearance in the open air before I was caged like a bird, a cover draped over my bars so that I could not see the light and could no longer sing. There would be Droon and Wahidi, of course, prowling the boundary, Markwick in his immaculate suit. Would the press be there to report on our team's achievement and to protect us at the end when we won? I had, at least, left a small legacy behind me.

Parwaaze had the *Kabul Daily* and I read the small boxed item.

The Afghan State Cricket Team (75) beat the Karta-i-Aryana Cricket Club (15) in the first preliminary match of the tournament. The Taliban Cricket Club (27) beat the Azlam Cricket Club (25). All the teams played fine cricket. The final match between the two winning teams will be played today at 2 P.M. in Ghazi Stadium.

It was the best Yasir could report on a game he didn't know at all.

"You saw the Talibs outside?" Jahan said.

"Yes." The team sighed in desperation.

"We still have to stick to our plan of getting you out," Parwaaze said, trying to reassure them.

"We have said our good-byes to our families too," Namdar said sadly.

"We'll miss them, but we'll return when the Talib have gone," Royan added.

"We have our passports and money," Qubad said

I slipped in to walk in their center when we left, and at the gate, Jahan and I spoke softly to Abdul.

"We might be away for some time. Look after the house."

"I will be here when you return one day," he said wisely, not his usual inquisitive self. "Let the doctor know if you're safe and she will tell me. I will pray for you."

Jahan gave him the keys to our front door. "Two of our cousins may come to stay the night, let them in."

The Talib fighters, young Pakistanis with hardened faces, watched us climb into the bus and followed it. I wasn't sure whether they had looked specifically for Jahan.

The bodywork rattled over every bump, but the engine sounded fine tuned. Jahan and Bilal checked the emergency exit at the back of the bus. It was stuck, but a heave opened it, and they closed it again. The driver, a young man in his midtwenties, wearing a blue *shalwar* and a black turban, watched in the mirror.

"What did they ask you?" Parwaaze asked him.

"Why I was here," the driver said. "I told them I was hired to take some people to Ghazi Stadium." He swung the wheel to avoid a crater and we clung to the plastic seats. "Nothing more. Why are they watching you all?"

"To make sure we reach the stadium safely," Royan said.

"They counted you as you got in and they will count you on the way back."

"We know. They frighten you?" Parwaaze asked.

"Only a fool isn't frightened of them." He watched us for a long moment before continuing with a friendly smile. "But like all men they have needs, and they're no different from us. How else can we pass their checkposts without satisfying them?" He rubbed a forefinger against his thumb.

The weather was gloomy, and as we moved, a dust storm blew through the windows and we covered our faces, trying not to breathe. When it passed, the air was a dusty dun color and it would take time for that to settle. The air was still murky when we reached the stadium. A few makeshift stalls were setting up to sell kebabs, naan, fresh fruits, and plastic toys.

The Jeep was there already. Our bus parked beside it and the Land Cruiser stopped some distance away. The fighters climbed out with their weapons and followed us into the stadium.

Veer was doing his stretching exercises and came toward us, looking for me, our eyes meeting, and mouthing our hellos.

Our fans were already in their places, twelve of the thirty or more of them dressed in exactly the same way we were. Among them was Hoshang, who gave us a sad wave. There were twice the number of spectators as yesterday in the stands and more were trickling in. Fathers were bringing their sons, but not their daughters, to learn the game. I recognized Yasir sitting by himself, smoking, looking bored. I wished I could go over and say good-bye. With the increasing numbers, five religious policemen also menacingly drifted in to monitor behavior.

Parwaaze moved toward our fans, and the team started to follow, but he gestured them to stay, as he didn't want the fighters to take notice of the matching clothes. He spoke to them and I saw them nodding and glancing toward the fighters, who settled themselves a few rows higher up.

Youseff ambled up the tiers to greet them as they laid their guns down at their feet, and he sat heavily. He offered them the first gift, cigarettes, and each took one and he lit them.

A groundsman, almost bent double with age and a gray beard

that flowed down his chest, shuffled over to us studying a scrap of paper in his hand. He pointed to the tunnel under the main stand leading out to the field. "You are in dressing room two."

"Who is in number one?" Bilal asked.

"The state team," he snapped. "You can bathe in room number four, room three is for the state team, and don't waste the water. Don't leave your dirt in there for me to clean up when I come tomorrow."

Our dressing room was spartan and gloomy, with a barred window filtering in dirty sunlight, and smelled of stale sweat. Two benches lined the opposite walls and above them, at head height, was a series of nails for the team to hang their clothes. We had no clothes to change into or out of and dumped our shabby cricket equipment in the center. Veer looked relaxed—he was used to such rooms from his cricketing days—while the others looked around as if expecting a booby trap.

"Babur will be playing, as my brother can't," Parwaaze told him.

"She . . . he is, that's fantastic," he said, grinning across at me. Then a quick frown. "It'll be dangerous for her."

"I'll be the wicketkeeper," I said.

"That's a great idea." The grin returned.

We heard the voices and clatter of the state team. Two of us stuck our heads out as they went into their room. Each one was carrying his new kit case, along with a bulging blue plastic bag. They looked very confident and didn't even glance at us as they went in. We counted thirteen, as they even had two reserve players who would watch from the sidelines like Qubad. They closed their door to change.

We went out together, with me in the center. There was a key in the door and Parwaaze locked our room and pocketed the key. Room numbers 3 and 4 were opposite our rooms and Qubad unlocked the doors for us to peek into. They were alike, with eleven taps and eleven buckets for us to wash ourselves with after the match. The small windows were barred and didn't even allow in a patch of light. He locked the doors again.

The air was clearing as the dust drifted away. Parwaaze and Veer led the way to the center of the football field to study the patchy, naan-colored surface, looking for cracks and bumps along it. The state team emerged out of the tunnel, immaculate in their cream trousers, cream long-sleeved shirts, new boots, and green caps. Their portly coach strode the length of the pitch, stopping here and there to press a thumb down on the hard earth. It hadn't changed since yesterday, as no one had rolled it. It was scuffed from the bouncing balls and the footmarks of the bowlers. I remained in the center, and, as if I were the sun, my cousins circled to keep me constantly there.

A black Nissan drove to the edge of the field, followed by a Land Cruiser with two Talib gunmen in the back. Markwick, hatless, his hair the color of river sand, was the first to step out. He capped his head with the same hat and wore the same suit, now slightly rumpled, that he'd worn yesterday. His shirt today was pale blue. Wahidi climbed out the other side, and the interpreter from the front passenger seat. The three came together and strolled toward us.

I backed away, as if there were an invisible force pushing me. Markwick was a head taller than Wahidi and they talked through the interpreter. Droon was still in the Land Cruiser and hurried to catch up with them. Wahidi introduced him to Markwick and the Englishman shook hands, smiling, with a man I truly hated.

And, even as they approached, Droon and Wahidi seemed to step into our present time, accompanied incongruously by a man they opposed. The two worlds lay, parallel, on this cricket field and the Taliban could move easily between them, not even conscious that they were doing it. But I could not move from mine to theirs.

My heart, mind, and body were rooted deeply in the present and I would wither and die in their medieval fantasy.

"Good afternoon," Markwick called out to us when he stopped at the edge of the pitch. Wahidi and Droon continued on, crossing it, and Markwick winced at this disrespect. "I am looking forward very much to watching this game and I know the better team will win. It's very generous of your government to send the winning team to Pakistan later today for further training, and I'm sure you'll return here to teach many others to play. I will strongly recommend to the ICC that Afghanistan should be accepted as an associate member when I return with my report."

I saw Droon look for Jahan, find him, and whisper to Wahidi. Then Droon gestured for Jahan to come across. Almost reluctantly, the team shuffled aside to allow a nervous Jahan out of our group. Namdar stepped in front of me in Jahan's place. Jahan reached them and looked so young and vulnerable against men whose profession was violence. Veer was still beside me.

"Which one's Wahidi?" he whispered.

"On the right," I replied. The two men I loved and the two men I feared on the same field.

"God, he's old and he's ugly," Veer said, disgusted. "I want to put a wicket through his heart, now."

"Don't move," I said, holding his hand tightly. "I've seen him shoot two people without blinking." When he glanced at me in surprise, I realized I had forgotten to tell him, blocking that horror from my mind.

With one mind, our team followed Jahan's every move as if we could protect him from any violence.

Wahidi took a step to Jahan, a foot away, to shake his hand, and they exchanged greetings, "*Salaam aleikum*," "*Waleikum salaam*."

"I am honored to meet you, my brother," Wahidi said.

Jahan took the hand, but, before he could let go, Wahidi drew him into a lover's embrace. "It is my honor, my . . . ," Jahan replied with little inflection and held himself stiffly, arms only half raised, not completing the embrace.

"I am very happy that you will consent to my marriage to your beautiful sister." Wahidi stepped back, releasing the embrace but holding the hand, as if Jahan would escape. He looked to Droon for confirmation, who nodded slyly. "Your sister is well?"

"Yes, well," Jahan managed. "She is in Mazar, returning very soon."

"We must talk about that." Droon's smile flickered like a serpent's tongue. He turned to his brother. "You must look after our guest while Jahan and I discuss this matter."

"We will come to pay our respects when she is home." Wahidi sounded soothing but there was an edge to his tone. "I wish to greet my future wife with all formality. She will make a good mother to my sons, who lost their mother recently. We have a beautiful house in Kabul in Wazir Akbar Khan and you must visit us often. Tomorrow, my brother will make the proposal and you will accept it."

Wahidi turned away to join Markwick. Droon remained until he was out of earshot.

"My men couldn't find your uncle's house," he said venomously. "You lied, and for that you will pay the price."

"I didn't lie," Jahan said with spirit, the team at his back. "I told you the exact directions. The Akbar business center, it's a new building half a mile west from the shrine, on the main road. There you turn right and after three streets . . . no, four streets . . . you turn left. After the third street, you'll see a postbox. You pass that and you'll see a large red building. There is a lane opposite it and my uncle Koshan's house is the fourth one. It's a very old, large house built by my great-grandfather and it has a large rosebush just inside the gate."

"You said the second street after the postbox."

"Third street, sir," Jahan insisted. "That was why I wanted to write it down."

"Where is she?" Droon demanded. "My brother wants to see her, I want to see her."

"She called this morning. Uncle has reached Baghlan and they will be here this evening, at the latest tomorrow morning. She will be here for our mother's third-day ceremony."

Droon couldn't control himself. He grabbed Jahan's *shalwar* front and lifted his other hand to slap him.

I started to raise my hand and took a step. I couldn't let him hit Jahan again.

"I—" was all that I could say. A hand clamped over my mouth, and Veer pulled my hand down.

"Stay quiet," Qubad hissed, and kept his hand over my mouth. The team pushed forward protectively.

Just then, Markwick came up behind Droon and Jahan.

"We're playing cricket," he said in the stern voice of a school-master, looking to Jahan and then to Droon. "We must start the game. It's half past two." He tapped his silver watch, not yet taking his eyes off Droon. "The light goes quickly here and I have a meeting after the match."

Qubad removed his hand from my mouth.

The interpreter stepped beside Droon and began to translate. He was dismissed with a flick of Droon's hand. Droon slowly released his grip on Jahan's shirt and stared at Markwick. We knew he would kill us for daring to interfere. Markwick was either brave or ignorant of the fact that he faced a murderous man with only a patina of piety. Markwick met Droon's malevolent stare with the slightest smile and Droon whirled away, his *shalwar* flapping.

"Are you okay?" Markwick asked Jahan.

Wisely, Jahan waited for the interpreter before nodding and stepping back to us.

"Captains," Markwick called.

He had the coin in one hand and in the other held a new, shiny cricket ball, his first and second fingers parallel to the white seam, circling the red ball like an equator, the reflexive grip of a fast bowler.

The coin spun and fell. Parwaaze called heads, and grinned happily when he'd called right. It was an auspicious start.

The team formed a huddle, draping our arms over each other's shoulders, closing out the world. I squeezed between Veer and Jahan.

"We have to play our very best," Parwaaze said. "We have a hard fight ahead of us and I know we'll win it." He turned to peer at me, and the team also craned in my direction. "And without Babur we would not be here. We cannot let her down. She taught us the game, she showed us how to love it and that it's a fine game."

"This will be the first time a cricket tournament is played in our country," I whispered to them. "In a small way we're making history, and not a blood-stained one. So we cannot lose. We will show the Talib we'll fight them even on a cricket pitch and beat them with our cricket bats, and not guns."

We all remained silent, heads bowed, until Omaid whispered, "Win, win, win," and we all took up the chant.

We returned to our dressing room for Veer and Parwaaze to put on their pads and gloves.

"I'll open with Parwaaze," Veer said. "Babur should bat number three."

"I was going to bat last."

"No, come in early, and try to stay in as long as you can so you're not seen in the stands with the others."

"Watch out for the Pakistani bowler," I whispered.

"He'll only be allowed three overs," he said as he strapped on the homemade pads. "If he picks up quick wickets they'll bowl him out. I'll try to keep Parwaaze at the other end."

Markwick and the state team coach, as umpires again, were waiting for the two batsmen. I didn't have to wait long to join Veer, as Parwaaze was out for five runs bowled by Wasim. Veer had hit up thirty runs against the other bowler. Poor Parwaaze was crushed.

As we passed each other, Parwaaze whispered, "Walk straighter and don't sway so much."

I never felt more alone on this long walk to the pitch. I imagined with each step that Wahidi and Droon were staring at this youth, their sharp eyes penetrating the disguise, running onto the field to grab me and bundle me away.

Veer waited for me and noticed my nervousness.

"I love you" were his first words. "I can't wait to get that beard off your face."

"Don't distract me, I can't think of that now." Then I saw his disappointment. "I love you, and we have to focus."

"Just think you're playing with Nargis and the others and that no one is watching the match," he whispered. "You're a good batsman, I saw you play, so just focus on the ball. Be patient. I'll score the runs. So don't think about anything else. And don't call the runs. They'll hear your voice. I'll call."

"Is that all?" I walked beside him to the pitch, looking around at the fielding side.

"No. I love you."

The pitch was scruffy and already pockmarked from the balls landing on it. I took my guard and looked around at the field placements. It was a warm day, the quiet was soothing, and I remembered those days with my college team and the feeling of serenity each time I went out to bat. I felt as if I had found my natural place in the world, here on a cricket field, crouched over my bat and surrounded by hostile fielders. I had two balls to face from Wasim. They came fast, bouncing high, and I let them whistle past me.

It was a pleasure to watch Veer bat. He had great footwork, a good eye, and he timed the ball sweetly. He hit a high ball and I held my breath as a fielder positioned himself for the catch. It slipped through his fingers and I did a little jump for joy.

I went over to Veer and whispered, "Don't take too many chances."

"It's the only way to win." He laughed.

Between us, we put on another thirty runs, with me contributing ten and Veer reaching his fiftieth. Fortunately, their fielding wasn't good at all. They dropped a few more catches and let the ball through their legs. But then, going for a big hit, Veer was caught near the stands. The score was sixty-five runs for two wickets.

"That was reckless," I scolded him quietly.

"Sorry," he said meekly. "Now you have to keep as much of the batting as possible. If we can get to ninety-five or more, I'm sure we'll win."

Jahan joined me as the next batsman.

"Don't be afraid and don't think of Droon. Remember what I taught you—play with a straight bat and just block the balls. I'll try hitting them."

"I know," he said testily.

When he took his stance, I watched anxiously. I wanted him to score runs too. He played the first ball with textbook perfection and I relaxed. The next one, he surprised me by aiming it between the fielders and we ran for two.

"Good shot," I whispered as we passed, and he smiled.

Together we managed another ten runs before Jahan, like Veer, became too impetuous and hit a catch.

"I told you . . . ," I scolded gently.

"Sorry . . . ," he replied as he trudged off.

I took Veer's advice, facing as many balls as I could, but my team collapsed at the other end. Namdar came last and, despite my advice, took a swing and, to our surprise, hit three balls into the stands. When we finished our fifteen overs, we had scored ninety-five runs.

We huddled again before taking to the field, and Veer told us, "We have to field not just well but brilliantly. We must catch every high ball and stop the ground balls from reaching the boundaries. It's the only way we can win this game."

Veer opened the bowling against Wasim, and they were naturally wary of each other, knowing that they were the ringers. We worried about him, as he looked too professional, and he played with aggressive confidence, hitting the ball to all corners.

When we heard the call to prayer, we and the spectators, around four hundred or more now, knelt quickly and bowed our heads. I peered to Markwick, as upright as a lone flagpole, the breeze teasing his tie. In the distance was another upright figure, a religious policeman looking at Markwick. He finally decided to leave him be, and knelt too.

We continued playing after the prayers. After each boundary, we clustered to discuss how to get Wasim out. Each of us had an opinion and gave it: "Move a fielder here, move another there, change the bowler, bowl slow, bowl fast. He will beat us by himself if we can't get him out."

Bowling from the other end, Omaid was spinning the ball, and the batsman either hit a catch, which was caught, or else the ball hit their wicket. He was so delighted each time.

But Wasim remained belligerent, the runs creeping up to catch ours, and we thought he would win the match.

His team was nearing our total and a shadow of depression

settled over my team. They were giving up, and even I began to think we would lose.

In our next huddle to talk strategy, I told them, "We have to think of winning, we must not give up. In cricket, anything can happen suddenly and there's still time left. Don't give up."

Veer looked determined as he ran up to bowl at Wasim. The bounce was higher than he expected, he swung, and the ball nicked the edge of his bat. I dove full length to my right, hand stretched out, and the ball smacked into my glove. It was the best catch of my life, and I lay looking up at the pale gray sky, thinking we had a chance to win now.

I jumped up, holding the ball high. Wasim looked back, and saw me holding the ball. He hit the ground with his bat in disgust and stalked off.

Veer ran to embrace me, but I backed away just before his arms enclosed me. "Not here, you can't, it's against the law."

"Fantastic catch," he said quietly, dropping his arms, and the others crowded around to pat me on the back. In the stands, our fans stood up and waved excitedly and called out, "Good, good."

We were so relieved at seeing Wasim go out, but he had brought his team near victory. Finally, we picked up the last wicket when they were at ninety-three runs.

"We won, we won, we won!" we shouted, jumping up and down.

It was nearing six thirty and dusk was sweeping into the stadium.

"We'll be going to Pakistan," Parwaaze said. "Thanks to you . . . Babur." Each one in turn repeated his words as they patted my shoulder tenderly.

Then we sobered. We had to include Jahan, who stood apart, worry on his face, looking toward the stands and the two Talib gunmen, now rising and stretching. We couldn't see Youseff.

Markwick, accompanied by Wahidi, strolled toward us, followed by minions and the interpreter.

"That was a very exciting game," Markwick said and waited for the translation. "You all played your hearts out, and I know cricket will take root now in Afghanistan." He turned to us. "You must return from Pakistan and teach as many boys as you can to play." He paused a beat. "We would also like very much to encourage Afghan women to play the game, as you know women's cricket is played in most countries too." This line, we noticed, as did he too, wasn't translated.

He went to the Afghan state team first. We followed the strict etiquette of cricket and the two teams lined up to shake hands. He went down the line, pausing long enough to say a few words before Wasim. The state team looked sulky at losing. Then Markwick came to us and also shook each hand, and then stopped before Veer.

"You played well."

"Thank you, sir," Veer replied, not surprising Markwick with his English.

I was next to Veer, smaller, and Markwick bent slightly to take my hand. I still had on my gloves to hide my softer hands and he shook the glove.

"That was a match-winning catch, young man. If you hadn't made it, they would have won. Congratulations."

I nodded mutely.

Veer and Wasim shook hands, talked and laughed, knowing they were the ringers. It was in the nature of cricket that we held no animosity toward each other. Three dropped catches by the state team off Veer had swung the match. We had caught all our catches.

"You played well," Wasim said to me. "If we'd had your wicket early, we would have won."

I ducked my head in acknowledgment and said in a whisper, "Thank you," and then retreated to Jahan's side, avoiding any further conversation.

The teams waited, looking up to the covered stand where Wahidi and the other officials had watched the game. Droon strode by with his brother, talking to him.

I mustn't move to Wahidi until Droon has left his side. No, don't think of that. I promised Jahan.

As if that was a signal, all the spectators descended from the stands to flow onto the field. Our fans reached us, patting us on the back, laughing and smiling. For a moment, it looked as if we had twenty-six players on our side until they moved away to allow others to flow between us.

Yasir pushed his way through the crowd, a notebook in his hand, a cigarette in his mouth, to talk to the winning captain.

"Do you believe cricket will be popular in our country?"

"Yes, it is a very good game," Parwaaze said. "It encourages every player to express his own personality and to think for himself as he faces the opposition all alone on a field."

Yasir made his notes and peered through the gloom. "I know you." He took the cigarette out, dropped it, and crushed it into the pitch. He lowered his voice. "You were with Rukhsana at the announcement. Where is she?"

"Mazar."

Yasir winced. "She should be elsewhere." And then he went to interview the Afghan state team's captain.

Wahidi's fighters cleared a way for him through the crowd, now ten to fifteen deep, and everyone fell silent when they saw the guns. Wahidi beckoned Markwick to stand beside him.

Where's Droon? Stop thinking.

"We in the Islamic Emirate of Afghanistan are very proud that we have now introduced cricket to our country. As Mr. . . ."

He leaned to the interpreter, who whispered back.

"As Mr. Micwek has seen, the game was played in good and fair spirits. It is a game all our young men can enjoy, as it is appropriate in its dress and in its behavior. He will have observed the enthusiasm of our people too who enjoyed watching the matches. Our staff ensured the smooth functioning of the tournament. Quite rightly, as I announced three weeks ago, the team will be sent to Pakistan for further learning and they will return to teach other young men to play and occupy themselves with this sport."

When that was translated, Markwick clapped, startling Wahidi, Droon, and the others. The crowd shifted nervously.

Wahidi continued, sending a silencing glance to his religious policemen. "Mr. Observer, now that you have seen these games, I hope you will tell the International Cricket Council to accept our application to join it as an associate member."

"I will do so with all my heart," Markwick said. "Mr. Minister, I was most impressed with the efforts of your government, and the players, for conducting such a splendid tournament. I hope you will hold one every year to nurture more talent so that one day Afghanistan can send a team to play cricket across the world. I would also like to thank everyone for their kindness and their hospitality to me."

Wahidi gestured to a follower who stepped forward with a package. Wahidi opened it and reverently took out a beautiful pale gray *patoo*. He unfolded the wool shawl and draped it around Markwick's shoulders. The ends fell down to his knees.

Markwick caressed the texture. "It's beautiful. I'll treasure it always, and it will keep me warm on a long English winter's evening. Thank you."

Darkness now was moving swiftly through the crowd, having already hidden away the outer circles. There was a half-moon, hazy behind the clouds, barely lighting the stadium. Wahidi took Markwick's arm in a friendly way.

"We will always welcome you to our country," he said as he escorted him, still wearing the shawl, to the Nissan now waiting on the field.

The crowd opened a path for Wahidi and Markwick, and when they reached the open rear door of the car, Wahidi shook Markwick's hand and placed his own against his heart, half bowing. Markwick, now familiar with our greetings and good-byes, quickly copied the action before getting in. Wahidi watched the car move off, and Droon joined him as a Land Cruiser now pulled up to take Wahidi away.

Wahidi turned to face us.

"I must congratulate both teams for learning to play cricket," he announced. "One day soon, Afghanistan will play in international matches, so we must make sure that we have good players." He beamed at both teams, holding the letter of authorization, and turned to us. "But we cannot send you to Pakistan to improve the sport, as we have already arranged for the Afghan State Cricket Team to go there for training. It will be confusing for the Pakistan Cricket Board if we send a new team."

TWELVE LIVES

"Gafoor," Wahidi called, and the captain of the state team hurried forward. "Here is the permission for the team to leave this evening. All arrangements have been made for your team's training in Pakistan." He addressed the state team. "My nephew Gafoor is the state's representative and you must all obey him."

The silence hung for a long moment. We couldn't believe his words at first and then we realized he had planned this all along. Droon knew too. I felt hollow and then angry. I glanced at the faces beside me. Qubad was near tears. Veer's face showed disgust at such a betrayal. In Namdar's face I glimpsed the anger passing quickly to panic and worry. The shoulders of those in front of me bowed under the weight of the pronouncement.

The crowd murmured finally, a simmering of disappointment and discontent that Wahidi had reneged on his word. They stopped when Wahidi glared around.

How could I even have thought of giving myself to such a dishonorable man?

Veer held my hand to reassure me.

Wahidi handed over the letter and embraced Gafoor. He did not even apologize to us for breaking his word as he hurried to his Land Cruiser. His fighters jumped in behind him and it raced out of the stadium.

"What do we do now?" I whispered.

"We all run for the border," Veer said harshly. "It's going to be a long, hard ride in the Jeep and I hope we'll make it."

We saw Droon approaching and Jahan going to meet him so that he wouldn't come too close to me, still hidden by Veer and my team. The state team scurried away toward the tunnel to get ready for their departure, not hiding their smiles. They didn't even look at us.

Droon crossed to Jahan and put an arm around his shoulders to draw him away from the others.

"See, I told you your team wouldn't leave the country."

Jahan seethed. "And your brother broke his word."

"He had not given it," Droon said and smiled. "When I meet your sister, in person, with my wife, you will be safe, but only then. She will be there in your house or else I will punish you despite my brother's affection for you as a brother-in-law. But until then, remember what I said. Tomorrow at what time is convenient for you?"

"Nine. I pray she will have reached us by then."

"Eight. I think that will be the best time. Tell your sister to be ready to meet my wife. I will bring the gifts. My brother will join us later to pay his respects to your sister."

I prayed I would not be there to receive them. Droon patted Jahan, more a slap, to remind him, and went to his Land Cruiser, waving as he drove away.

We waited for the silence once more, listening to the fading engine. Our fans and friends stood in despondent silence, waiting for us to tell them what to do. The groundsman was nowhere in sight. I looked for Yasir—he had to write this up—but he had left. Even if he had heard Wahidi, I doubt he'd have written the story.

But he was a stickler for facts and he'd write: "In the final match, the Taliban Cricket Club (95) beat the Afghan State Team (93) and won the tournament."

Our two Talib minders were waiting for the team by the main exit, cradling their guns. The religious police, their duty done, left the stadium.

"Jahan, we have to do this now," Parwaaze said. "You go with our cousins. One moment . . ." He counted; with Jahan there were eleven for the bus today. He pulled aside the youngest, around Jahan's age and build. "There must be eleven. You wait until Jahan gets out of the back door and then you climb in quickly." The boy drifted away, moving slowly so as not to be noticed. Parwaaze embraced Hoshang. "Make sure this works."

"We'll get our kit first, and you take it with you," Veer said, then told us, "Come on, we must hurry so the crowd is still around and Jahan can get out of that bus."

We hurried down the tunnel to our dressing room. The state team was just emerging from theirs, carrying towels and soap, laughing and bantering as they crossed to their washroom. They again avoided looking at us. We waited for them to pass before moving and glanced into their room.

A dim forty-watt bulb pushed the darkness to the corners. Green blazers, with a vague crest on the pocket, hung neatly from the nails. On the floor were the blue plastic bags in which they had been hidden.

"They knew all along and came ready to leave," I said bitterly.

The others were hurrying to collect our kit.

I stepped in and took down the nearest blazer. It was made of a cheap cotton-nylon mix, and the green, in this dull light, was anemic.

I put my hands into the side pockets and then into the inside pocket. I felt something in it and pulled out an Afghan passport.

Veer checked another blazer. It too had a passport in the inside pocket.

We stood for a long moment, staring at what we had in our hands.

The others came out of our room, carrying the kit, and saw what we held and then, in unison, looked at the blazers hanging up in the room.

I think we all counted silently—there were thirteen blazers, each with a passport in its pocket.

We looked at each other, and then to the closed washroom door. Our cousins and their friends waited at the mouth of the tunnel.

"Grab the other blazers," Veer said.

We thought with the same mind.

They rushed in, grabbed them, and, without checking to see whether they fit or not, slipped on the blazers. Mine was a size too large.

Parwaaze found Gafoor's blazer, Wahidi's permission neatly folded in with the passport. We took the thirteenth blazer too.

Without a word, Qubad darted across the hall and, as quietly as he could, turned the key of the state team's washroom, locking them in. We could hear the splash of water and laughter inside.

Namdar locked their dressing room too. They kept both keys, and when we locked our dressing room door we took that key too.

We hurried down the tunnel. Night had slipped its shawl over the stadium and the distant hills. The moon remained clothed in clouds. Our cousins looked at us in surprise. We passed our kit for them to carry and flourish so that the Talib would see it.

"Jahan, go with them," Parwaaze said. "We'll follow, with your blazer."

I prayed as hard as I could. Jahan moved with the others, and pretended to make conversation. They fell in with that, and they passed the Talib fighters.

I saw them counting as they followed the "team" out of the stadium. It was too dark to distinguish any faces. The crowd had thinned to thirty or forty still meandering around, while others crowded the stalls buying kebabs and naan to have as snacks on their way home. A neon light flickered at the far entrance to the main stand.

We followed as close as possible.

The "team" reached the bus and Jahan was the first one on; the others followed him, milling around, talking.

Inside, the bus was so dark that we couldn't even see him moving. We passed close to the side of the bus.

The Talibs counted eleven and then slammed the door shut.

Jahan opened the rear exit and jumped down. The cousin climbed in to take his place, then closed the door quietly as the bus started.

Veer tossed Jahan the blazer and he slipped it on as we hurried to the state team's bus, parked next to the Jeep.

Our team bus moved away slowly, too slowly, as if trying to make up its mind. The Land Cruiser crawled behind it.

Youseff appeared out of the night. "I paid fifty dollars to the driver to go slowly and also fifty each to the Talibs."

"Did they ask what for?" Veer said.

"A tip for looking after the team so well," he said and grinned, only his teeth visible. "They counted eleven in and that will keep them happy."

"Follow us. If this doesn't work, we may all have to travel by Jeep."

"And break my axles," Youseff complained.

The state team's bus driver climbed in wearily and started the bus without a glance at us as we climbed in and filed into the darkness. It had been a long day for him. The other bus had reached the exit and turned onto the main road, moving toward Karte Seh.

"Airport," Parwaaze said to our driver. "We are late. Hurry."

As the bus moved painfully slowly, we exchanged our blazers to fit our builds. I needed one that fit the slightest build, and we checked the passport in the dying light. The boy looked around my age, with a thin beard and a delicate face. In bad light, I could pass for him if I kept my head down. At the back of the bus was a dozen small suitcases.

We didn't exchange another word; we were all holding our breath. We kept looking back to see if a car followed us, but the road remained deserted except for Veer's Jeep and the billows of dust our bus churned up. The bus rocked, it rolled, avoiding the potholes, and the driver seemed content to take his own sweet time while I knew we were all screaming internally—hurry, race, speed up, hurry.

The airport was a few kilometers northeast of Kabul and our road skirted the city, passing through depressed neighborhoods. I sat hunched in my seat, clutching Veer's hand, imagining the state team finding their door locked, banging on it, breaking it down, and reporting what had happened to the sentry.

They would use walkie-talkies to pass on the information to Wahidi and Droon and, even at this moment, they could be sending their armed men to intercept our bus. Droon, with his suspicious mind, could at this moment be searching my home for me.

The police would also arrive at any moment. We would see their headlights bearing down on us.

"How long before someone frees the state team from the washroom?" I wondered anxiously.

"Long," Bilal said. "The security guard's in his box and, even if he hears them shouting, he will believe that they're the spirits calling out to one another."

"We'll make it," Veer whispered.

"I'm praying," I replied, and I was.

We were moving out of Kabul, the road straightening and

leading toward Jalalabad, a four-hour drive. Another hour beyond that city was the Pakistan border.

The traffic was heavy. Trucks sped toward us in the center of the narrow road and our driver held his own center until both swerved at the last moment. Other trucks and buses behind us tried to overtake him but he would not give way.

"The police." We heard the whisper from the back shiver through the bus.

THE CRICKET TEAM

A POLICE LAND CRUISER WAS RACING TOWARD US, its lights flashing, the driver blasting the horn for our bus to pull over. It had overtaken the other traffic and was soon parallel to our bus. We didn't look down at it and kept our heads averted as it pulled ahead.

Abruptly, it started to slow down and forced our driver to do the same.

There were four policemen holding AK-47s and riding in the back. Once it stopped, they would jump down and surround the bus. They would line us up and shoot Veer, Jahan, and my cousins. Then they would take me back to Wahidi. He would fire a bullet into my head for having dishonored him.

"We're finished," Jahan said from across the aisle and reached for my hand.

I held his and Veer's hands tightly, looking from one to the other, just their profiles showing in the dark. Veer tried a smile, but it came out crooked, like an out-of-focus photograph.

The Land Cruiser kept going and then we saw why it had slowed. A badly filled crater was in the center of the road and it drove over it carefully, just as the trucks did as they came toward us. Once the Land Cruiser reached the other side, it accelerated and its taillights faded swiftly into the darkness.

We released our collective breaths in a loud hiss of relief and began to laugh softly.

I peered back, trying to glimpse the city.

Kabul was in darkness, as no streetlamps worked, and it had slipped back into its ancient past, when our invaders rode through the mountain passes and descended on this hidden city. I felt a painful loss at escaping from the city I would always love.

I would probably never see Kabul again and prayed that my ancestors, my grandparents, my mother, and my father would forgive me for leaving them behind—if I did manage to escape.

The airport lights were not very bright, just enough to silhouette it against the night sky. The lights of the control room seemed to hang on an invisible tower. The bus negotiated the turns slowly, finally stopping at the entrance.

We hesitated, looking at the departures terminal, expecting to see armed men waiting for us.

Parwaaze finally led us out, climbing down cautiously, looking around, and we followed him. We each chose a suitcase from the pile and hauled them along with us. We checked the name on the spare passport and left it with the thirteenth blazer stuffed under a seat.

Veer went to Youseff and embraced him. "Wait to see if we get away. If we come running out, be ready to take off."

I had Veer and Jahan flanking me as we entered the neon-lit departures terminal. The Kabul airport was tiny compared to the Delhi one I'd flown into years ago, but back then it had hummed with passengers. Since the international sanctions in 1996, except for Karachi and Dubai, all international flights were banned and the terminal echoed with our hushed presence. It had a deserted air and it wasn't hard to imagine cobwebs hanging from the ceiling, and a gossamer shroud spreading over the check-in counters.

"Which f-flight are we on?" Qubad asked.

"There's only one flight tonight," Veer said, pointing to the board. "To Karachi." He whispered to me, "From there we'll take a flight to Delhi." He turned to the team—Parwaaze, Qubad, Nazir, Omaid, Royan, Namdar, Bilal, Daud, and Atash. "You'll all be safe in Pakistan?"

"Anywhere but Pul-e-Charkhi," Royan answered for them.

"We have two good friends in Karachi," Parwaaze said. "They'll look after us until we fly to Malaysia and catch that boat to Australia. They have good contacts to help us."

He led us to the check-in counter. There wasn't a queue.

We knew then in our hearts that the flight had been canceled. Wahidi had discovered our escape and sent orders ahead. The airport authorities would lock the doors so we could not get away.

A harried, young man in an Ariana Afghan Airlines uniform almost leaped toward us from an office at the back. "You are the cricket team?"

"Yes, yes," Parwaaze said with authority. "I have the minister's letter." He took it out with a flourish.

The man snatched it, not even looking at the content. "You're late. We must hurry." He turned to the cubicle. "They have arrived, sir."

A tall, elderly man, with a beard not quite gray, stepped out. A cigarette hung out of his mouth, curling smoke into his eyes. He wore a *pakol* but not a *shalwar;* instead, a suit, a size too large, hung on his frame. He surveyed us with a look of fury.

We cringed, stumbling back like small animals facing an omnivorous beast. The police would swarm in from hiding and arrest us.

"Where have you been?" he shouted without removing the cigarette. "I have been waiting for you for two hours. The flight is half an hour late because of you all."

"The bus . . . ," Parwaaze managed in desperation, also looking for the police.

"The stupid bus." He threw the cigarette at us and it fell far short of our feet. The action seemed to calm him and he pulled down on his jacket. "I am Hukam, from the Sports Ministry. You will all do what I say and I want no more trouble from any of you. Do you understand?"

We nodded mutely, relieved. There were no police to swarm around us. We weren't surprised by his presence, though we had expected a Talib fighter and not a bureaucrat who was impatient to start his two-month vacation from the office.

"You saw the match, sir?" Parwaaze asked politely.

"I didn't have the time to visit the stadium," he snapped and pointed to Parwaaze. "You are Gafoor?"

"Yes, sir, the minister's nephew."

"Good, we'll work well together." He shook hands with Parwaaze but not with the rest of us. "I want harmony. If anyone misbehaves, I will have to send you back. Understand?"

We nodded.

"I'm fining the team two hundred Pakistan rupees for coming late," he said.

"But we don't have any rupees," Namdar pointed out.

"It will be deducted from your daily allowance."

"So that's money already in his pocket," Atash whispered.

Hukam swung away, all in a hurry, to the airline official. "Check them in quickly." He strode toward the departure gate, not looking back.

"Passports, quickly, quickly," the official said and ordered the baggage attendant, "Get their luggage onboard at once." As he herded us toward immigration, carrying our boarding cards, he scolded us. "We held up the flight for you and you come so late.

How can I work like this?" He dumped the passports on the immigration officer's counter, along with Wahidi's letter. "Stamp them quickly."

He counted twelve passports.

The Ariana man checked his list. "I have thirteen passengers."

"Malang couldn't make it," Parwaaze said quickly.

The immigration official, relieved that he could go home now, flicked through the new passports and stamped each one without even looking at which one of us it belonged to.

Our official grabbed them and nearly threw the bundle at Parwaaze as he herded us out and down the stairs to the bus waiting on the tarmac. Some distance away was our plane, the steps about to be rolled back.

Hukam imperiously waved to have it returned for us to board.

Veer hesitated. The plane looked ancient, the silvery body dull and tired, the Ariana Afghan Airlines logo on the side. "What is that? Does it fly?"

"It's a Russian An-26 turboprop," Omaid said, proud of his knowledge. He pointed to another plane, even older, parked a little distance away. "And that's a Yakovlev Yak-40. I'm going to be a pilot."

I looked back, as did the others; there was still no sign of the armed men, no walkie-talkies screaming out commands to stop us.

We ran up the steps and into the plane. We caught a glimpse of Hukam sitting down in the business-class section, a privileged passenger. We avoided the angry stares of others, knowing they were friends of the government.

The stewards were unhappy with us for delaying the flight and pushed us down the aisles to find whatever vacant seats were available. I flopped down with Veer in the seat next to mine and looked out the window. The stairs rolled back and the engines started, vibrating through our bodies.

I saw the others also peering out anxiously, scanning the tarmac, trying to look beyond it, as if they could see the road and the racing cruisers. The plane lumbered forward slowly, gradually speeding up, and then it was airborne, banking over the dark city and sliding its way over the high hills and through the narrow passes.

We all held our breath, as we didn't believe we would escape. At any moment, airport control would command the pilot to return to Kabul.

We peered out, but all we could see was the dark land and the jagged peaks in the distance. I was leaving behind the country of my birth, all my ancestors, my history, my identity, my language, my people, and my culture for a future of exile in which I would have to find a tiny niche in which I could survive. I would always keep the past in my heart, as it can never be forgotten.

I looked at Jahan and my cousins and saw that their faces too were suffused with the same sense of loss, fear, and expectation. At least I had Veer, and I held tightly to his hand, willing the plane to keep flying to Karachi. It was only a two-hour flight and we kept checking our watches, counting the minutes, but the old plane was in no hurry.

It groaned and growled as if it was in pain and only wanted eternal rest.

I knew the plane was going to crash and we would die together; I knew the pilot was talking to Kabul air-traffic and getting orders to return; I knew Droon was waiting there.

I shrank into my skin when a hand clutched my shoulder.

"Well played, young man," Markwick said, looming over me. For once he was tieless but wore the same suit, now rumpled.

I nodded, staying mute, catching my lost breath.

He crouched down to save us straining our necks and looked over to Veer. "That was good batting. I thought the standard of cricket surpisingly high for a young cricketing country. And your team played almost professionally. Who coached you?"

"We have a great coach," Veer said with a smile toward me. "But he has a sore throat from so much shouting."

"Congratulations, coach." Markwick gave me a friendly pat on the shoulder and stood up, looking at us. "Cricket is a strong bond between countries, once it takes root. I think it will here." He leaned over to Veer. "If you should visit England, do look me up. You can find me through the MCC. My club team could do with you on our side."

"I will, sir," Veer said, and with a wave, Markwick retreated back to his seat.

"So you'll play in England now," I said.

"Only if you're on the same team." He blew me a kiss and sank deeper into his seat.

Before I could blow one back, he was asleep, and I remembered him telling me that he fell asleep in an instant because he traveled so frequently. He looked at peace, his sensual lips slightly parted, his breath steady. I wanted to shake him awake to be with me in these last moments. I looked around at the team. Apart from Jahan, this was their first flight and their faces were as grim in fear as mine was.

I was so tired and drained; I shut my eyes tight to stifle my imagination.

I woke when the plane suddenly banked, shuddering with the effort.

"Oh god, it's turning back," I said in a panic and shut my eyes again.

In that moment I saw Droon and Wahidi waiting at the Kabul airport, dragging me off the flight and carrying me away into the pitch darkness of their lives, where I would never see light again. Veer was there too, lying on the tarmac with a bullet in his head.

Veer laughed. "Since when did the sea move to Kabul?"

I opened my eyes and looked out. The sea was a silvery desert stretching out beyond the horizon and I smiled—there were no longer hills and mountains limiting my view of the world. Then the city appeared below, spread out like a bejewelled carpet in the darkness to guide us down.

The flight had taken slightly over two hours and bumped down in the Karachi airport.

Veer grinned to reassure us that we were in Karachi. The smile was infectious, a happy disease that first touched Jahan's tense face and lifted his lips and lit up his eyes; then it was on to Parwaaze, Qubad, Namdar, Omaid, and the others. I watched it spread to each face.

We wanted to burst into laughter, and we all stood up even before the plane rolled to a stop. We wanted to be the first off, the first to touch Pakistan, and only then would we believe we had escaped.

We waited for Hukam, yawning, to lead and we hurried down the steps and into the bus waiting to take us to the terminal. The air was warm and humid, caressing us with its damp tongue, but it smelled deliciously refreshing. We smiled at each other as we swayed in the bus, crowded in with other passengers, speaking not a word, yet the smiles said it all. Markwick swayed along with us.

As we got off, he waved good-bye. "I have a flight to London in an hour and I hope my luggage makes it too. Good luck." And he weaved away toward the connecting flights. We felt a small loss at seeing him go.

We queued at the immigration counter, behind Hukam, Parwaaze at our head, clutching the letter.

The officer looked at him and then craned his head to look down the line at us in our blazers.

"What sport do you play?"

"Cricket," Parwaaze said proudly and was surprised by his laughter.

The officer turned to his colleague at the next counter. "Hassan, the Afghans now play cricket." And he laughed too and looked at us as if we were aliens.

"We're here to be coached by your cricketers," Veer said.

"We have the best players in the world," the officer said, smiling.

A young man in a well-cut suit and a green-and-white-striped tie, with eager-to-please eyes, stepped out from behind the immigration officers.

"You are Mr. Hukam?"

"Yes, yes, Afghan Sports Ministry." Hukam put out his hand and they shook.

"I am Anwar Khan from the Pakistan Cricket Board. Welcome to you all. Now, if you give me your passports I'll have you all cleared." We handed over the state team passports, praying he wouldn't open them. He didn't, instead passing them on to immigration and saying with authority, "They're state guests. Stamp them quickly." He turned back to Hukam. "I'll meet you outside. There's a bus waiting."

We followed Hukam past immigration to the luggage carousel. It wasn't moving and we stared at it in silence. He checked his watch.

He told Parwaaze conversationally, "We will hold your passports until it's time to return home. So don't get ideas." He looked around. "Where is the toilet?" he demanded, as if we had hidden it away.

We looked around and Veer pointed to the far side of the baggage hall.

"Gafoor, you collect my case too. It's black with a white stripe," he ordered and ambled across to the toilet, lighting a cigarette as he negotiated his way through the other passengers.

When he reached it, he looked at us; we hadn't moved and he entered and the door closed behind him. We left the carousel and passed the customs checkpoint.

"We better get rid of our blazers," Parwaaze said.

We slipped them off and dropped them in a dark corner.

I removed the beard and started to stuff it in the blazer's pocket, but then had second thoughts. I still hated it, but I wanted it as a memory of the days when I was Babur, though I hoped I'd never need it again. I slipped it into my *shalwar* pocket.

Veer stroked my bare cheek. "At last."

"If only it was that easy for us," Parwaaze said, stroking his sparse beard. "We're all going to shave first thing in the morning." The team smiled and murmured their agreement.

We looked through the glass doors leading out and I sensed our hesitation.

We had only to take a few more steps, but like birds or other animals that see their cage doors opened, we were suspicious of the freedom beyond. Was it a trick? We looked back and couldn't see Hukam.

We had negotiated the maze up to this point, and the final doors would slam shut as we tried to pass through them. We were leaving the security of our familiar prison. My cousins had never left their homes and their families, and they were about to exchange familiar dangers for unknown ones.

Their faces were taut with anxiety. We stood rooted to the floor.

THE SENTRY HAD HEARD THEIR INDISTINCT SHOUTS AND believed that they were the dead spirits calling out to one another.

He had stopped his ears and closed the door of his sentry box. By the time Droon heard the news and called the Kabul airport, the flight had landed in Karachi more than an hour and forty-five minutes before. Now, he would be calling the Karachi airport to stop us from leaving the terminal. I imagined Droon racing to our house. He would smash in every door and find the secret room . . .

"COME ON." VEER TOOK MY HAND.

As a herd, we rushed the door and it opened.

It was only when we stood outside, surrounded by strangers, hearing an alien language, that we all began to laugh and clap and embrace one another.

I saw the faces of women everywhere, only a few veiled, revealing their beauty for all to see. I imagined Noorzia passing among them on her way to a distant city.

I wanted to cry, not out of despair, but for the sheer relief of escaping the predatory Droon and Wahidi.

I was free, I could love the man I wanted to love, live my life the way I wanted to live it.

Yet the heart is strange. A tiny flicker of compassion for Wahidi seeped in from this safe distance. I believe he had fallen in love with me and would mourn the woman who had not requited his love. But Droon would be relieved. He would find a new, younger wife for his brother, one who would not be such an obsession that she disturbed a man's mind. For him, women are a sinful vice.

But that feeling was extinguished in the instant we heard music from somewhere, a strange sound after so many years of endured silence, and the notes lifted our spirits even higher. Even though we didn't know the tune, we danced together, arms on one another's shoulders, forming a circle, still laughing like lunatics. We stopped finally even though the music hadn't.

"Look there." Parwaaze pointed to a man in a khaki uniform.

He was holding up a placard: PAKISTAN CRICKET BOARD WELCOMES AFGHAN STATE CRICKET TEAM.

We moved away from him quickly to mingle with the crowd. Even if Hukam charged out now, he wouldn't find us.

"We're going to Delhi first to get our visas and then on to New York," Veer said in the sudden quiet among us. "There's a flight to Delhi in four hours."

"I'm going to marry Veer," I said, looking at him and then at them, wanting their consent as well. Their eyes flicked to Jahan, and I caught the imperceptible blink, assuring them that he, my *mahram*, consented to the marriage.

"We're not blind." Royan laughed.

"You haven't let go of his hand since we left the stadium," Omaid said shyly.

"You have our blessing," Parwaaze said.

Then each one shook Veer's hand, placing their hands on their hearts.

"You all will always be welcome in our home," Veer said. He took out a roll of dollars, peeled off most of them, and held them out to Parwaaze, who shook his head. "You'll all need more money. I am family now."

Parwaaze took the money. "Thank you. And you come and watch us play cricket in Australia."

We all looked at one another, the light on our faces, wanting to remember every tiny feature of one another's faces so we would never, ever forget. I knew I would carry those memories all the way to my grave, even if I never saw them again. One by one, they stepped forward to embrace me. They held me tenderly, as if I were a crystal vase that would shatter at their clumsy touch, and I experienced the warm pleasure of love in their arms.

They whispered words into my ear and I replied into theirs, so that only one at a time heard me. Then they embraced Jahan and finally Veer.

My team stood together, waving as we entered the departures terminal. Then they melted away into the darkness.

"What did you say to each other?" Veer asked.

"*Khoda haafez*, God protect us."

ACKNOWLEDGMENTS

I MUST THANK SUKUMAR KARTHIK FOR HIS HELP, ADVICE, and support and for introducing me to many of his Afghan friends in Kabul. They were all, in true Afghan tradition, courteous, kind, and very hospitable, answering all my questions on living under the Taliban regime between 1996 and 2001. Among them Obaidullah Noori (who has one hundred cousins in Kabul), Noor Ahmad Darwish, Qudratullah Khan (who was so generous with his time), Dr. Obaidullah Sabawoon, Professor Abdul Karim Waseel, Najiba Ayubi of the Killid Group, Aunohita Majumdar, Kalyani Sethuraman, and Katharina Merkel. I listened to the life stories of many Kabul women, working freely under the present government, who preferred not to be named. I'm indebted to my driver, Zalmay, who protected and kept me out of trouble in Kabul. And much gratitude to Nick Webb, Mary Sandys, Anupama Chandrasekhar, and Bill Shapter who supported and encouraged me in writing this novel. I am lucky to have great agents in Kimberley Witherspoon and William Callahan, and truly fine editors in Lee Boudreaux, Abby Holstein, and Lorissa Sengara, who worked so hard to keep me on track.

In 2000, the Taliban regime, backed by Pakistan, did apply for associate membership to the International Cricket Council. The ICC did not respond until *after* the regime was defeated in 2001. The rest is fiction. Today, Afghanistan plays in international cricket tournaments and is an affiliate member of the ICC. There is also a nascent women's cricket team and a touring women's football (soccer) team.